THE TEMPLAR'S PENANCE

Michael Jecks

headline

First published in 2003 by
HEADLINE BOOK PUBLISHING

10 9 8 7 6 5 4 3 2 1

British Library Cataloguing in Publication Data

ISBN 0 7553 0170 6

Typeset in Times by Avon DataSet Ltd,
Bidford-on-Avon, Warwickshire

Printed and bound in Great Britain by
Clays Ltd, St Ives plc

HEADLINE BOOK PUBLISHING
A division of Hodder Headline
338 Euston Road
London NW1 3BH

www.headline.co.uk
www.hodderheadline.com

To paraphrase P.G. Wodehouse . . .

This book is for the builder and his wife,
without whose wine, food and conversation
this book would have been finished in a third of the time.

Thanks, Bob and Heather.

Glossary

Claveiro	Key-holder or castellan of a castle (in Portugal).
Espada	The symbol of the Knights of Santiago. The upper part was a cross, but the lower part was shaped like a sword's blade.
Frey, Freiles	'Brother', 'Brothers': the term given to knight warriors.
Furtum sacrum	The theft of a set of relics by a rival church was a recognised crime, but it was condoned as being a pious act. Our forefathers took the view that if the Saint in question objected, he or she had it in their power to prevent it.
Hidalgo	A low class of noble, a *hidalgo* was on a par with a reeve, probably, but was born to his position rather than elected. *Hidalgos* would often work in the fields with other townsfolk, which meant that they were looked down upon by other, higher nobles.
Malfechor	During the troubled early years of the 1300s, a raider or thief who preyed on travellers, villagers and anyone else they could rob or kill.
Maestre	Master – in Castile.
Mestre	Master – in Portugal.
Mudéjar	A Moslem living under Christian rule after the reconquest.
Pesquisidores	The title given to certain 'enquirers' in Castile from the early thirteenth century. Its literal meaning is: well-informed men who fear God.

Cast of Characters

Sir Baldwin de Furnshill A former Knight Templar who is well-known as a resolute investigator of crimes in Devon. It is a new experience for him to be investigating a murder in a different land, Galicia, without the support of his wife, Lady Jeanne, and his servant, Edgar.

Bailiff Simon Puttock Baldwin's friend for many years, the Stannary Bailiff from Dartmoor is less used to travelling and finds Galicia more intimidating than Baldwin does.

IN COMPOSTELA

Dom Afonso The son of a religious man, Afonso is burning with the determination to avenge his father's death.

Caterina The widowed sister of Domingo, and cousin of Joana, Caterina was rejected by her Christian father when she married her Moorish husband against his will. Now she is forced to beg in the streets.

Sir Charles Once a proud supporter of Earl Thomas of Lancaster, Sir Charles now has no protector and must find a living as best he can.

Domingo Leader of a small group of thieves, Domingo is distraught to witness the death of his son Sancho at the hand of Sir Charles; he is determined to exact revenge.

Gregory of Coventry   The ex-husband of Doña Stefanía, he has become a sad, disillusioned man. Now a cleric, he is appalled to see his ex-wife in Compostela.

Guillem   The clerk to Munio, who keeps notes and records all the *Pesquisidor*'s enquiries.

Joana   A lowly-born woman, she has been maid and confidante to Doña Stefanía for some years.

Margarita   Although she has the dark beauty of a Castilian lady, Margarita is in fact an Englishwoman from Oxford, who married Munio while he studied there.

María de Venialbo   A beggarwoman seen in the streets of Compostela. Like other mendicants, she is unpopular, for even pilgrims object to paying out good money to beggars!

Matthew   Baldwin made many friends when he was a Knight Templar, but most have faded from his memory over the last fifteen years. Matthew's is one face he recognises. When the Order was destroyed, Matthew was left with nothing, and now he must beg his daily allowance from pilgrims.

Munio   In the city of Compostela, there are elected official investigators, the *pesquisidores*, of whom Munio is one. He studied in his youth at Oxford, and speaks fluent English.

Parceval Annesen   Forced to go on pilgrimage to atone for the murder of a fellow merchant in Ypres, Parceval is anxious lest he be seen to be wealthy, and thereby robbed or captured and held

	hostage. To avoid this, he conceals his wealth.
Paul	Squire and general man-at-arms to Sir Charles, he also sees to Dom Afonso's needs.
Frey Ramón	One of the famous Knights of Santiago, Frey – or Brother – Ramón is apparently a devoted Soldier of Christ.
Don Ruy de Benavente	A knight forced to go into exile, unjustly accused of crimes against a young woman.
Doña Stefanía de Villamor	The Lady Prioress of the convent at Vigo is fearful that her money might be stolen, but still more worried about the contents of her purse. They are not hers, and she shouldn't have kept them.

Author's Note

It is impossible, I find, to hope to fire a reader's interest in a subject without already being intrigued by it myself.

I know that is not an astute observation, yet it's something many of my friends don't appreciate, because I have often been asked to write on subjects which are well outside my sphere of interests. As a crime writer concentrating on medieval England, I was bemused to be advised that I should write a novel about Formula One and Indie motor racing. 'Millions watch racing, Mike, you'd make a fortune!'

Thanks, Ramsey, but there are some things I do not *want* to write about!

The converse of this is also annoying. Sometimes I really do want to cover a subject in more detail, but can't.

When you have spent months of your life researching a subject until you really live and breathe it, it's very hard to discard the bulk of what you've learned in order that your editor won't tell you off for trying to preach about your era. Sadly, though, she's usually right. All the fascinating little details which get culled *would* have slowed the story down.

For example, there are two strands which led me to write this book. First is the difference (or lack of one) between English justice and law and the European model. The second is the theme of the 'warrior monk'.

Although the British have prided themselves on their system of justice over centuries, with the jury trial as the cornerstone of commonsense justice, in reality England was not unique in the 1300s. Our legal system was founded upon the same principles as other European states because we all came from pretty much the same roots: the Roman system. The real difference was that at this time, both the English and European systems were in a state of flux. Trial by ordeal had petered out, which meant that new means of testing people must be invented. This led to more investigations in which the judge and lawyers were actively questioning witnesses to get to the truth.

In the 1460s an exiled former Chief Justice called Sir John Fortescue wrote 'In praise of the Laws of England'. It was a piece which attempted to demonstrate the superiority of the English system over the French model. According to Trevor Dean in his excellent book *Crime in Medieval Europe*, Fortescue presented 'the English system of trial by jury as a guarantee of impartiality and truth'. Logically, Sir John said, a juror is safer than a mere witness called before a judge. A juror has money, land and status. A Frenchman need only acquire a companion who would invent a plausible story with him and, if they perjured themselves, an innocent man could be arrested and thrown into gaol. This, Sir John thought, was 'wicked'. The idea that a judge could also use torture, he said, was 'a pathway to hell'.

It goes to reinforce the view that in England 'everyone is innocent until proven guilty'. Sadly, all too often this is not true, especially now, with rafts of new laws being brought into being with little debate. In many cases, British subjects can be assumed to be *guilty* unless or until they can prove their innocence. Even the ancient right to silence has been removed. Senior politicians have said that it is as bad to let one guilty person walk free as it is to wrongly imprison an innocent one. They advocate more emphasis on the feelings of the victims of crimes rather than on the 'criminal's' protection.

But if you take away safeguards for some, it erodes the protection of all. There are too many cases of innocent men held in prison without parole because they refused to confess to their crimes and show suitable penitence. If they had admitted their guilt, they would have been eligible for parole, so if they had actually committed the crime of which they were accused, they would have been released much earlier! This is a clear injustice.

The concept that 'it is better to let one guilty man go unpunished than to condemn an innocent man' was not a smart, liberal Victorian invention; it was not even Fortescue's. It is an ancient principle from Roman law, and was an argument recycled often enough by Roman lawyers. If anything, Fortescue took it from continental legal systems.

*   *   *

Now we come to my second theme, the different forms of warrior monk who existed during the fourteenth century.

In the early 1300s, the Templars were destroyed, of course, but that wasn't the end of the various Orders. All through the age of the Kingdom of Jerusalem, Orders had sprung up in imitation of the Templars and the Hospitallers, with their own Rules and slightly pick'n'mix attitude to the more difficult commands. For example, the Knights of Santiago, who feature in this novel, were part of a very liberal Rule. Not only was consorting with women *not* frowned upon, but many *freiles* (Brothers) were married. On certain religious occasions they slept away from their women, but most of the year they lived happily as man and wife.

Warrior Knights – men prepared to fight for their beliefs – were essential in the religious Orders during the whole of the *Reconquista* – that period of reinvasion during which the Christians pushed the Moslem invaders of Spain and Portugal southwards until the Iberian peninsula became wholly Christian once more.

It was in 711 that Moslem troops crossed the Straits of Gibraltar and quickly spread throughout the whole of Spain and Portugal, apart from a few mountainsides in the north. It was only two years later that the Umaiyad caliph Abd al-Rahman appeared on the scene and forged this huge territory into 'al-Andalus'. Yet although he and his successors ruled this land, five Christian kingdoms also sprang up: Aragon, Castile, Galicia, León and Navarre. In 1031 the caliphate broke up into smaller city-states, and now the reconquest began in earnest.

This is the main thing that a modern person must appreciate: the Orders were not a strange, foreign group of men. Yes, they were intensely religious, giving up their lives in battle for, as they saw it, the greater glory of God; but they were still ordinary human beings, with the same beliefs as the average man in the street at that time. The difference was, they were utterly dedicated to God.

The wars in which they fought were long and bloody, causing suffering over centuries to people living in Portugal and Spain.

The Moslems launched raids over the Tagus, stealing cattle, food, and of course people: the slave markets needed regular supplies of fresh blood. For hundreds of years families lost their sons, and women, their food stores and money. The fighting was unremitting and the raids characterised by religious fervour on both sides. When the thirteenth century faded into the fourteenth, the Portuguese had only recovered the Algarve fifty years before. Yes, the Moslems had been forced back, so that their sole remaining toehold was in Granada, but over the seas were hordes more waiting to be called. This was no theoretical war, it was a ferocious series of see-sawing battles.

In this climate the military Orders flourished – apart from during the inevitable reverses. It is astonishing how often religious rashness could overwhelm good strategic minds. For example, in 1280 Frey Gonzalo Rodgriguez Girón, the *Maestre* of Santiago, met a huge force of Moors. Most men, being outnumbered, would sensibly refuse to join battle, instead scouting around for re-inforcements, but not a good Knight of Santiago. Like so many other religious warriors, Frey Gonzalo believed that if his faith was strong enough, pure enough, God would protect him and his men.

He charged, taking his little force of fifty-five knights with him. They were wiped out. Revealingly, a chronicler said that these were 'most' of the Brethren, which gives an insight into how few knights there were in some Orders. For this reason, King Afonso forced the Knights of Santiago to merge with the small Brotherhood, Santa Maria de España, which he himself had created a few years before.

There were knightly Orders of Calatrava, of Santiago, of Alcántara and Avis, amongst others. The Portuguese and Castilians were often at daggers drawn, trying to carve up the massive territory. One result was the dissolution of some Orders for political reasons. For instance, Santiago lost the Portuguese parts of its territories after pressure from King Dinis; the breakaway group became the Knights of São Thiago. Similarly the Portuguese elements of Calatrava became independent, at one memorable point demanding money before they would go to the support of their Brothers over the borders.

When the Templars were disbanded, their destruction led to two new Orders. On the ruins of the Temple there rose the new Aragonese Order of Montesa, an Order which kept the white tunic and red cross like the Templars. At the same time, King

Dinis in Portugal decided that he didn't agree with the Pope that the Templars' property should all go straight to the Knights of St John. They were already powerful enough. Instead he created a new Order, the Knights of Christ. This Order was to grow in importance and dominance for the next few centuries, becoming the leading missionary and imperial Order in the Portuguese empire. For those who are interested in historical buildings, their monasteries and churches in the Romanesque, Manueline and Renaissance style are quite breathtaking.

And the best, for my money, is the old Convento de Cristo and Templar castle at Tomar. It stands up on top of a great hill, an impregnable fortress whose scale has to be seen to be believed. The church itself is one of the few remaining Templar sites, unspoiled because when the Templars were destroyed, the Knights of Christ weren't foolish enough to wreck their buildings. They reused them.

If you have a hankering to visit an old church and complex to see what the Templars left, you would be hard pressed to find a more evocative place than Tomar.

There is just one geographical point I should make. I have shown Baldwin taking a boat all the way to Óbidos in Portugal. This is not a slip of the keyboard. Although now, if you are lucky enough to visit the beautiful walled city, you will find yourself driving up the coast on the road overlooking the smallish lagoon and then along the broad, flat plain, now that the sea has retreated. Until the fifteenth century, visitors would be as likely to arrive by boat. At the same time Peniche, now a town on the coast, was an island.

In reality it is hard to check most details about rivers and the coast, because with the 'Great Earthquake' of 1755, so much of Portugal was destroyed or changed. Lisbon was effectively shivered to pieces, and the Tagus (the Rio Tejo) moved so much that the Tower of Belém, which had been constructed in the middle of its flow so as to protect the way to Lisbon's harbour, now lies almost on the shore!

In this book I have speculated on what might have happened to the Templars. Few, unfortunately, came to what I should have thought a good end. Some, we know, were executed by the authorities, especially in France. Added to the deaths during torture, this must account for some hundreds. Others were given the chance of joining another Order, although not usually a military one. Some scholars believe that none would have been allowed to remain in a renamed Templar site (see Desmond Seward's *The Monks of War*, Penguin, 1995). Others believe that many remained or simply travelled to find other Orders which they could join and where they could wield a sword (see *Dungeon, Fire and Sword* by John J Robinson, Michael O'Mara Books, 1994, or *Supremely Abominable Crimes*, by Edward Burman, Allison & Busby, 1994). It is generally agreed that most of the men living in Tomar after the destruction of the Templars had themselves been Templars. They merely changed their name.

Possibly, some Templars were saved and installed in another Order, but it's equally probable that many ended their lives in misery and squalor, starving and perhaps more than a little mad. We know that is the case for the poor devils who had been caught in Paris.

Whatever the truth, I like to believe that at least some of these men were saved and escaped from the violent retribution of the French King Philip le Bel, fleeing in desperation southwards, where some, maybe only a very few, managed to create a new life for themselves in the warm climate of Spain and Portugal, among some of the friendliest people in the world.

Michael Jecks
Northern Dartmoor
September 2002

Prologue

It was an unnaturally cool morning in this part of northern Spain, when the youth who had got there first gave a whoop of triumph from the top of the rise which men called *Montjoie*, the Mountain of Joy. At least in those last moments before he died, the youngster knew absolute pleasure of a kind which he could never have known while slaving in the fields. He was only a damned peasant, after all, Gregory thought, watching him.

He was an unprepossessing specimen, this boy, with a face all scarred from the pox; he had the shoulders of an ox and flesh burned black by the sun and the wind. Gregory had an urge to snap at him for presuming to run on ahead of the group, but he swallowed his irritation. He would try to take the lad aside later and give him a bit of a talking-to.

It had been a longstanding ambition of Gregory's to be awarded that glorious title of 'King' just for having been the first to reach the summit and see their destination. Many pilgrims would pay it no mind, but Gregory did. He had wanted to rise early in the morning and come here to this hill and see the sacred city of Santiago Matamoros, Saint James the Moorslayer, shimmering in the distance, to stand on this knoll in splendid solitude, listening to the birds and drinking in the view while he offered his thanks to God. It was a dream which he had enjoyed periodically during the long journey here, and now it was gone. He had hoped that he could commune with God alone up here and find some comfort; merely catching a glimpse of Santiago was supposed to make a man more acceptable to God, after all, and Gregory needed all the help he could get.

It wasn't the boy's fault. Gregory could hardly blame him for taking the lead. It was just his luck! If only the group hadn't collapsed last night when they had stopped for shelter. They were all exhausted after stamping through torrential rain for hours; the weather here was worse than Gregory's worst memories. The refuge of a small barn had called to them, and then a cheerful woman had brought them a steaming dish of pottage. No, there was no possibility of their carrying on after that, which was why they didn't arrive at the stream until this morning.

The sun was feeble today, but compared with the terrible rains of yesterday it felt wonderful. At least they could walk in the dry. The dust had been settled by the dampness, so they didn't suffer the irritation of inhaling the stuff as their boots stirred it. Not like the South of France, where Gregory had coughed almost all the way, choking in the thickly laden air. Warmed and rested, the group had woken refreshed and ready for the last part of their pilgrimage. Some had only travelled a few tens of miles, but many had covered hundreds. Some, like Gregory, had walked perhaps more than a thousand to get here. God, but he'd needed to wash his feet!

This river, the Lavamentula, was enclosed in a small wood, and the warm, green-tinged light had a curious effect on them all. It was as though they all realised that they were entering a holy site. Light was sprinkled on the ground in pools of gold; the thin scattering of weedy plants beneath the trees looked somehow blessed as they were touched by it. In the clear morning's sunshine even the dark, barren-looking soil was given a glowing aspect, as though new life was about to burst from it.

One of the first there, Gregory had eagerly stripped and washed with the rest of them. After the journey, all were gritty and rank. Even with the weather so cool, they had built up sweat from many days of travelling, and the pilgrims all needed to scrape themselves clean. Gregory himself felt the bathing to be almost a spiritual experience, a preliminary ritual so that he might arrive at the Saint's altar cleansed. There was a curious silence as he rubbed vigorously at his armpits and groin, an

expectant stillness broken only by the sound of trickling water –
and gasps as cold water shocked cringing flesh.

While he wiped himself dry, he watched the others. He was
struck more by the differences between them than by the super-
ficial similarity given to them by their broad hats and capes. Yes,
they all wore the same basic clothes, many with the cockleshell
symbol of Santiago, but their attitudes were clearly at odds with
each other.

Some splashed enthusiastically like children, bawling loudly
at the cold, spraying each other and laughing, while others stood
silently contemplative, preparing themselves for the day, ready-
ing themselves for actually seeing the church, perhaps sad that
the end of their journey was at hand, reluctant to consider that
soon they must turn about and return to the mundanity of normal
life, to bickering or scolding wives and squalling children. Some
would no doubt be feeling the same emptiness as Gregory,
realising that they would never know such a sense of purpose
again. Perhaps there were some who were happier. Maybe there
were some fortunate enough to be experiencing the inner peace
that only a pilgrim who has dedicated and risked his or her life
willingly can know, the calmness of one who has achieved a
great ambition.

Not Don Ruy, though. Gregory reckoned that few groups of
pilgrims would have had a knight like Don Ruy joining them
on their travels. None of the knights he had ever known in his
past had been aware of their failings. Yet this one, Gregory
thought, sometimes seemed to radiate sadness, as though he
was the victim of a great injustice. At those times he would
break down, turning away from the other pilgrims as though he
feared to pollute them with his mere presence. At least one
knight was aware of the shameful state to which his arrogance
had brought him. That must explain it – simple shame. Perhaps
Don Ruy could recognise his soul's needs. Not many knights
could.

At this moment, Don Ruy's attention was fixed upon the
frolicking travellers like a man surveying a procession of dogs

before they were set upon a bear. Or perhaps, Gregory thought, he was like the bear itself, waiting while his tormentors paraded before him. There was something in Don Ruy's eyes that reminded Gregory of a convicted felon awaiting his death – like so many of his own friends, the men with whom he had served in the Templars.

Others there were easier in their minds than Don Ruy, Gregory felt sure; *all* must be easier than Gregory himself. His own guilt was so overwhelming, he could never feel peace. He had made his oath, sworn it before witnesses, and then tried to renege. And then there was the second source of guilt: his act towards his wife. The act that had cost him his marriage.

It was why he had so desperately wanted to be the first to catch sight of the city, as though merely seeing it before anyone else could give his personal pilgrimage a particular sanctity and potency. He would never know now. The peasant boy was King, not him.

Gregory had thought that since he was first in the water, he'd be the first out and off up the hill; he'd be King. But no! The peasant lad scarcely washed himself; just a quick dip, in and out in a minute, and back into his clothing. Hardly clean; hardly pious.

He did not bother to dry himself. Gregory saw the boy throw on his shirt and tunic, snatch up his cloak, scrip and staff, and hare on ahead of them all through the trees. Others were moving off too, and Gregory realised, with a leaden sinking in his belly, that he was too late. He had missed his opportunity.

At the top of the hill now, he stared hungrily along the plain towards the great city of Compostela, but it didn't arouse even a frisson of religious pleasure. Nothing. He felt a keen desolation, a dreadful sense of loss. His life for the last weeks had held meaning solely because of his focus, his ambition, to reach the city. Now that the end of his journey was literally in sight, it revealed the utter paucity of any other aspect of his life. He had lost his wife, his fortune, and now, he felt sure, his immortal soul.

While he stood there leaning on his staff, a hand over his face, his back bowed, the others were already streaming down the incline towards the city, a mass of joyous humanity. Only two remained at his side. One was Don Ruy, the knight who wore his pride like armour protecting him from the lesser folk about him. The other was Parceval Annesen, a weaselly-looking Fleming with a sallow complexion, thinning hair and bent shoulders. There was a great weight on that Fleming's shoulders, Gregory thought. He looked like a man who'd been buffeted heavily by the gales of misfortune and had all but gone under. It took one to know one, Gregory thought bitterly. Parceval had been luckier than most, though. At least he didn't suffer from loneliness. Apparently, one night he'd chatted up a woman pilgrim on the way here, and Don Ruy, so it was rumoured, had walked in on him while he was bulling her. Gregory hadn't even *seen* her. Just his luck! He'd been asleep and minding his own business, like a real pilgrim should.

So far as he had seen, the knight and the scruffy Fleming had exchanged scarcely a word, but that was no surprise. A weedy type like Parceval would be scared stiff of someone like this knight, who could sweep your head off as soon as look at you. No, a scruffy little churl like Parceval would never dare engage a man like Don Ruy in conversation, and a great hulking knight like Don Ruy would not demean himself by addressing someone like Parceval – especially if he'd walked in on the tatty little man while he was stuffing a whore.

Gregory fixed his eyes on the stream of excited people rushing ahead, listening to their shouts and laughter, wishing he could be a part of their joyous throng. He was so tied up in his jealousy and self-pity that at first he didn't realise there was anything wrong; didn't hear the subtle change as first one, then another man screamed with fear.

'Sweet Mother of Christ!' Parceval hissed suddenly.

The foul exclamation made Gregory recoil with shock. That a man should speak thus within view of holy Compostela! He was about to command Parceval to drop to his knees and beg forgive-

ness, when he caught sight of the man's expression. That made
him turn back and scrutinise the plain ahead.

There was nothing obvious at first. Not that he could see,
anyway. It was just a crowd running down the hill delighted to
be in sight of their destination. Nothing. Maybe someone had
tripped, that was all. Then he saw a flash of something glinting
in the sunlight between some trees. There was a creaking of
leather and shriek of exultation, and there, cantering towards the
left flank of the pilgrims, was a force of men-at-arms, a motley
band, armed with swords and axes, one or two wearing a pair of
greaves or a breastplate, some with simple helmets. There was
no uniform to them, no single colour of tabard or tunic, only a
general scruffiness that was in itself a proof of their nature. At
their front rode an older man with a hunched aspect, kicking his
horse onwards, his heels drumming against the flanks. He had a
mad, grinning face, Gregory thought, and an odd way of holding
his head, as though one side were too heavy.

'*Malfechores!*' Gregory heard Don Ruy hiss, and the knight
unsheathed his sword.

The small bands of robbers and thieves had grown fearfully
since the famine, especially here, because of the turbulent
politics over the last few years. They did not fear God's wrath
and would happily attack even pilgrims. Gregory wanted to flee,
but when he turned to glance over his shoulder, there was another
band behind them, three strong-looking men on great rounseys.
'Lost! We're lost!' he groaned.

Even as Gregory fell to his knees, overwhelmed with defeat,
he saw the knight's teeth gleam. Don Ruy planted his feet
firmly apart and gripped his sword-hilt with both hands, the
point aiming at the three men. Parceval was at his side, his
staff gripped tightly in his fists, his face showing his anxiety,
but yet fixed and intent. It was the sight of the miserable little
churl sturdily challenging their foe that made Gregory realise
how weak and pathetic he had become. The reflection stiffened
his spirit. He stood, taking up his own staff and holding it as he
had once been taught. It was a polearm, a weapon, and a man

who could use it offensively was safe from most attackers. That was what he had been taught, anyway, and right now, just the feel of the thing in his hand was enough to give him some confidence. He saw Don Ruy flick a glance at him in which surprise vied with amusement, but he didn't care; he had been a knight himself once.

However, the three horsemen took little notice of the group. The first was a heavyset man with a badly pocked, square face. As if to conceal his scars, he wore a thin dark stubble, which only served to make him look more intimidating. His brow was low and simian, and his eyes gleamed with what Gregory recognised as fanatical rage as he stared at the carnage on the plain. Pockface was clad in clothes that looked as though they had been expensive, but that was some years ago. His tunic was faded, his cloak threadbare, and his hose were holed in both knees; his mount looked strong and well-cared for, but the harness and fittings were dull and marked from sweat and scratches, showing that they too were old and well-used.

Behind him was another man, slighter of build and calmer in appearance. He had the long, regular face, fair hair and blue eyes of a northerner, and he peered ahead with less rage, more calculation. His clothing was newer than his companion's, and the horse he rode looked to be of better quality.

The third man was plainly not a knight. Short and plump, this fellow snorted and spat a thick gob of phlegm onto the ground at his horse's hoof. His hair was black with white feathers at his temples, and he had the quizzical look of one who has seen enough fighting and death in his time. Behind him he led two packhorses, both heavily laden. He shifted in his seat, squinting ahead and resting a hand on the blade that sat in the rough, undecorated scabbard at his thigh. He glanced in Gregory's direction and the latter saw his eyes narrow as he took in Don Ruy, but then his fierce, dark eyes met Gregory's as he addressed his two companions in a light Scots accent.

'Aye. Well, are we goin' to join in or just sit and watch all the long day?'

With that, the fair man gave a high, giggling laugh, and then suddenly he drew his sword, whirled it about his head a few times, and slapped it sharply on his horse's rump. In an instant he was off, racing down the hill, his sword flashing in the sunshine like a torch in the wind, hair streaming behind him. The man-at-arms clicked his tongue, but he had already dropped the reins of the packhorses, and his rounsey was moving to follow the fair-haired knight.

The warrior with the pockmarked face muttered a curse under his breath, spat, and then raked his spurs along his mount's flanks. Before the other two could get far, he was level with them, his mount straining at the gallop, and Gregory could hear his hoarse roar even over the thundering of hooves.

By now, the band of *malfechores* had scattered the pilgrims, and two had stopped to take up bundles where they had been dropped. As Gregory watched, he saw a sudden gout of blood, and saw the 'King' spinning, a rider raising his sword for a second hack. Suddenly a great slab of the King's head seemed to separate from the rest of his body, a third of his face and skull falling away to lie on his shoulder, exposing the pink and grey horror of his brain. There was a fine, pumping mist of red, and then he fell, thrashing, to the ground. His attacker lifted his sword in triumph, but then the three were on them.

First was the madly shrieking fairhead, who galloped full tilt at a group of four who were circling a pilgrim and taunting him. With a sharp sweep of his blade, he took the head and a shoulder entire from one man, rammed the horse of a second, bludgeoning the rider from his seat, and then stabbed a third through the throat; the dour man-at-arms came a little way after him, ducking below an ill-judged thrust like a tumbler, and stabbing viciously once, upwards beneath his opponent's chin, so that his sword appeared through the top of his victim's skull, then withdrawing it swiftly lest it become snagged as the corpse slumped and toppled from the saddle. Finally there was the apelike warrior, who gave a bull-like bellow like a *berserker* of old, and charged straight at the thickest mass of *malfechores* with a sword in one hand and a long-handled knife in his other. He rode with his reins dangling, gripping his mount with his thighs alone, guiding the horse by sheer force of will, apparently, or so Gregory thought, as his two blades flashed wildly, already red with the blood of his enemies. Gregory saw one man stabbed and bludgeoned from his horse, only to be trampled. Unconsciously, he had clenched his right fist, and was following the blows when he realised what he was doing and shamefacedly unfurled his fingers.

The battle was over in moments. Suddenly the evil-doers were bested, and leaving nine of their friends dead on the field, the seven survivors fled.

Last to go was their leader – the man with the curious set to his head. He screamed as the fair-haired warrior slashed at a young rider, and a thick jet of blood burst from the young man's leg. The boy went white, and suddenly slumped, like a bullock struck with a spike in the skull, slowly toppling from the saddle, while the fair man hacked at him as though in a fury.

The leader shrieked like a demented woman, and might have ridden back into the midst of the carnage, but his mount was unnerved by the smells and noises of death, and with wildly rolling eyes, it turned and fled the field, cantering after the others.

Screaming with fury at seeing this new quarry escape, the fair man spurred his horse after them, but Pockface cast a look of exasperation at the heavens, sheathed both weapons, and set off after him, catching up with him and apparently remonstrating, throwing a hand back as though to indicate that their responsibility was to the wounded, not to killing any more. Gradually the two men slowed, and the fair man turned his horse's head back to the battlefield, although his body language spoke of his reluctance.

Gregory himself now hurried down the incline to see if he could help any of the wounded, and soon he was on his knees praying for the hurt and the dead, walking from one to another. It took some while and it wasn't until he had eased the pain of the worst wounded and given some solace to those who would die, that he could rest. Then, when he glanced up, he saw the fair man standing nearby, a slight smile on his face.

'My lord,' Gregory stuttered, 'I . . . I don't know how to thank . . .'

'Pray, do not mention it, friend,' the man smiled. 'It is the duty of all to protect and serve pilgrims.'

'You fought well,' Gregory observed, gazing about him in some astonishment. He felt dazed. The action had been so swift, the rout of the felons so absolute, that until now he had scarcely had time to take stock. Now he recalled the ferocious battle with a twinge of jealousy. It was a long time since he had witnessed – let alone experienced – such a magnificent charge.

Near his knee was a hand, next to the long-bladed knife it had held, while its young owner lay a short distance away, his eyes glazed like those of a dead fish. Gregory would have felt sorry for him, but this was not one of the pilgrims: this was one of the *malfechores*.

A little farther away lay a dead pilgrim, bearing an obscene abdominal wound that had been augmented by a vicious slash across his throat. As Gregory himself knew, corpses would often receive three or even four blows after death. As lines of men met in the clash of arms, those in the front would fall and be trampled, and as the battle rolled forward over them, the wounded – yes, and the already dead – would be stabbed or struck by the second line of their enemies, and the third, just to ensure that they wouldn't suddenly spring up and attack from behind. Swift and brutal, it was the way of things, but in this case it looked unnecessarily cruel. The fellow couldn't have survived with that terrible wound – no one could. There was no need to make sure of him by cutting his throat. He was no soldier, merely a pilgrim.

Gregory could remember him. A rather dim-looking fellow, but always cheery enough. He had no boots, but never complained, just gave an occasional suck-in of breath when a thorn stabbed his foot, or a stone gouged a hole in his heel. A simple, happy boy, he didn't deserve to die like this.

They were evil devils, these *malfechores*. All too often a single malcontent gathered a gang about him and set out on an orgy of violence before their brief period of fear and domination was done. Just like that hunchback, Gregory thought. He glanced about the field and saw no sign of the man. Typical, he felt, that the leader should flee, leaving his companions to die on the field.

The three strangers had saved their lives, and Gregory was deeply grateful, yet his attention returned to the corpse of the slender young robber. He would have liked to see this boy grow to maturity, lose his desire for blood, lose his urge to rob the poor pilgrims who passed by here. Gregory had seen too much of death and killing.

'Are we to get on, then?' It was Pockface again. He was riding about the field, staring at the bodies of the dead and wounded with a ferocious scowl, but Gregory felt sure that it was not an indication of anger, simply the way his face looked at rest. Where others might appear happy, or vacuous, this man would only ever look full of ire.

'I think we should await Paul's return, Dom Afonso,' said his fair-haired comrade. 'He has only been gone a little while.'

Afonso grunted, then swung himself down from the saddle and stood gazing about with his eyes narrowed. Gregory suddenly realised that the man was afflicted with poor sight.

'Come, Afonso. It will not be long before Paul is back again. Then we can go and find an inn.'

'Not soon enough for me.'

His accent was curious, a hard-sounding tone that held a mix of different tongues. Gregory couldn't place it. For now, he was content to know that these men were safe.

'Mmm. Well, while we wait . . .' Afonso said, after a moment's pause, and walked around the bodies. While Gregory watched, he rolled over the body of one pilgrim and opened his scrip. He stared at the few coins in his palm. 'Hardly worth the effort, Charles.'

'Every little is worth the effort,' the fair man grinned as Afonso made his way to the next body. 'One should never leave money and goods lying around, in case another robber may happen upon it and enrich himself. That would never do!'

The chuckle in his voice made Gregory glance at him. Although the man called Charles had a fixed smile on his face, there was something in his eyes that made Gregory shiver.

He had the eyes of a man with no soul. The eyes of a mercenary.

Never had he known such horror! Hidden, Domingo watched the men moving among the bodies, his heart pounding, the blood roaring in his ears.

He and his men had waited here for more than a day, just to attack the band of pilgrims, and this group had appeared out of nowhere and destroyed his little force. They had sprung upon him and his men like wolves upon a flock, and he had been forced to dart sideways, leaving the lad there in the mêlée. He'd thought his boy would escape, would follow him as he pelted off away from the fight; no one stayed near a battle like that, not when there were knights joining in.

Now, more than half of his men were dead, all because of the accursed three who had appeared so suddenly.

Domingo rolled away and sat with his head in his hands, sobbing bitterly. Among the dead was his own son, Sancho. It was all his fault; he had taken on this attack, and he had lost. If his horse had obeyed his commands, he could have ridden back and maybe saved his boy, even at the expense of his own life. It was a trade he would gladly have made, but it was not to be.

He had enough men left to charge again, but they wouldn't. That much he could see in their eyes. As a fighting band, they were destroyed. It was no good even thinking about using them again. Now Domingo would have to go back and tell her that he had failed her.

THE TEMPLAR'S PENANCE 13

The thought wasn't pleasant, but it was better than sitting here, staring out over the corpse of his son.

'I shall kill them. I swear it!' he vowed.

Chapter One

On arrival in Compostela, Baldwin knew immediately that coming here on pilgrimage had been the right thing to do.

Just the weather was balm to his soul. The sky was larger here in Spain. He had noticed it before – it wasn't as immense as Portugal's, but definitely vaster than poor England's. The plants looked greener here, the trees more robust, the buildings more comfortable. It was all because of the climate, which was warm and reliable. In the summer there was sun, in the winter there was cool. Rain fell in season – but it was always warm rain. In Devonshire, Baldwin knew that the rain was always chill, being blown in off the sea.

He snuffed the air like a dog. There were the scents of rosemary, thyme and other herbs from the markets; the warm fug of many people crammed together in the heat, the smell of roasting stonework and heated timbers. Good God, he said to himself, how could I have lived without all this for so long? It was good to have returned to his old clothing. Today he was clad in white again, with a fine linen material that accentuated his body underneath. After the horror of the mad monk at Gidleigh, during which episode he had been forced to kill one man in order to defend another, he felt as though he needed every little bit of assistance that he could win, because he felt dirty. There was a deep, ingrained stain on his soul, because the man he had defended was more guilty than the attacker could ever have been.

A nasty matter, that one. Bitter and devastating. He craved forgiveness, some solace for his unwitting homicide, and hoped that here in Santiago's great Cathedral he might find it.

The massive entranceway, the *Pórtico de la Gloria*, was enough to distract him and he looked up at it in awe. It was magnificent – daunting. Over a hundred years old now, it had been carved between 1168 and 1188, and the stonework was richly decorated with figures of prophets and apostles, each of them welcoming the pilgrims. Saint James himself was placed sitting prominently above the central column as though watching over all the poor folk as they reached this, his memorial.

'A bit ornate,' muttered his companion.

'Different, that is all,' Baldwin said, refusing to argue. In his opinion there was a grandeur about this entrance that showed how well men could honour God when they put their minds to it.

Simon Puttock glanced up and his face twisted doubtfully. This experience was wholly new to him, and he wasn't sure that he was enjoying it. He had been keen to come here at first, because it seemed a great adventure. Simon had never travelled abroad before. True, he was well travelled compared with almost everyone he knew, but this was the first time he had been somewhere where all the people spoke a different language. It made him feel very exposed, as though he stood out wherever he was. Like a pilgrim, perhaps, but as he told himself, he felt more like a blasted target, walking about on a field waiting for the archers to loose their arrows. It was as though everyone was pointing at him, gauging the distance before firing, and it made him jumpy and unsettled.

Seeing Simon jerk his head to one side, staring suspiciously at a pilgrim jostling him, Baldwin had to laugh for sheer joy. It was hard not to feel delight here, among so many people thronging the church. Their joint pleasure and relief on reaching their goal was enough to make the tiredness fall away from Baldwin like a man shedding a mantle.

Not so his friend, he knew. Simon, a tall man in his middle thirties, had the ruddy complexion of one who spent many hours a week on horseback in all weathers, but now he looked pinched with nervousness. Riding had given him his solid strength, the strong muscles in his legs and at his throat, but good food and a liking for good ale had fattened his belly and made his jowls grow over the years. The extensive travel of the last days had reduced his paunch, although it had not improved his temperament. That had grown more fiery with the weather as they had approached this southern city.

Baldwin was sure that Simon's moodiness stemmed from his feeling out of his depth. For the first time, Simon Puttock, Bailiff of Lydford, was aware of his own impotence. Here his voice would not summon officers to do his bidding; he had no power. Instead, almost anyone who understood the local language was better off than he, and this made him fretful, as though it reflected upon his lack of education. But he had been educated by the Canons of Crediton Church in Devon; he could speak, read and write Latin, and could understand much French, but he could make nothing of the language here in Galicia in the far north-west part of the Kingdom of Castile.

His dark-grey eyes still held a measure of the stolid common-sense and piercing intelligence that Baldwin had noticed when they had first met all those years ago in 1316, but here the sparkle was dimmed, because Simon felt lost. Baldwin could easily comprehend his friend's state of mind. He himself had been aware of that curious sense of 'otherness' which afflicts the traveller on occasion.

Not today, though. Today Baldwin was determined to know only pleasure. He had never before been to the great city of Saint James, and wished to make the most of his visit. More than that, he also wanted Simon to enjoy himself.

'Look at all these people! Hundreds of them,' Simon muttered.

'Yes. This is a popular place for pilgrims like us.'

'And for knights.'

Baldwin followed his gaze and saw several men who must surely be knights. One, wearing a light cloth tunic of slightly faded crimson, was clearly a secular man-at-arms. His shock of fair hair shone brightly in the sunshine and he met Simon's gaze with reciprocal interest, as though he was gauging Simon's ability as a fighter. A short distance away, stood another man wearing a clean white tunic with a red cross on his shoulder. It was at him that Simon stared.

'He is a Knight of Santiago,' Baldwin informed him. 'A religious Order devoted to protecting pilgrims.'

'The cross looks odd,' Simon noted, then looked up to see that the shoulder's owner was glaring at him, as though affronted that a mere pilgrim should dare peer so insultingly. He was a strong, heavy-set brute to Simon's mind, with prognathous features and swarthy skin.

'It's made to look like a cross above, but the lower limb is a sword's blade,' Baldwin explained. 'They call it the *espada*.'

'They don't like people staring at them,' Simon noted.

'Knight *freiles*, that is, "Brothers", are as arrogant as you would expect, when you bear in mind that they are a cross between chivalric, honourably born knights and clerics. They feel that they have all right and might on their side. You know the motto of the Knights of Santiago? It is: *Rubet ensis sanguine Arabum* – may the sword be red with the blood of Arabs.'

'That miserable bugger looks as if he'd not mind any man's blood on his sword,' Simon said, adding thoughtfully, 'although perhaps that's because of his guilt.'

'Guilt? Why do you say that?'

'Look at him. He's with those women. One's a nun, from the look of her, but the other is too bawdily dressed for that. I wouldn't mind betting . . .' Then Simon recalled where he was, glanced up at Saint James's welcoming features high above him and cleared his throat.

Baldwin, seeing his brief confusion, chuckled. 'She may be his wife.'

'What? He's a Knight Brother!'

'The Order of Saint James allows their *freiles* to be married,' Baldwin said, but with a note of disapproval in his voice. He personally believed that religious Orders should all conform to the same principles of poverty, obedience and chastity.

'At least I can admire his taste,' Simon mused. 'That young woman is a delight to the eyes.'

'And I think the good knight has noted your admiration,' Baldwin warned.

They both turned away. To cause anger in a strange city was foolish, and anyone who did so by upsetting a man protecting his woman was a fool.

'I don't know why I allowed you to persuade me to come here with you,' Simon said mournfully. 'Look at me! I'm a Devon man, through and through. What am I doing all this way from my home and family?'

'Be content. We might have travelled all the way on foot like so many others,' Baldwin reminded him.

The memory was not enough to soothe. 'You think that makes me feel any better?' Simon snapped. 'And don't snigger like that. I've never felt so near to death in my life before.'

'I only feared that you might intentionally hasten your end,' Baldwin chuckled.

'Hilarious.'

Their initial journey had been violent, as they aimed for la Coruña, and Simon's belly had roiled in response. He had sailed many times, as he had said to Baldwin before they first boarded their ship at Topsham, but he had never seen seas such as those they encountered on their way here. Baldwin, he was sure, had felt poorly, but that was nothing compared with the prostration which Simon experienced. Following the advice of a sailor, he had remained in the bowels of the ship, and although he tried to lie down and sleep, he could find no ease. Blown from their course, they made landfall farther east, near Oviedo, to Simon's eternal gratitude, while Baldwin had remained up on deck for the entire journey, and denied any illness.

'A fine officer you will be for the Keeper of Dartmouth!' Baldwin chuckled.

'To be the Abbot's man in Dartmouth I won't ever have to set foot on a ship,' Simon retorted. He was soon to become the Abbot of Tavistock's representative in Dartmouth, now that the King had granted Abbot Robert the post of Keeper of the Port of Dartmouth, a lucrative position for both Simon and the Abbot. 'Anyway, even you agreed that the sea was about the worst you'd ever seen.'

Baldwin showed his teeth in a brief smile. He was slightly taller than Simon, and although he was prone to run to fat, he drilled daily with his sword and clubs to keep his belly flat and his chin from doubling. It had not been a conscious effort to keep trim, but a continuation of his regime of training. Baldwin had learned weaponry when he was young, but later he had joined the *Poor Fellow Soldiers of Christ and the Temple of Solomon*, the Knights Templar, and while in the Order had learned to respect their attitude towards constant practice with weapons. Only by using the sword and lance effectively as a part of God's army could a knight bring honour to himself and to God, Baldwin believed.

But then the Templars were destroyed.

When the Templars had been arrested, Baldwin had been distraught. For two years he had travelled about Aragon, Navarre and other lands, hoping to find a new purpose to his life, for until Friday, 13 October 1307, when the Templars of France were arrested and imprisoned, he had believed utterly in his Order, and had no other life than that of a Knight Brother. But then, when the Pope himself declared the Order dissolved in his bull *Vox in Excelso*, in 1312, Baldwin was left without home, faith or hope. His Order existed solely to support God and the Pope; the Pope was the man to whom all the Templar Knights ultimately gave their loyalty, yet this Pope had destroyed them. God had allowed him to see the most holy Order brought to destruction.

It was in memory of his Order that Baldwin still wore a small beard that followed the line of his chin. Few English knights affected a beard, but Baldwin felt it necessary, even if it did itch here in the warmer climates. He wanted to honour his dead comrades. It was for that same reason that he wore a Templar cross on his sword. The symbol of his faith was strongly engraved on the bright blue tempered blade, a constant reminder to him that he should use the weapon only to the glory to God – or his own defence. Sadly, it was this same sword which had led to this pilgrimage. He had used it to kill the wrong man. The memory made him shudder, as though someone had walked over his grave.

Like all knights who had trained with lance and sword from youth, Baldwin was of a broad and muscular build. His face bore just one scar, from a raking knife-cut, but apart from that his features were unmarked. There were deep lines at either side of his mouth, but the main signs of his anguish at the loss of his Order had faded since he had been married to his Lady Jeanne two years ago – and especially since his daughter Richalda had been born. Since then his brown eyes had grown calmer, although they could at a moment's notice achieve a powerful intensity. Some said he could see through a man's soul when he studied them closely.

It was not true. Baldwin ran a hand through his hair. Once black, now it was threaded through with silver, just like his beard, although his eyebrows themselves were in fact still all black. No, it was not true. He could sometimes tell when a man lied, he could sometimes feel when a man was behaving dishonourably, but nothing more than that. All he possessed as a keen investigator of crimes was his knowledge of the world; that, and his unswerving loathing of injustice. Those two were all he needed as Keeper of the King's Peace, because Sir Baldwin believed with every part of his soul that it was better that ten men who were guilty should be set free than that one innocent man should be punished. There was no more fundamental rule that governed his life. Years ago, when he was a callow young Templar Knight, perhaps he would not have believed so fervently in this principle, but now he had no doubt. Since seeing friends imprisoned, tortured to death, or slaughtered by slow roasting over a charcoal fire, his perspective had changed, because he knew that they were innocent.

Baldwin shook himself. This was no time to be thinking such grim thoughts. He was here because he had killed a man, an innocent man, and his pilgrimage was his way of atoning for that crime. Standing here in the Cathedral, his mind should be bent solely on the reason for his coming so far, not rehearsing the list of crimes against him and his comrades.

His eyes rose at that thought and he found himself gazing up into the eyes of the statue of Saint James. Then he felt a curious sensation: a tingling along his spine, not at all unpleasant, and he became aware of a conviction that here he need not beg forgiveness: it was offered freely. In Saint James's eyes there was compassion and kindness – and understanding. Baldwin's raw mood faded, and he found his normal optimism returning.

He was content. 'Come, Simon. Let us go in.'

Gregory had entered the city with his soul weighed down by the recent attack. It had been so swift and ferocious, especially the way that the three strangers had joined in . . . it made him feel dull and uneasy, like an old man who is reminded of the magnificence of his youth when he sees other young men chasing women or drinking, and knows that all his own abilities are gone for ever. Just his luck that the first chance of protecting pilgrims would arrive when he was too old to help. Ironically, he still felt as young and virile as ever.

The feel of the horse between his thighs was, to a knight, almost a religious experience: separate, yet a part of him, rearing and plunging among the multitude of armour-clad men, turning and pounding off on massive hooves to a fresh point in the line of battle, seeking always to be there at the front. There was that raw, unalloyed delight of feeling one's sword slice through a man's arm, shoulder or skull, of relishing that power to end life, impregnable in one's suit of steel. Yes, there was real joy in killing. He could remember that.

Here, inside the cathedral city, those urges were wrong. Gregory didn't need a priest to tell him that. Here men were supposed to appreciate the kindness and generosity of Saint James and, through him, Christ. Death and bloodshed were anathema to the cult that had given birth to this marvellous cathedral.

He passed through the *Pórta Francigena*, the French Gate, and walked down the *Via Francigena* towards the Cathedral, musing on the fact that these places were so-named purely because so many pilgrims came here, like him, straight from France. It was strangely stirring to think of so many travellers passing this same way.

The roadway was lined with street traders of all kinds – hawkers in gaily coloured clothes shouting, a few brazen women leering at the men, although they waited more for those who had already visited the Cathedral – perhaps because they had learned from experience that a pilgrim needed to refresh himself spiritually before trying to slake his more natural desires.

Gregory hesitated at a wine-seller's counter then purchased a small cupful at an exorbitant price; he didn't grudge the fee. It felt so good to have almost reached his goal. He only hoped that he might find some peace when he arrived in the Cathedral. If only he'd been made King – but then, as he reminded himself, he would be lying dead on the plain now if he had, with the other pilgrims who'd been caught in the ambush.

Setting his cup upon the board, he was about to rejoin the line of pilgrims when he stopped. There, a scant yard away, he had seen *her*, he was sure! Certainly it must have been her; there couldn't be two women in the world with that peculiar heart-shaped face, the same tip-tilted nose, the high angle of the cheek, the rich, ruby mouth and little chin.

She was wearing a pleated wimple and fine-looking tunic of some light material, as befitted so wealthy a woman, and she was riding a good *ambler*, a horse trained to walk with the legs at each side moving in unison, first both of the left side together then both of the right, to give a gentle, rocking gait that was more comfortable than a horse's usual motion.

Gregory felt as if he was in a dream as he followed after her, along the rest of the roadway and up into the square at the northern side of the Cathedral. It was easy to keep her in sight, because she was one of the few pilgrims on horseback. Most had left their mounts back at the stables near the gates so that they could make the last few yards of their journey on foot. Not her, though. Oh no, my lady Prioress wouldn't want to sink so low.

Only a peasant would walk, she'd have said. Poisonous bitch!

She stopped in the square when she saw the milling crowds there. Gregory had heard that this place was called 'Paradise' by the people who lived here, but no thought of that came into his mind as he watched his ex-wife dismount and leave her horse in the hands of a loitering stablehand. Gregory's attention was entirely bound up with *her* as she climbed the stairs slowly towards the central column, preparing to put her hand in a niche in the stone to give thanks for her safe arrival.

Her! Giving thanks to a Saint, like any pilgrim, Gregory thought bitterly, when it was she who had made him foul with sin. *She* shouldn't be allowed in a place like Saint James's Cathedral; *she* should be barred. It would be just his luck if she were to accuse *him* of guilt, and he was refused entry, he thought glumly. If only he could hate her; but he couldn't. She was beautiful, and he adored her.

If only, he thought, he didn't still love her. Doña Stefanía de Villamor, the woman who had been his wife.

Gregory was not alone in spotting her. Although Parceval had not set off until some time after him, he had not halted for wine or food and arrived in the square at the same time as the anguished penitent.

Parceval had caught sight of Gregory staring at him several times during their journey, and at first it had worried him, thinking the old dolt had recognised him, but he felt sure now that he was secure. It was only the snobbery of an older man staring at his social inferior. Bloody bastard. It was embarrassing enough, having to wear this filthy clothing, and assume the shabby appearance of a peasant. But it was, after all, what he had intended. No one who knew him as a wealthy merchant would recognise him like this, surely.

Ah, it was good to be back in the warmer country of Galicia. The last time he had been here, it was a little later in the year, at a time when the local people were harvesting their fruits and grains. Now, in the early summer, it was certainly damper, but at least the rain was warm – far better than the miserable conditions which had prevailed in Ypres when he left. That had been far colder. Christ Jesus, yes. Although the circumstances of his departure might have coloured his feelings.

About his neck was a small skin filled with water, and he took a swallow now as he made his way through the crowds, darting between pilgrims and wanting to curse as one stood on his foot, another bumped into him and a third pushed him aside on the way to a pie-seller. If these people had any respect, they would surely make way for him. He was rich, damn them all!

Not so rich now, of course.

It was so unfair that he should have been made to pay. In his eyes, the killing – he refused to call it murder – was completely justified. Hellin van Coye had deserved death, and Parceval had dealt it out. The whole town had supported his action, and although he had been forced to pay compensation to the widow – who was grateful to him for making her a widow and ending her living hell – and must complete this penitential pilgrimage to Compostela, that didn't change his basic belief that he was innocent of any crime. Even now the thought of Hellin's crime made him feel faint. Hellin, the man who had killed Parceval's soul. He could feel the sickness wash through him, as though it was washing through his soul, polluting him still. Please, God, he begged silently, forgive me when I have completed this pilgrimage. Don't forsake me when I need Your help so badly!

He felt the bitterness bubble up again, and tried to force it down. There was no point in anger now. He had done what he needed to do, and that was that. He was here to show his remorse – ha! Remorse for the death of that devil's spawn? With a cynical shake of his head, he told himself that when he returned to Ypres, that would be enough to earn him rewards from people who would assume him to be still more decent a man with whom to do business, because he had made this journey (a notably expensive trip, after all). And if some refused to deal with him because of his 'crime', others would come to him because he was known to be someone who would stand up for his rights and his property, surely a notable citizen.

The tears were back. Him *notable*, after all his crimes?

He brushed the tears away and took a deep breath. There was no reason for him to feel guilt. Guilt was for the guilty. He was here to show that he was accepted as an innocent not only by the city's ruling élite, but even by Saint James himself. He had not *meant* to do anything wrong. It was the fault of beer – and of Hellin van Coye.

Pleased with this conclusion, he squared his shoulders. Just then, gazing ahead, he caught a glimpse of *her* – the Doña Stefanía – and his heart began to beat a little faster. He could remember every curve of that delectable body from the time they had met. Beautiful. The memory hadn't dimmed. Christ alive, no! If anything it was thoughts of her which kept him awake in the early hours.

'Doña Stefanía,' he murmured to himself. She wouldn't have forgotten him; she couldn't have. No, so why not renew their acquaintance? Forgetting entirely the attack in which he could so easily have been killed, Parceval began to forge his way through the crowds, but even as he thrust himself onwards, he realised that he would never be able to reach her before she got to the Cathedral's doorway. There were simply too many people here in the square.

Cursing under his breath, he was bemoaning his bad luck when he saw the lady start to climb the stairs that led to the great doors. All there were slipping their hands into the niches about the main column, atop of which Saint James himself sat gazing down with a welcoming expression on his stone face. While Parceval watched, he saw a man arrive at Doña Stefanía's side, a stolid, slightly hunched man, with a curious way of holding his head, as thought it was too massy on the left side to be supported.

'Get away from her, you bloody bastard!' he muttered.

Chapter Two

On arriving at the great column, Simon and Baldwin knelt and reached in with their hands, in the ritual of holy greeting to the Saint, Baldwin gazing up at the Saint with a murmured prayer, soon after repeating the *paternoster*.

Simon was bemused to see his friend so overcome.

Sir Baldwin de Furnshill, as he well knew, had been a Templar, and Simon also knew that his friend was deeply embittered by the destruction of his Order. It wasn't the kind of act that could ever be forgiven: Baldwin had been a driven man since the end of the Templars. Before that, Simon reckoned, Baldwin must have been focused on the ruin of the Moors who had evicted the Christians from their most holy city and forced them from the Crusader kingdoms in 1291 when they kicked the last of the garrison of Acre from the Holy Land. Baldwin was deeply religious, though he detested the Pope and eyed the Church askance, and Simon reckoned he must have been a ferocious enemy of the Moors.

Since that terrible year of 1307, Baldwin's life had utterly changed. He had lost his friends, many of whom were murdered by the French King's men and the Church's own 'Hounds of the Lord', the Dominicans, who manned the inquisitions and tortured the poor warriors, most of them unlettered, who had been held for so long. Men who had devoted their lives to God and His Holy Land were persecuted by another of the Pope's own Orders. It was no surprise that Baldwin had been so deeply disgusted, nor that he blamed the avaricious instincts of a corrupt and ignoble King and his lackey, the Pope at Avignon.

And yet Baldwin still trusted and believed in God. Simon wasn't so sure whether, if he himself had undergone these same trials, he would have been able to maintain the same faith as his friend. Baldwin seemed convinced that the Pope was responsible, and that had left him untrusting of politics and power, but he still had a strong belief in God and God's determination to protect His own.

Simon sniffed. If it had been him, he might have renounced his religion entirely and joined the ranks of the Moslems in the face of such dishonour and treachery. Others had, from what he had heard. Poor devils, once they realised that their own faith was turning against them, they bolted and found comfort in the ranks of the Moors. At least there they were respected.

Baldwin had strode on into the nave and Simon withdrew his hand from the hole in the column, cast an apologetic look skywards to where the Saint's figure now seemed to peer down with a more forbidding expression, and scurried after his friend.

Parceval didn't recognise the man at Doña Stefanía's side, but Gregory did, and as he saw the tatty-looking figure bend towards his ex-wife and murmur in her ear, he felt a worm of unease uncoil in his gut. Like the painful ache in his bad shoulder that invariably predicted a change in the weather, this feeling left him convinced that he would soon know more of the man he had seen leading the attack against the pilgrims.

He had thought the man was a mere outlaw, a felon set on stealing the few belongings of the pilgrims on their way to Compostela, and when the attack had failed and the survivors had been routed, he fully expected the leader to have bolted like the cowardly scum he must be, and he had; he had fled the field without standing by his men.

Gregory observed the two as closely as a man some hundred feet away could, and felt sure that the robber glanced about him as though checking that they were unobserved, and then, he thought, they passed their hands together as though touching – a clandestine signal of affection, he assumed at first, but then he looked at the man's hunched back and twisted neck, and his air of utter misery, and revised his opinion.

As he watched, he saw the foul-looking scoundrel stow something away in his purse. What could it be? A token of her affection?

The idea made him wince. His wife was of noble birth, and was painfully aware of the barriers between serfs and those who were freeborn. She would have looked down upon a squire, from her elevated position, let alone upon a miserable cur like this one. No, it couldn't be a sign of her love. Perhaps he was her servant . . . but no. He was not steward to a nunnery, not from the look of him, not unless affairs in Castile had changed greatly since his last visit.

But it could, he reckoned, be a payment.

There was some irony there. It was just his luck that he should have been close to being attacked by one of his ex-wife's own servants.

But that made no sense! Why should his wife pay a felonious son of a bastard Breton pirate and a Southwark whore money? It made no sense at all.

For Caterina, seeing her brother Domingo was a relief. He was a figure who had always loomed large in her life, up until her marriage, and spotting him in the square with his head held at that curious angle – the result of a fall from a pony when he was very young – made her heart lurch as though this in itself was a sign that her luck was about to change.

'Domingo! Domingo!' she called, but he paid her no heed.

That was odd. Domingo, always a man to have a finger thrust up to the knuckle in any pies available, was habitually cautious, always keeping a weather eye open for any officials. It was most strange to see him apparently deaf to her voice. Not like him at all.

Caterina pushed her way through the crowds until she was a great deal nearer, her forcefulness earning her curses and one hack on the ankle. At last she got close to him, just in time to see how he was ordered away by the Lady Prioress.

Caterina had heard much about her, of course. Doña Stefanía de Villamor was spoken of in hushed voices by Caterina's family, mainly because she had enjoyed a rather sordid history, being a married woman who gave up the world for a place in the convent. Not everyone liked her. They thought her to be a grasping woman, remote and unfriendly, with her eyes firmly fixed upon whatever pleasures she could win for herself on this earth, rather than the gains she would make in heaven.

That, so far as Caterina was concerned, was fine. She too had lost faith in heaven. All she wanted was a little peace here on earth.

'Domingo!' she called again, this time a little more peremptorily as he made to pass by her and go back out into the square.

His face was black with ingrained dirt, sunburn and a kind of grim misery that was so palpable, she felt his look strike her like a blow.

'Go away, peasant!' he snarled.

'Domingo, it's me – Caterina.'

'It can't be,' he declared, scowling at her closely.

'You look terrible,' she said gently. 'What is the matter?'

'My son. He's dead.'

'Sancho?' She listened aghast as he told her of the ambush on the pilgrims. 'But why did you attack them in the first place?'

He wouldn't meet her eye. 'It was for a good reason,' he said evasively. 'But the bastards cut my poor Sancho down as if he was nothing more than a calf. Just struck him down like a calf.'

She opened her arms to him, and he went to her, his sister, the widow who begged in black in the great square at the foot of the Cathedral. The sister who was dead to him.

When the two men had finished their prayers at the shrine of Saint James, they made their way out through the Cathedral to the northern square.

Simon was mentally drained after visiting the Saint's shrine and kissing the relics. The incense used had affected him like a strong wine, making him warm and comfortable, yet the rest of the experience had been unsettling. Although the words spoken by the priests were the same Latin ones he knew and expected, the intonation and accents were strangely different, as though being pronounced by children or untutored priests who were pretending a greater understanding than they truly possessed. To think that they should be guardians of such a magnificent cathedral!

And it *was* truly magnificent. He absorbed as much as he could, walking about the place after they had given their thanks for their safe arrival, drinking in the pictures and symbols all about. At the south portico he saw the Virgin Mary and he stared at her with adoration, admiring the way that the artist had depicted her with her child in Bethlehem, the three kings nearby, offering their gifts, and finally the angel warning them to leave and not return to Herod because of his evil plan.

There were other pictures, too. Simon's judicial soul rather enjoyed the scene painted near *The Temptation of Christ*. It showed *The Woman Caught in Adultery*. In her hand she held the head of her lover, which her husband had hacked from the body, ordering her to kiss it twice a day if she loved the man so much, even though it was putrid and rotten. Of course he found the punishment repugnant, but Simon privately wondered if there weren't some women who could benefit from such a salutary lesson in justice. He'd seen some during his lifetime who were little better than whores. With that thought came the reflection that many men deserved the same treatment.

The tomb of Saint James was magnificent, and Simon was intoxicated with the gold and rich crimsons. The altar cloth itself must have been a good nine by twenty or more handsbreadths in size – huge! Surely the patron who gave that must have been rich beyond imagination. The whole place was massive but beautifully proportioned, bright with light and constantly humming with the noise of hundreds of people talking and murmuring prayers.

This was the busiest time of the year, Simon had heard, and as he stared out over the multitude in the square, he acknowledged that he himself had never before seen so many people gathered together in one place. It was two days before the great feast day of Saint James, and it appeared to him as though the whole of Christendom had gathered here in order to honour the city's patron saint.

Of course, many of these people were only here to provide services for pilgrims. There were money-changers, people offering lodgings, shoe-sellers, wine-sellers, men selling herbs and spices – and everywhere were the folk hawking cockleshells, real or made of lead or pewter, to celebrate arriving at Saint James's Cathedral. Some fellows simply loitered around, Simon noticed, and he saw some of them spring up and stride over to a man leading a horse. There was a short discussion, and one lad took the horse away, over the paving slabs, up towards a beautiful well, next to which stood a large trough. Another man brought up a bucket of water and filled the trough for the horse, standing at its side as it drank its fill. This was clearly where riders left their mounts when they were in a hurry, Simon thought.

When he and Baldwin had first left the Cathedral, the sun was like a blast from an armourer's forge after the cool stone shelter within, and Simon had felt his energy being sapped as the first rays struck his heavy woollen tunic and cloak. He was sweltering in moments. Now he was less aware of the sun's warmth as he stood gazing out over the great square.

People were everywhere, dressed for the most part in their ordinary, day-to-day clothing: peasants in rough unmended hose and tunics that were all but rags; wealthier freemen with their pathetic bundles but more colourful jackets and shirts; merchants clad in expensive velvets or fine linens; knights with their slightly poorer quality clothing, but the swagger of the man-at-arms; clerics with their robes and slightly bowed heads. The scene was filled with reds and greens, ochres and yellows. Faces were blackened by the sun, shaded by their great broad-brimmed hats, many already wearing that symbol of Saint James, the cockleshell. Some wore real examples, the pale pink colour showing up clearly, while others had dull pewter versions which they would have purchased from the vendors along the Via

Francigena or from a thousand other places all along the route here from Tours, Vézelay, Le Puy or Arles.

'My God,' Simon murmured.

'Has the heat affected you?' Baldwin asked quickly.

'That must be the seventh time you've asked me that so far today,' Simon noted.

'It is important, Simon. You are not on Dartmoor now.'

'Dartmoor can be hot enough in summer.'

'Perhaps so, but here the temperature is that much warmer, and people do collapse from the heat. It affects everyone differently.'

'I can cope with heat,' Simon said confidently.

'Perhaps in England, but here you should be careful. It is something that my Order taught: always take refreshment when you can, for you need more in the sun. During my first years in these warmer climes, I had to be taken from my weapon training several times because of the heat. It is a terrible malaise, Simon. You become weak and sickly, dizzy and disorientated. I was thoroughly laid low and had to be given a cool bath and plenty of water.'

Simon pulled his hat over his brow without comment. It was, to his mind, a foolish piece of headgear. The felt of the brim was swept up and folded over to form a long peak at the front, like a duck's beak. It was designed, so he had been told, to keep the sun from his eyes, because it could weaken his vision. He was sure that this was another old wives' tale, to be treated no more seriously than the other tales he had once heard, of fevers being passed on by foul waters, when all knew that they came from vapours in the air; or the idea that taking blood wasn't good for a man, when all knew that letting some blood was the only way to balance a man's humours.

'What I need right now is some liquid inside me – and I *don't* mean water,' he said with determination.

'I doubt you'll find any ale here,' Baldwin said.

'They must have something to slake the thirst.'

'Yes . . .' Baldwin agreed doubtfully, eyeing the nearest wine-seller. Then he saw a cart with a larger barrel. 'Ah – cider!'

Simon followed the direction of his gaze. 'Yes, that will do perfectly. A pint or so of that will definitely help clear my head!'

Caterina led her brother away from the tumult at the Cathedral gates, and out to the square. A line of trestles stood in the shade of some chestnut trees and she took him along here.

The man selling cider and a thin beer didn't seem to care that Caterina was a beggar. He ignored her black clothing and veil, but waited until he saw that there was some money in Domingo's purse before serving them.

'What happened?' she demanded.

Domingo told her all about the attack, how he and his men had swept down only to be repulsed when the three strangers slammed into their flank, five men falling in the first few moments.

'It was evil! The fair man, he could have been a devil. A devil with yellow hair.'

She said nothing. In her life she had already experienced enough misery – she had lost everything. It was hard not to feel sympathy for her brother, though. His bereavement was all but unbearable, she knew. It was obvious in his eyes, and she squeezed his large, horny hand.

In a moment, he had snatched his hand away. Seeing the hurt in her eyes, he gave a twisted grin. 'I shouldn't be with you.'

'I was comforting you, Brother.'

'But you are no longer known to our family. You married against our will, and when you did that, you left us for ever.'

She felt the blow like a dull stab over her heart, but the pain was brief. Soon it had dimmed, like the memory of her husband's death.

He had been such a handsome, bold fellow. Brash, too, she could admit to herself now, from the vastness of the years. A young soldier in the service of the King of Navarre when they first met, she had been attracted by his courage and his stories of adventures near the mountains. He told them with a mock seriousness, but in each story there was a bawdy ending, or a sharp edge that showed him to be self-deprecating in attitude, a good trait in a man whose entire life was bound up with searching for honour and fame.

They had known each other only three days when they ran away and married. Caterina's father had refused to acknowledge her afterwards because for him, there could be little more dishonourable than that his own daughter should marry one of 'them'. He and his family had learned to cope with the continual raids, had learned to fight back and defend themselves, and now his daughter was marrying one of the enemy.

'You should never have married him,' Domingo said roughly. She knew he wasn't a man who could show love readily, and yet he meant to be kind. They had not spoken in years, and he was finding it difficult to talk to her, she knew.

'How is Joana?'

He grunted. 'Your cousin is much as she always has been – loud and demanding. Seems to think she can order people around for no reason. She asked me and my boys to come east, to guard her mistress; now my Sancho is dead, she's completely lost interest. Just wants . . .' He broke off, rubbing vigorously at his eye. 'Always wants things her own way or not at all. That Lady Prioress has turned her head. Gives Joana her old dresses, and then the silly mare thinks she's got the position to go with it.'

'She was once my best friend,' Caterina said sadly. Now she'd be lucky for Joana to acknowledge her in the street.

'You shouldn't have married a *mudéjar*,' he said harshly.

She wouldn't have if she could have helped herself. The thought of wedding a man who had Moorish ancestry was appalling to her, and yet when she saw him, his white smile, his lazy grin wrinkling those deep brown eyes, his tanned, dark face, when she felt his solid frame and those wiry muscles beneath, Caterina had simply congealed with desire. He was perfection, and a kind and attentive husband to boot.

But Domingo could never see beyond the colour of his brother-in-law's flesh. No matter that he had renounced the religion of his father and grandparents, that he had become a

Christian; to Domingo, he was still the enemy, and Caterina was sure that on the day Domingo had heard of Juan's death, he would have danced with joy. If she had enough cruelty in her, she would have asked about Sancho – and then *she* would have danced before him for the death of his own son. Except she wasn't cruel enough – or perhaps she was too drained with exhaustion to work herself up to such an emotion.

'He died in the famine?' Domingo grunted.

She nodded. 'He was in France with his lord, six years ago now.'

Six whole years. Since then, nothing to live for. Only survival. The mere thought of all those years gone was daunting, as though she had blinked and a quarter of her life had disappeared. She had been married for five years, from fourteen to nineteen, five wonderfully happy years. And since then, her life was empty.

'Yeah. And he died there,' Domingo said laconically. He had finished his pot of cider, and now ordered another. He didn't offer Caterina a second drink. 'Best thing. Saves you from being pointed out and laughed at. It's better.'

'I'm better off being a beggar?'

Since Juan's death, everything had fallen apart. Her son had died, her daughter had been adopted by Juan's sister, and Caterina had been left desolate. No money, no home: Juan's master wanted no women about the place. There was nothing left for Caterina, so she had packed her few belongings and returned to her home a little south of Compostela. But her father rejected her, denying that he knew her.

'I had a daughter, but she is dead to me. Be gone!'

There was nothing else for her but to come here, to the city, and make the best of things. She begged, and occasionally, when a man was interested, she sold her body for the cost of a meal, using the name María to protect her daughter. In her time, she had serviced many men, for as her resources dwindled and she began to feel the pangs of hunger, she learned that nothing was so precious to her as life itself. Only someone who had experienced hardship like this could understand how valuable life was, she sometimes thought.

Just then, Domingo's head shot up. 'There he is,' he spat. 'The murdering bastard!'

'Where?' She followed his gaze and saw a man on a tall, high-stepping horse. It might have been an Arab, from its spirit, a beautiful, glossy beast that scorned the feeble humans all about its massive hooves.

'He's the man who killed my boy,' Domingo grated, and he stood up.

'Will you get him?' she asked with some trepidation. She had never seen Domingo in this mood before. He looked like a man on a suicide mission, who would dare an entire army for his own justice.

He made no response, but sprang over a low wall, and then pelted away across the square, darting in and out of the people standing before the Cathedral.

She cried out, but he was already out of hearing, and as she felt the intimidating presence of the cider-seller looming over her, she dug out the few coins in her purse and dropped them on the table, before quickly striding away on her long legs.

Domingo ran at full tilt, but in moments he was swallowed by the crowd. Although the fair knight was on top of a horse, Domingo was too low with his hunched back to be able to keep an eye on him. He ran on until he came to where the rider had been, and stopped to take a squint about him. Clambering onto a low wall, he saw one man riding along an alley.

Filled with eagerness, Domingo leaped lightly from his perch and hurtled along an adjacent alley until he came to an intersecting lane. Down this he went, his heart swelling, whether from the exertion or from the thrill of tracking down the man who had slaughtered his son, he didn't know.

He felt the fury churning in his belly, begging for release. In front of his eyes, he had a picture of his son as young Sancho was slashed and stabbed, then toppled white-faced from his horse. The memory made him want to kill the fair man with his bare hands – pull out his entrails, rip out his beating heart from his breast, tear off his tarse and cods and stuff them in his mouth, before slowly slicing off his entire head, so that the man could feel every moment of his death. He wanted agony – true, all-encompassing agony – inflicted on the man who could murder his son.

At the end of the road, he stood with his back to the wall, unsheathing his knife, holding it in two hands as he tried to control his breathing, and then, as the hoofbeats approached, he licked his lips, said hoarsely, 'For you, son,' and stepped around the corner.

The horse reared and its rider, a red-faced Castilian with a yellow hat, let out an oath and Domingo's rage left him. Still swearing, the man rode on, and Domingo slumped against the wall. He would kill the murderer, though. He *would*.

'I swear it, my son,' he vowed, and then sobbed drily.

Chapter Three

Doña Stefanía felt calm and soothed as she left the Cathedral, her head bowed in humility, her hands concealed in the sleeves of her habit. The little disappointments were fading from her memory, as was Domingo's incompetence. She shouldn't have trusted him to try and perform a simple task. A man with so many fighters behind him, and the lot of them were bested by a trio of mercenaries? Pathetic! Why did she have to put her faith in idiots? She should form her own retinue. It wasn't as though she couldn't afford it, she mused. She knew why she didn't, though. It was simply that the cost of keeping a force of men would be prohibitive in the longer term, and all too often the men could become more trouble than they were worth. Especially in a convent like hers, in which there were too many attractive young women.

There must be no hint of impropriety about her place, she reminded herself, patting her purse gently. The Bishop would never allow her to remain there if he heard so much as a whisper of misbehaviour. That thought brought up the inevitable memory. It was, she thought, like a piece of dog's excrement that she couldn't scrape off her shoe, no matter how hard she tried. If only she hadn't been so rash, so driven by her lusts. Then she wouldn't have had to try to have the fool killed before he could spread tales of her salacious urges, and Domingo wouldn't be sulking because of losing his damned son!

'My lady.'

The voice made her heart lurch, and she was all but expecting to be told that she was to go with a guard to see the Bishop, when she realised who it was.

'Señor,' she said coldly, with a slight dip of her head in the direction of the knight in his tunic of Santiago. Frey Ramón, she groaned inwardly. So devoted – and so *dull*!

Spanish, she knew, was the most beautiful language, but this man's Basque accent was so strong he sounded like a peasant from the mountains. In response her dialect reflected her nobility as she spoke with a deliberately pronounced Castilian clarity that sounded like small bells of crystal. 'You are good to have waited.'

'It is my pleasure,' he said, and cast an anxious look at Joana, who stood a little behind Doña Stefanía.

He had the dim-witted devotion to Joana of an ape, the Prioress thought scornfully. And for some reason her maid gave every sign of reciprocating his feelings! It was a curious thing, she had often found, that women who were in every other way perfectly sensible and wise, could show in their choice of men a sad lack of commonsense. Joana was intelligent, she had beauty of a sort, and her appearance was fine, wearing as she did Doña Stefanía's own cast-off dresses. Today she had on a magnificent blue tunic with bright yellow embroidery at neck, cuffs and hem. Most men seeing her would think her a lady in her own right, with her calm, brown eyes and olive complexion. Her mane of dark hair was decorously concealed beneath her spotless wimple, but there was just a slight hint of the long braids beneath, just as the length of the tunic showed how long were her legs, and the belt nipped in nicely to show off her hips, waist and the bulge of her bust. Yes, with her smiling oval face and full lips, any man would be pleased to have her at his side.

There was only the one reason why she wanted him, surely: his money. Frey Ramón might not be a great lord with huge estates, but there was one thing certain about a Knight of Santiago, and that was that such a man would never be forced to beg for his food. She could wed him, comfortable in the knowledge that she would have time to herself, that she would gain not only a husband but also servants and staff and that she would never have to work again. A fair enough exchange, Doña Stefanía thought.

It would be cruel to separate the two, judging from Frey Ramón's languishing expression, but Doña Stefanía had no wish to throw them together either. She wanted to talk to Joana if she could, ask whether she was serious about this fellow.

'I think,' Doña Stefanía said, after a moment's thought, 'that it would be most pleasant to take a short ride now. You know where I am staying, Señor. Perhaps you could come and meet me there?'

'Um . . .' He threw a longing, confused glance at Joana, and Doña Stefanía sighed to herself. It was hard, when dealing with dolts. She would advise Joana to give him a tumble, if she desired, but really, when she had enjoyed herself with him, she would have to throw him over. Surely she must realise how dull-witted the fool was!

Frey Ramón mumbled his response like a carter's boy, and it was all she could do to maintain her smile as he ducked his head in a deep reverence, before walking away backwards. No matter his birth and the colour of his tunic, he was still an unmannered oaf, like a serf. Any man could swear to poverty and obedience when he knew he could wed and enjoy the natural pleasures of a man and woman, and Frey Ramón, was a man like any other. Ramón of the hairy-arse, she thought of him. The idea of his embracing Joana made her shudder.

'Are you seriously intending to leave my service to marry that *imbecile*?' she hissed.

Joana's eyes took on that heavy-lidded look of obstinacy which Doña Stefanía recognised so well.

'You can look at me like that, if you want,' she told her maid tartly, 'but it won't change anything. Look at you! You could have your choice of many fellows. You don't have to stick to *him*! He's so . . . so silly!'

'And you think that you behave better?'

It was a slap in the face. The lady took a sharp breath, but then let it out gently. 'Very well. I am no paragon of virtue, perhaps, but that doesn't mean that you need throw yourself away on a fellow like him.'

'He suits me. He would do anything I wanted,' Joana said, 'and that serves my purpose for now.'

'For now maybe, but marriage is for a lifetime, not for a few moments of idleness.'

'Perhaps.'

'Is that beggarwoman waving to you?'

Joana glanced up and along the way to where Doña Stefanía had seen the tall beggar. The sight seemed to surprise her, and then she gave a cold smile. Murmuring a word of apology, she left her lady, as though making for the beggarwoman, but turned away at the last moment when she saw Ramón and paused to talk with him instead.

Foolish, Doña Stefanía thought, her mind still locked on the riddle like a terrier fighting to get the marrow from a beef bone. Why couldn't she have picked a fellow with a brain and looks? There were enough of them about. If Doña Stefanía herself decided to choose a man for her personal use, she would be sure to select one who was on her own level.

At the thought she gave a twisted grin. The last man with whom she had slept wasn't at all the right sort. If she was honest, Parceval Annesen the Fleming was a scruffy peasant at whom she would not usually have glanced, but there was something about his persistence. It was just as though he had fallen in love with her, and that was enormously complimentary. He did at least have manners; he was extremely polite. And although Doña Stefanía wouldn't usually have entertained any thought of sleeping with him in the normal course of events, while away from her priory, and with the thrill of his obvious infatuation, she succumbed and let him take her. At the time she had thought it could be dangerous: and now . . . Well, she had been proved right! She had no wish for a man to come and blackmail her – and yet that was exactly what had happened. It was unfair!

Perhaps, she thought, that dullard Ramón was *not* so unsuited for Joana, after all. At least he was devoted to her, from what Doña Stefanía could see. Watching the two of them now, she saw the little caress Joana gave him – a fleeting touch on the forearm, no more. There was no need. He was enraptured, smitten, hooked. Bowing to Joana, he walked away backwards for a few paces, as though intending to fix every aspect of her upon his mind, reluctant to leave her presence.

Doña Stefanía pursed her lips. What an idiot. He was just like a lovesick youth. Yet he made Joana happy, and that was good.

Joana was talking to the beggarwoman now, a tall woman who looked much like Joana herself, apart from the heavy black material of her habit and veil. There was no hunching to her shoulders, no palsied hand shaking beneath the noses of passers-by; in fact, she had the carriage of a noblewoman. Doña Stefanía thought she could herself have been a lady.

It was annoying that Joana would still go and talk to people who were below her station. It was always a mistake, Doña Stefanía thought sourly. It made those to whom she talked feel as though they had some importance, which was entirely spurious. Better by far to leave them to their own kind.

There she went again, laughing with the beggar. Joana would always have a word with even the lowliest. For many people who knew her, it was a part of her charm; for Doña Stefanía, this ability to talk to any person, whether a whore, a beggar, or a queen, was a sign of the girl's foolishness. One should always remember from whence one came, and stick to one's equals while serving one's superiors. That was the whole basis of society. If peasants started to think they were equal to lords and ladies, there would be rioting. Better that the peasants should know their place. Better for everyone. Peasants didn't enjoy being treated like equals, they preferred certainty. But a person's station in life mattered less to a woman like Joana, the Doña assumed. After all, she was born a peasant herself, so there was less stigma for her, talking to the dregs of society. The Doña herself would have found it very difficult to talk to some of the folks that Joana sought out – like those beggars. Nasty, befouled people that they were. Most of them were perfectly healthy, too. They only begged because they were lazy.

It wasn't only Joana who went to the beggars. Another group of pilgrims had just entered the square, and Doña Stefanía saw a monk, two merchant-types and a tall woman in black all reaching into their purses. Fools. All they were doing was showing the beggars that there was money to be made.

'Doña? Doña?'

She took one look at the grubby out-thrust hand and commanded, 'Begone.'

'Could you spare a coin for an old man?'

'No. If you want alms, claim them from the Cathedral.'

He was frowning now, peering determinedly. 'Doña Stefanía?'

She turned and looked at the black-clad beggar, slowly taking him in, up and down. 'What do you want? I have no money for you.'

'I remember you. You were wife to Gregory.'

She drew in her breath. 'I do not know you,' she said. The insolent son of a Moorish slave!

'I used to be a knight, Lady – Sir Matthew,' he whined. 'I knew your husband.'

This creature used to be a knight? It hardly bore thinking of. Some knights occasionally suffered loss, when their master died or they were thrown from their positions because of some real or imagined misdemeanour, such as trying to bed the master's wife. That was the most common cause of a knight's urgent separation from his place of bed and board. This fellow did not fit her picture of an adulterous servant, however. Nor did he look like a knight, even one who had lost his position and livelihood.

'Go away, little man! I do not know you,' she snapped.

Matthew stood unmoving for a long moment after the Doña had walked away with her nose in the air.

Only ten years ago he had been a man of honour. He was called to meetings with great lords, his opinion was sought by the rich and powerful, his support enlisted.

In that one decade, his entire life had been pulled apart; his position in the world had been whisked from beneath him and his status utterly eradicated. There was nothing he could do about it. There were no allies for a man who had been a Templar. Eleven or twelve years ago, he would have been able to report the behaviour of that vain Prioress to her Bishop and felt sure that she would have learned to regret her rudeness.

A couple of traders were watching him unsympathetically, he noted, as though they were preparing to evict him from the square. He turned and walked away between the stalls, until he reached a clearing, and there he almost stumbled into a pair of arguing women.

'Caterina, look at the state of you! I'm shocked that you've sunk so low.'

'What would you expect, Joana? My father won't support me, therefore I am destitute. What else can I do?'

'What of your husband's master? You gave up everything for your man. Wouldn't he look after you if he knew the depths into which you have sunk?'

'Look after me! How many masters accept responsibility for their servants' widows?' Caterina said scathingly. 'There is little enough chance of that.'

'There may be a way for you to earn some money.'

'How? From your mistress? I doubt it!'

'Perhaps so,' Joana said slyly. 'I may be able to help you.' She nodded as though with satisfaction, but then noticed a shadow gliding forwards. 'Domingo? Is that you?' she demanded.

'Yes. I missed the bastard! He got away, but I'll—'

'Shut up about him,' his cousin ordered. 'We have more important things to worry about.' She became aware of Matthew and demanded: 'What do *you* want?'

'Me? Only alms,' Matthew said, trying to fit a suitably humble tone to his voice. It was hard, God, but it was hard.

Domingo moved towards him. 'If you don't disappear, old man, I'll make you – got that?'

Matthew squared his shoulders. A flare of anger ran through his bones like quicksilver, making him recall his past, as though his youthful strength might return to him and give his muscles the power they once enjoyed. He clenched his belly and felt his shoulders drop, a leg slipping back into the approved position for defence. Yet even as his body flowed automatically into the posture, there was a twinge in his ankle and a stabbing pain in his thigh. If he were to try to fight this man, he would be killed within seconds.

That stark reality hurt. Even after the destruction of his Order, he had known that he could fight off an assailant: now even that was taken from him. His stomach was empty, not only from lack of food, but from the emptiness in his soul. He felt like a warrior who had been left on the field after a battle, watching with empty eyes as the scavengers arrived – the crows, foxes, rats and men and women, thieving what they wanted from the corpses. He was the last alive, the remaining member of his unit. And now he had been dishonoured by a felon whom he would have killed with one hand tied behind his back when he was a younger man.

His head hanging, he turned and stumbled away. At last he looked what he knew himself to be: an old, broken man.

Joana watched him shuffling away, then turned to her cousin again. 'So, Caterina, you'd like to win my lady's favour, would you? I think I might be able to help you there.'

'What do you mean?'

'Never you mind for now. Later, when the sun is two hours past its highest, meet me again. There is a ford north of here where many women do their washing. I'll tell you then. I promise it will be worth your while.'

Caterina held her gaze steadfastly. 'Very well, but I beg of you, don't make me hope for something which you can't provide. Please, I am content now.'

'*Content?* Look at yourself! A stale widow, no use to anyone. No money, no property, nothing,' Joana said with disdain. 'If you want my help, do as I say. Otherwise, be damned! Now leave me.'

In the face of her cruelty, Caterina held her head high, but as she turned, she couldn't help a shuddering sob from racking her frame. It was only with an effort, Joana noticed, that she kept herself from breaking down and weeping. The maid was somewhat disappointed not to hear evidence of Caterina's grief as the beggarwoman passed in among the stalls and out of sight.

'Poor bitch,' Domingo muttered. He was still wiping his eyes, and now his voice sounded thick.

'Oh, you're not going to start weeping again, are you?'

'I'm not weeping! I don't weep! I seek the murderer of my son, and when I find him, I'll make him regret ever trying to harm a hair on my Sancho's head.'

'Very brave, very commendable,' Joana said. 'Right – did you take the mare like I told you?'

'Yes, and put her back in the stable.'

'Good. Then go. I shall find Doña Stefanía and comfort her, and then take her place.'

'Are you sure of this?' Domingo asked hesitantly. 'It may be dangerous.'

'Domingo,' she returned impatiently, 'you are a fool. You worry about yourself and leave my safety to me.'

And with a new sense of purpose, Joana strode off to seek her mistress.

Doña Stefanía's annoyance grew as she wondered where Joana had gone. The maid was nowhere to be seen. Maybe she had made a tryst with Ramón, and had forgotten the time, or perhaps she had forgotten about Doña Stefanía's appointment. Either way, she was late, and that was intolerable, today of all days.

Time was moving on. She had to find her mount, the Prioress thought, patting her purse. Where on earth was that peasant with her horse? Gazing about her with a crease forming on her perfect, broad forehead, she felt a rising disquiet. Thefts from pilgrims were always a problem. Women were robbed, knocked on the head, raped, sometimes taken and kept imprisoned by uncultured villeins who sought better quality wives than the women of the villages in which they lived. Well, that was fine. Men were at risk too, she knew. Only the other day she had passed

Lavamentula, and was told that it was a famous place for robberies, with pilgrims having all their clothes stolen while they bathed in the waters.

It would be no surprise if her mount had been stolen. Men had eyed it with interest in several towns as she passed through. The horse had cost her a small fortune. Ambleres were always hideously costly, and a popular target for thieves. Damn the lad, she wasn't going to see it taken by a beardless boy!

Aha! Thank God. There he stood – over near the well, just where she'd told him to take her mount before she went up to the Cathedral. The thought was hardly in her mind before she was on her way over to him.

Seeing her mistress, Joana lifted her skirts to hurry over and join her.

'Where is my horse?' Doña Stefanía demanded as she reached the lad.

'*Your* horse?' he repeated, a faintly anxious expression rising to his face. He was a typically swarthy, unhealthy-looking serf, vacuous and incompetent – and right this minute as nervous as any felon caught filching a lord or lady's purse.

'Yes,' she said tightly, '*my* horse. I left her with you while I went into the Cathedral. Perhaps you remember now?'

'But the man . . .'

'What man?' she snorted. His manner was shifty; why she had left her mare with him, she didn't know. Looking at him now, it seemed obvious he was a wastrel. He'd taken her mount and probably sold it already. 'Where is my horse, you thief?'

'My lady, please don't shout!' he begged, his hands up, but it was too late. There was whispering and now a space opened about them as the crowd became willing and eager witnesses. Among the voices, Doña Stefanía heard muttering as other pilgrims realised that this fellow had not just robbed any old pilgrim, he had taken a lady's horse, and a lady of the cloth at that. There were many who would be ready to hang a man for that.

'You have my horse? Good. Where is it?' she said, her voice cold and relentless.

'But you asked me to deliver the horse, and I did.'

'What do you mean?' she scoffed. 'I told you to keep the horse for me and I would pay you when I had visited the Cathedral. Now you suggest I asked you to sell it and keep the money yourself, I suppose? You do know the penalties for those who rob pilgrims?'

Turning, she saw Joana behind her. She opened her mouth to command her maid to seek an official to arrest the peasant, but now the momentum of her speech was lost and the groom's desperate voice was winning support from others in the crowd.

'No, lady!' he pleaded. 'When you were going inside, your man came here and told me to give him the horse. He said he would take it to you because you felt faint and were going to ride to an inn. He paid me, too.'

'What man, eh? I see no one! Joana? I want you . . .'

'He took the horse and led it away.'

'A likely story!'

Now a basket-seller spoke up. 'It's true. I was here when the man came up. The boy was reluctant to hand over the horse, but this man, he accused the boy of calling him a liar. What else could the lad do?'

'What sort of man was this?' asked a suspicious-looking fellow who stood with his thumbs in his broad belt.

'Looked like a felon, but he had something about him, you know?' the helpful basket-seller said when the boy plainly wasn't going to reply; he was overawed and terrified that he could be accused and found guilty of theft. 'He wasn't tall, but hunched, and very broad about the shoulder, like one who's used to work – but his hands weren't dirty, so he was more like a knight than a peasant. Had a head that was sort of tilted to one side, like this, as if he had a pain in his neck.'

There was some sympathetic noise from the crowd. Clearly most felt that the lad had done his best, and any boy who was threatened had a right to protect himself.

'That's all very well, but how do I know you aren't in league with this fellow yourself?' demanded the Prioress.

'Lady, I am only trying to help.'

'Of course you are!' she said sarcastically, and threw a look at Joana. The description was all too familiar – but why should Domingo take her horse? More probably, this 'witness' had seen Domingo with her earlier, and thought this was a good way to deflect attention from the kid. Except there was an indefinable tone of conviction in his voice.

'The horse might be found,' Joana said. 'Shouldn't we go and look? In which direction was it taken?'

Doña Stefanía could have stamped her foot in frustration. This was not how she had intended spending her afternoon. Glancing over the crowds, she wondered where that oaf Frey Ramón had gone, but it was too late and he had disappeared. He wasn't here, and neither was her mare.

'Ballocks!' she said viciously in English, but the folk about her merely stared uncomprehendingly.

Joana alone understood, and she was waiting when her lady joined her and spoke from the corner of her mouth. 'It was *him* took my horse, was it, your damned cousin? Why should he steal *my* horse?'

'If he did,' Joana said soothingly, 'I assume it was because he saw it held by a stranger and sought to protect your property.'

'Don't give me that,' Doña Stefanía snorted. 'He's a thief and a leader of thieves. When he saw a horse waiting with a groom, he saw a profit to be made, and that's all.'

'Perhaps I can find him and ask . . .'

'Ask him what?' Doña Stefanía hissed with frustration. 'There's no time – look at the sun. No, there's no choice: I'll have to use your mount, Joana.'

'Doña Stefanía, let me go instead.'

'Why?' the Prioress demanded with some surprise, and frowned with indecision. There were advantages to sending Joana: it was the hottest part of the day and as Joana knew, Doña Stefanía would always prefer to remain under shelter with a jug of chilled wine rather than gad about in the heat of the sun. And as for going and meeting this man . . . But it was she that he wanted, not Joana: it was *her* secret that he held. Besides, to stay away would be a tacit admission of fear, and Doña Stefanía had a hatred of being thought a coward. She was a noblewoman, after all.

'It would be safer for you,' Joana replied. 'If there is only one of us, it could prove dangerous, but I don't mind.'

'Safer?' Doña Stefanía stiffened and then pulled out her rosary, the cross dangling. 'I fear no felon! I have God to protect me.'

'I know, Doña, but think what a capture you would be to a man who had no scruples. If he was not prey to the fear of God, you would be a magnificent prize, wouldn't you?'

The blackmailer, Joana told her, had asked for the contents of her purse, which surely meant solely the money. No one else knew what she carried, or so she hoped. Maybe Joana was right. There was no need to put herself into danger. She should at least keep her physical body from his clutches. There was little she could do to protect her good name now. Not even Saint James could save her reputation if that bastard got it into his head to ruin her, but that wasn't the point. She had no desire to be raped, tortured or captured just to satisfy her stupid sense of duty and honour.

She nodded her agreement, spun on her heel, and found herself facing Gregory.

'Oh, God! Not you again!' she exclaimed dramatically, throwing both arms into the air, and then hurried past him before he could stop her.

It was one thing for her to be forced into the painful transaction of paying a man to keep a secret, but it would have been quite another, should her ex-husband hear of her misbehaviour!

Chapter Four

They could smell the potent brew from several yards away and Baldwin eyed the cart with the barrel racked atop with a certain anxiety.

Simon saw his look. 'I don't care. It's refreshing. Cider always is.'

'Very well, but when we have finished, we must look for somewhere to stay the night. Rooms will be difficult to find.'

'Rooms!' Simon expostulated. 'After last night in that hell-hole of an inn, I'd prefer not to bother, thanks all the same! I'm covered in flea-bites and the lice are still squirming along my spine. No, let's just find a pleasant, shady riverbank and stay there.'

'I doubt whether the people of the town would be too pleased about vagrants sleeping out of doors,' Baldwin pointed out.

'You think someone would dare accuse *me* of being a vagrant?' Simon growled. 'I'd soon teach the miserable bugger to—'

'Look!' Baldwin said hastily. 'There's a place up there.'

'It's a bit rickety-looking,' Simon said doubtfully.

It was a large tavern, built into the side of a hill, so that on the ground level there was a cattle-shed, while the entrance to the place was on the next level. From the look of it, there was plenty of space inside, with a small chamber jutting out over the alleyway to provide toilet facilities.

'You simply don't like anything built by a foreigner,' Baldwin said lightly, 'but I'd rather a room in there than another night in the rain or being arrested as a vagrant.'

Simon grunted, but he couldn't disagree. No one liked tramps sleeping rough, and he had no wish to be arrested.

They had reached the cart of the wine-seller, and at this moment their conversation was interrupted by the arrival of a slim, short woman with black hair and gleaming eyes. She nodded encouragingly at them.

'Cider,' Simon said, holding up two fingers.

'Simon,' Baldwin remonstrated, 'not all people here will speak English.'

'Sí, señor,' she nodded and was soon back with two large jugs.

'See?' Simon said triumphantly. 'It's easy to get what you need when you show a little understanding.'

Baldwin smiled. He knew that in a city like Compostela, many traders would be used to the curious languages spoken by pilgrims from all over the world. A moment later, before he could frame a reply, he became aware of a woman behind him. She was hunched over, dressed entirely in black, a hood thrown over her head, veil covering her face like all beggars, a palsied hand waving before her as she wailed and wept, bemoaning her fate, her bare feet dusty as she shuffled through the dirt. She approached the two, her crying increasing in volume.

A woman like that, Baldwin mused cynically, would be more of a challenge in communication. He was wrong.

'Bugger *off*!' Simon said unsympathetically, and without missing a note, she moved away like a ship turning across the wind, seeking a fresh target. 'I hate being confronted by beggars. You know that most of them are professionals, trying to gull the innocent out of their hard-earned money, yet some will always help them.'

'There is a motive – you have heard of charity?'

'Yes. And I give a good tenth of all my income to support people like her,' Simon said, '*if* she is genuine. But most beggars aren't, as you well know. If only they'd take up work, they could get by. It's people like her who prey on crowds, knowing that among all the people she only needs . . . what? One in every twenty or four and twenty? That would bring her plenty of money for herself and a family of eight squalling brats. If she was really

that desperate, the Cathedral would look after her. I'm sure there
are alms enough for her at the doors after each meal. The
Almoner wouldn't see her starve if she is needy.'

'Perhaps. And yet I think that the famine here struck the
peasants more cruelly even than in England.'

'Baldwin, you are growing soft. No, we suffered badly
enough. Remember cannibalism, God save my stomach! That
occurred in places like Wales and Kent – and Devon,' he added
meaningfully.

'I remember.'

'There you are then.'

Baldwin grew aware of another dark, shambling figure
standing a short distance from him, and groaned to himself. He
disliked spurning genuine beggars, but was sure that Simon was
correct and that the black- and grey-clad shapes that moved and
moaned among the hordes in the square were opportunists and
no more. He turned away and sipped at his cider, hoping that the
fellow would be daunted by his back.

Then he felt a creeping chill like a snake slithering slowly
down his spine as he heard the man speak. At first there was no
recognition, but then something of the voice snagged on a
memory, and Baldwin realised that he knew this man. There was
a cough, and he heard a voice say gently, 'Sir Baldwin, you
wouldn't ignore an old comrade, would you?'

Baldwin felt more comfortable when he was sitting with his
back to a wall in a shaded room off the square.

The innkeeper had welcomed Simon and himself effusively
when they approached, but his attitude altered as soon as he
caught sight of the limping figure behind them. Holding out
both arms, he made brushing motions at the beggar like a man
waving away a fly, and Baldwin had to move between them,
staring coldly at the innkeeper until he backed down and allowed
them all inside.

It was a pleasant little spot. Not far from the Cathedral, so
that they could see the great building looming over the roofs, it

was sheltered from the heat of the sun, but even so Baldwin was relieved when a jug of water was deposited before them by the host. He glowered at the beggar as though he expected to be stabbed as he turned his back, then reluctantly set a second jug, this containing a harsh wine, before them all. Three cheap pottery cups joined the jugs, and the keeper turned from the party as though glad to leave them.

'Did you know me, Sir Baldwin, did you – after so many years?'

Simon was gazing at the man with an expression of mingled doubt and distaste, and Baldwin could understand why. 'Brother Matthew,' he said gently. 'How could I forget you?'

'Easily, I'd imagine,' the man said sadly, looking down at himself. 'Not many would want to associate with such as me now.'

'You are no less honourable now than you ever were,' Baldwin said.

'No. I am far less honourable,' Matthew corrected, remembering the terrible desolation he had felt when he realised he dared not defend himself against the bully in the square. 'I used to be a knight, and now I can't even protect myself from attack. I am a beggar, pleading for my daily bread and water. I am that which I myself used to spurn. God knows how to bring down the mightiest, doesn't He?'

Baldwin put a hand out and touched the beggar's wrist. 'Those of us who were fortunate enough to serve God as we did will be honoured when we die, Matthew. All the crimes committed against us during our lives will only serve to increase our favour in the eyes of God.'

'I hope you are right!'

Simon looked away. The man's hood had fallen back now, and the tears were falling unchecked. It was somehow not merely sad. There was something Simon instinctively disliked about this Matthew.

He wasn't as repulsive as so many beggars were. There was no sign of physical disability about his face and limbs, which was a relief. Simon cordially detested the sight of the lepers and cripples who populated so many cities. Even here in Compostela, or perhaps especially here because so many would come to beg the Saint's aid, there were unnumbered men and women, hooded and concealed so as not to scare away those from whom they begged their alms. Fortunately this Matthew also appeared to bathe regularly, for there was about him none of the sour stench which Simon tended to associate with mendicants; nevertheless, for all that there was some aura about him which showed the depths into which his spirits had sunk. He was surprised that Baldwin couldn't himself feel the horrible emanation. It was like a miasma about the man.

Matthew had once probably been tall, but it was hard to tell now. He was hunched over, his head held so low that his unshaven chin all but touched his chest; however his face was still quite comely, marred only by age. His hair was that curious silvery yellow which showed that once he had been fair, but his features were burned as brown as an ancient oaken timber by the sun, and his skin looked about as soft. Simon thought that his eyes might once have been a bright cornflower blue, not that it was easy to gauge. Matthew was so used to peering into the bright sunshine that his eyes were habitually narrowed in a squint. That he could see perfectly clearly, Simon guessed, because his attention was forever moving, glancing at the table and picking at a crumb of bread, then going up to gaze at people in the crowds outside, back to the innkeeper, and then across to Baldwin or Simon.

He had suffered, though. Simon could recall all too clearly just how impressed he had been with Baldwin's appearance when they had first met, and now he was struck in the same way by this Matthew. There were deep tracks at either side of his mouth as though a carpenter had gouged them with his chisels. His tall brow was lined with proofs of care and fear, and his square jaw was clenched in rest as though there was no peace to be had for a man who had been so cruelly betrayed.

Yet there was something about him that grated on Simon's nerves: a faint whining tone to his voice, as though he was now so thoroughly habituated to his role as a beggar that he couldn't stop himself from trying to plead for money. Simon looked forward to getting away from Matthew. The man was twisted and ruined by his experiences.

'You did not try to find a new Order?' Baldwin asked now.

'I was in our preceptory at Pombal in Portugal,' Matthew said with a writhing movement as though the bench was uncomfortable. 'When the arrests were made in France, like so many of our brethren, I couldn't believe the accusations, but then we were arrested as well.'

'They took you into custody – but they did not torture you?' Baldwin asked gently.

'No. We were fortunate. King Dinis held us and set his own officials in the castles and towns, but he didn't misuse us. When our Father the Pope ordered that there should be an enquiry, King Dinis set up his own special court which found us innocent. But behind the scenes, he had agreed with the Kings of Aragon and Castile that they would all adopt a common policy. When the Pope commanded the Order to be suppressed, the three Kings had a special case. The Hospitallers didn't get the Templars' lands – they went to new Orders.'

'This King Dinis created a new Order,' Baldwin observed.

'He called it the Order of Christ,' Matthew agreed. 'It's based in Castro-Marim near the mouth of the Guadiana, to protect the Algarve. It was Dinis's father who won that back from the Moors only fifty-odd years ago with the help of the Temple, and Dinis always feared losing it to a fresh attack.' He stared down at the table before him. 'He took all the Templar castles and towns and gave them to his new Order. Castelo Branco, Tomar – all of them. Some he kept for himself, like Pombal and Soure. I suppose he was scared that there might be another power rising in the land if he let the Knights of Christ take all the Templars' lands.'

'Like the Hospitallers,' Baldwin muttered to himself.

'I was lucky. I was released when it was decided that I was innocent, but since then I have wandered as you see me now, penniless, destitute. I had no horse, no master . . . all I had once possessed I gave up in order to join the Templars, holding to my vow of poverty, so when I was thrown from my home, I was utterly bereft.'

His eyes had been dry for some little while, but now they filled once more and a single tear fell from his right eye, shooting down the darkened cheek and splashing on the table.

'Many were less fortunate,' Baldwin observed sympathetically.

'Many were *more* fortunate,' he countered. 'They died.'

Doña Stefanía watched Joana ride off towards the Porta Francigena and made her way back though the crush towards an inn. She had to hold her annoyance in check as she passed through the crowds, trying to preserve her dignity as best she might. Hawkers shouted, beggars pleaded and wept, urchins scampered, one stepping heavily upon her sandalled foot and crushing her big toe, but she kept her lips pursed and made no comment.

The beggars here were a dreadful nuisance. Children with withered arms, crippled men without limbs, women weeping, declaring themselves widowed and asking for food on behalf of their starving children. They were nothing to do with her. Her own responsibility was to the folk of her priory of Vigo and its manor, and she looked after them as well as she could, with some of the drier husks of bread and the carefully garnered remains of the meals, collected up and distributed to the needy at the convent's gate. She and her Sisters were generous, as they should be, but there was no reason why she should also support the poor of Compostela. That was the duty of the townspeople here. Doña Stefanía had limited funds, and these were already allocated. And now some must be scraped together for this accursed blackmailer.

She hoped Joana would find him and carry out her instructions. The maid was devoted to her mistress, of course, devoted and fiercely protective, so probably she would be successful. If

Doña Stefanía herself had gone, she might have broken down in tears, which could have been disastrous. It would show this fiend of a blackmailer what a hold he had over her. She had tutored Joana carefully in the time that they had; be calm, be cool, state the position and see what he says. There was nothing more she could do. Soon Joana would be with him, and a short while later Doña Stefanía would know his response. No doubt it would cost her a fortune, the devil! Well, he could *go* to the devil if he demanded too much!

For now, there was no point in worrying. Doña Stefanía was nothing if not a realist. The die was cast and there was nothing more she could do. She might as well take her ease. After this morning's efforts, she surely deserved a good pot of wine, and it might calm her nerves. Yes, a good pot of wine.

A small smile played about her lips as she sat down at a bench and signalled to the innkeeper. In a corner, she was astonished to see two respectable men – a knight and a prosperous yeoman – sitting with a beggar! A repellent fellow with hunched shoulders and downcast gaze, as though he was scared to meet the eyes of any others in the room – or maybe he was merely ashamed, she amended. He had the appearance of a man who wore his befouled clothes and the grime on his hands and face like a thin patina to conceal his genuine status. When he picked up his cup, he sipped it like a lord; when he spoke, he waited until his companions had stopped before speaking. And he didn't pick his nose, she noted. That was an improvement on many others.

Later on that day, she noticed him again, this time in the street, and he gave her a chill smile, ducking in a bow that was so courteous, it might have been given by a knight. That was when she realised that it was the man Matthew who had accosted her in the square. She barely acknowledged him, of course. A Prioress had no need of companionship from a mere beggarly peasant, after all, but then a short while later, he walked past her, and her nose twitched. He might look disreputable, but at least he didn't stink like some; in this climate men often smelled worse than hogs. This fellow had the odour of citrus about him, and some spices, as though he had rubbed them into his skin to take away the stench of sweat. It made her look at him again, wondering.

There were always men who were born to a certain position and who then lost all, some from gambling in tournaments, others from gambling on politics and being forced into exile. This fellow could be one such man – someone who had been born to a good position, but who was then forced to beg because he had somehow lost the favour of his master.

The observation made her feel a vague sympathy for him. If he had been born to nobility, he deserved her compassion. Anyone of rank who had sunk so low as to depend upon the gracious gifts of others must be deeply humiliated. To be like that, she told herself, was worse than being dead. The disgrace must be intolerable.

Not that all men could appreciate such finer feelings, of course. Her ex-husband Sir Gregory was one such example: he had none. No *humblesse*, no shame. No understanding of others, the devil! Ah, but why should Doña Stefanía trouble herself over him? When all was said and done, he was a mere churl, no better than a serf, and it was unlikely he would learn of the blackmail.

The idea that he might get to hear of her behaviour secretly appalled her. He could make all sorts of trouble for her, especially now, with the little box so securely held in her purse, she thought, a hand going to it and stroking it through the leather. Merely to touch it like that made her heartbeat slow a little. Yes, Gregory could have caused untold harm if he had heard. He mustn't ever learn of her fornication. It would all have been so easily resolved if Domingo had succeeded, the damned fool. All he had to do was kill Ruy and, regretfully, her tatty little lover Parceval, and all would have been safe. Instead the fool saw to the death of most of his men, including his own son, and since then his mind was turned more to his own grief than to what she needed from him. That was why she had to pay this blackmail.

It all came down to money. Always did. People had no interest in anything else. They wanted cash no matter what it cost others.

Certainly Sir Gregory had never concerned himself about others. From the look of him he was short of money now. He could have been a friar. Maybe he was! That would be a joke. A loud, roaring, rich knight reduced to poverty.

It had been a terrible shock to see him on the way here. Blasted man! In all the lands of Christendom, why did he have to come here? Maybe it was because he wanted to atone for some of his past offences. There were certainly enough of them.

She was bemoaning her fate when she realised that a man was approaching her.

'My dear lady! I felt sure it must be you as soon as I saw you in the crowd. Such elegance and grace could never be duplicated on this earth. Dearest lady, may I kiss your ring?'

She turned with a start, her heart leaping into her mouth, and gaped. 'My God – Parceval!'

The Fleming bowed with as much grace as he could muster, smiling at the expression of shock on her face. 'You didn't expect me here?'

'I didn't, no. Not so soon. You made very good time.'

'Well, a man in a hurry can always find a means of speeding himself on his way,' Parceval said easily. He tugged his purse around his belt so that it was under his belly, and reached inside. Pulling out some coins and peering at them shortsightedly, he held one aloft for the tavern owner to see and peremptorily demanded wine.

'Yes,' he continued, 'we set off at dawn and it was only later I asked where you were and was told you were staying behind. That was – oh – three days ago? You travelled quickly.'

'No, I set off before you,' Doña Stefanía said. 'I arrived here at noon yesterday.'

'You must have hurried,' Parceval said, but inattentively. He was watching the tavern-keeper.

It was fortunate that he didn't catch sight of Doña Stefanía's face as he raised the coin again. Had he done so, he would have observed rather less pleasure at their meeting than he might have wished.

For her part, the lady was appalled that her lover had material-ised here. She had enough troubles without this, but then another thought struck her and she stared suspiciously at his heavy purse.

She had hurried here, leaving in the dark to avoid meeting this man and his companions as soon as the blackmailer had made his demands. Frey Ramón had left with her, happy to be with his Joana, and delighted to be there to protect them both when Domingo's men were left behind.

When she met Parceval two weeks ago, he had told Doña Stefanía that he was a penniless pilgrim.

How, then, had he come to be in possession of so much money?

Chapter Five

Just as Parceval was sitting down with Doña Stefanía, Baldwin and Simon were rising to leave the same place with Matthew.

'Take a little of this, old friend,' Baldwin said gently, holding out his hand.

'No, Sir Baldwin. You keep it. You may have need of money on your travels. It is many leagues from England, as you will know. Many a weary mile to walk. How long did it take you?'

Baldwin held out the handful of coins for a moment longer, but seeing the proud expression in Matthew's eyes, he shrugged. 'We came by boat from Topsham. A merchant brought us in a matter of days. Sadly we were blown from our course, and ended up in Oviedo, so we had a walk of it from there.'

Matthew gave a smile that was all but a wince. 'It is good to hear that you are successful, Sir Baldwin. I would not like to think that all my comrades were as unfortunate as me.'

'I fear that many are,' Baldwin said sadly.

'Perhaps,' Matthew said. 'Some survived, though. In Portugal, some still hold positions of power and authority.'

'I had heard that,' Baldwin said. 'In some of our old forts.'

'Yes. In those which Dinis the King gave to the new Order of Christ, there are some men who were simply given the opportunity to change their title. All he did, when all is said and done, was take the words "And the Temple" from their name. Now they are "Soldiers of Christ". A tiny change. Such a little thing, and the Pope will accept them. While men like me, honourable men who did all we could to support the Pope, are shunned and left to beg like lepers!'

Baldwin touched his shoulder as he spat the last words. Matthew's jealous grief was all too apparent; like so many

Templars, like Baldwin himself, he felt the prick of betrayal. Clement V had been their only ruler on earth, after the Grand Master himself. They had all been proud that they answered to the Vicar of Christ himself and no other man. It was partly that pride which had ruined them, Baldwin knew, because the jealousy it instilled in others helped to ensure their destruction.

'But perhaps . . .'

Baldwin smiled encouragingly. 'Yes?'

'There could be former Templars in positions of authority in Portugal. If a man could find them and report them to the Pope, he might reward such loyalty . . .'

Baldwin felt his heart stop within him but when he spoke his voice was soft and kind. 'I hope no one would ever consider such a wicked act. What would be the point of persecuting innocent men to the end of their lives? You might just as well say that men could hunt me down . . . or you, old friend.'

Matthew gazed up at him with a dreadful expression of loss on his face. 'Oh Christ, what am I become!' he wailed.

'Please, do not upset yourself . . .' Baldwin began, but Matthew cut him off with a dismissive gesture and a weakly smile.

'Do not worry about me, Sir Baldwin. It has been good to see you again – very good – but I must be going now. If I remain with you, people will wonder what sort of man you are, and there will be little chance of your finding a room for the night. No innkeeper wants folk who mix with my sort. You could catch fleas and all sorts from me!'

He gave a brave, sad grin, and pulled his hood up over his head again, setting off along a narrow alleyway as though intending to avoid all other people.

A pathetic creature, was Simon's thought, but he kept his silence. One look at his friend showed him that Baldwin was deeply affected by the chance encounter.

'So many of us,' Baldwin mumbled. 'I wonder how many still wander the lands like him?'

'Were there many? I thought all your comrades were installed in monasteries or got placed in the Hospitallers,' Simon said hesitantly. He was unwilling to continue the conversation if it might trouble his companion, but he was intrigued. It was rare that Baldwin would discuss his experiences in the Templars. Even now, neither actually mentioned the name of the Order, not while they were in the open. If Baldwin had been discovered as a 'renegade', a Templar who had not been captured and who had never suffered a punishment nor been forced to submit to the Inquisition, he could be arrested here.

Baldwin gave him a troubled look. 'Some escaped to monasteries, I think, although I do not know how many. There are so few whom I have met and spoken to, like Brother Matthew there. He is older than me. When his wife died, he joined the Templars and, being childless, gave all his possessions to the Order. I remember meeting him when I had only recently joined myself. He was a tall, powerful man then. My heavens! He has changed.'

'What happened to those who weren't . . .' Simon didn't know whether to say 'executed' or 'burned', but he wanted to spare Baldwin's feelings.

'Many had already died. There was one old man, I heard tell, who was tortured so badly, they roasted his feet over a brazier until his feet were gone. Can you imagine that, Simon? He had to be carried into the Inquisition with a sack in his hand, and when he was asked what was inside, he showed them: it was the charred bones of his own feet! How could a Christian do that to an old man whose sole offence was loving God, and being prepared to lay down his life for God?'

His voice was pained. Simon knew that Baldwin was tormented with the thought of his friends being forced to suffer.

'You know, Simon, those men would never have submitted to any agony that the Moors could inflict on them. Any pain, any cruelty, would have been shrugged off. But these torturers were their own kind, they were all Christian – *that* was what made them give up. The Inquisition was composed of men like them, men who had taken the same vows to God and before God. That was what really destroyed them, the fact that it was the very same men whom they had fought to protect, who then betrayed them. Such brutality! Such dishonour!'

'You think most were killed?'

'No. Some, I heard, escaped the arrests and fled to Lettow, to join the Teutonic Order. Some, I believe, went to the Hospitallers for, to be fair to them, many Hospitallers were appalled at what was done to the Templars, just as so many Orders in Castile, Aragon, Navarre and Portugal were. It was so obvious that the accusations were false.'

'Yes,' Simon said, although he privately had his doubts. He could never tell this to Baldwin, but he believed that the allegations were quite possible. If the Pope could believe the stories, Simon was prepared to give him the benefit of the doubt, because the Pope had more advisers than he. 'So two Orders accepted renegades?'

'More than that. But in places like, oh, like Pombal or Soure, none of the old Order could be allowed to remain, because it might seem that the King was condoning the re-emergence of the Temple. He couldn't afford to do that, so he evicted all the knights and their sergeants.' And many, as Baldwin had heard, bitter at their dishonourable fate, had committed the all-but inconceivable crime of renouncing their religion and joining the Moors. Perhaps some had not actually given up their faith, but they had certainly gone to fight for the enemy. Baldwin could not blame them for that, not when their own religion had seen to their persecution.

'So no Templars remain in their castles?'

Baldwin pulled a face. 'I have heard that some places still have Templars. Many of the old ways continue in towns like Castro-Marim. Perhaps that means a few of my old friends survived the purges, just as Matthew himself did. I should like to go there to find out. Portugal is not so very far from here . . .'

His face was wistful. Simon saw his profile as Baldwin stared out southwards as though he could gaze through the walls of the buildings and far-distant hills and see a place he could remember from his youth. He looked so preoccupied, Simon was reluctant to break into his mood, but they had a pressing need.

'Baldwin, we still have nowhere to sleep.'

'You said we could sleep by the river.'

'You said we shouldn't.'

Baldwin chuckled drily and then gave himself a shake, as though he could shed his grim thoughts like a dog shaking itself free of water. 'Very well. Let us see if we can find a loaf of bread, a cheese, and a skin of wine. Then we may take them out of the city for a short way and rest by a quiet river unobserved by any. If it is dangerous, so be it. Today has been too lovely to think that we could be harmed by people.'

Simon smiled and walked with Baldwin to the vendors in the square, but all the while he kept shooting little glances at his old friend. No matter what Baldwin said, his face did not express pleasure in a lovely day. Rather he looked pensive and melancholic.

It took her almost an hour to get rid of the fool. Parceval was persistent, of course – well, she knew that – but really, the great dunderwhelp should have been able to see that she had other things on her mind. But no, he sat there languidly, ordering wine and trying to make her drink her fill, as though he was determined to get her so maudlin drunk she'd submit to another fumbling prodding when it grew dark.

'I am not thirsty, and I must soon go to the Cathedral to pray,' she said briskly at last, when all her attempts at subtle rebuffs failed – for she might want his companionship again later.

Her bluntness made him blink, but then he gave a rueful grimace and stood. 'I see I am not in your favour today, my lady. I am greatly sorrowed for that. My apologies. Perhaps you will permit me to see you again?'

'I should be delighted,' she said, unbending a little now that he was actually going to leave her. She gave him a warm smile. 'I apologise, but I must have a little time to clear my head before praying.'

'But of course.'

His mildly aloof manner told her in no uncertain terms just how he felt, like a young swain who was rejected on the first attempt at wooing. He would live. In the meantime, Doña Stefanía had other things to occupy her mind.

First among these, of course, was: how was Joana, and how had the rendezvous gone? She should know soon. Second, and a close second at that, was: where had the Fleming found his money? He was suddenly in possession of large amounts of gold, if the weight of the purse was anything to go by, yet when she had first met him out on the road, he had declared his absolute poverty. That was part of his attraction to her at the time. It was no smutty lust which had made her notice him, but the fact that he came from a different land, a completely different class and was therefore highly unlikely ever to meet her again; this meant that she could afford to take the plunge with the reasonable hope that she was safe from discovery. Only she and Joana had known that she had submitted to Parceval's clumsy attempts at seduction, so far as she knew, until later, when the other man walked in, anyway: Señor Ruy.

That damned knight had appeared at the chamber's doorway and had stood there stock-still as though shocked; she had seen him. Her view had necessarily been confused, being upside-down at the time, but she had recognised him. Parceval continued bulling like an ox on his cow all the while, hoarse grunts bursting from his throat at every thrust, oblivious to any interruption – to be fair, she herself hadn't stopped encouraging him at the gallop – and Señor Ruy stood there staring, drinking in the sight and sounds of their lovemaking. In a curious way, his silent presence stimulated her still more. It gave the Doña an especial thrill to think that she was exciting the knight while helping her lover to a climax. She had felt safe in the dark of the room, thinking that the man couldn't recognise her. All he would know was that a couple had been rutting.

Then he turned and marched away, just as Parceval gave a

loud groan, called upon God in his guttural voice, erupted, and collapsed panting sweatily on top of her.

In reality, she hadn't cared much about the knight at the time, and soon after Señor Ruy left, Parceval recovered enough to tease her to a fresh bout and she found herself responding enthusiastically. That was then; *now* she was worried.

The next day she saw Señor Ruy talking to another pilgrim out in the yard of the place, and realised with a jolt of horror that the man to whom he spoke was Gregory, curse his cods – the man she'd divorced; the man who knew she was a nun. Hardly the sort of fellow she wanted to hear about her nocturnal escapades. Just then Parceval appeared and saw her, all but shouting out to her, his face beaming, and she had hurriedly ducked away from him before Gregory could notice her. The little man had given her enormous sexual pleasure, true, but he was a scruffy churl, penniless and clad in worn clothing that would have shamed a *mudéjar*.

It was immediately obvious that she must flee the group as soon as possible, and it was her good fortune that the others decided to remain at that village, to rest and visit a local shrine. All that day, Doña Stefanía had kept herself away from the others and the next morning, she, Joana and Domingo and his men all rode off long before dawn, their destination: Santiago de Compostela.

In a way it was lucky that she had seen Gregory before he had seen her. Perhaps by now, Gregory had heard of Parceval's nocturnal exercises – the two men might even have talked together! The Prioress cringed at the thought. She had concealed her real name to Parceval, but if she were to stay with the band of pilgrims, she would have been pointed out, and it would only have been a matter of time before Gregory heard the gossip. She knew enough about men to predict that Parceval would enjoy boasting about his conquest. The eager little fellow! she thought with some affection.

Then that disquieting thought resurfaced: Parceval had been poor then. How *had* he suddenly managed to find so much

money? Where had it sprung from? It was curious that he was
suddenly in funds, just as she was losing her own.

Joana – *where was Joana?*

Joana had indeed reached the place chosen for the rendezvous,
but at first there was no sign of anyone there.

It was a pleasing spot, a quiet glade a little distance from the
roadway, near to the river, and for a while she just stood on the
bank watching the water drift past. Laughter came to her from
upstream and she stood back, shadowed by the branches of a
tree until she could see the source: some young women were
approaching with baskets of laundry propped against their hips,
probably heading for their favourite spot. Soon they had passed
and Joana could relax again. She didn't want anyone else to see
her here. That could only lead to embarrassment.

The bag in her hand was heavy and she stared at it wondering
how he could carry it away without it being noticed. But then
she reflected that he would have his own leather satchels to
transfer the money to. A man who was used to travelling, he was
bound to be accustomed to concealing money so that others
wouldn't notice it. Anyway, he was a knight. He must be used to
fighting and protecting what was his. Heaven help the footpad
who tried to pick *his* pocket!

Joana took a deep breath and sighed. Her heart was pounding.
Strange to tell, she was petrified. This was a new experience for
her. After all, he wasn't going to hurt her; she had the money,
and that was a guarantee of her future. Yet she still felt nervous,
in case her confederate, when he arrived, would be enraged.

Doña Stefanía would be on tenterhooks by now. She would
have drunk at least her first cup of wine, if not more. Suddenly
Joana wished she was there, with her mistress. She could have
killed for a taste of good wine, for a crust or two of bread dipped
in olive oil. Her belly felt empty, as though she hadn't eaten for
a week, and yet she was well enough. Still, when she looked at
her hand, she could see it was shaking.

'So, my lady!'

The hand on her shoulder made her squeak in alarm, but then the hand gripped her hair roughly, and she felt her head being pulled back and upwards until she was staring into his face, saw the fiercely smouldering eyes gazing down into hers.

That was when she knew she was lost.

Simon was first to hear the scream.

It exploded into his mind and shattered his dream of lying in bed with Meg, his wife. He wasn't in his bed, he was lying in the shade on a grassy riverbank in a foreign country. Shocked into full wakefulness, he shot upwards like a startled lark and stared about him.

Baldwin stirred beside him, and Simon prodded him with an ungentle foot as he listened, utterly absorbed. Flies hummed near, a large black one aiming for his face, and he waved it away, frowning with concentration, his other hand hovering near his sword.

They had been here for at least an hour, from the look of the sun's shadows, sitting and eating their bread and cheese in quiet contemplation, drinking wine chilled by the river, the skin left dangling by a thong in the waters. Once they were done, both men lay back and chatted desultorily until they submitted to the warmth of the afternoon sun and fell fast asleep.

'What is it?' Baldwin grumbled.

Simon was almost sure that the scream had come from farther upriver. 'A cry – up there somewhere.'

'Nothing now,' Baldwin yawned.

'Wait!'

Shrill and terrified, the cry came again and again, shuddering on the still air like the call of a strange bird.

Baldwin was on his feet, hand on his sword, already sprinting towards the sound.

Simon hurried along behind him, his sword out, the blade flashing as it caught the sun. The blade had been so well-used over so many years, that there was nothing left of the high polish which it had once possessed, in stark contrast to Baldwin's newer one. That flashed with a wicked intensity whenever the sun caught it, the carefully tempered, peacock-blue metal glinting like a well-cut and polished jewel.

Their path took them through lank, straggling grasses, wild flowers of white and yellow, under great trees and through drying puddles, and although it was not a great distance, Simon soon found his heart was pounding more vigorously than he had ever known it do before. He put it down to the strength of the wine, and perhaps the fact that he had eaten too much cheese, but he was sweltering in his rough tunic and cloak and would have felt no damper had he thrown himself into the river.

But all thoughts of his comfort disappeared as they ran through a small grove, past a donkey braying wildly, and some skinny chickens which fled, squawking, and found the two girls.

Neither was more than fourteen, Simon guessed as he leaned down, both fists on his thighs as he tried to catch his breath. Both were plainly petrified, but as Simon began to find his wind, he realised that a large part of their terror might stem from the fact that two foreigners had suddenly burst through the trees and materialised in front of them with drawn swords. He tried a soothing smile, but was rewarded with a fresh screech of panic.

It was Baldwin who calmed matters. He carefully thrust his sword back into its scabbard, motioning to Simon to copy his example, and then stared about him, ignoring the two girls. After a moment, they pointed and, to Simon's mind, jabbered incomprehensibly. Baldwin appeared to understand, and strode off in the direction which they had indicated.

The place was apparently the spot where some of the local women would come to wash their clothes. There was a broad sweep of the river in a loop, and because it was upstream from Compostela itself, the waters were clean and not befouled by the ordure thrown in by the thousands of inhabitants and pilgrims. The well-trodden path led down a grassy little bank to the water's edge. There, some large flat grey rocks provided scrubbing boards while the branches overhanging the place gave drying facilities. From the look of the shards of pottery, many women came here, did their laundry and then supped wine while they waited for their washing to dry overhead. It must have been one of the few relaxing times of the day for them, Baldwin thought to himself.

All this he took in with one glance, but then he smelled the foul odour of death. There was a loud buzzing, and he saw a small cloud of flies. He only had to go a short distance, a matter of ten yards. There he stood among some longer rushes and grasses, and Simon saw him stop and stare sadly down at his feet. For once, he didn't instantly crouch and touch the body. This time he stood stock still before silently beckoning Simon to join him.

Reluctantly, knowing from Baldwin's stillness as much as from the obvious fear of the two girls that this must be a murder victim, Simon went to join him. He never could understand the knight's objective approach to bodies. Baldwin was always, so he said, keen to learn as much as he could from a corpse, and after his experiences during a siege when he was a mere youth, he had picked up much about human bodies when sudden violent death was visited upon them. He had told Simon before that if an intelligent man could observe a body correctly, that body could speak of the murderer. There was more to be learned from a corpse than the mere number of wounds or their depth.

When Simon reached his side, he saw that Baldwin was contemplating the body of a young woman with the figure of a Madonna lying at his feet, head nearest him, body pointing to the river. From her hands and trim figure, she had been well-born. Certainly her hands had not seen much hard work. The flesh was clean and pale olive, like a wealthy lady's, with few calluses. Her dress was a blue tunic, very well cut, with expensive-looking embroidery at the neck, wrists and hem, but blood had soaked into it, turning it into a reeking, blackened mass.

She lay in some long grasses a short way from the river itself. Her arms were at her side; the back of her right hand was scraped, as though it had been rasped with a rock. A nail was torn away. Her head was turned towards the right shoulder, and a thick puddle of blood surrounded her dark hair, in which the first strands of white showed at the temples even through the thick gobbets of gore. Her legs were spread in the unmistakable posture of lovemaking, the skirts thrown up and over her belly revealing the dark triangle at the junction of her thighs. Simon glanced down and saw the marks of blood on the soft inner flesh. He swallowed hard.

This poor woman had not merely been raped; she had been bludgeoned to death, as though her attacker was enraged by her, as though he wanted to remove every sign of her. Her shoulders, hands and face were a mass of ruined flesh, as though the killer wanted to destroy her utterly.

Chapter Six

For Simon, the next half hour or so was disturbing in the extreme. The screams of the two girls had brought some farm labourers running from a field a short way off, and now five men stood scowling grimly at Baldwin and him. A sixth was retching near the river, and being comforted by one of the girls, who was still dreadfully pale, but seemed grateful for the opportunity of forgetting her own horror and concentrating on someone else's. Another man had gone with her friend into the city to fetch help.

In England, Simon would have known exactly what to do and say. He was not the First Finder, he was the fourth witness to arrive, after the two girls and Baldwin, and could be sure that he would be fined, but that would be the limit of his expense. But he wasn't in England, he was in Galicia, and he wasn't sure what the law said about the treatment of witnesses. However, he knew perfectly well that his neighbours in Devonshire, where he lived, would infinitely prefer to accuse a stranger than think that one of their own could have committed a foul murder such as this. If a local jury accused a local man, it was because he was possessed of a 'common fame' – an unenviable reputation for theft or robbery or simply mindless violence.

Here, Simon had little idea how matters would stand. He believed in the superiority of the English legal system, in which a man was innocent until proved guilty. In foreign parts, so he had heard, that rule didn't hold sway, and sometimes a man could be held until he had been tortured to seek the truth. Simon was appalled by the thought that an inquest could rely on the evidence of a man who had been systematically crippled, but he knew that it happened abroad. Baldwin himself was proof of that. The Templars had been tortured, generally one at a time in

front of their comrades, so that each should know exactly what
was in store for them, should they refuse to confess.

Torture was not routine, apparently, but that was of little
consolation, because all knew that the ways of foreign laws were
flawed.

Simon licked dry lips as he and Baldwin waited, trying to
avoid the hard stares of the peasants. One in particular was
holding his long-bladed knife at the ready as though wishing
that one of the two would try to escape.

Simon found he could remember some of the other things he
had heard about the legal system abroad. Often, a court case was
based on one man accusing another. If he could bring one other
witness to support his contention, the case was decided in his
favour – unless the defendant could bring more people to support
him. From what Simon had heard, it all came down to numbers.
Clearly it was a mess, because if two men were prepared to cook
up a story between them, they could get an innocent man
convicted. And then, if the latter refused to confess, he would be
tortured until he admitted his guilt!

In England the law was more effective, because the jury itself
determined the guilt or innocence of the accused. The jury would
report offences to the judges and, if they knew who had committed the crime, the jury would accuse him. Then it was up to
the Justice to impose the penalty. Thus all the folk of the vill
were involved; the jury comprised all the adult males, after all.
And *Englishmen* at that, he reminded himself, glancing at the
man with the knife.

It seemed hours before there was the sound of a crowd
approaching, although Simon was sure, from looking at the sun,
that it could only have been a short while. Then he saw a drifting
of dust over the low trees towards Compostela, which gradually
grew. At the same time, he was aware of his heart beating faster.

This was a novel sensation. He shot a look at Baldwin and
saw that his friend was frowning meditatively at the corpse, and
although he glanced up a few times in the direction of the city,
he was plainly unconcerned about his own or Simon's safety.

Simon wished he could feel Baldwin's confidence. No matter that he was innocent as a newborn lamb, it was the mere threat of being caught up in the machinery that was so intimidating, especially if the victim was gripped in a foreign system. Still worse if he, the foreigner, did not have a grasp of the language. From now on, Simon swore that he would always treat any strangers at home with more than usual courtesy and kindness, explaining to any man who appeared before him the whole system in which the fellow was caught.

The procession which at last came into view consisted of a man at the front with a broad hat concealing his face, while at his side walked a priest, also wearing a wide-brimmed hat against the sun. Behind them creaked a small cart, obviously prepared for collecting a body as a door was laid upon it. A fair group of onlookers were straggling alongside this makeshift cortège.

The first man tilted his hat up as he reached them, peering at the peasants intently before turning his attention on Simon and Baldwin.

He was a tall man, his shoulders slightly bowed, and he had a narrow, hawk-like face, with high cheekbones and a thin gash of a mouth. The eyes in his browned face were very dark; there was a ferocity in them that Simon found intimidating. It was perhaps because the man rarely blinked, which gave him a strangely reptilian aura.

This man studied Simon for some moments, then turned and subjected Baldwin to the same slow survey, before snapping out a question. Baldwin knew some Castilian and a little Galician, but he wanted to ensure that there was no room for misunderstanding. He looked at the priest and spoke in Latin. Simon knew that language from his studies, but Baldwin and the priest spoke so swiftly that he found it difficult to keep up. The priest translated to the inquisitor, listened to the reply, and translated that to Baldwin, who responded and pointed to the girl witness who had remained behind with them.

There was much shaking of heads as the inquisitor spoke to her. Soon her companion, the girl who had fetched him, was brought to the front and he questioned the two together, then the peasant men, all of whom now appeared obsequious, a fact which confirmed Simon's belief that this was the local investigator or judge.

The man nodded at last as if he was content with all he had heard, and crouched at the head of the body. As he did so, a cloud of flies rose from the corpse and he waved them away irritably, pulling out an orange from his scrip and holding it beneath his nose.

Baldwin, Simon saw, was watching him with interest, and even as the man rose to his feet and stood over the body, Baldwin was already staring farther off, in the direction of the water. 'We should go and look at the trail there,' he said to Simon. 'I should like to see whether there are any signs in the mud at the side of the water. Perhaps this woman or her murderer stood or struggled on the bank.'

The investigator gave him a piercing look, as though he had interrupted his thoughts, then spoke to the cleric, who sighed and translated again for Baldwin. Baldwin replied in Latin, and the investigator walked carefully around the body, gazing at the ground nearer the water. At last, after staring concentratedly for some while at something, he looked up and motioned to Baldwin.

Simon walked with his friend and found that the investigator was pointing at a large stone lying near the riverbank. It lay on a piece of mud, looking entirely out of place, as though a man had tossed it towards the water, but missed by some feet. If there were any doubts that this was the murder weapon, the smears of blood all over it dispelled them.

'The murderer killed her, then chucked the rock back here,' the Bailiff murmured.

'I expect he intended to hurl it into the river,' Baldwin nodded.

The two were so involved in their observations that they had momentarily forgotten the Galicians with them. Now the investigator spoke again.

'So, Señors, you were right to think of the mud at the water's edge.'

'Yes,' Baldwin said, and there was a faint smile on his face as he turned to the man. 'I congratulate you on your English.'

'Scarcely a surprise that I should speak English,' responded the tall man with a sniff. 'I studied at Oxford.'

The body was soon loaded on the door and carried to the cart. Then, while the crowd watched, the investigator spoke rapidly to the clerk, who had installed himself at the cart, and who scratched with a reed at scraps of parchment which had been bound together with a thong to make a thick bundle. When he was done, the investigator returned to Baldwin.

'Señors, I am called Munio. I am one of the six *pesquisidores* of Compostela. You would call me an "enquirer" in English, I think. I must investigate this death.' He added with a humourless smile, 'You agree that she would not have killed herself like this? Please, your names?'

When the two had told him who they were and explained that they were pilgrims, he held out a hand for their letters of *testimoniales*. Glancing at them, he read for a few moments before passing them back. 'You are welcome, but I am sorry that your pilgrimage should have ended in so sad a manner. Did you see or hear anything?'

Simon explained how he had been disturbed by the screams of the two girls and that he and Baldwin had rushed here to offer aid.

'You appear interested in the matter,' Munio said. 'It is not often that a man suggests where the *pesquisidores* should look.'

Simon could see that the man retained some suspicion of them, and he began to simmer with annoyance at this affront, but even as he opened his mouth to complain, Baldwin put a restraining hand on his forearm.

'Señor, in our own country we are both very experienced in looking into homicides. I am a Keeper of the King's Peace in Devonshire and often sit as a Justice of Gaol Delivery, while my companion here is a Bailiff of the King's Stannary in Dartmoor under Abbot Robert of Tavistock. We often work together in order to secure the punishment of murderers.'

'I see.' Munio drew in a breath and stared about him. 'If you can assist me in this matter, I would be glad. These peasants do not recognise her face – I doubt she would recognise herself. But they do not know this dress either. Perhaps she was a pilgrim. Is she known to you?'

Baldwin and Simon exchanged a look. They had not seen this woman before. Both shook their heads slowly, and Munio sighed. 'As I feared. It is hard to find a killer when the victim is not known. He could be a man desperate for a woman, could be unknown to her. Mere random death.'

Simon had listened, but now he shot a look back at the body and spoke up boldly. 'I don't think so. I've never seen a body mutilated like that before. It's as if someone killed her in a frenzy – someone who went berserk. Perhaps a jealous lover, striking her in return for a rejection? Or someone who wanted to conceal her identity?'

Baldwin nodded but he felt there was another possible explanation. 'In a city like this, where there are so many pilgrims, one might have decided to attack a woman to satisfy his desires. Perhaps it was another pilgrim who travelled here with the victim?'

'You think to accuse yourselves?' Munio said with a faint smile. 'But perhaps you are right. Perhaps one of the many pilgrims here became overwhelmed with the urge to possess a woman, and this is the result.'

'She rejected his advances,' Simon pointed out. 'Those scrapes on her hand – they look like marks made when she tried to defend herself.'

Munio nodded slowly.

'The peasants saw no one?' Baldwin enquired.

'No.'

Baldwin looked at them. When he and Simon had run here, they had passed no one. There had been no peasants, nor any other travellers. 'We dozed in the sun before we heard the girls' screams. It is possible that another man or men passed us while we slept.'

'Sí! So the murderer could have returned to the city.'

'Yes,' Baldwin said, but his mind was playing through the scene before him. A man had come here, molested the woman and killed her. 'Perhaps she walked here with the murderer. You should ask at the gates whether the keepers remember a woman dressed like this, and whether she walked alone.'

'I shall have it done.'

'And if he killed her here,' Baldwin said pensively, walking back to the body on the cart, 'it must have come as a surprise to her, for there is little sign of a struggle.'

'Only the scrapes on her hand.'

Baldwin nodded vaguely, but he was already exposing the woman's forearms. 'And here, on the underside of her forearm,' he said.

'Sí. What of it?'

Baldwin stared down at the arms. 'Perhaps nothing, but her assailant may have been unsure – nervous, perhaps – because it means that she was not killed with the first blow, but was able to hold up her hands and defend herself.'

Simon shrugged. 'I have seen women who have been able to hold their arms over their heads even after having massive injuries. Perhaps this is one such woman. Maybe she had a strong skull and thick skin.'

Baldwin nodded.

'In any case,' Simon continued, 'if you're right and this woman *was* adored by a man so that he formed a desire for her so strong that he was prepared to rape her, maybe his hand was reluctant. It's not surprising that he wouldn't want to kill her. It's an odd man who wants a woman so much, he'll murder her just to possess her.'

'It's a stranger man still who is so determined to possess a woman that he does not mind the fact that she's dead,' Baldwin pointed out gruffly.

'Maybe she wasn't dead when he had her,' Simon countered. 'He could have taken her by force, and then realised that she wouldn't forgive him, so he beat her. Maybe she taunted him, saying she'd have him arrested as soon as she got back to the city.'

'Come, Simon! How many rape victims have you known who have not shown extreme fear and loathing afterwards? Few would dare to taunt their attacker.'

Simon gave a fleeting scowl. 'I have known women who were not that scared of their rapist beforehand. Some had so little expectation of being attacked, they told the man that he'd best be off, before they told their father and brothers, and all too often the fellow's run. I've seen it many times. Familiarity breeds contempt, and the mere fact that a man wants to get inside a woman's skirts doesn't mean she's petrified of him, not if it's a man whom she knows well. If it was a man this poor girl had come to know on the way here on pilgrimage, perhaps she didn't fear a murderous assault until it was too late.'

'It is possible,' Baldwin admitted, but reluctantly. In his experience, women were all too prone to terror when they were raped – no matter how well they knew the assailant. 'But let us investigate the land about here and see whether there are any signs which might assist Señor Munio.'

Simon was happy to leave the body in the cart and join Baldwin.

The ground was hard and dusty, dried out already by the mid-day sun. It was only at the water's side that there was still moisture, but here there was only the mark of some feet walking to the water, then away.

'Small feet,' Baldwin noted.

'Perhaps it was this woman,' Munio said. 'She came here to fetch some water, and was attacked as she walked away.'

'Yet there is no container,' Baldwin mused. 'Does that mean that the killer took her water? Maybe he knew he must flee, and because of that, he took her skin or pot with him.'

Simon was less interested in the land by the water, and more in which direction the killer had gone after the murder. 'If he killed her and was struck with remorse, I'd have thought he'd have run straight to the Cathedral to beg forgiveness, but this doesn't look like a sudden attack that went wrong. It's more as though the man was overwhelmed with fury, to have done so much damage. Perhaps he just ran straight away?'

'There's no sign of footprints,' Baldwin said, peering about.

Simon was walking in a circle at some distance, trying to see whether there was any mark in the dry soil or clue left in the scrubby plants. He then extended his search by some yards, but found nothing of interest. It was only when he looked in the shade of a small tree some forty yards distant that he saw the first of the hoofprints.

One set was broader, belonging to a bigger, heavier horse, for where they crossed the other hoofprints, they were set deeper into the soil. 'Baldwin!'

The knight and the Galician investigator joined him. Baldwin touched the dusty marks gently. 'There's little doubt that these are recent,' he concluded. 'The rain would have destroyed them, so I assume these horses were here *after* the rains.'

'This tree – surely they came here and tied their mounts to it?' Simon suggested.

Baldwin frowned. 'A man could have ridden here with her, and when he saw that they were alone, he decided to take advantage. He and she stopped, probably to take refreshment from the waters, and both tied their mounts to the tree. But then he revealed his genuine desires.'

'Perhaps.' Señor Munio jerked his head to the cart, and the cleric began storing his parchment, inks and reeds in his scrip. 'But it's all guesswork. For now, I must return to the city and question the gatekeepers in case they saw someone like this woman leaving the place earlier.'

Baldwin smiled. It was clear enough that the *Pesquisidor* expected Simon and he to join him. In his position, Baldwin would have demanded the same. 'There is another possible explanation,' he said. 'I heard today that this morning there was an attack on a group of pilgrims just outside the city. Perhaps this was another band of thieves, who simply happened upon a young and attractive woman and decided to enjoy her body.

Maybe it was not her horse: there were two men, one with a smaller horse than his companion's. They had travelled here together and caught sight of this pretty young woman. One captured her, the other tied their horses, and then they both raped her. Overwhelmed with fear for their own lives in case she denounced them, they then beat her to death.'

'It is as likely as any other explanation,' Munio shrugged.

'And as a story, it holds this advantage,' Baldwin said. 'If you spread this tale and the real killer is in Compostela still, he will think himself safe. That might give you more time to discover the truth.'

Simon nodded, and gruffly said, 'And thank you for not arresting us.'

Munio's face was curiously still as he glanced at the Bailiff. 'There is still time, Señor.'

Chapter Seven

As the sun passed slowly across the sky, Doña Stefanía grew anxious. What was taking Joana so long? The place of the rendezvous had been chosen because it was almost in hail of the city walls, easy for both to get to, easy for both to escape from.

The bastard, making use of her shame in this way! It was disgraceful that a knight should act in such a manner, demanding cash in exchange for his silence. Not that it would necessarily be the end of the matter. Doña Stefanía was a woman who had lived in the real world all her life, even if nominally she was supposed to be cloistered now in her abbey. As a lady, before she took up the cloth, she had travelled widely, and she still did so at every opportunity. She was not naive enough to believe that a black-mailer would make his demands once only and then forget her indiscretion. No. Any man who was foul enough to rob her in this manner, would try it more than once.

She was really worried now. It was growing late and there was no sign of her maid. What had happened to Joana? The meeting should have been over hours ago.

After some little while, she heard a rumour passing along the street and glanced up, wondering what the noise might portend.

It was a curious noise, almost hushed, as though the crowd was talking more, but less loudly, out of some form of respect, and she wondered for a moment or two whether this might be a religious procession; however she knew that there was no religious significance to the day or to the hour. In any case, a procession would emanate from the Cathedral itself, not from the Via Francigena. That way led only to the outside world.

It was as though that mere thought had suddenly sprung a hideous fear upon her. Overcome with dizziness, she sank back onto the bench from which she had risen, a hand going to her breast.

'Doña?'

Looking up, she found herself gazing into the concerned eyes of Don Ruy.

'My lady, I didn't mean to alarm you,' he said hurriedly, 'only to ensure that you were well. You appear pale. Have you had a shock?' And then he gave her a smile. 'Would you like me to seek your maid?'

The twist to his mouth was ghastly. She was sure that he was implying something . . . that he was somehow threatening her. He must have had his money, damn him! Joana had been there – hadn't he seen her? Was she still waiting there for him? She stared at the knight transfixed, but no words came.

It was as she was about to demand what he wanted of her, that the behaviour of the crowd caught her attention. All were staring towards a corner of the square on her left. She was struck by the sudden quietness. It was as though there was a cloud of trepidation engulfing the square from that end.

Standing again, and moving swiftly away from Don Ruy, she stared in that direction. Rolling slowly across the pavings was a cart, and behind it came many men, while in front of the donkey pulling it was a solitary cleric, hands joined together in prayer.

Doña Stefanía felt her heart begin to shrivel. She glanced at the knight again, a dreadful fear overwhelming her. 'Where is she?' she cried hoarsely. 'What have you done with her? Where is my maid?' Then, without waiting for his reply, 'She told me she was seeing you,' she went on wildly. 'I know why, too, so don't try to deny it.'

As the thoughts swirled in her mind, she grew aware that Don Ruy had moved a little closer to her, and then she made that fateful leap: if Joana wasn't back yet, it was probably because she *couldn't* come back. Don Ruy had stopped her.

'You have killed her!' she gasped, and before he could lunge and grab her, she span around and, picking up the skirts of her tunic, hurried off through the crowds. The only thought in her mind was to get away from him before he could kill her too.

In front of her the crowds seemed to thin, and before she knew what was happening, she found herself pelting into the middle of an empty space. There stood the cart, and in front of it were four men – the cleric, one Galician and two foreigners, to judge from their dress – all watching while four others lifted a door from the back of the cart and laid it on a table.

From her vantage point, Doña Stefanía could see a pair of thighs lying on the door, and a face that was a horror of blood. A man rearranged the clothing to cover the corpse's legs and render her decent before she was placed in plain view of so many men. It was, the Prioress thought, a kindly act, the sort of thing a father might do for another man's dead daughter; protect her modesty. The body might have ceased breathing, but that was no reason to be callous. Someone somewhere must have loved her.

That was the last thought, that someone must have loved this woman, for clearly from the well-formed calf and shapely ankle, this was no man's body, before she saw the hem of her old tunic and knew for certain that Joana had been murdered.

'Doña?'

She turned to see that Frey Ramón stood a short way behind her, his ugly face twisted with anxiety. She felt as though the entire scene was being shown to her through a glass. It seemed to move, the colours altering, and swirls of mist rose up before her, while the regular lines of paving began to dance. And then they grew larger, and even as she heard a warning shout, the pavings seemed to leap right up towards her.

Baldwin heard the gasp and turned just in time to see a tall, elegant woman lean to one side, and then fall to the ground as though all sensation had been cut off instantly.

'Simon!' he called as he made his way towards her, but then he saw that another man was already there.

It was the brute Simon had noticed before, the Knight of Santiago. He knelt at the woman's side and looked about like a man lost, staring around for assistance.

'Friend,' Baldwin said soothingly. 'Let me help.'

The man looked Baldwin up and down, then shook his head and began shouting for, 'Joana! Joana!'

Baldwin stared in helpless appeal at Señor Munio, and was relieved to see the *Pesquisidor* nod and stroll towards them. He spoke rapidly as he came closer, and the knight snapped something back, but then seemed to regret his words and spoke again, hanging his head.

'What is it?' Simon asked after a few moments during which the Knight of Santiago grew conspicuously disturbed.

'He says that this lady is always accompanied by her maid,' Baldwin translated. 'I think that this noble knight is betrothed to the maid, and he is concerned that she is not here.'

Baldwin glanced at Munio. 'Do you think we should let him see her?'

Munio sighed but agreed. There was no joy in this work. He touched the knight softly on the shoulder. 'Come, Frey Ramón. We have found a poor woman murdered. Please come and see her, in case you know who she might be.'

'Me? Why me?' Ramón demanded. 'Leave me here with Doña Stefanía, and I shall protect her until my woman arrives. She will not be long. Can you hear anyone trying to break through the crowd? She cannot be far away.'

'Come with me.'

Frey Ramón was irritated by his insistence. The man was a mere public official, after all. A *hidalgo*. He might be a low form of noble, but he still worked with the peasants in the fields. The knight was about to give him a curt refusal, for no Knight of Santiago need answer to a petty *hidalgo*, when he saw the expression on Munio's face.

Slowly rising to his feet, Frey Ramón squared his shoulders. Ignoring Munio and Sir Baldwin, he marched past them to the table. There he stood motionless for a moment. The dead girl's tunic was immediately recognisable and he felt as though someone had slammed a hammer into his breast. All the breath was knocked from him. Over the corpse's head had been thrown a blanket, and Frey Ramón motioned to one of the men to remove it. What he saw beneath the material was so horrific, it was all he could do to ask the man to cover her up again. 'Her face . . . She has no face,' he gasped when he could speak again.

He became aware that Munio now stood at his side. Without turning his head, Frey Ramón said, 'It is her. It is my fiancée Joana.' He bent and collected up the body. 'I shall take her to the Cathedral. Please look after Doña Stefanía. Now she has no maid, she will need to be protected.'

Munio muttered his sympathy as the warrior monk of Saint James strode away towards the Cathedral, the pathetic bundle carried so steadfastly in his arms – the arms that would once have held her as a lover, Munio thought to himself. He was struck with sadness at the sight of such restrained grief.

Then he clapped his hands together. 'Come! What is everyone staring at?' he shouted. 'There has been a murder, but there's no need to gawp. Any man who knows about this sad event should come to speak to me now. As for the rest of you, you can go about your business!'

At the Cathedral end of the square, Gregory was peering over the heads of the watching crowds as Frey Ramón strode past, his head high, but his eyes speaking of his appalling loss.

'What has been happening here then, old friend?'

Gregory jerked in shock at the sound of Sir Charles's voice. The man had a knack of springing up without warning. It was just Gregory's luck that he should be looking away when Sir Charles appeared. Taking a deep breath to calm himself, he said, 'I fear that some woman has been murdered.'

'Ah. The sort of thing that happens all over the world,' Sir Charles said with a sympathetic shake of his head as Frey Ramón passed them. The knight sighed as though meditating on the swift passage of a life, then said more brightly, 'Hey ho! But life must go on! So, how are you this fine afternoon?'

'I am well, sir. I thank you again for your assistance this morning.'

'It was nothing,' Sir Charles said quite sincerely. 'It was no more than a fleeting action.'

Listening to him, Gregory stiffened in dislike. It was as though the other man was uninterested in the lives or deaths of the pilgrims, but had simply become involved because he had seen the opportunity for a battle. Some knights were that way, Gregory knew. He himself had once been equally selfish, with a disinterest in other men's lives and works. Like other knights he had enjoyed his wine, chased the women, and sought only earthly delights. And there were few pleasures greater than slaying your enemies and seeing their comrades fleeing the field, leaving you and your fellow knights in sole occupation.

Yet he had changed. Since that terrible time when he had lost his wife, he had grown more philosophical, more open to other people. Certainly, he knew glancing at the fair-haired man at his side, he had never been so callous as Sir Charles.

'Are you here on pilgrimage?' he asked.

Sir Charles peered at him as though he had forgotten he was there. 'No. I am on my way to see if I can help my friend Afonso. He wants to kill a man,' he said blandly, smiled, and was gone.

Gregory puffed out his cheeks and slowly relaxed. Thank God the man was gone. He was an unsettling fellow. Surely even when Gregory himself had been at the height of his self-confidence, he had never been as arrogant as that. Sir Charles seemed to be content to go through life as though he was careless of any man's feelings. That was no way to live. It was like being possessed of a deathwish.

Perhaps it was only his way of joking, Gregory wondered, but then he shook his head. The fellow had seemed perfectly serious.

Gregory felt uneasy suddenly, standing with his back to wherever Sir Charles had gone. In preference, he moved forward through the crush. He had seen Frey Ramón carrying the body out of the square, and there had been a stillness in the crowds as though it was a rare, terrible event. Funny how foreigners could react, he reflected – not for the first time.

Folk were beginning to resume their normal activities now. Hawkers began to shout their wares again, men bawled for wine at the taverns, and Gregory found his way was easier. Soon he was up at the front of the crowd, staring with vague curiosity at the men gathered there. A cart was being led away by one peasant, and a cleric was standing talking to three men while a physician was bent over a figure lying in a dead faint on the ground. The physician straightened, then set about striking a spark from his knife and a stone, blowing onto tinder. Gregory suddenly felt a dim recognition stirring in him. The bare arm which he could see looked rather familiar.

From closer, it was a great deal more familiar. There was a birthmark near the wrist. Oh, surely it couldn't be her – not his wife!

The physician had at last made the tinder catch, and now he blew on it. When he had a large enough flame, he lit a candle, shielding it from the occasional gusts in the square, then held it near the unconscious woman's face and burned a few feathers.

As the reeking smoke entered her nostrils, Doña Stefanía retched, then coughed and moaned loudly. She pushed the noxious odour from her, and even as the physician smiled and tossed his feathers away, she winced and sat up. 'What . . .'

She was assailed by sudden nausea, and had to close her eyes for a moment. 'What is happening?' she asked dully, and then she began to weep as she remembered the body of her maid, remembered that shattered remnant of a face.

Simon was saddened to see a noblewoman brought so low by circumstances, but he could easily understand her feelings. A pilgrim, many miles from her home, the only companion she would have had was her maid, and now the latter had been snatched away. It was a fearfully lonely life for a woman, no matter how well-filled her purse, if she were left alone. Bad enough to lose a husband, but in some ways Simon thought that for a woman, losing a maid or manservant was worse. The companionship was usually easier and more genuine between master and servant than that which prevailed between married partners.

No one could doubt the genuine sadness of the woman. She had collapsed at the sight of her maid, and now she wept uncontrollably. It was the sort of behaviour that no one of her station would normally indulge in. They wouldn't want people to think they were so weakly as to become too closely attached to their staff. All too often people did, of course: the number of widows who married their husbands' stewards was eloquent proof of that.

Rather than contemplate the wailing woman, Simon turned away. Nearby was a woman clad in black, wandering among the crowds. He watched her irritably, half aware of Baldwin arriving at his side.

'Another ruddy beggar,' he grouched. 'There seem to be more of them than pilgrims.'

'Do not be too harsh,' Baldwin remonstrated gently. 'Some are genuine enough.'

Simon winced. 'I'm sorry, Baldwin. I didn't mean to pass comment on your old companion. He's obviously all right.'

'Not many would agree with you,' Baldwin said moodily, scuffing a boot on the paving and sending a pebble skittering over the slabs.

'There is one thing that *is* beneficial about beggars, though,' Simon said. 'Come with me.'

Surprised, Baldwin obediently followed Simon to the edge of the crowds. The beggarwoman in black was moaning gently, a hand wrapped in filthy linen held out to any who passed within her range. There was a repellent odour about her, with a faint hint of lemons, as though she had slept beneath a grove of citrus. Simon caught sight of a pale face beneath her hood, but averted his eyes automatically. One didn't meet their gaze, because that lent their begging legitimacy and let them feel that they could ask for more money.

'You speak English?' he demanded gruffly.

'Sí – a leetle, Señor.'

'You walk about the crowds here. Did you see the woman with the blue tunic before, the woman who was killed?'

'I saw her with the Doña there. She was maid to her, called Joana.'

Baldwin smiled as he understood Simon's reason for questioning this beggar. A beggar could pass through a crowd unnoticed, ignored, as irrelevant as a cur, but might still notice others and make comment about them.

Simon saw his understanding dawn. 'Today, did you see her leave the city?'

'Sí. She left by the Porta Francigena after lunch.'

'Was she alone?'

There was a long pause, and then the woman spoke as if reluctantly. 'I think she was with a man. Perhaps I am wrong, but he was behind her – a tall, dark knight. I have seen him. He is called Don Ruy, I think. A pilgrim to Compostela.'

'You think he and she were going to a rendezvous?' Baldwin asked.

'I do not think she saw him, but he had eyes only for her.'

'They were both walking?'

'No. Both were on horseback.'

'We may need you to speak to the *Pesquisidor*,' Simon said sternly.

'I am always here in the square,' she said sadly, and her hand rose a little.

Simon grunted, but he reached into his purse and pulled out a coin. 'Very well. What is your name?'

'What need has a beggar of a name?' she asked softly. 'I have lost my husband, my home, my station. But I have been called María. My father called me that. You may, too. María of Venialbo.'

'Very good,' Simon said and dropped the coin into her palm.

Chapter Eight

Domingo had watched dully while the men with the body on the cart passed, going towards the Cathedral, but it meant nothing to him. Nothing did, not since the death of Sancho. Life itself had lost its meaning. All that mattered was finding the fair man and executing him. Standing with his men in front of the tavern, he drained his cup and belched.

They had been waiting here as he had told them, and now that the little cavalcade was done and the body had been carried away by Frey Ramón, they all felt the anti-climax. They turned to drinking more cider or wine, thinking about finding some food and maybe a woman. One of his men had told of a serving girl at an inn up the way who had a saucy smile that promised more than mere conversation, or he was a *mudéjar*!

Domingo sat on a wall with a pot of wine and drank steadily.

This place was too far from home. He'd never have come here if it wasn't for that bitch of a Prioress. She'd tempted him with money, him and his men. She needed protection, she said. And Joana had added her voice to the Prioress's. She told her cousin that she needed his help: without some sort of guard, there was no telling what might happen to Doña Stefanía and her. They were carrying something, she hinted, something which was so valuable, they must have men about them to guard it.

It was enough to pique his interest, naturally. Joana knew perfectly well how her cousin made his living; Domingo captured travellers and held them hostage, sometimes wounding them if their families were too slow to pay, occasionally killing them when the whim took him.

His son, poor Sancho, he was a good lad. Not the cleverest, even Domingo wouldn't suggest that, but he was tough, ruthless and loyal, provided you didn't take your eyes off him. If you did, you might learn just how ruthlessly ambitious he was. Not the sort of man you would let behind you.

But he was Domingo's son, and to Domingo a blood tie between man and son was sacred. His duty to find and kill his son's murderer was equally sacred.

The attack was strange. He still wasn't sure why the Prioress had instructed them to attack the pilgrims. It was days since she had tried to join the band, days since she had opened her legs to the shabby little creep in the shed. Oh, Domingo knew all about that. He'd seen the churl go in there with the Doña, saw the tall knight walk in and hurriedly leave; later he'd seen the Prioress slip out, walking a little more bandy-legged than she had for a while, and with a huge, grateful smile on her face. But any shame or anger she felt at her subsequent treatment must have faded by the time she told Joana to have Domingo attack the pilgrims.

'Attack them and kill all,' Joana had said.

'Why?'

'She wills it.'

That was all. Joana had swept around in her nice new blue tunic as though she was going to flounce from his fireside, but Domingo wasn't so easy to impress. He grabbed her arm and pulled her easily to him, bending her arm behind her back. '*Why*, I asked.'

There was a prick at his belly, and he glanced down to see that in her other hand she gripped a short knife. 'Let me go!' she said through gritted teeth.

'You'd not kill a chicken with that,' he said, and then his hand moved. He took the blade in his open hand and twisted. Her face was wrenched with pain as he tightened his grip, squeezing her fingers tightly into the wood. He could feel the blade cutting into the fatty skin at the edge of his palm, but his expression didn't alter. Pain was something he was used to. 'Well?'

'A man has threatened her with blackmail.'

He released her with a feeling of anti-climax. Blackmail was a good way to earn money, he knew. He wondered what scandalous thing it was, that she was paying to keep quiet. If he could learn it, it might benefit him. However, he did think that it was unnecessary to kill all the others just because the Doña wanted one man dead. Not that it mattered.

But now it did matter. It mattered a great deal, because his own boy was dead. Poor Sancho; it was terrible to think that he'd never be able to rely on the lad at his side in a fight. Sancho was dead and gone for ever.

The thought brought a huge gobbet of grief into Domingo's breast. To lose it, he stood and sniffed, gazing about him like a man idly stretching. He could feel the tension in his men, as though they knew what he was going through and feared that he might explode into violence. They had seen his rages before. Curiously, he felt no need. For once in his life, fighting would not assuage his spirit. It couldn't.

In the square, he could see the men discussing the dead woman in the blue dress. It was nothing to him. Others mattered not at all, compared with poor Sancho. When they returned to their little church in their home town, Domingo would have to make an offering in Sancho's memory. Their town was poor, but at least the priest was on the side of the poverty-struck peasants. They had little enough to look forward to, as he knew – only the annual cycle of labour on the land, unless they could break out like Domingo and find work elsewhere, making use of their physical strength in the service of whichever lord or lady offered the most money.

That was when he saw him, over at the far side of the square, peering down at the body with a clinical interest.

It was the fair one, the tall, easy-looking bastard. He was with the other, the one who'd ridden into the fight with two blades flashing; while the fair one killed Sancho, the other one had slaughtered others. Domingo's son Sancho was killed as he struck down a pilgrim, and then the fair man rode over his poor body, trampling it in the dirt like the carcass of a dead fox. As though there was nothing to worry about, killing a man like that. There was nothing but shame in leaving a man alive who could behave in such a manner towards Domingo's kin. This was a deed that could only be punished with blood, with the man's blood.

Dropping the cup and letting it shatter on the stone floor, Domingo stood up straight, twisting his head as he contemplated the bastard. He thought he was powerful, Domingo saw; thought he was superior to all others, probably. Well, Domingo would prove him wrong. He would cut out the man's heart and eat it. He'd open his belly and throttle him with his own bowels. He'd . . .

'Domingo? What is it?' One of his men was watching him warily.

'Him – the fair one. He's the man who killed Sancho.'

'You are sure?'

Domingo barely glanced at him, but reached out with the speed of a striking snake, took hold of Azo's shirt and pulled. The other was a thin, unhealthy-looking youth of nearly twenty, his face a mass of acne, and he looked terrified as Domingo held him close enough to see the sweat of fear starting from his forehead. 'Yes,' he hissed. 'I am sure. I watched him slaughter my son like a pig. You think I would forget his face?'

'We can do nothing here in the city,' another man cautioned. 'If we do, we'll be found.'

'I want his head. The man killed my boy. I want him to pay.'

Azo felt himself being released and stood back, watching as Domingo touched his old wooden-handled dagger. 'They were fearsome fighters,' he said hesitantly.

Domingo sneered at him, then hawked and spat at his feet. 'So am I!' he snarled as he walked out and followed after the fair man. However, when he reached the square, the tall figure had disappeared. He took one alley at random, hurrying up it and staring about him, but although he followed it to the old city's wall, he saw neither hide nor hair of his quarry.

Feeling the hilt of his dagger, Domingo licked lips which were dry with expectation and swore softly.

'I shall find you, murderer of my Sancho. On his grave, I swear I shall find you, and cut you to pieces!'

Simon felt torn as he watched the grieving figure of Ramón walk slowly through the crowds, carrying his murdered fiancée to the Cathedral. Even when he was lost to view, the moving of heads showed where he was. 'Baldwin, we have to ask him what's happened here,' he said quickly. 'Perhaps he knows of someone who was obsessed with his fiancée and might be guilty of this crime.'

'Look, this is nothing to do with us,' Baldwin countered, but his interest was obviously piqued.

'The lady can't be questioned yet: she'll need some time to recover from the shock. But that man, he was clearly very fond of the girl. Come on! Let's go and speak to him – see if he can think of some reason why his woman should have been murdered.'

Baldwin glanced at Munio, but the *Pesquisidor* was arguing with a skinny man at the cart. It looked as though he was the cart's owner, and was demanding payment for the use of it. 'It is his investigation, not ours,' he said reluctantly.

'And he's not pursuing the one man who might help,' Simon snapped. 'Come along!'

Baldwin gave up his reservations. As Simon said, this man could have some useful information, and it would be sheer folly to let him disappear without trying to learn whatever they could from him. He nodded and the two darted off through the crowd.

It was hard to see him, but they were able to push their way through the people without difficulty, their clothing and swords tending to give them more authority than most pilgrims, and when they were through, Simon pointed. Far off, in the south-western corner of the square, they saw Ramón with his bloody burden, passing about the corner of one building and disappearing from sight.

Baldwin instantly pelted off after him, but Simon suddenly felt a little wobbly on his legs. The heat was like a furnace. It felt as though he was in a forge, and trying to run in such a temperature was mad. He moved forward as quickly as he could, but he had a tough time of it. By the time he reached the corner of the roadway, Baldwin was already waiting, an expression of half-annoyance, half-concern on his face. 'Are you all right?'

'I felt a little odd,' Simon admitted. 'I'll be all right in a minute.'

Baldwin glanced over his shoulder. 'We've missed him now,' he said with disappointment. 'Do you want to rest a moment?'

'No, I want to find the blasted man.'

'We cannot do that now. He could be anywhere,' Baldwin said.

The alley stretched before them for several hundred yards, with other lanes turning off to the north and south. The man could have taken any number of turns, either into lanes or entering a doorway.

'God's cods,' Simon cursed bitterly. If only his sudden weakness had not attacked him, they could have caught up with the man.

They were walking back towards the square and Munio. Simon puffed out his cheeks and moved his belt. It felt too heavy and hot about his waist, and he could feel the prickling of sweat beneath it.

'Are you sure you are well, Simon?' Baldwin asked.

'Yes, yes,' he replied tetchily. 'I just feel a bit hot, that's all.'

'So long as you are sure. You look almost yellow.' Baldwin decided they must find a tavern as quickly as possible. His companion looked quite unwell.

'So there you are! I have been looking for you!' Munio bellowed angrily. 'Come here, and don't run off again.'

Ramón entered the little chapel and carefully set the body down before the altar. It was not usual for women to be permitted in this place, and it was still less normal for a man to perform this last, most intimate service, but he didn't care.

Carefully, he removed Joana's tunic and undershift, and when she was naked, her slim, well-formed body lying neatly, he fetched a bucket and filled it from the well. He could find no cloth, so he tore a large piece from her tunic, and soaked that to clean her. There was little enough to clean. As he wiped at her brow and skull, he could feel the broken shards of bones shifting beneath his fingers. A large flap of flesh had been removed from her cheek, and her face, her beautiful face, had been so savaged that it was impossible to recognise her. No one, not even her mother, would know her.

Not even her lover, he thought, and with that the tears began to flow in earnest.

'My friend, may I assist you?'

The soft tone interrupted his weeping, and Ramón jerked up, staring at the figure who stood in the dark. Apologetically, the man stepped forward, as if realising that he was almost completely hidden in the shadows. 'My name is Gregory. I hope you don't mind that I followed you here. I knew her, you see. Only a little, but enough to honour her.'

Ramón covered his face with a hand, then wiped at it and sniffed. 'I loved her.'

'Let us tidy her, then. It is the last service we can do for her.'

Ramón accepted his aid, but reluctantly. He wanted Joana all to himself, and wanted to do this for her alone, but having another man with him, especially one who wore the pilgrim's cockleshell, was soothing. And the man certainly had the skill of preparing a body.

When Ramón had finished washing her, cleaning the dirt and sweat from her feet and legs, under her armpits, around her breasts, he finished by removing the last traces of blood from her thighs. Then Gregory took the bucket, now pink with her blood, to her head, and gently dangled the sodden hair in the water, rubbing the long tresses between his fingers. When he had the worst of the blood out of it, he went out, rinsed the bucket, and returned with it refilled. He soaked her hair again, until at last it had recovered its silken sheen. Only then did he take the bucket out and throw away the last of the water. When he came back, he carried a thick bolt of linen. 'A lady outside asked if you wanted some cloth to wrap her in.'

They clothed her, setting her out neatly with her hands crossed over her breast, and then knelt together and prayed for her.

'How did you know her?' Ramón asked when both stood again, staring down at her still form.

'I used to know her mistress,' Gregory said quietly. 'She seemed a kind, charming girl. And generous. I saw her giving alms to a beggar this morning.'

'She was ever big-hearted,' Ramón said, gazing sadly at the still body of his fiancée.

By the time that Simon and Baldwin left Señor Munio, it was growing dark. The *Pesquisidor* had taken them to a small tavern. There he had spoken to them both, with the cleric taking notes, drinking copious quantities of wine and grimly munching on dry bread and olives. Nothing that they told him could ease the sour temper into which he had sunk since hearing from the gate-keepers that no one could remember a lady dressed like Joana leaving the city. It seemed as though he would have an unsolved murder on his hands, and his expression told of how much he disliked unsolved crimes.

Baldwin was intrigued by the cleric. He was scribbling on scraps of parchment that had been cut from pages when the latter were squared, and the knight was impressed that use could be made of such small pieces, instead of discarding them. The cleric was a serious soul named Guillem. He smiled rarely, but when Baldwin spoke in his fluent if somewhat rusty Latin, he beamed. It was, he said, good to speak to a man who had an understanding of the Holy tongue. His enthusiasm made Baldwin feign a certain dimness – an automatic reaction. He dared not be discovered as an escaped Templar.

'Who was that woman to whom you spoke – the beggar?' Munio had asked Baldwin.

'She called herself María of Venialbo,' Baldwin said. 'Do you know of her?'

Munio shrugged and grunted. 'I've a good wife to look after me – I don't need her sort. Anyway, a woman who turns to begging or whoring will always change her name so that she doesn't bring shame upon her family – *if* she has any remaining.'

He sighed and looked thoroughly out of sorts. Baldwin knew how he felt. In his own investigations, there had been times when he had realised there was little likelihood of finding a culprit, and he too had known despair and annoyance at the thought that a guilty man might go free.

Simon had been getting jumpier and jumpier as the questioning went on, and his trepidation had been obvious to Munio. 'So, you are sure you can tell me no more?' the *Pesquisidor* asked searchingly.

'We've told you all we know,' Simon stated resolutely.

'Then you can go.'

Simon had paused with his mouth slightly open, and then shot a look at Baldwin.

Catching sight of his expression, Baldwin smiled. 'What – do you want to stay here?'

'I thought . . .'

Munio knew what was passing through his mind. 'You thought you'd be grabbed and arrested, maybe dragged off to a cell and tortured, didn't you? You English! You think that every other land is without compassion and meaningful law. The only way is the English way; the only law is English law. Listen, my good fellow. We don't torture people here unless there is good reason. If someone is found red-handed and denies guilt, he might be tortured to get at the truth – but not when there is no reason to suspect a man.'

Simon felt his nervousness fade as he watched the investigator moodily crumbling a crust between his fingers. He had heavy hands with thick fingers, the hands of a man who was used to working. 'What will you do now?' the Bailiff asked.

'Ask if anyone else knows this person, María. Joana's mistress, for a start.' Munio had permitted Doña Stefanía to leave on compassionate grounds, on the proviso that he could speak to her properly the following morning. She had walked away disconsolate, shuffling like a woman suddenly aged.

The only help the Prioress had been able to give them was to tell them that Joana had been with her for many years. She and a cousin of hers lived not far from the Prioress's estates at Vigo. Another cousin called Caterina lived hereabouts in the city, but that was the limit of her knowledge of her maid's family. As far as she knew, Joana had no enemies; she was honest, dependable, and had her mistress's absolute trust. The two of them had just been to Orthez on business, and were on their way home to Vigo. And now . . . now the Prioress would have to return alone, and break the news of their Sister's death to the other nuns in the convent. It was a terrible day, truly awful. She didn't know how she would be able to make the journey alone.

Baldwin ended with the impression that if Joana was still alive, her mistress would be berating her for her selfishness in being killed.

'None of the guards at the gates saw this woman, you said?' Baldwin mused.

'That is right. I described her and her distinctive blue tunic, but none noticed her. It came as no surprise. Many hundreds of people walk in and out every day by all the gates. This is an important city.'

'Yes. And yet I should have thought that a bored guard would have noticed a pretty young woman in her prime, with wealth stamped all over her. From the look of her, she would have been a woman with style.'

The *Pesquisidor* grunted. 'Perhaps. But all too often the gate-keepers sit in their little chambers and gossip; they don't watch the people outside. Why should they? All they are supposed to do is see that people coming to sell goods pay their tolls, but if they're doing that, it's hard for them to keep an eye on people leaving the city as well.'

Baldwin nodded. 'This Ruy whom María spoke of – perhaps we could find him. If he stayed with her, he could be the guilty man. There may be blood on his sleeve . . .' Then Baldwin had another thought. 'We should ask at the stables. We know that two horses at least were present at the murder scene. Joana's mount must have been stabled somewhere in the city, and she herself rode out on it. You may be able to discover where her horse was kept, and that way learn whether the groom saw anyone suspicious – like this Ruy.'

'It is a good idea,' Munio said drily. 'Which is why I sent two messengers to enquire at the stables as soon as we returned to the city.'

Baldwin smiled. 'You are a sensible man, Señor. You know how to investigate as well as any.'

'As well as an Englishman, I suppose you mean. I dare say that is a compliment,' Munio growled, but there was a faint smile on his face as he stood and beckoned the cleric to follow him. 'I thank you for your help. If you can advise me – if you have any new ideas, I would be most grateful.'

'Any help we can give, we offer freely,' Baldwin said, rising and bowing.

'I am glad to hear it. After all,' Munio continued, eyeing Simon, 'I shouldn't like to think I could miss out on the aid of two English investigators!'

'What did that mean?' Simon demanded suspiciously when the *Pesquisidor* had gone.

Baldwin smiled. 'Do not take his words personally, old friend. I think he likes the English. Otherwise, why should he have lived and studied so long in our country?'

'I don't care. He seems to be making fun of us,' Simon muttered, but without rancour. He was merely glad to be free, out in the open air, and taste the local wine. 'Still, this wine is good.'

Baldwin nodded. 'Perfectly acceptable, yes.'

'You are still thinking of the dead girl,' Simon said. 'So am I. It's hard to believe that any man could do that to a woman.'

'Yes,' Baldwin said absently. 'And especially if the man was unknown to her. Why mutilate her so brutally? Perhaps it was done by a man who had been snubbed by Joana.'

'Could be,' Simon acknowledged, and waved a hand at the tavernkeeper, indicating their empty jug. A wave of contentment rose and engulfed him as he relaxed and leaned back against the inn's wall, stretching his legs before him. 'I don't mind telling you, Baldwin, that until that miserable bugger informed us that they don't use torture on just anyone, I was waiting for him to put our thumbs in a vice. Phew!'

Baldwin grinned. 'Foreign travel can be dreadfully alarming.'

'Don't take the rise out of me!' Simon threatened. 'I am happy to be here. Look at this place! Warm, no midges, a gentle breeze, good wine, pleasant folk – what more could a traveller want?'

Perhaps, if you were Joana, your life back, Baldwin thought, but he didn't say it out loud. Instead he said, 'Tomorrow we should rest, ready for the return journey.'

'It seems odd to have come so far, and to know that all that remains to us is to return.'

'Most pilgrims walk all the way here, dependent upon the good will of inns and other people throughout, and once they arrive they take a meal or two, rest, and then go home again, knowing exactly how dangerous and exhausting their return journey will be,' Baldwin mused. 'We were lucky to be able to take ship almost all the way.'

'Quite so,' Simon said. 'And I think that it is entirely reasonable for a pilgrim to rest here, especially since so many hostelries are duty-bound to feed and water them! But it seems odd for us to just turn about, walk to the coast again and find another ship to take us home. We have only just arrived.'

A servant placed a dish laden with roughly sliced rings of sausage on their table. Simon took a piece and chewed. 'It's good! Like a smoked sausage at home.'

Baldwin took a slice and the two chewed meditatively for a while.

'Bugger!' Simon exclaimed.

'What?' asked the knight.

'We still haven't found a place to stay this evening,' Simon pointed out.

'I am sure there'll be a space at that inn we saw earlier,' Baldwin said confidently.

Chapter Nine

Sir Baldwin and Simon were still sitting in the tavern when they saw Frey Ramón pass from the door of the Cathedral. He moved like a man in a nightmare, his features drawn and blanched. His white robe was smeared and beslubbered with gore from carrying Joana's body, and there were tearstains on his cheeks.

Baldwin motioned to the innkeeper and stood. 'Frey Ramón,' he called out. 'Please join us.'

'I have no wish to be sociable,' the knight said. His eyes were restless, as was his soul, Baldwin thought. The man was torn by horror and loss.

At least he understood English. That was a relief. 'There is little comfort in the compassion of a stranger, and yet I would speak with you,' Baldwin told him. 'If we can aid you, we should like to do so.'

Frey Ramón looked a little confused by some of Baldwin's words, but he understood the sympathy in his tonc. He ducked his head, and appeared to make up his mind. 'I am thankful for your kindness. Perhaps a little wine?'

'Please be seated,' Baldwin said and motioned towards a stool.

'I was to have married her next week,' Ramón sighed.

'I am terribly sorry.'

'She would have made a perfect wife for a Brother. For me.'

For a moment Baldwin feared that Ramón might burst into tears, his emotion was so plain, but then he gratefully took the cup Simon had poured and drank half in a gulp.

'Did you meet her near here?' Baldwin enquired.

'It was on the pilgrim route from Tours. I had been to Orthez and was returning when I met her, and I fell in love with her immediately. To see her, to feel her sweetness and generosity, that was all I needed. I knew she was meant to be my wife.'

'When did you last see her?'

'Here, in the square. We went into the Cathedral, and when we left, her mistress told me that they were to go out for a ride, but that they would be back later. I said I would meet Joana when she returned, and her mistress gave us her blessing. It would obviously be an honour for her to have her maid wedded to a Knight of Santiago.'

'Of course,' Baldwin said without emphasis.

'But she never came back. I didn't see her again until you brought her back on that cart. Her face, her head . . .' He swallowed.

'Did you ever argue with her?'

'You think *I* could have hurt her like that?' Ramón cried out.

'No. But it is a natural question. Others will wonder if you don't answer.'

'I never argued with her. I could not. It would be impossible. She was always so sweet and kind.'

'Did she have enemies?'

'No! You don't know what you are suggesting! How could someone like my Joana have enemies?'

'She was a good woman, I am sure,' Baldwin said comfortingly.

The sudden flush which had risen in Ramón's face seeped away. He stared down into his cup, which Simon refreshed for him.

Baldwin took a breath. 'I have heard of another knight in the town. Perhaps you have seen him – a Don Ruy?'

'No. I have never heard of him.'

'Do you know of other people whom she knew, people who are here in the city?' Baldwin enquired.

'There was one. A man who calls himself Gregory. I think he is named Gregory of Coventry, an English name, but he speaks Galician fluently.'

'Do you know where we might find this man?'

'He was in the chapel with me just now, helping me to lay her out ready for burial, but I do not know where he is staying. He is a pilgrim. He said that he met my Joana because he knew Doña Stefanía.'

'Where did she and her mistress travel from?'

'They live south of here, but they had gone to Orthez. I returned with them yesterday. Doña Stefanía had been travelling with a band of men, but they left us the day before yesterday. I find it hard to understand how men could desert two women like that. For the sake of their own mothers, for the sake of Holy Mother Mary Herself, they should have protected my Joana and her lady. But at least *I* was there, and for that I should be grateful. Although now . . .'

Frey Ramón drained his cup and refused when Simon offered to refill it. 'I must go. I shall pray for my poor Joana in my chapel. I would not go to pray for her drunk. I thank you both for your kindness.'

Standing, he bowed, turned and walked away, crossing the square. Baldwin and Simon watched, and neither spoke a word as the man disappeared from sight.

Later, when the two were rolled up in blankets, having negotiated a space for themselves in an old stable at an inn, Baldwin snoring gently, Simon staring up at the ceiling, pensively considering reasons for a woman to be killed and her features so comprehensively ruined, Frey Ramón sat before the altar in his Order's chapel, and bent his head. He wept. At his side, the chapel's priest sat and prayed with him, stolidly speaking the prayers of the services for the dead woman, occasionally glancing sideways at Ramón as the man's grief overwhelmed him. Once he put a hand out to touch Ramón's shoulder, but the knight shrugged it away.

There was no end to Ramón's grief. Confused, shocked, seeing the whole of his future life destroyed, he was unsure what he should do after the terrible events of the day.

'God, give me peace!' he begged, but he knew that God

couldn't help him. The answers He must give could only lead to Ramón's destruction.

It was almost dawn when he stood and made his obeisance to the cross. He would have to leave. There was no place in Compostela for a man like him. He had made his decision. He would go to Portugal and hide himself there.

After he had gone to his room and collected his few belongings, he returned to the priest and paid him for his vigil, then gave him a little more to arrange for the burial.

'You must see that she is treated honourably,' he stated. 'Have her buried like an honourable woman. A good, kindly woman. A woman who was loved,' he added, his voice choked.

Then he turned on his heel and walked from the place, never to see it again.

Simon woke in the middle watches of the night, groggy and chilled, with the faint sense that something was wrong. He had to pull his cloak back over himself, from where it had fallen.

Their room was an old wine storage barn, containing huge casks of wine, which was occasionally used for guests when there was a glut of visitors. Simon and Baldwin were not the only men staying; there were several other bodies lying rolled in cloaks on the floor.

The barn was a good forty feet long, and the roof was more than ten feet above their heads, giving a feeling of airiness or, as Simon reckoned at this godforsaken time of the night, of draughtiness. He could feel a rumbling in his belly. His bowels were unsettled, and he wondered if it was the rich food which he and Baldwin had tried the night before. One more piece of information which Baldwin had cheerfully shared with him was that people who travelled abroad could contract diseases from the bad air. Baldwin had seen it often in the warmer climates, so he said. Simon had no wish to go and experiment with the garderobe here in the dark, but he was uncomfortably aware that he might soon have little choice.

It did not appeal. The toilet here was like others he had seen in England, but the whole structure looked extremely dilapidated. In his home, that didn't matter. The outhouse was a light shack which was positioned over a hole in the ground, and every few weeks a new hole would be dug and the shack lifted over it. The muck could be dug out and used as manure, while a fresh crop was collected. Here, though, the toilet was a wooden projection from the wall of the barn. Because the barn had been built on a hillside, although the guests entered from the road's level, when they walked out to the far side of the barn, they were one storey above the roadway. Here the owner had constructed a room which was in reality little more than a series of rotten-looking planks placed over the void and supported by the building on the opposite side of the alley. The intrepid person who wished to make use of this convenience, must dangle their buttocks over one of the two holes, trusting to faith that they would hit the target, which was a large wooden enclosure into which the muck from the cowshed underneath the wine store also drained.

Simon was not keen to experience this in the pitch dark, and he turned his mind to other matters in an attempt to forget the growing urges.

The dead woman had been murdered in a particularly brutal manner. It was possible that her lover could have done this. Ramón was her lover: it could have been him. Then there was the knight Don Ruy, who had followed her from the city. He could have been jealous because the girl shared her favours with Ramón and not with him. Or it could have been a passer-by, who had seen Joana there and decided to force himself on her.

Lost in thought, Simon yawned lengthily. Soon his breathing calmed and he slept once more.

In a large communal guestroom in the Cathedral's precinct, Doña Stefanía lay wide awake.

She was in a big, comfortable bed with a soft, plump mattress, trying to ignore the snoring coming from the far side. Her bedfellow was a whuffling, snuffling heavy breather, whose periodic snivels were an atrocious interruption to a lady who was used to the privacy of her own room. Doña Stefanía was tempted to heave a shoe at her.

Still, before long she would be able to return home to the convent at Vigo. That was the thought that consoled her through the long hours of darkness. At least when she got there, she would be able to set up the new chapel, with the Bishop's help, and display the relic.

It was all up to the Bishop. He might be reluctant. It had been known before. Sometimes a churchman was not happy to thieve another's relic. Not often though, she reminded herself. A man would be a fool to thwart the Saint's own will. In fact, no man would dare. She wasn't sure, but the Doña had the impression that the Bishop of Compostela was not the sort to worry himself about that argument. He would reason that if he decided that the relic was not for Vigo, the Saint was making his opinion felt. However, it would be a big feather in his cap, were he to retain the thing. If it added to Doña Stefanía's prestige, it likewise added to his own.

She was content with that. The thing must remain with her, at all costs. It was the only way to ensure that her convent survived.

A particularly loud snuffle made her bite back a caustic response. If only Joana was still here! She could have taken up one of the spaces in the bed, and the two of them together would have been intimidating enough to drive off another, unwanted companion.

Poor Joana. All this was her plan, and now she would never see it come to fruition. She had been so keen for it to happen. Yet all had started to go wrong when she met Ramón. From that day on, Joana had grown more peevish and difficult – perhaps because of something he knew about her?

The thought was worth considering. He certainly seemed to have some sort of hold over her. Perhaps that was the matter: he was a difficult, jealous lover. Perhaps he wanted more than she was prepared to give him, or had decided to take more than she wanted to give. What if she had gone to the meeting with Ruy, and Ramón saw her return? Would he not be enraged to think that his woman could have gone secretly consorting with another knight? It was eminently possible.

But if that was the case, then where, she wondered, returning to the main point, where was all her money? Someone had taken it.

But *who*?

Simon was suddenly wide awake again, his belly rumbling urgently. It was almost pitch black outside, with no more than a faint luminescence to indicate the roofs and yards. As he reluctantly climbed to his feet, he could feel the beginning of a griping pain in his belly; there was no doubt that his bowels were out of order.

It was an unwholesome prospect. There was something about illnesses of the belly that always alarmed him. He had a morbid fear of them, which was exacerbated by the distance from home, as though any such disease must be more virulent, the farther he travelled from Devon. It was not an irrational phobia, for diarrhoea could kill an adult as easily as a child, when the balance of the humours was disturbed. Some years before, Simon had witnessed the death of his own son, Peterkin, and the horror of that gradual fading away would never entirely leave him.

Here, in the middle of the night, he was struck by a sharp sadness. For perhaps the first time in his life, he actually pictured his own death. He could imagine Meg, his wife, hearing of it from Baldwin, he could see her weeping, his daughter Edith sobbing uncontrollably, his servant Hugh stoically sniffing, a fixed scowl twisting his features. He might easily die here, over the next few days, and never see any of them again. The thought was hideous. He had to put the idea away from him! He wasn't going to die here, he would return home to see his wife and daughter, and he would be fine again.

Naked, Simon pulled a jack on against the cool night air, and then had to step carefully over the seven or eight prone figures who littered his path on the way to the rear wall. Before he was halfway, he could see nothing. There was only a deeper blackness before him than that which lay behind.

The door to the noisome little room was a thick blanket suspended by rings hanging from a pole. Simon had to feel his way along the wall, stumbling against one of the massive racks which supported the casks, and then his finger, fumbling, felt the edge of a length of cloth. He pulled at it and walked cautiously forward, but as he moved, his foot snagged on a plank and he tripped forward, cracking his head painfully on a projecting stone.

After a few moments which were filled with an awfully pregnant silence, all the obscenities which sprang to his mind appearing woefully inadequate, Simon took a deep breath and reached forward. This time he carefully felt around the area and found where the planks lay in which the holes had been cut. Finding one, he turned, reversed into position, and sat thankfully.

From here, suddenly the room looked as though it was filled with a silver light. The open doorway was a bright rectangle, and as he felt the boards settling underneath him, he wondered fleetingly whether he would plummet to earth sitting here.

Thankfully, he and the boards survived and he made it back to his sleeping space without mishap, but even then he didn't fall asleep immediately. He lay wrapped in his robe on a bench, hands behind his head, and stared out into the night, thinking mostly of the dead body, but also of the devastated face of Frey Ramón. He had said he last saw Joana in the square.

Could the man have been lying? Was he capable of murdering his own woman – and if so, why?

The next morning there was the sort of dawn Baldwin remembered from his service in the Templars. Small, thin clouds floated high overhead; the sky was a perfect, silken blue, impossibly beautiful. It made the limewashed buildings shine as though they had been deliberately created to make the eyes ache.

For once, Simon woke before Baldwin, and was out in the yard sluicing water over his head and shoulders when a mangy cur entered their room, cocked a leg over Baldwin's baggage, then went on to sniff and dribble over Baldwin's head.

Waking, the knight always thought, was a reinvigoration. It was a process by which the body stirred itself from near-death back to life; however, being woken by a flea-bitten mutt which had just pissed over his clothing was less invigorating than he would have liked. Roaring at the little creature, which folded back its ears and streaked from the room like a dog catching a speeding arrow, Baldwin sprang from his makeshift bed and surveyed his clothing. The dog had not had a good life, and the yellow spray stood out on his linen shirt. It stank.

'Good morning!' Simon called.

'And a nice joke that is, I am sure,' Baldwin retorted grumpily.

'What joke?'

'Saying it's a good morning. What's good about it?'

But his bad humour faded when he stood at the doorway and could see the sun bursting through the branches of pale leaves, dappling the little yard with shadows that moved gently as the breeze blew. There were soft colours here, pale yellows and ochres, and flowers Baldwin had known when he used to live in the South: plants with rich purple blooms, others with bright red leaves, and olive trees with their tiny, green-white star-shaped flowers. The sight caught at his heart. He felt as though he had come back home, as though he had only been half alive in all the time that he had been living in England.

He had missed this. The scents on the air, the sound of people laughing and talking unhurriedly, knowing that today would be warm again. If there was to be rain, it was no matter. The rain was needed in order to preserve the plants. And if it rained, it would be warm, not the chill mizzle they were used to, out on Dartmoor.

The last time he had been to Southern Europe was so long ago, he could hardly recall it, and yet seeing Matthew in the square had brought it all back to him. Now, with the soft breeze stirring the leaves above him, Baldwin felt oddly excited. It was in a warm climate where he had first felt the urges of lust, chasing girls along alleys in the sunshine to snatch a kiss or rolling in the long grasses with the sun warming their naked bodies. Suddenly aware of a poignant longing for her, he wished his wife Jeanne was with him.

At the inn, the keeper's older daughter took Baldwin's pack and promised to launder it. The people of the town went upriver a short distance to where there was a series of rocks on which their washing could be beaten and then left to dry, she said.

'I hope she's careful,' Simon commented as she departed.

Baldwin, who was feeling a little constricted in one of Simon's cast-off shirts, grunted. 'Why?'

'It sounds like the place where we found Joana yesterday. I wouldn't like to think that there could be another murder.'

Baldwin set his mouth. The death of the woman was a terrible reminder that no matter how holy the city, men still harboured motives to kill. 'I wonder if Munio will ever learn who killed her?'

'I doubt it.' Simon cast a look at Baldwin. 'I was considering it last night while you snored. The sad fact is, any number of people here could be felons, so how could you tell? A pilgrim is automatically to be assisted by all, regardless of age, sex, or whether he has *murdered* even. A murderer would be safe from the rope until he returned home to face the law. And that's what gets to me: so many people here have set out on their journey for precisely that reason – because they are guilty of something. That's why pilgrims come here, after all, to atone. They commit some terrible sin, and travel all this way to pay for it.'

'True enough, I fear,' Baldwin responded sadly; it was certainly true in his case. 'Many towns in Europe will impose a pilgrimage on a murderer.'

The two left the place and walked through the shaded alleyway out to the square. This early in the morning, there were fewer people abroad, and Simon and Baldwin saw that the inn where they had drunk with Munio the night before was open and ready for business. They sat at a table under a large tree and were soon happily chewing coarse bread and dried meat, washing it down with a smooth, sweet cider.

Simon gave a contented belch. 'What if every single pilgrim here was a killer? We'd have our work cut out then!'

Chapter Ten

It was while the two friends were leaning back, feeling the soporific afterglow of a good meal, that Baldwin saw his old colleague Matthew again.

The former Templar walked slowly among the tradesmen, speaking to no one, which made him stand out from the other beggars there. Men and women clothed in black all moved with the same lethargic pace, but most offered a greeting to the traders standing there in the crowd. Not Matthew. He walked with his face averted, as though he hated to see how much the people there detested him. In his past he had been a warrior monk, someone notable for his religious dedication, his integrity and his honour. Now he had become a shrunken man.

Baldwin had long ago developed the ability to isolate his logical mind from his emotions. It had been necessary when he saw his friends dying in the hellish Battle of Acre, and had grown still more necessary while he was a renegade knight, avoiding capture as the King's men hunted down all those Templars who had escaped their traps. Watching Matthew today, he was struck by the fact that the beggar was the most solitary man in the square. Whereas others were disabled to varying degrees or had obvious deformities, it was Matthew, albeit physically whole, who appeared the most cut off. It was curious, but Baldwin felt he understood. A man like Matthew, proud and haughty as he had been, would find it intolerable to have changed into someone who was despised or pitied. That, for him, would be worse than any form of torture.

Baldwin wondered if Matthew would, in fact, have fared better if he had suffered from some of the cruel injuries inflicted on the other Templars. It might have helped him to create a bond with other folk. Then again, perhaps not. Some men were arrogant and, whatever the circumstances, would not see fit to mingle with those whom they considered below them. Matthew was formed in that mould. While other beggars walked together, he kept himself aloof.

They were a lively group, these beggars, Baldwin noticed. A pair of legless men over at the entrance to the square were talking loudly to a deaf fellow, who bent his head, a hand cupping his ear, while he frowned comically, trying to understand what they were saying. Meanwhile a woman who had lost an arm cackled with a young mother, whose children were scampering all over the place. There was a man with a dreadfully disfigured face, who kept it half covered so as not to upset people, yet who burst out laughing uproariously at some joke passed to him by a young servant who lounged at his side. Then there was a small gathering of women nearer the Cathedral, all holding out their hands and piteously calling upon any passers-by for alms; although if they received nothing for their efforts, their cries soon became screeches of outrage. It was a common trait for beggars to hurl imprecations at those who ignored their pleas.

The woman María was there, Baldwin saw. She was a little taller than the rest, and probably louder than all the others put together. Her harangues were more spiteful, too, and her knowledge of Galician sewer-language was, to Baldwin's ear, impressive.

'They won't do well if they keep shouting at people like that,' Simon commented drily.

'Maybe they feel they have little to lose,' Baldwin guessed. 'If a man will not help them with alms, they see little need to show respect.'

'It's damned disgraceful.'

'It is not honourable, no – but if you were forced to beg, how would you behave? At least this way, abusing those who refuse to help them, they feel a little satisfaction, I imagine. Revenge upon the people who shun them.'

Simon grunted without conviction, and Baldwin's attention

returned to his old comrade. Matthew was near the Cathedral wall now, and he squatted at its foot, his hat tilted slightly back, surveying the crowds like a man who sneered at the antics of children. Catching sight of Baldwin, he half lifted a hand as though to acknowledge him, but then let it fall, as though reminding himself that he was no longer the equal of Baldwin, and could not expect recognition. Had their positions been reversed, Matthew would have refused to acknowledge him, Baldwin was sure, both because he would refuse to have any dealings with a beggar, and because he wouldn't confess to knowing a Templar. That might be dangerous. Baldwin was sure he should feel upset by this, but somehow it served only to increase his vague feeling of comradeship with Matthew, as though it was their differences which bound them together.

The sun was high in the sky and the heat was growing when Doña Stefanía appeared from an alley behind them. She walked to a table at a corner, shaded pleasantly beneath a great tree, and sat quietly, as though entirely humbled or devastated.

Simon and Baldwin exchanged a look.

'I should like to leave her in peace,' the knight said slowly, 'but what of others who might be harmed by Joana's murderer? The killer might even now be stalking another young woman.'

'There's little point in our becoming involved,' Simon countered. 'It's nothing to do with us. There's no merit in upsetting a Prioress, or whatever she is, just to find out something which is of no importance to us.'

'No importance?' Baldwin snorted. 'Come on, Simon – the truth is always important.'

'You know what I mean. We have no authority or jurisdiction here. It's sad that a girl was killed, but what of it? Girls are raped and murdered every day. We should concentrate our minds on returning home and helping our own folks there.'

'Yes,' Baldwin said, unconvinced.

Simon stared about him sourly. 'And anyway, no one even speaks bloody English here. I don't think I could be any use whatever.'

Baldwin chuckled. 'Little change from life at home in Devonshire, then.'

'Oh, you think so do you?' Simon demanded in mock anger, but as he did so, he caught sight of the lady. She had suddenly shot upright in her seat and was staring at a tall, dark knight. 'Who's that?' he wondered aloud.

'I wonder why the lady trembles so at the sight of him?' Baldwin murmured.

Simon was certain of one thing. 'She's petrified of him. Come on, let's see what the matter is.'

Baldwin was nothing loath, because the man who had approached Doña Stefanía was clearly terrifying her out of her wits. He stood near her, a hand resting on his sword hilt in a non-threatening manner, but Baldwin still felt it was right to intervene.

'Doña Stefanía,' he called as they came closer. 'We saw you sitting here. I hope you are feeling better after the dreadful shock yesterday?'

He stopped and smiled at her before turning his attention to the knight.

His first impression was quite favourable. From the look of him, the man came from a wealthy family. His sword's scabbard was richly decorated, and his clothes showed that he possessed money and delighted in spending it. Today, though, he was not enjoying the benefits of his position. It was plain that he was labouring under some great inner stress from the way that he breathed so heavily, his breast rising and falling like a man who had run some distance in the heat, and yet it was his face that attracted Baldwin's interest.

He wore a hunted expression. When he heard Baldwin speak, he turned to the English knight with a startled mien, rather like a dog caught stealing meat from the table, as if he fully expected some form of punishment.

'We have not met,' Baldwin said.

Doña Stefanía was recovering her poise. Now she lifted her chin haughtily as she introduced them. 'This man is Don Ruy de

Benavente – *he says*,' she said in a voice which clearly declared that she herself doubted his word.

Baldwin introduced himself and Simon, who stood a short distance away, listening with complete incomprehension. He had been determined to make an effort to learn a little of this language on the ship coming over, but the sickness which assailed him had made that a hopeless venture, and since arriving in Compostela there had been little time for him to gain even a smattering of the language. All he could do was watch and listen, hoping to gain some sort of understanding of what was being said.

'Did you travel here together?' Baldwin asked politely.

'No, Don Baldwin,' Don Ruy said. He appeared to have recovered himself a little. 'We met briefly on the journey, but did not travel together. My group was not in favour of feminine companionship on what was intended to be a penitential journey.'

'Indeed? Then your companions must have been a very pious band,' Baldwin said. Inwardly he condemned the man for his priggish attitude.

'Perhaps. I think most of us sought to find some spiritual peace on our way.'

He stood like one who was waiting for an interloper to depart and leave him to continue his conversation, but Baldwin turned to Doña Stefanía with a sympathetic smile. 'So, my lady, did you sleep well? I trust that sadness did not unduly disturb your slumbers?'

'I scarcely slept a wink,' Doña Stefanía snapped. 'How could I? No maid to help me disrobe or see to my hair . . . it was appalling. And so sad that Joana should be murdered like that,' she added with a wave of self-pity.

'I can only express my deepest sympathy,' Baldwin said.

'And I too,' Don Ruy said stiffly. He made as if to move nearer the lady, but she blanched noticeably and shifted herself farther up the bench. It was only a small movement, but Simon and Baldwin saw it, and Simon took a step to one side, so that he could threaten Don Ruy's flank if he should think of attacking her.

Don Ruy glanced at him, and there was frank disbelief on his face as he realised what Simon's aim was. He took a short pace back, turning to face Simon more directly but saying nothing. Glancing at Baldwin and then Doña Stefanía, his expression looked accusing.

'Simon, stay your hand,' Baldwin said in English, before speaking to Doña Stefanía. 'My lady, it is clear that you are perturbed. Is there anything I can do which would help you?'

'There is nothing,' Don Ruy said. 'A misunderstanding, that is all. Leave us. We must talk.'

Doña Stefanía shuddered and looked appealingly at Baldwin. 'Please, Sir Baldwin, don't leave me with him. I . . .' she swallowed heavily. 'I fear he means to kill me.'

Frey Ramón felt exhausted. His knees ached, his eyes were gritty from lack of sleep, and he tightened the girth on his mount like a man in a dream, although this dream was a nightmare. All he could think of was that poor, shattered body, now lying quietly at rest in her grave.

The horror of seeing her lying there on the trestle in the square would never leave him, he felt sure. It was terrible, the worst sight he had ever known. The woman to whom he was engaged, brutally slaughtered like that, left to water the soil with her own blood. He had felt a part of him die when he saw her.

This journey would be long and hard. He had surrendered his position in the Order by running away, but he couldn't regret it. All he could do was go far away and try to find some peace. There were other Orders he could join. Perhaps he could make his way to the sister Order of Santiago, the Knights of São Thiago. They had broken away from Santiago a few years ago, but they still wore the same emblems and held to the same Rule.

'São Thiago,' he muttered. 'Or the Order of Christ?'

'Eh?'

'Nothing,' he told the groom, an older man with the pinched features of one who lives in constant pain. 'I was thinking aloud.'

'They say that the Knights of Christ have taken over from the Templars,' the groom said helpfully.

'So they are rich and arrogant, then,' Frey Ramón said.

'No more than the other Orders,' the man said. Frey Ramón had removed his Order's tunic, so he wore no distinguishing marks that showed him to be a Knight of Santiago. 'But I've heard that the Knights of Christ are the most honourable of the lot. They turn their noses up at any fripperies, refuse too much food, and spend all their time training to kill Moors.'

'I don't care,' Frey Ramón said. He could not help but slow in his work. He had the horse saddled, and he turned to his bags. There was a little food and a skin of wine, and he had a spare shirt and a tunic in another. With his great cloak to wrap himself in at night, he had all he needed.

He had thought that the Order of São Thiago would serve him best, because he knew the Rule. It was bound to be much the same as that of Santiago, since it was an offshoot. But one reason was also because he liked the idea of being married. Now that was an impossible dream. Certainly he would never marry now. The memory of that poor, destroyed body prevented his ever finding peace with a woman, so he might as well hurry south, escape his memories, and find meaning in action, fighting the Moors.

If he were to seek action, he should join the Order which promised the best chance of fighting and serving God.

He cocked an eye at the groom. 'You know much about such matters, friend.'

'My daughter, she married a Portuguese and lives near Tomar. She came to visit me last month.'

'Which Order do you think is nearest the Moors for fighting?' he asked.

'That is easy. The Order of Christ has its headquarters at Castro-Marim. That's down in the Algarve.'

'The Algarve?' Frey Ramón repeated. That was territory which had only recently been reconquered. Frey Ramón racked his brain and felt sure he had heard that Castro-Marim was on the

River Guadiana, near the sea, but on the edge of the King of Portugal's territory, near Africa and the Moors who infested that land. 'And this Order has a castle at Tomar?' he asked.

'Yes. They took over the old Templar castle there,' the groom said. 'I saw the place once. Right on top of the hill over the town. A magnificent castle.'

'It sounds very pleasant.'

'Yes. But it is a hard ride, Señor. Perhaps eight days if you ride like the wind.'

A few hours later, the land opened before Frey Ramón, and he took a deep breath. This was the future for him. His past was gone and done, and all he had to look forward to now was an uncertain future as a warrior. He asked for no more.

There were some memories he would never be able to forget. The first time he had met Joana, the feel of her flesh when they first lay together, that silken hair, so glossy and black.

Then there were the other memories, such as the sight of Joana last night. He would have to ride for miles to escape from that. Perhaps he never would. The dreadful, macerated remains of his fiancée would always be in his heart, as though it was his fault she had died, as though he was responsible.

As, in a way, he supposed he was.

Doña Stefanía was appalled at her predicament. There was no one to help her here, not now Joana was gone. No one here whom she felt she could trust; nobody to advise her.

Perhaps she could have spoken to a cleric – but that was a stupid idea! she scolded herself. No priest would want to help her once he heard that she had succumbed to her carnal lusts on the way here. Worse, he would want to hear more about her sins, to be assured that she repented, and would probably insist that she remain in the Cathedral until a suitable guard could be found to defend her honour on the way home. Humiliating! The rumours would spread like wildfire, if she knew the way that gossip was passed about in a Cathedral like this. There was no such thing as a secret, only a story half told.

A story like this one, she thought miserably.

It wasn't only blasted clerics who loved a good tale, either. This strange bearded English knight looked as avid as any acolyte for a bit of smut. Damn him and his torrid imagination! He was probably no better than Don Ruy, she speculated, glancing at Baldwin. Or if he *was* more trustworthy, what about his companion? Simon looked grim enough to be a *malfechor* so far as she was concerned. He was the sort of man whom she would like to have in front of her, in *her* court.

'Lady?' Baldwin said gently. 'You have made a serious allegation against this man. Should I call for the *Pesquisidor* to hear your tale?'

'No!' Don Ruy said hurriedly. 'There is no need. As I said, it is all a misunderstanding, nothing more.'

Watching him, although he couldn't understand the words, Simon felt that the man was too emphatic. He sounded almost desperate.

Baldwin was struck with the same impression, but before he could speak, Doña Stefanía licked her lips and agreed. 'I should prefer that this story does not go any further, Sir Knight.'

'Very well, if you are sure,' he said. 'But if you feel your life is in danger, I should have thought that you would want the matter aired.'

'Once it is aired in front of you, perhaps the danger will recede,' she said with a faint blush rising from her breast to cover her features. 'I fear I succumbed on the journey here. You know how some men can sprinkle compliments and blandishments into their speech?'

She looked away, feeling her face starting to redden still more alarmingly. This was harder than she had feared; yet if she was to protect herself, she must tell her story. She had a sudden flash of inspiration. 'A man did so with me on the journey here. He wanted to talk to me about my faith, he said, and for many days he spoke with me, asking my advice on issues of the Gospels, telling me of his own deep convictions and love of Christ. How could a woman like me, devoted to His service, a Bride of Christ no less, fervent in her love of Him, not respond to a man who professed the same dedication and adoration? I listened, I laughed, I was overcome. In short, I agreed to meet with him and talk about some matters he wanted to discuss in private. Alas! Oh, that I should have put myself in any man's hands! I should have realised my danger. I am only a weakly woman, but I had thought that my cloth would protect me. Alas! *Alas!*'

'Do you mean to tell me that this man seduced you?' Baldwin growled, glaring at Don Ruy.

'Me? I did nothing of the sort!' Don Ruy declared, torn between anger and confusion.

'Not him, no,' Doña Stefanía said, although with a trace of reluctance, for that would have made, she realised, an excellent end to her story. Yet she had already chosen the line of her tale, and it was better, she felt, to stick to the story she had already mapped out in her mind. 'No, it was another man. A lowly pilgrim, someone of a very different class. All unaware of my danger, I agreed to speak to him in private, and my innocence was my weakness. As soon as I entered his chamber, he took hold of me in a strong embrace and began to smother me with kisses. In no time, he had me naked, and assaulted me vigorously, not once, but many times. This knight came in and saw me, he must have done, and although I implored him to aid me, he ignored my entreaties.'

'You said nothing to me!' Don Ruy protested.

'How could I speak? He was . . . I was . . . in a difficult position!' she declared with an embarrassed vehemence.

'Why should that make him decide to harm you?' Baldwin asked, bemused, but trying to save her from further shame. 'Had you refused Don Ruy's advances?'

'I made no such advance!' Don Ruy stated with a pained voice.

Doña Stefanía cast a cautious look about them. No one was near enough to give her cause for concern. 'No. He made no improper advances of that nature, Sir Baldwin. Instead, he offered to ruin me!'

Don Ruy was staring at her with eyes filled with astonishment as though disbelieving his own ears, but Baldwin felt that although the lady's story was far from the unvarnished truth, there was some element of veracity there – else why should she have recoiled so obviously from the man?

'Sir Baldwin, he sought to improve himself at my expense. The very next day, he approached my maid and demanded money. He threatened to tell the Cathedral authorities that I had willingly submitted to the coarse and indelicate attack of the other pilgrim, and that I was therefore indecent. Unless I paid him a large sum of money, he would tell all about me. There! What else could I have done? And now I throw myself on your pity and honour!'

'You agreed to pay him?' Baldwin asked.

'But this is madness!' Don Ruy burst out. 'I never spoke to you, I never mentioned the contents of your purse, nor did I threaten anything!'

'You deny this?' Baldwin said.

'Yes. Entirely!'

'He is telling the truth,' Doña Stefanía sneered. 'He is so courageous, he avoided me, but gave me the message through my maid. She told me so that night, and to escape his clutches, we fled before dawn the next morning. I never dreamed that he would follow so close upon our heels, but the day before yesterday he arrived here and met my maid, proposing a rendezvous so that I could go and pay him.'

'I only arrived here yesterday!' Don Ruy cried.

'You told Joana the day before!' she declared.

'I did not!'

'He told her to make me meet him at a point on the river, and to bring plenty of gold, for he had need of money for lodging. He dared to jest with me about the expense of staying in a city. I can only feel contempt for a man who could be so callous to a poor nun. And then, because some man had taken my mount, and I couldn't go myself, my maid went in my place, and . . . and we all know what happened to my poor Joana!'

As she gave herself up to her grief once more, Baldwin

watched the knight closely, but saw nothing other than confusion and rising anger. There was nothing to suggest that he was guilty. And yet the maid had died in carrying the money, presumably, to the man she thought was blackmailing Doña Stefanía: this knight. 'What do you say, Don Ruy?'

'That this is all invention. Why should I demand money? I have sufficient. I saw this lady with her paramour, but thought little of it. I didn't even realise it was her, it was so dark. It was only the next morning when I heard her maid talking and laughing about her mistress, that I realised who it must have been lying beneath Parceval. We all know that women are tainted with original sin, and that they can use their wiles to snare men, but I didn't even consider it. I was the loudest voice among my companions of the road arguing that we should have no women among our party, for they only sow dissension. My God! We all know that well enough! This woman has spun a tale to trap me – for what reason, I cannot imagine.'

'Where were you last afternoon?' Baldwin asked.

'I was here in the city.'

'Is there anyone who could vouch for you?'

Don Ruy looked at Baldwin with loathing. 'I was alone in my chamber.'

'You see, we have heard from another witness that you left the city, on a horse. You were seen following a young woman, this lady's maid, who was murdered a short while later.'

'I know nothing of this!' Don Ruy spat.

'I knew it!' Doña Stefanía shrieked, and pointed with a shaking finger. 'You took my money, and you killed my messenger! You'd have murdered me as well, if I'd been there, wouldn't you? *Murderer!*'

Chapter Eleven

As he waited, Sir Charles stood in the shade of a great vine that had been trained over some beams. He had plenty of time, but he did wish other men would be a little more punctual.

Behind him, sitting at a table with a jug of wine, his man-at-arms Paul worked at honing his long-bladed knife with a stone. The edge had grown dull with fine rust during the downpours of the last couple of days and Paul, who was nothing if not meticulous with his weapons, had undertaken to give them all a good polish. His bow was already beeswaxed, the string carefully treated and packed in a waxed cloth to keep it dry; his arrows had been inspected individually, the line of each checked for curves, the fletchings stroked to see that they remained flexible. Now he was putting a fine edge on his knife again. 'A man who looks after his weapons knows that they will look after him,' he was proud of reciting. It was one of the lines he had been taught many years ago when he had been a squire in training, and he had the annoying habit of bringing up such homilies every so often as though they carried the weight of Gospel truth, rather than being the utterings of a rather boozy and impecunious country knight.

Paul had been brought up in Gloucestershire, where his father had installed him in a noble household so that he might learn the arts of war, but then his old man had made a classical and unfortunate mistake. Just at the time that the lonely, widowed old King was falling for attractive young women, Paul's father had made a joke about one. His fall from grace was rapid and he had plummeted so far, he had to leave the country.

His son, though, had flourished. Paul was adept with all weapons and soon learned the finer skills of horsemanship. He was one of those men who have an immediate affinity with horses, and could guide his mount almost without conscious effort. Better than that, he was also a thoroughly efficient squire. In the thick of a battle, he never lost his nerve or panicked. Sir Charles was happy to fight knowing that Paul was behind him as a support. If Sir Charles lost his horse, Paul would be there with a remount; if Sir Charles lost a mace, his axe or sword, Paul would canter up with a new one. He almost seemed to know in advance when a weapon was required, and appeared at the instant he was needed, never too early, never late. He was the perfect squire.

They had met when Sir Charles had been a knight in the service of Thomas, Earl of Lancaster, and had remained together even after the trials caused by Boroughbridge.

Earl Thomas was a great lord, and uncle to the King, Edward II. It was said that he was the richest man in the kingdom after the King himself, and Sir Charles believed it. If anything, Earl Thomas was the wealthier of the two. He had none of his nephew's spendthrift habits, like throwing money at his latest boyfriends, playing with peasants, pretending to act on stage with his pretty boys and the like. It was true that Earl Thomas's wife had run away, but the Queen herself would have done so too, if she had had the chance. At least Earl Thomas's woman couldn't complain about being deserted in her own bed. Queen Isabella didn't even have the opportunity to take a lover, since all the courtiers were of the King's sexual persuasion, or so Charles had heard.

It was certainly true that Earl Thomas knew how to win loyalty. He might be more careful than the King with his money, but he didn't hoard it. He believed in the old system, in spreading his wealth and distributing largesse. Earl Thomas had thrown banquets which put the royal ones to shame, held tournaments in which the prizes were greater than any elsewhere – especially since the monarch had sought to ban them. Everything that Earl Thomas tried, he achieved, and living as part of his household meant that some of his glory was reflected upon Sir Charles. He and Paul were very content there, with plenty to eat, even during the famine, good quality weapons, women to bed, and two new tunics each per year. Few men were so well looked after.

Sir Charles was not troubled by the actual sequence of events. All he knew was that one day, his master, Earl Thomas, had lost favour with the King. He neither knew, nor cared, what possible cause there could be. It didn't matter a damn. What happened was that the two men had fallen out, and suddenly the King attacked. Earl Thomas's life came to an end at Boroughbridge, when his men tried to flee by passing over the bridge, only to be opposed by that bastard Andrew Harclay. He and a small force of dismounted soldiers held the bridge and prevented their escape. The King caught Earl Thomas, and executed him.

When the disaster struck, and when they heard of the defeat of the army, Sir Charles and Paul realised that there was no point in their remaining. There was not even a widow to protect; she had left six years before. Sadly, the knight and his man-at-arms joined the long lines of broken men marching away. There was no telling how a vengeful King would treat them, and Sir Charles and his squire left the country, taking a ship to France.

The pair initially hoped that they would find a new master very quickly. There were always petty wars going on up and down Europe, and Sir Charles started out confident that he would be able to find a post which would suit his skills very soon – but apart from a talk with a man who said he knew Roger Mortimer and had planned Mortimer's release from the Tower of London, hinting that he would raise a host to defeat the King himself, there was no offer of a position. Even war appeared thin on the ground. Sir Charles reluctantly concluded that either the man was mad, or stupid. He would need more than a couple of disgruntled knights and their squires to be able to attack England and supplant the King. The fool was even boasting that he had the support of the French King and his daughter, Isabella, who was Queen of England – but Sir Charles couldn't believe that. What would the Queen see in a fellow like Roger Mortimer?

Sir Charles and Paul soon left Paris. It was not a city in which they felt comfortable, and after hearing the recruiting story of Mortimer's man, they agreed that they should seek employment elsewhere. If there were men trying to build an army, the King of England's spies would not be far away, and rather than have Edward believe that he was the King's determined and sincere enemy, which would probably lead to a short life and death in a darkened alley, Sir Charles chose to ride eastwards. He had heard that there was money to be earned in Lettow. The Order of Teutonic Knights was keen for new companions, and there were rumours of vast wealth to be won.

It was while he was on his way there that he met Dom Afonso.

Sir Charles had been bemoaning his shortage of funds. The last of his plate had been pawned in Paris for a pittance, to buy bread and cheap cheese, and he and Paul had nothing left. Neither was prepared to starve or suffer the pangs of thirst, and so, when they saw a deserted tavern by the side of a road, they entered and drank their fill. Dom Afonso was there too, a grim-faced man with staring eyes. Sir Charles saw him and wondered what sort of a man he might be, but then some French peasants entered and Sir Charles's fate was sealed.

It was the rudeness of the peasants that upset him. He was unused to churls walking into a room disrespectfully and barging past. No English peasant in Lancaster would have dared do that. Astonishing behaviour. Quite extraordinary.

The first man to do it was a swarthy, barrel-chested fellow with a cast in one eye. He saw what sort of man he had pushed, but said nothing, merely carried on, waving to the tavern-keeper. After him came a pair of men, both carrying bills in their belts. Then a scruffy little urchin.

It was he who precipitated the fight. The young lad stumbled and fell with his full weight on Sir Charles's foot.

'You clumsy little bastard!' he roared. His big toe felt almost as though it had been broken, and he jumped to his feet while the boy squeaked in alarm. As Sir Charles grunted angrily, the lad was grabbed from behind and pulled away, and suddenly the knight saw that before him were three men with their bills in their hands. Behind him, he knew, were more. He had no idea how many, but Paul could deal with most of them. He had faith in his squire's ability.

'*Anglais?*' the swarthy man said sweetly, and than spat at Sir Charles's foot.

That was all it took. His rage rushed over him, and in the time it took for his face to flush, he had drawn his sword. It flashed wickedly in the enclosed room, catching in a low beam, and then he was running at them, stabbing, slashing and hacking. So fierce was his attack that one man stumbled over a stool and died where he lay; a second tried to get close, and lost his head in the attempt, leaving only the swarthy man. He appeared to shrink in size before Sir Charles's assault, suddenly realising his mistake in spitting, but the knight knew no pity. His sword swept up, slicing open the Frenchman's belly so that coils of purple-blue fell from him. The man had time to glance down in horror, before the blade reversed and removed his head.

Behind him, he heard Paul's blade ringing against another, and he spun around. Paul had two men before him still, but when he saw that his master was alive and well, he pressed his own case, and in a moment both were dead, one making a loud noise as his boots hammered on the floor in his death throes. It was irritating, so Sir Charles knocked a table over them, silencing their staccato rhythm.

Only then did he realise that the innkeeper himself was nowhere to be seen. The grim-visaged man still sat at his table, chewing on a hunk of bread, but there was no sign of anyone else. Sir Charles felt a curious sense of foolishness, standing with his sword drawn and ready, surrounded by slaughter, while a few feet away from him, unaffected by the mayhem, sat this odd-looking fellow. He cleaned his blade on the shirt of one of the peasants, and sheathed it. Only then did he see a pair of bare feet sticking out near the wine barrels. Peering closer, he saw that it was the tavern-keeper, and in his back was a wicked-looking long-bladed knife.

'He was going to brain you,' Afonso said courteously, pointing to a large club, and then walking around Sir Charles and retrieving his dagger from the man's back. He wiped it clean on the man's shirt, then threw it up. It whirled glittering in the light, and he caught it by the tip of the point, then up it went again, and this time he caught it by the hilt, swiftly stowing it away in his sheath. He stood there gazing down at the keeper's body for a moment. 'I wouldn't have a knight attacked from behind. That is not honourable.'

Sir Charles commanded Paul to prepare their horses while he searched the place, hoping to find a stash of coins, but found only a few of low denomination. As he knew, all too often the trade in a place like this would depend upon a form of barter. There were some sausages drying in the chimney, and some bread on a table, and Sir Charles and Paul sat and ate, ignoring the stink and gore of death all around them, and both eyeing the stranger with slight suspicion.

'My name is Afonso.'

Sir Charles introduced himself and his man, and then asked what Dom Afonso was doing in this place.

'I thought to ride to find fame and fortune. Now I return home. I tried the joust, but,' he shrugged emphatically, 'I lost. So now I return to Portugal.'

Sir Charles nodded sympathetically. Those who lost a joust would often lose their armour and horses too, because a joust could develop into near-war; participants could get nasty and demand a ransom to release their prisoners.

'The jousting can be difficult,' he said.

'Yes. But I had to leave my home to find a man.'

'Ah. The gentleman has a name?'

'He was called Matthew. I only knew him as Frey Matthew.'

'Brother Matthew?' Sir Charles repeated. 'I have not met such a man.'

'He was rumoured to be a great fighter with lance and spear, but,' Afonso looked glum, 'I failed to find him, and now I must return to my home. I have to find more money.'

'We need money too,' said Sir Charles. 'You have far to ride?'
'First I go to Galicia, to Compostela. There I shall pray to
Saint James to let me find this man Matthew and kill him. He
will understand why. I am avenging a terrible wrong. Brother
Matthew is a traitor to his master, to his comrades, and to
God.'

Sir Charles had never travelled so far before. To take leave for
such a long period would have been troublesome to his master,
but now he thought that the journey could be pleasing. The more
he considered it, the more the idea had appealed to him. It would
be good to join this man and visit the famous Cathedral of
Santiago.

'May we travel with you?' he asked.

The dour-faced Portuguese glanced at the bodies on the floor.
There was a humming sound as blowflies sought out the blood
and started to crawl over them. Then he held out his hand and
nodded.

They had packed the remaining sausages and a loaf of bread
each, filled some jugs with wine, and then made their way out to
their horses. Excusing himself for a moment, Paul re-entered the
inn when he had loaded their prizes on the packhorse, muttering
and tutting to himself, and while Afonso and Charles waited,
they heard a short shriek which ended abruptly.

'Nearly forgot the little sod who hurt your foot, Sir Charles,'
he said when he came out again, wiping his blade clean on a
piece of rag.

The recollection made Sir Charles smile. Paul always remembered any unfinished business. Ever efficient, he was the man
who went about the dead of battlefields first, always on the
lookout for better shirts or boots. 'You can't afford to wait until
the rooks have landed,' was his favourite phrase after a fight.
Crows he admired. Like him, they went alone or in pairs; rooks
were those from nearby vills, who invariably sprang up afterwards in great numbers, massing and robbing wholesale when
they had done nothing to share in the profit.

He was drawn back to the present, to his seat beneath a great vine in Compostela, by Paul saying, 'So now we've got here, where do we go next Sir Charles?'

'You find this city boring?'

'No. It's got wine and women. That's enough for me while there's a little cash in my pocket. But the money we have won't last long.'

'True enough. We need a chance of making some more,' Sir Charles said.

It was the eternal problem. In the days when they had been kept by Earl Thomas, life had been a great deal easier. Now, acquiring funds had become their chief occupation.

'If we don't get some money soon, we'll have to think of selling the packhorse.'

Sir Charles shook his head. 'That would be as stupid as throwing away my armour. Without our mounts and our weapons, we're no better than mercenaries. At least while we have these, we can call ourselves chivalrous.'

'In that case, we'd best find someone rich who doesn't mind sharing his wealth,' Paul said.

Sir Charles nodded. 'Yes. And if he does mind, we'll have to persuade him otherwise,' he grinned.

Just then he caught sight of Afonso appearing through the crowds, moving with his usual rolling gait, a little like a sailor. Sir Charles somehow felt that the Portuguese man had suffered more than he, but Afonso had volunteered nothing more about his past, and he was not the sort of man to blab confidences willy-nilly. He was rather like Sir Charles – self-sufficient, calm and satisfied with his own company. While Sir Charles and Paul were with him, he was content to be their companion, but if they were to leave today, he would not care.

That was his usual demeanour, but today something had upset him, Sir Charles could see. His face was set, and he shouldered a man from his path in an unwarranted display of anger. The man opened his mouth to remonstrate, but then closed it again when he took in the broad back and worn sword of the knight.

'My friend, what is the matter?' Sir Charles asked mildly.

'It is nothing. I saw a man I had not expected, that is all,' Afonso said.

'I see,' Sir Charles said. 'When we first met, you mentioned someone whom you wished to find. Is this him?'

'Yes!' Afonso swore and spat out, 'Matthew!'

'Would you like me to come with you and see him again?'

The offer of his assistance in attacking this man, who must surely be an enemy of Afonso's, did not produce the result which Sir Charles had expected. Instead of giving thanks, Afonso rounded on him, eyes glittering.

'No. You leave him to me! He is the cause of me being here, and I'll kill him myself!'

Doña Stefanía sat back, her heart pounding as she studied the now-pale knight. 'You didn't think I would be able to muster the courage to accuse, did you? Well, I have. I accuse you, Sir Knight, and I hope you will be forced to pay for your vicious crime!'

'I have done nothing, woman!' Don Ruy snarled, but Simon was sure that this was not the reaction of the discovered felon, rather the furious denial of a man repudiating his accuser.

'You killed her!' she shouted, and there was a kind of delight in saying so, she discovered. It was as though she had found some form of comfort in being able to declare her maid's murderer's guilt.

Don Ruy did not retreat or cower, though the other two men closed in subtly. It was the knight called Baldwin who spoke.

'You have been accused, and you deny the charge, but you give us no explanation of why you are wrongly accused. Will you not explain how someone could think that they saw you, when you say you did not leave the city?'

That's it! Doña Stefanía thought gleefully. Let him wriggle out of *that*!

'I did leave the city for a short while,' Don Ruy said stiffly. 'I hired a mount from a stable and rode out for exercise. I hadn't thought it would matter – but then I didn't expect to be accused

of murder for talking to the good Doña Stefanía either,' he added
with a bow to her.

He was impressive, she admitted. Suave and calm, even when
accused of such a dreadful crime.

'Where exactly did you ride?'

'I rode out along the river northwards.'

'Did you come to a clearing?'

Don Ruy considered. 'The ground was flat, and I don't recall
one in particular. There was a stretch which looked a little like a
ford. I passed by a place where women were washing their
clothes.'

'A ford,' Baldwin repeated in English for Simon. 'He says he
passed a place that was a ford, where women were washing their
clothing.'

'So?'

'I hadn't noticed that it was a crossing place.' Returning to
Don Ruy, he said, 'The ford – did you see anyone near there?'

'I saw two horses tied to a tree.'

'Was there a man there, or a woman?'

'Over on the opposite side of the river, walking together,
away from me. I didn't see their faces. I don't know who they
were.'

'Come, Don Ruy! You must remember the girl at least. She
wore a blue tunic, with embroidery at the neck and hem.'

'Very well. Yes. It was the beautiful dark-haired servant of
Doña Stefanía here,' he said with a faint smile. 'Yes, it was
because of her that I rode up that way. I noticed her at the city
gate, and from interest, I trailed after her up the roadway. She
went on ahead at speed, but I slowed because my mount had a
stone in its hoof. At first I thought that it was a miserable
creature that had been foisted on me, but when I had it out, the
beast rode all right. Still, when I got to the ford she had gone
already.'

'Gone where?'

'Over the river, like I said. One of the horses was hers – I
recognised it. It was hot, and what should be more natural than

that she should cross the river in bare feet to cool them, before walking with her man?'

'Which man?'

'She was with Frey Ramón when I saw her.'

Doña Stefanía felt the world tottering about her. 'No! This is ludicrous! How can that be? Don, how do you know the good Brother Ramón? *Do* you know him?'

'I know him well enough, and his horse,' snapped Don Ruy irritably, and turned to face Baldwin. 'Our bands of pilgrims were together at Tours until four days ago. His horse is black, with a white flash on the left shoulder that extends up the neck almost to the head. He has a grey ankle on the right rear leg, too. It was his horse, all right. And he was there, too, walking with Joana over on the other bank of the river. I knew her from the journey here to the city. She was with Doña Stefanía. It was her I overheard telling of the Doña's . . . *indiscretion.*'

'What were they doing there?' Doña Stefanía said, ignoring his last words. 'They were supposed to meet back here.'

'Perhaps,' Baldwin interrupted her, 'we should wait until we have an opportunity to ask the good Frey Ramón.'

'Joana promised she was going straight to meet this Ruy,' the Prioress persisted. 'What was she doing with Ramón? If Ruy saw Ramón, he might have thought that she had brought a guard or a witness, and left her there. He might not have negotiated. It doesn't make sense.'

'I did not ask to see her, I didn't ask for money, and I didn't go there to haggle!' Don Ruy said firmly, reddening. 'Look, they were obviously lovers, with their own little rendezvous on the other side of the river, away from the road, where they could take their ease in privacy. Where is the mystery in that?'

'What then? Did you ride on?' Baldwin asked.

'No. I turned back immediately and made for the city. Then, because I was not tired, I cantered about the walls for some exercise. A little later, when I returned to the gate, I saw one man leaving.' Don Ruy frowned. 'I don't know if you had heard, but my group were attacked on the way here by a set of felons who drew weapons and hurled themselves at us. Luckily there were three men-at-arms who happened upon us as the attack was underway. They charged the *malfechores* and put them to flight, killing several of them. The man I saw leaving the city was one of our attackers, I think. A hunched man with his head held at an odd angle. He didn't see me, and rode off along the road, the same way that I had taken.'

'What did you do then?'

'I came here to a tavern, sat and drank off some wine. I was hot by then. The weather was most warm.'

'Did you not bludgeon her to death?' Doña Stefanía burst out. 'You wanted her, you waited until Frey Ramón was gone, and then you killed her, poor child, so you could rob her!'

'I have told you, Doña, that I returned to Compostela, put the horse in the stable, paid the groom, and came here for a drink. I was only gone for a short time.'

'You say that the two of them were there together, but why should that be?' the Prioress repeated – but then realised what she had said. Suddenly the thoughts crowded in upon her thick and fast. 'Joana could have made up the whole blackmail story in order to feather her own nest,' she said wildly. 'She might have spun the whole story to me just to make me give her my money, which she would then share with her man. But now she's dead – and where's the money? My God! Her man! Ramón, where is he? Perhaps *he* killed her and took all the money!'

She leaped to her feet, and although Baldwin tried to calm her and persuade her to sit, she refused, but instead bolted off towards the Cathedral.

Chapter Twelve

At a tree some tens of yards away, Parceval heard her screech and glanced up with a sudden coldness in his chest as though he was going to witness *her* death again, this time while he was sober. It made his bones feel as though they had turned to lard, his blood seeming to clog in his veins, as though time was standing still, so that he could extract every last tiny moment of horror from this scene.

The drinking horn which he had grasped fell from his nerveless fingers even as his eyes fearfully took in the sight – and a tidal wave of relief flooded over him.

He watched as the Prioress pelted across the square towards the Cathedral, his fingers beginning a brief fluttering as though nerves had been trapped and were now renewed as the sensation returned to them, but inside, all he felt was self-loathing and sickness. She had been so perfect, his daughter, and now she was destroyed utterly. All because of Hellin van Coye. 'Damn you, you . . .'

But there were no words foul enough to suit Hellin van Coye. Parceval waved at the wine-seller and acquired a fresh horn, paying with a gold coin. In his distraction, he waved the man away without checking his change, and realised later that he had given the potman more than enough for three jugs, and although he felt annoyed to have wasted money, he had plenty more. No, the only thing that concerned him was that others shouldn't realise how much cash he carried with him. That was a real problem. He didn't want people to even remotely suspect that he was no more a scruffy peasant than the Bishop was. Hellin had friends all over the world, and one of them might take it upon himself to ensure that Hellin's murderer didn't have to worry himself about the return trip to Ypres.

He would protect himself against any attacker, he vowed, surreptitiously fingering his knife's hilt. As he repeated his oath to himself, his gaze drifted over the people in the square and just for one moment, he saw a face staring at him, and he felt as though Hellin's ghost had paraded in front of him.

It was the face of a man who was looking for someone. Parceval slowly edged backwards, into the shelter of a chestnut tree, and stared fixedly at the point where he had seen the man. No, he was wrong. It had to be a fellow looking for a friend. The face was familiar, anyway. Where had he seen the man before . . . Aha! It was Gregory, the priest who'd walked with their group from before Orthez. That was all right, then. Phew! There was nothing scary about him, nothing in the slightest.

Parceval felt the worry falling from his back like a weight. For now, he must return to the room he had hired. The woman who owned it was a terrible old harridan, who stared at him as though assuming he was going to walk off with her best bed and blankets. Stupid bloody bitch! Her stuff was adequate, but no more. At least it meant that he had a base.

He stared once again at Gregory. There was nothing wrong with keeping an eye on him, just in case. And if Gregory turned out to be any sort of a threat, he'd break the bloody bastard's head!

Don Ruy stood with Simon and Baldwin for some while after the Prioress had left them, apparently still in a state of shock from her accusations. At last he surrendered himself to bellows of laughter, sitting and holding his flanks helplessly.

'She is mad!' he choked at last, glancing at Baldwin. 'Does she mean to accuse every man in the city in rotation?'

'I had thought that she wanted the knowledge of her carnal adventure to remain hidden,' Baldwin said, gazing after her curiously. 'It is almost as though she would admit to sleeping with a man in order to deny murder.'

'Perhaps the thought that a man could have robbed her, and then done away with her maid, has made her so angry, she can only see the immediacy of her need for vengeance.'

'Perhaps. In the meantime, what would you say of this Ramón?'

'Him? A grey, unintelligent man, but honourable enough.'

'Would you think him capable of killing his own lover and taking her mistress's money?'

'That is a foul suggestion. I should be unwilling to accuse any knight of such behaviour.'

'The Doña was happy to accuse *you*.'

'I know, but I cannot understand. How could she possibly accuse me of such a terrible thing?'

'She was entirely convinced, I should say,' Baldwin said. 'What did you think, Simon?'

'Me? What do I know?' Simon said with some asperity. 'I can't understand a word you're saying. But I think this man is more concerned than guilty. He doesn't look like a felon to me, and if he's so hard up for money that he needs to blackmail, how on earth did he afford those clothes?'

Baldwin smiled slightly and related the story that Doña Stefanía had told. 'When she left us, she looked as though she was rushing off to the Cathedral to pray to Saint James, to ask him who had robbed her.' He then added as an afterthought: 'And murdered Joana, of course.'

'I don't know what she said about things,' Simon said pensively, 'but I'll tell you this: she was glad to get that story off her chest. If anything happens to her now, it's this knight who'll suffer for it. No one else would be considered.'

'No. I wonder what parts of the story were true?'

'The sleeping with a pilgrim was true. The flush that came to her face was genuine, or I'm a peasant. After that, I don't know what she was talking about, but the anger and fear in her eyes when she looked at this knight was real, I'd reckon. She looked terrified, and obviously believed that her maid had been murdered by him – if she believed that story about the blackmail.'

'Yes, but do *we* believe it?' Baldwin said, glancing at Don Ruy de Benavente again.

'If I could understand a word of what was being said, I'd be able to advise. As it is, though, how the hell should I know?' Simon groused. 'You twitter on with these others so quickly, I don't know what's going on.'

'Do you need help, Masters?' asked a new voice.

Baldwin turned round. 'Good day to you Matthew. I think that the short answer to that is "Yes", but we can't ask for it just now. The girl who was murdered was apparently carrying a large sum of money, and we are trying to find it.'

'You think *he* might have it?' Matthew asked, staring at Don Ruy.

'Stranger things have happened,' Baldwin chuckled and watched as the beggar moved off again among the crowds. When he turned back to Simon, his expression was pensive. 'You are right – this is nothing to do with us. Perhaps I should simply tell that to Munio and leave the whole thing to him.'

'Just ask Don Ruy: did he try to demand money?'

Baldwin shrugged and did so.

'Me? Of course not!' the man snapped, his patience gone. 'I certainly saw her *in flagrante* with that peasant Parceval, the nasty little man from Flanders, but I wouldn't dream of demanding money from her. Why, I wouldn't do that to the lowliest serving girl, let alone a Prioress – *if* she is one! She says she is, but she behaved more like a whore from *Malpertugio*! I wouldn't be surprised to hear that she is less honourable than she avows. I saw her, after all, with her legs spread as wide as a whale's mouth, ready to engulf any man who came near. It was just the bad luck of the peasant that she caught him.' He laughed briefly. 'Snared like a man in a bear trap.'

'You mentioned *Malpertugio* – the "Evil Hole" of Naples where they have the fleshpots,' Baldwin said. 'You have been there?'

'A few times. It's a fine city. I don't go to the *Malpertugio* myself, of course.'

'Of course not,' Baldwin said suavely. 'Yet the Prioress was engaged in that form of entertainment.'

'And not as an unwilling victim as she pretends,' Don Ruy stated. 'She was enthusiastic as hell. In fact, I didn't realise that she was the Prioress. When I walked in on them, she was underneath him with her head towards me, and seeing a naked woman upside down . . . well, it's not so easy to recognise someone you hardly know. It was only later I realised who it was.'

'Why? Did you wait and see who came out of the room?'

'No, of course not! As soon as my eyes had accustomed themselves to the light and I realised what they were up to, I left them to it. Not knowing who it was, I had no interest. It was merely two adults rutting in a shed. No, I only realised the next day, when I heard the Prioress's maid talking to another girl. They were giggling about it. I suppose all servants when they are alone laugh about the peccadillos of their masters and mistresses. It must amuse them no end.'

'And you thought you might be able to take advantage of her yourself?' Baldwin suggested.

'No! I am here on pilgrimage, not to fornicate!'

His outrage seemed unfeigned. Baldwin shot a look at Simon, but his friend was merely gazing at the two of them with an expression of bemusement. 'So what then? The Prioress says you tried to blackmail her. You say you did not. She says you demanded to see her yesterday, you say you did not. Yet you were there at the place where this woman died. Tell me, why *did* you follow her? To demand sex?'

'I am a pilgrim,' Don Ruy said steadily. 'I do not need to explain myself to you or to anyone.'

'No, but it might be easier if you were to do so. Perhaps I could see your pass? You have authorisation from your master to undertake the pilgrimage?'

'I see no need to show you or anyone else my credentials!'

'Very well. I shall mention this conversation to the *Pesquisidor* and leave the matter there.'

'I am not scared by your threats.'

'It is not a threat,' Baldwin said, bored with his prevarication. 'It is merely that I seek to assist the officer of the law in this city. If there is something he should know, I will tell him – it is my duty. You admit that it is suspicious that a woman of the cloth appears to believe you were blackmailing her; that her maid went, so she thought, to see you, and was murdered; and that all her money is gone. And you admit that you followed after the woman, but can't tell us much about what you were doing. Can you really be surprised that I think you would do well to explain yourself?'

'I am innocent of this crime!' Don Ruy declared, but then appeared to reconsider. Reluctantly he slipped a hand into the bulky purse that dangled on his belt. 'I am unfairly accused – an innocent man, but you seem determined to expose my shame. Here, read this.'

He passed a parchment to Baldwin, who took it up. He turned to Simon. 'This says that he was found guilty of raping a woman in Ghent in Flanders.'

Simon stirred and eyed the man intimidatingly. 'He's a rapist? And the dead maid was raped, wasn't she?'

'Yes,' Baldwin agreed, reading. 'And he was sent on this pilgrimage to make amends for his crime.'

Don Ruy understood some of their words and now he burst into an angry denunciation of his conviction, but Baldwin had to hold up his hands to slow the torrent. 'Don Ruy, please speak more slowly. Let me translate for my friend here.'

'The woman I was accused of raping was in fact my wife,' Don Ruy said heatedly when Baldwin motioned to him to continue, and pulled a second page from his purse. While Baldwin studied it, Don Ruy continued, 'The accusation was a false one, designed to embarrass me and prove that my marriage was null. I was accused of abducting her and raping her, but she was a willing lover for me, and it was her father, who sought to ruin my reputation, who deliberately brought me to this farce.'

After relaying his words to Simon, Baldwin said, 'This second sheet confirms your marriage to the woman. So you deny the rape?'

'Of course! But the court chose to ignore my statement. The Bishop himself told me to leave and undertake the pilgrimage.'

'Why the Bishop?'

'I was in his service. The matter was an embarrassment to him.'

Baldwin sipped at his wine. 'I fear that the officers of this city would be keen to know all this. Yet you cannot tell me exactly what you were doing yesterday, so that I can clear you of the murder.'

'I was alone. What else do you want me to say? I didn't try to blackmail anyone, I haven't raped anyone, and I certainly didn't murder that girl or steal any money. It's ridiculous to suggest any such a thing!'

'Ridiculous or not, it is what Doña Stefanía has claimed. Word of her accusation may well reach the ears of the *Pesquisidor*, and if it does, he may decide that you should be held here for trial. The word of a noble Prioress in a religious city like this could be enough to see you hanged.'

Don Ruy said nothing, but stood and inclined his head very slightly. He was about to walk away when Simon, who had caught the gist of Baldwin's words, interrupted quickly.

'Don't let him go yet! Wait, Don Ruy! Let's say this girl was with her lover. She's dead now. Did he see someone else there, apart from Frey Ramón?'

Don Ruy listened to Baldwin's translation. 'No, I saw no one else. But I wasn't looking.'

'So either Ramón killed her himself, or someone else was hiding there.'

'Like the felon I saw leaving the city,' Don Ruy muttered.

'Why did you not try to have him arrested for attacking your band of pilgrims earlier?' Baldwin wanted to know.

Don Ruy stared at him. 'You seriously ask that? This man was a felon, on my honour! Yet it would be my word against his. If I were to draw my sword against a man who looked like a local

Galician, I should expect to be captured and hanged for starting an affray in a cathedral city and for insulting Saint James. Look – the man was leaving the city. What purpose would my confronting him have served?'

'It might have saved the woman's life,' Baldwin said coldly. 'If you are right, and this man killed her.'

Don Ruy flushed. 'My inclination was to avoid any involvement with women,' he said, pointedly thrusting the parchments back into his purse.

'You say the Prioress is mad to accuse Frey Ramón. Yet some men have been tempted by less money.'

'By that, you mean that Joana *did* intend to rob her mistress? But Frey Ramón is a monk. He has renounced money.'

'Perhaps,' Baldwin said, unconvinced. It was possible for any man to grow to desire money – and just as possible for a woman to steal from her mistress to give to her lover. Still, he told himself that there were other possibilities – for example this lopsided-headed felon of whom Don Ruy spoke. If such a creature were to come across a maid carrying a fair sum of money, it would be easy to imagine his stealing it, and getting rid of her afterwards in a brutal way . . . yet Baldwin still disliked the fact that Ramón had lied to them.

'Tell me,' he said at last, 'if you overheard Joana giggling about her mistress, could another man have heard her, too?'

Don Ruy frowned and looked away. Eventually he found his voice again.

'You think someone learned of my seeing the Prioress *in flagrante*, then made up the story of my blackmailing her so that they could take the money when it was paid? It is a convoluted theory.'

'Not if you spoke of it to another,' Baldwin said. 'Perhaps the blackmail was real enough, and only the name of the felon was concealed. *Someone* knew of the Prioress's affair with this peasant, and that someone was surely with your band when you came here. He made up the blackmail story in order to rob the Prioress more easily.'

'I told no one,' Don Ruy insisted.

'Very well. But of course the Prioress's lover knew you had been there.'

'And blamed me while he sought to rob her,' Don Ruy muttered.

Baldwin nodded slowly. 'Yes, Don Ruy. If you are as innocent as you say, then the killer, or the blackmailer, could be one of those who travelled here with you. He had to kill Joana, because she saw him and could denounce him. Were there many in your party?'

The knight had stood to leave. Now he dropped back into his seat again. In the sunshine, Simon thought he looked like a man who had been up too late the night before. He also had the air of a man who had been living rather too well. Simon wondered whether he had been with another woman the night before. There were such wenches even in a cathedral city, he guessed. Then again, he realised, a man might feel guilt after committing a murder. That was emotionally draining.

'I believe the Prioress and Joana had been to Orthez, and they travelled on to Compostela with a large group. I joined their band at Burgos. She and her maid left us some four days ago to travel on ahead, I don't know why. I and the others continued and we arrived yesterday.'

'Not the day before?'

Don Ruy said irritably, '*She* was on horseback; *I* was on foot! We made good time, but no, she is wrong.'

'And she left after you saw her caught in the act with her peasant lover?'

'Yes.'

'There's something I still don't quite understand: you walked into the shed without knocking, knowing full well that it was her chamber?' Baldwin asked.

'No, of course I didn't know! I had been praying in a shrine not far from there. When I returned, it was dark, and I entered the place thinking that it would make a rude shelter for me for the night. As soon as I understood what was happening in there,

I left. Next morning I rose and heard the maid Joana talking about it to a companion, and realised who I had walked in upon. The next day my companions and I moved on. Her lover came with us. He is not an honourable man,' he added disdainfully.

Baldwin frowned. 'Yet she arrived here before you?'

'As I said, my companions and I were on foot. She and many of *her* group were on horseback,' Don Ruy pointed out again. 'She must have overtaken us.'

'Or she spoke the truth and left before you?'

'Possibly. Who knows?' He looked bored with the subject.

'All your group are here in the city now?' Baldwin asked, prompted by Simon.

'No. The party was so glad to see the city ahead of us that many started running off down the plain towards it, and as they did so, they were attacked by the outlaws.' He gave a slight shrug. It was a common enough occurrence. 'The murderous devils tore down the slope at my companions, hacking them to pieces. It was a miracle, but the rest of us were saved by three men who weighed in and slaughtered the attackers.'

'A random attack against such a party?' Baldwin asked. 'It scarcely seems the behaviour of a rational gang. Was there anyone among you who could have deserved such a treatment?'

Don Ruy stared into the distance meditatively. 'They were mostly a gaggle of peasants. Even the man with . . .'

'With Doña Stefanía, you were going to say?' Baldwin guessed.

'Even he was a scruffy little devil,' Ruy said equably. 'I was the only knight, and there was one cleric, a well-built fellow who could have been a fighting man of years ago, before he took up the cloth. But apart from those two, no. The rest were all churls of one form or another. It gave me no pleasure to endure their company for so long, I assure you.'

'So of the men of your party, how many survived?'

'Seven were killed, another five were wounded badly and remain in the Cathedral's hospital. None of them could have harmed the girl.'

'The two, the cleric and the peasant – do you know their names?'

'How should I?' Don Ruy said dismissively. 'I did not care for them.'

'Don Ruy, I think you should consider very carefully,' Baldwin said. 'I do not think you appreciate your position! You have been accused of rape, blackmail and murder by a convincing witness, a Prioress. And you are here because of an abduction and a rape . . .' he held up a hand to stem the sudden outburst. 'It is what your papers say, Don Ruy! If you wish to be declared innocent, I suggest you begin by aiding us rather than putting blocks in our way.'

'I am here because of an injustice,' the other man spat. Then he admitted grudgingly, 'The priestly-looking man was called Gregory. I didn't speak to him. The other was called Parceval. A Fleming.'

Baldwin had been roughly translating for Simon every so often, to keep him in the picture. Now Simon said, 'This Parceval who slept with her might easily have seen that she had money and concocted this story.'

Don Ruy was dubious. 'He could have stolen it there and then.'

'If he had, she would have known who had robbed her. It would have been easy to see to his capture,' Simon pointed out.

'Yes,' Baldwin said. 'She might have been unwilling to accuse him after a night of passion, but he couldn't bank on that. Also Joana could herself have been the cause of her own death. She told others about her mistress's affair – you yourself say you learned the woman's identity because you overheard Joana mention it to someone. To whom was she talking, incidentally?'

'I do not know. The two were in a chamber and I was outside. I heard the comment and a guffaw of laughter, but then I left. I do not like acting the spy on private conversations.'

'A shame,' Baldwin said unrepentantly, continuing in English for Simon's benefit. 'Perhaps someone else was told by this

Parceval and saw a chance of making money; he threatened to blackmail Doña Stefanía about her peccadillo.'

'I am troubled by Joana's part though,' Simon said thoughtfully.

'Oh? Why?'

'Someone presumably spoke to her to warn of the blackmail, but who? And why should she assume it was Don Ruy, unless he went to her himself? If he had a servant, I should suspect *him*, but Don Ruy travelled here alone.'

'Unless Joana did intend to rob her own mistress and invented Don Ruy's blackmail attempt,' Baldwin said.

'Then there is the nature of her death,' Simon continued. 'This was a strange attack. It might have been committed by a berserker.' He looked over the crowds of people. He saw Matthew, and was about to wave, but it would have been an incongruous action. In any case, Matthew was joining with other beggars for once. He was sitting next to a large woman, María de Venialbo.

'Or someone like the Fleming,' Baldwin nodded, speaking for him, 'who was unused to killing. They wanted to stop her blabbing about the blackmail, but they panicked at the sight of blood and went into a frenzy.'

'Aye. Unless it was just someone who hated the girl and sought to murder her.'

Baldwin looked up suddenly. 'No. The Doña said that *she* had been intending to go, but her maid advised against it, and went in her place. If the motive was hatred, the culprit was someone who detested Doña Stefanía herself, not Joana, and sought to kill *her*.'

'Bugger!' Simon exclaimed. 'That means she could still be in danger.'

'No, Simon, it means she *is* still in danger.' Baldwin scrutinised the people crowding the square. Where yesterday he had seen only happy, satisfied pilgrims and contented hawkers, now he saw a seething mass of humanity, a mix of hatreds and motives to kill, and in there amongst them all, was a murderer.

Someone who could bring themselves to slaughter a Prioress.

Baldwin gave a long, puzzled sigh. Just then, he saw Don Ruy, who had left them and was now engaged in earnest conversation with the beggarwoman María across the square. After a short discussion, María took a coin from the knight and resignedly followed him when he strode away.

Chapter Thirteen

Doña Stefanía bowed her head in the small lady chapel of the church and before she could frame her words, she felt her shoulders begin to shake uncontrollably.

Her sin was appalling. Yesterday she hadn't been able to worry herself about it, because she was too tied up in the fact of Joana's murder, but now she realised the enormity of her act. She had given away the life of her maid to save the little box in her purse.

How curious that she should have realised what she had done because of a stray word by that evil felon, Don Ruy. He had said it before the two Englishmen, commenting that he hadn't tried to win the contents of her purse. An odd way of putting it, that. He hadn't said he'd not tried to take her money, but *the contents of her purse*. Somehow, he had divined what she carried.

She couldn't pray like this. Instead, with shaking hands, she reached into her purse and pulled out the little box. Perhaps the sight of it would calm her. A prayer to him might also help.

From the outside, the box was perfectly ordinary, a shining pewter cube, with only one piece of ornamentation to show its importance – a cross carved into the lid, its outline filled with gold. At the centre, where the cross's arms met, there was a large ruby. The gold and the ruby together showed the value of the contents. Doña Stefanía allowed her tears to moisten the metal, and then, with fumbling fingers, she unclipped the clasp and opened it, staring inside.

As usual, she was overcome with excitement at the sight. Inside was a small piece of bone, maybe a half-inch long, discoloured from its long burial. She took it out reverently and kissed it, then put it back. It made her entire body tingle, just like sex with Parceval. She felt slightly faint, as though she had taken a drug which enhanced the senses; it was always the same, whenever she was this close to the relic.

'Saint Peter, I am so sorry,' she whispered. 'I had no idea. I thought all he wanted was money, nothing more. It never occurred to me that he might want this as well – your own finger.'

She heard a step and hurriedly snapped the lid shut again, dropping the box into her purse. If someone was prepared to kill Joana, might they not come and find her as well? Perhaps it was this that they wanted, not the money which Joana had carried to her death?

If only she hadn't been tempted to rut with that peasant, she would not have feared the blackmail. And the blackmail itself had led to this: to Joana's murder and Doña Stefanía's trepidation.

All because of the finger of Saint Peter. Her priory's most precious – *its only* – relic.

Gregory was content. He had spent much of the morning in the Cathedral's square, and the result was, he was happier than he had been in many long years.

There was a wonderful sense of fulfilment here in the sunlight. Pilgrims who had travelled for hundreds of miles were arriving and giving thanks for being able to see this marvellous building, giving praise to God for allowing them to achieve their goals. As he watched them, his spirit was renewed.

The only thing that smudged the scene was the curious glimpse he'd had of that fellow Parceval. He remembered the churl from the journey here. He couldn't very well forget the man, since Parceval had survived that terrible attack, just like him. Strange, but he'd found himself disliking the Fleming on sight, and from the way that Parceval ducked behind a tree when he spotted Gregory, he felt the same.

Still, he wouldn't allow one idiot to ruin his day. He was having far too much fun. Especially once he left the square and entered the Cathedral again.

This place was magnificent. Gold gleamed everywhere, and

the rich crimsons set it off perfectly. In a place like this, it was easy to imagine oneself that little bit nearer to God.

In fact, he felt better than he could have hoped. That terrible desolation had gone, replaced by a renewal of love, faith and hope. Gregory had thought his life was more or less ended, that there was nothing left for him. It seemed that God Himself had turned His face from him just when Gregory needed Him most.

But that was rubbish – he could see that now. When the others went streaming down the hill towards the city, only to be cut down by the outlaws, he realised that his survival was proof of God's forgiveness. Why else should He have saved him? Obviously it was a sign that God still loved him.

That awareness was wonderful. Where he had felt horror at being divorced from God's love, now he was once more closely united. All was well.

Slowly drifting with the crowd, he walked like a man in a dream. Incense didn't so much waft as billow from the enormous censers swung by powerful-looking young novices, and he inhaled a lungful of the aromatic smoke by mistake, suddenly overtaken by a coughing fit. Pilgrims eyed him dubiously, either considering him to be an unhealthy specimen, or wondering whether this was a fit brought on by a demon. There were a few who watched with interest, hoping to be able to attempt to exorcise him, or witness another doing so, but unfortunately (for the witnesses) he soon recovered. He rested his back against the cool stone of a column and contemplated the great windows ahead.

He was there when he heard a sudden intake of breath, and looked down to see Doña Stefanía. Dear God, he thought. Why was there always a serpent in Eden?

'You again!' he spat.

'Where else, my once-husband?' she said coldly.

It was lunchtime when Matthew glanced up at the sky and decided he needed a drink. That was the trouble with a place like this. The square was good for alms, for there were so many pilgrims passing through each day, but begging was hot, dusty work, and when the sun beamed down like this, it was unbearable. He felt as though he was melting in his black clothing.

Ever and again his mind took him back to the tavern last night, to the light playing gently over Sir Baldwin's features as they chatted. It was the first time that Matthew had felt someone's sympathy since the destruction of their Order. Usually all he felt was waves of revulsion when people saw him in the street.

He knew it was normal for ordinary people to loathe beggars – he would have done so himself. They were commonly the bone idle, incompetent and congenitally stupid – but surely people should see that he was different? He had the stamp of a warrior monk on him, he had been responsible for many lives, he had commanded men, and he had served his Pope with honour and distinction. His sole offence was to have been marked out for misfortune. He had not acted against the Lord God, he had not offended any of His commandments. All he had done, he had done in God's name for God's glory.

That was his firm belief. When he was younger, when he had served the Pope, things had seemed so simple and straightforward. There was good and evil, and the two were clearly delineated.

Matthew tramped over the square towards the alley that led north. A short way up here, he knew, was a small inn where folk like him were treated kindly. The owner was a decent woman who sought to support those who needed her aid. She had a soft spot for Matthew, he reckoned, for she always had a pot of wine and water for him, and sometimes there was a sausage to go with it or a slab of bacon.

Yet his mind was not on the blessed joy of a filled stomach. Rather, it was still fixed on Baldwin's generosity of spirit. It seemed that the knight still adhered to the oaths he had taken so many years ago, and still felt comradeship for Matthew; it was as though he didn't see the torn rags of a beggar, but smelled the purity of a clean soul beneath. At the memory of Baldwin's expression, Matthew's eyes filled with tears. He felt a thick, throat-blocking sense of guilt and foolishness at what he had done.

He couldn't speak to Baldwin again, he decided. There was too much shame in doing so.

He walked along the narrow snickleway with the slow gait of a man made drowsy from the heat. Perhaps later he would leave the city, go back upriver again, and take a cool dip. Then he could lie on the bank and dream of the past, of his glories and honour during those great days when he lived in the Pope's fortress at Avignon.

How vain are the dreams of man, he thought. None at Avignon would recall his face now, let alone his deeds. He was an historical embarrassment, that was all.

As he passed a tree, he thought he heard something behind him, but his mind was so fixed upon the idea of water and the delicious sensation of coolness, that he paid it little heed. Only when he heard a scream from a woman, and saw the man suddenly appear, did he realise that his end had come at last, and it was with a brief feeling of relief that he saw the blade of the dagger right before him.

He made no effort to defend himself. He had been a coward once: this time he could embrace his fate willingly. He actually smiled as he felt the point pierce his breast.

'Christ's cods, but it's hot, isn't it?' Simon muttered as they passed along the alley leading to the gate.

Baldwin glanced at him. His friend was wiping at his brow with a sleeve, and his face appeared redder than usual. 'Simon, we ought to get something to drink before we do anything else.'

'Oh, in God's name, I'm all right,' Simon retorted. 'You're worse than Meg. My wife's always telling me to take it easy when I have to go on a long journey or anything. Anyone would think I was a feeble cleric or something.'

Baldwin smiled, but he was not going to be refused. There was a well in a garden nearby, and Baldwin asked the man leaning against the wall there whether they might drink a little from it. He grunted his assent. Baldwin drank his fill, then insisted that Simon do the same. 'You have never suffered from sunstroke – I have,' he declared. 'It is worse than you can imagine, and it can be dangerous. It is not worth taking the risk.'

'Very well,' Simon said. He was prepared to humour his friend, and to be fair, he was thirsty. Next to the well was a small sewer, and he availed himself of that too, turning his nose up at the smell of faeces in the hot, still air.

'Right,' he said when he was done. 'Let's summarise what we know so far. We have a dead maid. She was there at the river, we know or think, with her fiancé, Frey Ramón. However, he denies this and says the last time he saw her was in the city.'

'We only have Don Ruy's word for Frey Ramón's presence at the murder site.'

'Yes – and he himself was sent here because of a rape.'

'But with a parchment that declares he was innocent.'

Simon nodded. '*If* it was real – and not a forgery!'

'True,' Sir Baldwin sighed. 'We also have this mysterious matter of the blackmail. Remember, Ruy alleged that a known outlaw with a hunched head left the city that afternoon, too.'

'So our chief suspects so far are Ruy himself, Ramón and this felon.' Simon shrugged. 'Where on earth could the Prioress's money have gone?'

'Find that and we find the murderer,' said Baldwin.

'Where are we going now?' Simon asked as Baldwin set off again.

'To look at some of the stables about here,' Baldwin said. He was peering up the road, towards the unmistakable sound of neighing and snorting. 'I want to make sure that the noble Don Ruy was telling the truth about hiring a horse. There can't be that many stables here, and if he decided to hire a mount on the spur of the moment, surely he'd pick a place that lay on the way to the gate.'

'Didn't Munio say he had sent men to check the stables?' Simon said, hurrying to keep up and panting a little.

'No. Munio sent to learn where the maid's horse was stabled, and whether she was followed. I want to see where Ruy found *his* mount. After all, he may have followed her *after* seeing her on her horse. There is nothing to say that he followed her to her stable. In any case, I think you and I can question stablemen more effectively. We have more facts about the murder at our disposal.'

'You suspect him, don't you?'

Baldwin looked at him. 'Did you see his face when he spoke of Joana? There was hurt there when he told how she'd tethered her horse with that other man's. We heard that he was staring at Joana when they left the gate, according to the beggar; also, he admits he was chasing after her.'

'Interesting. That all means he didn't see Ramón on the way out, only her. So was Ramón already there and waiting at a prearranged rendezvous?' Simon mused.

'Perhaps. I do wonder about him. Could Ramón have killed her for the money?' Baldwin thought aloud.

'He looked to be utterly bereft at the scene yesterday.'

'True.' Baldwin stopped. 'Let's ask in here. Perhaps things are about to be clarified for us.'

The building had a large yard, railed to stop horses escaping, and a simple barn behind, set out with rings in the walls to enclose the horses. Inside, rounseys and cheaper pack beasts stood and chomped on their straw. The groom arrived in moments, happily took Baldwin's proffered tip, but could not help them. He had not served any man yesterday, let alone a knight.

They left and walked farther up the lane. The next two stables were no more helpful than the first, but when they reached the fourth one, the little, pinched-faced man took Baldwin's money with a suspicious glower. Simon thought it made him look less like a human and more like a deeply unhappy goblin, similar to the ones being carved on Exeter's new Cathedral.

Baldwin asked whether a knight had called in yesterday afternoon, and the man nodded suspiciously. 'What of it?'

'We wanted to ask about his horse. He had it for much of the afternoon?'

'If he's the man you mean, he took it out in the early afternoon. I told him to be careful, because of the heat, and he said he was going up along the river so the horse could drink and get shade when it wanted.'

'I see. And which horse did he take?' Baldwin asked glancing along the lines of mounts.

'His own. A dark one, with a splash of white on its shoulder and neck. Why?'

Baldwin tried to control his excitement. 'This man, he came back later? Where is the horse now?'

'He's taken it with him – off to Portugal, I think. Probably to Tomar. That was where he was talking about going, anyway.'

Baldwin rapped out some more questions, then turned at last to Simon. 'He says that the man's name was Ramón.'

'He's bolted! He's taken the money and gone!'

'Slow down, Simon. He could merely have been so distraught at his fiancée's death that he decided to flee the city. It is, after all, in Compostela, where his dreams came to nought.'

'Did he say he would return?' Simon enquired.

'No. He has gone to Portugal, this man thinks.'

Simon licked his lips. 'Ask about other travellers who have come in here recently and stabled their horses with him.'

After much talk, the groom admitted to some others. One in particular was a handsome mare which had arrived the day before. A man with a badly hunched back had brought it in, and left it. He hadn't said when he was going to want it. It was just down the second aisle.

The groom led the way between massive rumps of horseflesh to a pretty little amblere, which stood sedately cropping at a bundle of hay, eyeing the men curiously.

'Very pretty,' Baldwin said with a smile, patting her backside.

'She'd be a lovely beast for a lady,' the groom said innocently.

'I am sure you are right,' Baldwin agreed affably. 'Tell me more about this man who brought it in to you.'

* * *

Munio was in his hall with his clerical secretary when the call came to him, and he sighed as the priest packed up his scrip and some parchments with the air of a man who had seen it all before and knew he would see many more deaths before his own.

Every year, five or six men were elected to the post of Enquirer in Compostela, but Munio would be happy when his own period of office was complete. Usually, he spent his time in arranging sales of the strong local wines, for he was a merchant of some repute, but this last year had been difficult because he had been busy with investigations.

It was a dolorous task, observing the results of crimes, enquiring of the victims what they had seen, how they had been treated. All too often they would be shaking, scared, injured, with blood seeping from filthy rags bound about knocked heads, or over the stumps of fingers where they had tried to deflect a blade. And all too often they were dead, like the poor girl yesterday.

Death was the most depressing part of it all. It was not unnatural to be upset by the death of a young woman, but Munio felt the same sadness whether it was a child, a youth or an old person. His mournfulness had increased greatly since he became *Pesquisidor*. There was no sense in the early death of a fellow before his time. Or *her* time.

All were used to the misery of loss. No one could have escaped it, especially after the dreadful famines which affected the whole of Castile in the years from 1301. He had heard that other places had suffered too, especially since 1316, but the loss of so many in his own town was enough woe for him. There was only so much sadness a man could cope with.

There had been good times, it was true. He had fallen in love, he had married, fathered a pair of boys who were even now apprenticed to a friend who would teach them discipline and the rudiments of business, and his wife Margarita was a loyal, sensible, contented woman, who was a source of delight to him, and a continual relief. Without her, he would never have been able to cope with the stress of the last few months looking into so many crimes.

It was hard to believe that so many people who were only here to show their religious convictions or to beg forgiveness for a crime could cause so much mayhem, but that was the case.

And now there had been another murder.

He followed the young man who had found the corpse, and stood over the bundle of filthy clothes, his nose twitching at the metallic smell of blood. It repelled him as ever.

'Who would want to kill an old chap like him?' he wondered aloud.

'There was another beggar here. She screamed when he fell,' the lad said. He was a short fellow, with the crooked leg that spoke of rickets when he had been a child. His pale, shocked features were pox-marked and scrawny, as though he hadn't had a filling meal in weeks.

'Where is she?' Munio asked.

'Dunno. I heard her scream, and saw this man fall, and then she ran off. The murderer must have stabbed the old sod and then bolted back down that way,' he said, pointing back towards the square.

'Did you see who the beggarwoman was?'

'I've seen her, yes, but I don't know her name.'

'Oh, good!' Munio sighed with weary acceptance. In his experience, people who thought that they recognised someone near a crime, whether it was a witness or the perpetrator, were invariably wrong. In the heat of the moment, they always seemed to impose their own bigotries or hatreds on the scene and, in short, saw what they expected to see. It was rare that he had learned much of any use from 'witnesses' to a crime – except where the criminal was caught red-handed.

Usually, of course, that was what happened, he reflected as he hunkered down beside Matthew's body. The man who killed was there, tripped over or grabbed by passers-by, and held until the *Pesquisidor* arrived. Normally, there was the smell of old wine on the man's breath and he confessed bitterly, his motive some imagined slight or insult in a tavern, or some ancient feud reignited by alcohol.

This was not that kind of death, surely. 'You say she screamed when this man fell, and *then* the killer approached him?'

'Yes.'

'So he was already on the ground before the man reached him?' Munio said, brows raised. 'The killer saw him fall to the ground, and then stabbed him?'

That he had been stabbed was not in question. There was a sharply cut section of material in the front of his breast, a little to the side of the breastbone. The knife must have been thrust in forcefully and it had penetrated the heart instantly so far as Munio could see, because there was little blood. When he lifted the robes and pulled the shirt aside, there were no other stab wounds that he could see. The old man's thin ribcage stood out plainly, the ghastly slit where the blade had penetrated showing as a dark cut with a dribble of blood.

It was a miserable figure, this corpse. At least the woman yesterday had been fully fleshed. This man was skinny, each bone defined. His chin was covered in a grey stubble as though he hadn't been shaved in a week or more, although he was proud enough not to want to remain unshaved. Most beggars accepted their status and grew long beards. Not this fellow.

Matthew, Munio thought to himself. He had seen the man often enough, as had everyone who lived in the city. His stumbling gait was well known to all, as was his independence. He always stood apart, as though he was too proud to accept his lowly position. Munio was not the only man who had wondered about Matthew's past. Odd. He was the one beggar who remained unbending and unsociable, yet he was the one whom all knew best. He was a loner, but that made him significant. It made him seem important.

There were other differences between Joana's corpse and his. She had died as the result of a maddened attack, whereas Matthew had been disposed of in a simple, direct manner. A single stab wound, and that was that.

Munio considered that contrast as he sat back on his heels. Perhaps Joana had not merely cast off a past lover; maybe she had taken another woman's man, and the spurned mistress had taken her revenge? In contrast, this beggar Matthew may have been cut down because he had known something, or seen something.

Whatever the reason for his death, Munio was not sanguine about finding his murderer. The sad fact was, that when there was no killer caught at the time, it was unlikely that anyone would be found later.

Was there a chance that the two deaths were in some way linked?

Munio stared down at the body. It was not very likely. The methods of death were so different, the means too, and any connection between an old man and a young, fresh woman was all but inconceivable.

'So you heard her scream, saw him fall, and then the murderer went to him? Very well. Now we should seek the woman.'

A woman who was terrified for her own life, since she was a witness to a murder. Munio sighed to himself. Someone who was that scared would be hard to find.

Chapter Fourteen

Running away from the place, Afonso knew that his attack was mad, that he had been a fool, but he couldn't help it. When that bastard son of a Moorish slave and a Venetian whore, that piece of hogshit, Matthew, had wandered away from the square looking so smug, Afonso had felt the strings of his gut and bowels start to tighten like he was about to be sick. He couldn't help it. He'd chased off after him, running along the alley.

But he'd taken a wrong turn somewhere and found himself in a dead end. He had to run back, then up the next connecting lane.

It was a grim place, stinking of piss and shit, and he'd slapped his sandals through pools of damp, trying not to think of the mess that fouled his feet, ankles and shins. The smell was enough to hint at what lay all about. He was relieved when, diving round the corner of one house, he found himself in a wider opening, and was able to look about him in the blindingly bright sunshine.

Left was a tavern with a single tree outside, a cobbled yard a little like one of his own, back in the village where he had been born – in Gradil, in Portugal. In the road next to his father's olive farm, there had been a place much like this, a small building with a triangular court before it, and one solitary olive tree, he recalled. From there, on the side of the hill, you could look eastwards over the broad space of the land, with the olive trees and grapes ripening on the vines. It was always peaceful there, quiet and good. A man like his father could sit and gaze at the view with a jug of his best red wine beside him in the hot summer evening, while a few pieces of fish or meat cooked on his open fire.

For an instant Afonso felt his heart fold in upon itself. That was where he would still be now, if it weren't for the Templars – and for Matthew in particular. It was as he turned that he saw, coming from the opposite direction, Matthew and some beggarwoman. Immediately he had drawn his dagger and rushed at the old sod.

Matthew was dead. That was the main thing, the only thing that mattered. Matthew, the murderer of his father, had died; although his passing was far too easy and gentle for Afonso's taste. If the latter could have had his own way, he would have made the traitor suffer much more.

It was curious, that expression on his face, Afonso thought. Almost as though he was glad. Perhaps he had known that he was going to die like that someday. He had certainly guaranteed that he had enough enemies.

In the square, Afonso glanced about him before making off towards the lane that would take him back towards Sir Charles and Paul. Once there, he would pack and prepare to leave. There was no point in hanging around here for someone to find him. No, he would throw all his things into a bag, then make his way south, away from this city.

Sir Charles was sitting with his back to a tree, a large pilgrim's hat with a cockleshell symbol pinning up the brim to protect his eyes from the glare of the sun, when Afonso arrived. The Portuguese stood a moment contemplating him, then cleared his throat loudly enough for Sir Charles to hear.

The knight merely smiled under his hat. He had heard Afonso's feet approaching and had instantly come awake, just as he always did. He was too well attuned to the possibility that an enemy from long ago, or even from recent times might arrive to kill him. 'You look tired, my friend.'

'Sí. I am a little,' Afonso said. He looked along the lane, back the way he had come, but no one appeared to have followed him. 'I think I have had enough of this place.'

'Ah. You have seen your friend again. He will trouble you no more?'

'He will trouble no man.'

Sir Charles looked approvingly at him. There was about Afonso no sign that he had just brought a man to swift or violent death, no blood on his tunic or sleeves, no mark on his hands. If he had been asked, Sir Charles would have said that this calm, collected man before him was guilty of nothing – but then he had seen Afonso kill before. With that dagger of his, he could draw, spin the blade up and catch it, and then hurl it so smoothly and quickly that it could penetrate a half-inch of solid hardwood. He had seen it. Just as he had seen Afonso's knife kill the tavern-keeper who was going to brain him in that tavern in France. There had been no blood on Afonso then either. It was a very effective weapon, a knife thrown at speed.

'So, are you ready to leave?' he asked.

'I have nothing more to do here,' Afonso said. 'I shall return to my home.'

'Down to Portugal?'

'Yes.'

'Extraordinary!' Sir Charles stood and dusted his backside. Glancing up at the sky, which now had thick, fleecy clouds moving slowly across it, he sniffed. He put a finger into his ear and delicately removed a little wax, inspecting it with curiosity. 'There seems little of interest in this town to me. A pleasing altar, it's true, but precious little else. There's not even a decent brothel. I know . . . why don't I join you?'

Afonso nodded calmly. Sir Charles was a dangerous man, but he had proved himself honourable enough. He and Afonso had been together for some months, and they had not exchanged a cross word. Both were slow to take offence with a companion. He had noticed before that there were fewer arguments and fights between men who were genuinely equals. 'I would be grateful for your companionship,' he said politely.

Sir Charles nodded, then shouted for Paul to prepare to pack and go. He smiled at Afonso and said, 'Friend, you have the air of a man who has achieved something with his day. A weight has fallen from you.'

'Yes,' Afonso said. It was true. He had not been able to satisfy his lust for vengeance, but at least the man was dead. Now his father could rest in his grave at last.

Again the expression on the old man's face came back to him. Gratitude for seeing that his debt was at last discharged? Relief that his grim existence as a beggar was about to be ended? Perhaps he had come to realise how foul his act had been, and welcomed the tardy arrival of justice.

Or was he just glad that the waiting was over?

The groom could help them no further, but the two men left the stable and set off with the certainty that they were following the right trail.

There were another three stables along this road.

'Christ's Blood!' Simon said, wiping the sweat from his forehead again. 'They have more horses per head here than any city I've known.'

Baldwin nodded absently. 'Yes, it's the same with all the big pilgrim centres. They have so many people arriving, and they have to cater for them all. It's worse here, because Saint James brings in so many travellers for each week, but I think that at this time of year, getting close to his feast day on 25 July, the place must have at least double its normal population. Local businesses have to provide accommodation and food for all the men and women, and also for all the beasts which they bring.'

Two boys were playing with a ball. As it rolled down the road, Simon aimed a kick at it in passing, but he missed by some inches. That was odd, but he put it down to the weather. Never again would he complain about the sun when he was parched and riding over Dartmoor. This was a heat he could never have imagined, had he not come here. He must be hungry, too; his belly felt empty. 'My gut thinks my throat's been cut!' he grumbled.

The next stable was where they found Don Ruy's horse.

'Yes, masters, he came here last afternoon, hired a horse and went for a ride. Was out almost until dark.'

The groom was leaning on his rails as he spoke, a happy, smiling man in his late fifties, from the look of him. He had a face like a walnut and, to Simon's eye, appeared as wiry as a Dartmoor shepherd. Although he was leaning talking to the two, he seemed to have eyes in the back of his head, because he suddenly broke off and roared, making Simon jump, although the Bailiff wasn't as startled as the boy who was supposed to be mucking out a couple of stalls. The lad stopped eavesdropping and bent to his task again, while the old groom, who had not so much as turned his head, winked at Baldwin.

'You have to keep them on their toes.'

Baldwin grinned. 'I have a young servant who needs the same attention. Tell me, this man yesterday – how did he seem when he came back? Did he seem disturbed in any way?'

'I'd say he was sad – you know, like a man who has learned that his dog's just died.'

'Which means we are a little farther forward,' Baldwin said to Simon as they walked back later.

'Perhaps. We may know where the Prioress's mare has gone, and we know where Don Ruy and Frey Ramón's horses were kept.'

'And there is Joana's mount, too,' Baldwin said suddenly. They were near the first stable, and he saw the wrinkled little man inside. 'Holá! One last question, señor. That mare – was there ever another mare with it?'

'There was another, yes. A pretty little thing,' the man said, walking out to them. He had some twine about his belly, and he stuck a thumb in it as he stared at them both consideringly. 'A maid came in here for it, and took it out yesterday after lunch. Haven't seen it or her since. Pretty maid, she was. Slim, tall, black hair. Lovely.'

'And so,' Baldwin smiled, 'this is presumably where Joana's own mount was left.'

Simon nodded moodily.

'What is it, Simon?'

'It seems quite a coincidence that the shifty fellow who took the Doña's mare chose to store it here with the Doña's maid's horse, doesn't it?'

It was later that evening that Baldwin heard of the death of his friend. At first, he disbelieved the story. It seemed so unreasonable that he could have found an old comrade only to lose him again almost immediately.

He and Simon were sitting in a tavern in a small court some short way from the square, and they had eaten their fill of good stew, soft-crusted bread, olives and a light, fresh wine. Afterwards they sat back, Simon belching softly. 'Not bad wine, this. Better than the French stuff I sometimes buy in Lydford. This is on a par with the quality wines they sell in Exeter.'

Baldwin sipped and nodded. 'I think they have more flavour here. Either that, or the drink which we normally buy has been adulterated.'

Simon grunted and stretched. 'It's strange. This Galician air seems to make you more tired. I could ride twenty or thirty miles at home and still feel ready for a few quarts of ale, but here I sit about all day and have a little wine, and suddenly I'm exhausted.'

'The heat can do that to you,' Baldwin said. 'I did warn you.'

'It doesn't seem to hurt others.'

'The people who live here grow accustomed to the temperature.'

'No, I meant the other pilgrims.'

'They walked or rode here, spending time to get used to the gradual increase in temperature. You and I arrived on a ship after a short journey. We are more likely to be affected.'

'If you say so.' Simon cast a knowing look at him. 'You aren't interested in this at all, are you? You are still thinking about that dead girl.'

'I cannot help it.'

'Nor can I,' Simon said. 'You know, those injuries worry me. Joana was recognised instantly by her mistress, Doña Stefanía, and yet I wouldn't be able to swear who on earth it was. It's almost as though Doña Stefanía had ordered her death. She recognised the girl because she knew who had been killed.'

'She was the right height and wearing familiar clothes,' Baldwin pointed out.

'Clothes alone! Is that enough to make a reasonable identification? No!'

Baldwin leaned his forearms on the table before him and met Simon's gaze. 'I too feel oddly uneasy. It is as though I am forced to remain a spectator, when my soul is crying out that I should be there helping. You and I must have more experience in seeking out killers than any man in this city, yet we have no authority to do anything, while a murderer is loose somewhere near us.'

'It doesn't mean we can necessarily help. I doubt that I'd be much assistance to anyone; I can't even understand the language!'

Baldwin watched him drain his cup. 'Yet you can still see when a man is lying, can't you? You are adept at hearing when someone is dissembling.'

'Oh, I don't know . . .'

'It is often said that a blind man will hear more acutely. Some philosophers believe that when a man loses one faculty, his mind works more concentratedly with the others. Thus, a blind man may hear better with his ears and feel more with his fingers. It follows that you may be better attuned to hearing a man's deceit when you have no understanding of his words.'

Simon gave him a pitying look. 'You think so?'

'What of that man Ruy?'

'Sir Ruy? There's a prime example. I have no idea whether he lied or not.'

'Nor have I.'

'There you are,' Simon said, leaning back and closing his eyes. 'It's a handicap, not being able to speak the language. If even you couldn't see where he lied, he fooled you too. Perhaps you need to be fluent in a language to spot a man's dishonesty.'

'I am not so sure. My linguistic skills have to be scraped up from the recesses of my memory, which means I cannot listen with the ear of an inquisitor to the tones and inflexions of a man's voice. Now: I believe Don Ruy could have lied to us.'

'He could have, I suppose, but why? Do you mean he killed the girl? He has a record for rape, of course. But we both know that what he was accused of was really eloping, if he was telling the truth. His documents support him.'

'*If* he told us the truth,' Baldwin agreed. 'Then we should consider whether he was *not* lying to us.'

'That means the Prioress was lying, and I won't have that.'

'It does not necessarily follow, Simon. There is a third possibility: that neither did.'

Simon considered. 'She said that he saw her, which he admitted; she said that he blackmailed her, which he denied. Either he did, or he did not. Simple.'

'But she did not say that he went to her directly. That was the point of my questions to him. She said that her maid was told. Now, perhaps her maid did not actually meet Don Ruy face to face, but instead spoke to a third party who pretended he was speaking on behalf of Ruy but was in reality acting on his own cognizance. When the maid told her mistress, she would naturally speak of the Don, not some servant. Thus the Prioress was assured that it was him, Don Ruy, who was blackmailing her, when in reality it was nothing to do with him. Therefore, neither lied to us, and both were telling us the truth.'

'So who could this mystery man have been?'

'The peasant, Parceval – he knew Ruy had walked in. Look, he could even have dreamed up this blackmail story with Joana herself. She helped him invent it in order to rob her mistress – but then her partner killed her to take the full amount rather than share it with her.'

'You believe that?' Simon asked doubtfully.

'Not really, but it is a possible explanation, along with others, like Ramón killing her and fleeing with the money, Ruy's lustful rape and subsequent murder, or a felon's robbery and murder of her.'

'I cannot get away from the fact of Ramón's fleeing the city, and Ruy saying Ramón was there with her.'

'Really?' said Baldwin. 'I cannot myself get away from the hunchbacked felon. He took Doña Stefanía's horse back to the stable, which is why Joana had to go to the ford – and die. And Ruy saw a man who looked just like that, attack his companions and then leave the city in time to kill the girl.'

'I should like to speak to the peasant Parceval to see where he was when Joana died,' Simon said. 'Perhaps we should find Munio and tell him what we have discovered?'

'We tried that this afternoon, remember?' Baldwin said drily. He was a little put out by the *Pesquisidor* because he and Simon had sent a boy to find Munio to tell him what they had learned from the Don and Doña, but Munio had sent the lad back to say that he was too busy to see them right at that moment. 'His reply bordered on the insulting.'

'Maybe he was merely very busy,' Simon said soothingly. 'I expect he has many calls on his time in a city as lively as this.' He languidly beckoned to the daughter of the innkeeper and asked her if she knew where Munio lived.

Fortunately, she knew a little English from the pilgrims who flocked to the city, and could answer. 'Yes, he lives only a short way.'

'Would you send a boy to ask him to come and join us?' Simon said.

When she had gone, calling for her brother, Baldwin gave a twisted grin. 'I hope you are right. Perhaps he will come here now. Or maybe he will decide again that he has better things to do than come to meet with us, a *busy* man like him!'

His doubts were soon to be dispelled. After a few minutes, there was a cough behind him, and a voice said, 'So. You wanted to speak to me, gentles?'

'*Pesquisidor*, I am glad to see you,' Simon said effusively, standing and indicating a seat near him.

Baldwin saw why when he himself stood. Behind Munio stood a beautiful woman. She was taller than Munio, with dark skin and hair as black as a raven's wing. Her face was long and fine, with high cheekbones and a straight nose leading down to a thinnish mouth, but any solemnity that it gave her face was given the lie by her large, luminous eyes, which were filled with kindness.

'This is my wife, Margarita,' Munio said. 'We were walking when your messenger found us.'

'Please be seated,' Baldwin said, bringing a seat up for Margarita and then motioning to the serving-girl.

'You said you had something to talk about,' Munio enquired.

Baldwin thought he looked very tired, as though the events of the last day had worn him down, and he felt a fleeting guilt that he had considered the man to be too lazy to bother to visit him when he asked. Munio's face had a drawn appearance, like one who had slept little and thought too much.

It was Simon who spoke. 'It is this murder. We wondered whether we should trouble you, but it seemed only fair to tell you.'

Munio jerked upright. 'You know about the beggar?'

Baldwin smiled. 'No, what beggar?'

'Only an old man. He was killed today not far from the square. Poor old devil. He was a loner in life and died the same way.'

'A shame,' Baldwin said.

'He was so noble-looking, too.'

A chill hand seemed to settle over Baldwin's heart. 'You can't mean Matthew?'

'You knew him?'

'An older man with a grey beard? Narrow features, pale-grey eyes, had been fair-haired once, and had a deeply lined face with dark, sunburned skin?'

'There was only the one man begging called Matthew that I know of.'

Baldwin felt strange and a little dizzy. It had been many years since he had last encountered a brother Templar, and to have met

Matthew only yesterday and learn today that he was dead, was a terrible shock, outrageous: it could have been torn from a Greek tragedy. It was as though the very last bond with his past had been sliced through and he must now sail on an uncharted sea without any aid to navigate. In a way, he felt he could glimpse the mournful loss that Matthew himself must have experienced over these last few years. Baldwin felt so bereft that even the memories of his wife and daughter failed to touch him.

Simon could see Baldwin's distress, and quickly broke in to change the subject. 'One thing I never asked you, señor, is how long you lived in Oxford? You speak English so very well.'

Munio set his head to one side deprecatingly. 'I spent seven years in Oxford, when my father sought to have me educated as a philosopher, but then he lost his money and I had to make my own way in the world. I persuaded a merchant in the city to let me learn how he plied his trade, and some while later I managed to set myself up as a merchant in my own right. I came back here with my wife because it was the city I grew up in. I have always loved it.'

'Your wife is not from here?' Simon asked.

'No,' she laughed. 'I come from Oxford.'

Simon was astonished. To find a man who spoke English was pleasing in a foreign land, even if they had first met while the man held some suspicions of him, but then to learn that this beautiful woman was also English was a delight. 'I can understand how you speak my language so well, having so charming a tutor,' he said to Munio.

Munio gave a grin. 'When a man has a wife nagging at him, he learns her language soon enough.'

'I don't nag,' she scolded, but with a trickle of laughter in her tone, and she glanced gratefully at Simon.

Baldwin had recovered sufficiently to pour the wine that had arrived at last. 'This Matthew – how did he die?'

'It was murder,' Munio said, and his eyes lost the humour which had flared in them for a moment. 'A youth heard a scream and turned to see him fall. A beggarwoman was a little way behind him and must have witnessed the incident, but I haven't met her yet. The youth saw a man run at Matthew, pause, and then run off. When he reached the beggar, he was dead, a wound in his breast. It must have punctured his heart.'

'It takes only an inch or so of steel to stop the heart,' Baldwin said inconsequentially. 'Did he see the man who stabbed Matthew?'

'No. The man was facing away the whole time. The lad said it could have been anyone. There are so many pilgrims, and they are changing every day, so it would have been a miracle if he had recognised the man.'

'What of the beggarwoman? Did she recognise him?'

'I haven't spoken to her yet. I was seeking her when your messenger told me you wanted to talk. I was very busy. My apologies. I didn't intend to be rude, but I think my response might have seemed so.'

Baldwin gave a flick of the hand as though discarding any possible upset. 'You had much to deal with.'

'What was it you wanted to tell me?'

Simon saw that Baldwin wasn't quite recovered from his shock on hearing of Matthew's death, so he began to tell Munio of their conversation with Doña Stefanía and Don Ruy.

'So there are two other men from Don Ruy's band of pilgrims with whom we should speak,' Munio summarised. 'This peasant who ravished the Prioress, and the priestly man, Frey Ramón, wherever he might be.'

'There is a third man, of course,' Simon pointed out. 'The felon. We know Don Ruy saw him. Perhaps he had something to do with all this! It is too much of a coincidence that he should take back the horse *and* then be seen leaving the city. He made sure Joana went to pay the blackmailer, and then followed her.'

'Yes,' Baldwin said, trying to set his mind to the problem again. It was hard. All he could see was the careworn face of Matthew as he had seen him yesterday. It was only one day ago, and that made it so much more difficult to believe that the man was truly dead. There was an emptiness in his soul. It had been fine to learn that his old friend was alive, to see a comrade from the days of his youth, and now that last friend was dead. 'I shall find him,' he growled.

'Who?' Simon asked, but then he looked at Baldwin's face and understood.

'Munio, could I see Matthew's body? I wish to say farewell to an old friend.'

Chapter Fifteen

Doña Stefanía got up from her kneeling posture and made her way out of the chapel. This was her third visit here today, and she would spend as much time here as she could over the next days. She had to make sure that her decision was right.

It had been hard, deciding to steal the thing, but better that than seeing the priory collapse. That was her overriding concern, the survival of the priory. It was not a task made any easier by her nuns. Usually, a Prioress should be able to hope for the assistance of her Sisters, but in the convent of Vigo there were too many arguments as her nuns vied for power. It was frustrating, but there was little peace in her home. That was part of the reason why she had acquired this thing.

There was a tingling in her breast at the thought. She had borrowed the relic from Orthez to help her convent and it had worked, bringing in many people from about the lands. Vigo was some way south of Compostela, and had always suffered from a lack of pilgrims, but with rumours of the relic's miracles carefully disseminated by Doña Stefanía, suddenly folk made the short journey from Compostela down to her convent. People who had never heard of the place before had suddenly started flocking there.

When the demand came for the relic to be returned, she hadn't believed it at first. However, the request was confirmed by the Bishop of Compostela, and it was impossible to ignore. When she had asked to borrow the sacred relic, she had said she would want it for some years, and the church at Orthez had apparently had no objection. But now, after seeing how much profit Doña Stefanía had made from the relic, they had apparently changed their minds. One of the priests had passed by her convent, and when he saw how many travellers were stopping there, he obviously took back highly favourable reports about the success of her venture. After that, it took but a few days for the church authorities, especially that pathetic old cretin Sebastián, to decide to demand the return of their relic, Saint Peter's finger bone.

They should have been more polite. As it was, they were rude and discourteous, and that got her goat immediately. She swore that she wouldn't return the thing to them, no matter what they demanded. In fact, she screwed up the parchment and hurled it into the fire. Damn them and their legalistic rubbish! They had forgotten that Doña Stefanía was the daughter of a lord, once wife to an important knight, or they wouldn't have dared write in so curt a manner.

She had been white-faced with fury, almost incoherent with rage when Joana had found her. Joana, the angel, had come in with a tray when Doña Stefanía had just consigned it to the flames, and soothed her with that calmness and calculation which were so much a part of her.

'They demand the return of their relic? Then you must return it.'

'I shall not! The thing was promised to us for years. Just because they can see that we're better suited to attracting pilgrims, that doesn't mean that they should have it back! It's why the thing should stay with us in Vigo. It's worth a fortune to us here.'

'It is said that the Saint himself can decide where his relics stay,' Joana said thoughtfully as she poured wine and passed the goblet to Doña Stefanía. 'Perhaps the Saint would prefer to remain here with us, in the quieter atmosphere of the convent. That might be why he has favoured us with so many pilgrims when he did not treat Orthez with such generosity.'

Doña Stefanía felt her mouth drop open. Of course there were many stories of churches and cathedrals stealing each others' relics, and then claiming that they possessed them by right of the Saint's own wishes – for if the Saint did not wish to be there, he or she could miraculously move him- or herself to another location – but it hadn't occurred to Doña Stefanía to use that argument. Now, though, as Joana crossed the floor and placed the jug on the cupboard, she considered the idea and began to see its merits.

'They'll soon beg for the Bishop to return it if we refuse.'

'Oh, I think the best thing would be to go to Orthez and give them back their relic in their box,' Joana said, 'but then come back to Compostela and ask the Bishop what he would advise.'

'That's no good! If I deliver it to them, we'll never get it back.'

Joana ignored her scathing tones. 'They won't have it back. You will give them the box, but with another small bone in it. We shall keep the original bone here, in our own little casket. We can have one made specially for it. Then, when you come home from Orthez, you can stop at the Bishop's palace and ask him for his support. All you need do is point out that the Saint has made his will clear by showing you how to deceive the men of Orthez. Surely no Bishop would go against the plain will of the Saint himself? And then you can come back here to our little convent, and arrange a feast in honour of the Saint who has so honoured our little chapel.'

The scheme was breathtaking in its simple beauty – and in its purity of revenge against Orthez – but Doña Stefanía felt a certain irritation that the suggestion had come from her maid and not from herself.

There were plenty of precedents for such action, after all. There were stories of an English church which had lent a relic to a French one, but who then had demanded its return. The French sent back a relic, but later, when they were trying to tempt back more pilgrims, they let it be known that in fact they had sent back an imitation and had kept the original. The pilgrims dried up in the English church and began to drift towards the French church again, but then the whole story grew more confusing when the English declared that they had never sent the genuine relic in the first place. Knowing that their French brothers were unreliable in sending back loaned relics, the English had sent a copy themselves. The French had stolen a fake.

This could have been true. Certainly Doña Stefanía knew perfectly well that the French and English clergy were about as unfriendly as their secular lords; all were at daggers drawn over the English territories like Aquitaine, which the French King had confiscated only thirty years before. Since then there had been continual disputes in the English lands. French churches also vied with each other for possession of relics. Vézelay had the relics of Saint Marie Madeleine, but Aix-en-Provence claimed that these had been stolen from them.

Yes, it was a bold plan, Doña Stefanía acknowledged. More, if they could pull it off, the Bishop himself would have to approve. Otherwise, he was overruling the Saint, and that would never do.

In less than an hour, Doña Stefanía and Joana had sketched out the plan. It was much as Joana had originally suggested, but with some minor amendments. First, Doña Stefanía was not prepared to let the genuine relic out of her sight, so she had asked for this little box to be made, and now she carried it with her all the time; Joana had also suggested that there should be a small guard to protect the 'relic' which they would deliver to Orthez. That was why Domingo and his men had gone with them, travelling up through Castile and Navarre to Aragon and then over the passes. The smug, fat priests in Orthez had been slimily grateful, thanking her with such obvious contempt, that it had been difficult not to laugh at them. They were so obnoxious, with their clear disregard for her and her convent, and so delighted to have their bauble back, that she longed to tell them that she had exchanged their relic for an old piece of pig's bone which she had found in the rushes on the floor of her refectory and left in manure for a week to stain it a rich, dark colour.

Joana and she had collapsed in tears when they left the town, but not for the reasons which the fat clerics would have expected or understood.

In Doña Stefanía's purse nestled the piece of the Saint's finger still in its little casket. It was there now, and she pulled it out to look at it once more. The gold of the cross gleamed in the candlelight and she kissed it reverently. This was the saving of her convent.

It was late. She must return to her room, for she didn't wish to tempt Providence by going abroad alone in the dark, unlit streets. The place was full of pilgrims, which meant that there were bound to be cutpurses and other vagabonds wandering about. Pilgrims were easy prey to the nightwalkers of a large city. Walking out through the great door, she went down a side street, and had just turned up towards the square when a low voice almost made her heart stop.

'My lady.'

Her hand rose to her breast, and she felt suddenly light-headed with fear, but relief washed over her when she saw that it was only the grim figure of Domingo. He had been behind her, and now he overtook her.

'I wondered who it was! Foolish fellow, leave me alone,' she commanded. 'I am going to my room.'

'I lost my son for you, lady,' Domingo snarled. 'Don't patronise me.'

'I didn't tell you to have him killed,' she snapped. 'If you were a better leader, he would be alive yet. Now leave me before someone sees us. I don't want anyone to know that you are with me – understand?'

'My men need food and drink but we haven't any money.'

'So?'

'Lady, you brought us here. It's your fault we starve. We need some money.'

'What happened to the sum I paid you? I gave you plenty of gold before we left Vigo.'

'That was enough for us to live on for a month, but we've been travelling for fifty days now. It took twenty-five days for us to get to Orthez, and another twenty-four to come here. What do you expect us to live on – grass?'

'I don't have any more cash with me now.'

'You have a full purse there, lady.'

'There is little in it,' she shot out, a hand covering it.

Domingo was tired of her commands and penny-pinching. He had lost companions to Sir Charles and Dom Afonso, including his own poor lad, and now he needed food, and was desperate for wine. This woman, who had hired him and his men for the whole journey, hadn't warned it would take so long, and now she was prepared to see them go hungry. With a quick sense of the injustice of her actions, he growled deep in his throat, then grabbed her sleeve and drew her to him. She gave an incoherent squeak of fear, and then his hand was on her purse.

It was impossible! He couldn't! 'No! Don't touch that! There's nothing in it!' she said and flailed at him with her fists.

'Do you really think I'm that stupid that I don't know what you carry about in your purse?' he sneered. 'I know what you took out and stared at each night, Doña Stefanía. Me and my men, we guarded you all the way up here, even though you treated us like shit! If you want to have our protection still, you can pay for it.'

'There is only the relic, you fool,' she hissed. 'Touch that, try to steal that, and the Saint will see you die in the most foul and degrading manner!'

He stared at her a moment, and she was sure she'd won. Her argument carried the authority of the Church, and she rose to her full height. Clearly the threat of a Saint's enmity was enough to cow even the dimmest churl. 'Now leave me, you idiot. I shall be returning to Vigo soon, and I want you and your men to be ready to come with me.'

'You want us to come too?'

'Of course.'

'I see. You call *me* a fool, Doña, but you stand there like a stuffed tunic talking about us coming to guard you on the way back to Vigo, but you're prepared to see us suffer until you're ready to go? Think again. You have enough in that purse to buy us all food and drink for a year, don't you?'

'Don't be so stupid!' she said, but then she realised that he had drawn his little knife from his belt, and she saw the wicked gleam of steel before her eyes. She slumped with terror. Never before had anyone drawn a dagger on her. It was terrible. She herself had hired this felon, and now she was suffering the consequences; he would *kill* her! Her mouth fell open but she couldn't even scream, her terror was so complete.

'Shut up, bitch!' Domingo hissed. The blade moved, she snapped her eyes shut, and felt the hideous dragging at her belly. Then he released her. Drained, her legs collapsed beneath her and she fell to the floor.

'Christ's Bones!' Parceval muttered as he saw the lady slump down. A dark shape stood over her – a large, threatening figure – and as Parceval shouted and began to run towards her, he saw the evil glint of a blade. He immediately slowed his pace.

In the past he had killed, yes, but he wasn't a very competent fighter. When he killed Hellin van Coye, he hadn't worried about Hellin's ability to strike back; he'd made sure of that by knifing him in the back when the man was walking away. Not the most honourable assault, perhaps, but Parceval wanted revenge, not a tribute for courage and honour.

This man looked big and Parceval didn't want to be brought before God quite yet. There was too much to enjoy on earth before that. He shouted again, moving his arms threateningly, but not moving forward. To his relief he saw the thief bolt, and when he was sure that he was safe, Parceval went on to the body.

'Doña Stefanía,' he breathed.

She was weeping uncontrollably, but there was no sign of blood. In his experience a man or woman would leak alarmingly from a slight scratch, whereas a serious wound, like the one he gave Hellin, might give rise to very little bleeding. That was worrying, for she might be about to die, and if she was, he didn't want to be near her in case he got accused of her death. As these thoughts were running through his mind, and he glanced along the alley considering escape, she looked up, her face streaked with tears.

'Oh, Parceval! He stole it from me!'

Her voice didn't sound like that of a woman who was gasping her last, and Parceval felt relieved.

'My dear, dear lady! How are you?' he said. 'I heard the fracas, and although I ran here as fast as I could, he escaped! Who was it, did you see? If I catch him, he'll regret his actions! I'll cut his throat for him, acting like this to a Lady of the Church! Has he no faith?'

'Leave him,' Doña Stefanía said urgently. 'Don't pursue him, he is deadly.'

'You know him?'

'I . . .' she hesitated, but fear made her blurt out the truth. 'Yes. He was my maid's cousin. He and his men were protecting me on my way to Orthez, and back again.'

'They were not with your party when you joined us,' Parceval pointed out.

'I told them to keep away, but to follow at a distance. I thought that such a disreputable group might make your companions refuse to let me join you.'

Parceval nodded. Clearly she feared attack or robbery by the man and his companions – not unreasonably, from what he had just witnessed. Well now, he thought, this is better than the other day when I saw her in the square. He was about to speak again, when she submitted to another bout of sobbing. 'My lady, please. How can I serve you?'

'I don't know . . . Take me to a tavern, somewhere I can have a little wine. I am so unsettled . . . I feel terrible.'

He saw her hand pat at her side, as though feeling for something, and then he saw the thongs, obviously sliced through, and realised that her purse was gone. So now she was bankrupted. With nothing but the clothes she stood up in, she would be delighted for the comfort, and perhaps companionship, of a man. Especially a man of means. He smiled and held out his hand. 'Come, lady. Let me help you. But you shouldn't go to a low tavern. Come with me and I shall see you well provided for.'

She accepted his hand, and when she stood, he was

enormously relieved to see that opposite, a short way up a narrow little alley, there was a torch burning. He realised it had been the reflection of this which had made the attacker's knife shine so alarmingly.

'Are you hurt?' he asked, content now that her answer would be negative.

'No. Only my . . .' She dissolved into tears, and this time he was in a better position to offer her comfort. He took her head in one hand and bent it to his shoulder, while with the other he encircled her waist. Then he stood still as she wailed and moaned quietly into his neck. 'I trusted him! I've lost Joana, now him . . . who can I trust?'

Tonight he need not pay the exorbitant charges of the prostitutes, he reckoned. This woman was desperate, and he was sure that, from past experience with her, he could give her exactly the kind of solace she required.

He was rather glad he'd come along this alley. That figure had been very alarming, but things had turned out well. With that thought, he shot a look back in the direction the man had run off. If he appeared again, Parceval would ditch the woman and flee, he decided, but then he calmed himself. There was no sign of the fellow, and Parceval, if he played his dice aright, would have the opportunity of plenty of exercise without running!

That night, Simon woke with an intense griping sensation in his belly. 'I'll never get a decent night's sleep in this blasted country,' he grumbled as he picked his way over the slumbering bodies, tugging his blanket tighter about his naked shoulders on the way to the garderobe.

Squatting on the creaking wood, he brought his weight away from the moving timbers. It was partly to take his mind off the quality of the workmanship that he reminded himself of the investigation so far.

Baldwin, he knew, was shocked by the death of his friend Matthew the beggar. Learning that an old companion had been murdered had clearly stolen his concentration. Simon had a conviction that if either of them was to learn who had killed Joana, it would be him.

It was odd, the bond that service in the Order created between men, he thought. All the men he had met who had been in the Templars had seemed more intelligent than other knights, and Simon wondered fleetingly whether that was a sign of the recruitment policy of the Order, or a sign that they did enjoy some special training. He would probably never know. Even Matthew, who had sunk so low, still had a degree of cunning and intelligence that was higher than some knights Simon knew. Most knights, when it came down to it, would find it hard to locate their arses with both hands!

With that thought, there was a tortured squeak from the timbers and he hastily stopped chuckling.

Don Ruy had looked like an honourable knight, but he was flawed, if his Bishop was to be believed. But then, the Bishop might have been partial. If the girl's father was politically important in Don Ruy's town, the Bishop himself may have been influenced to punish the knight unreasonably. Politics mattered.

If Ruy was telling the truth, then it was possible that Ramón had walked with his fiancée, then killed her and stolen the money. Certainly Ramón had fled the town one day afterwards, which could be taken as an admission of guilt – although Simon himself could well understand that a man who had just buried his raped and murdered woman would want to flee the place which held such foul memories. Then again, surely a knight would want to find the culprit and kill him?

There was the other man: the felon who had been involved in the attack on the pilgrims, and who took the horse to the stable. How could that tie into Joana's death? There were plenty of attacks on pilgrims, after all. Robberies and rapes were common enough.

Simon wondered whether the man had actually left Compostela to go and find the girl Joana. If he had, he might have come across her after Ramón had seen her; after which he killed and robbed her. Perhaps he had led an attack against the pilgrims because he wanted to kill her before, or to kill the Prioress, and he killed Joana when the Prioress didn't appear? The two women had joined this group of pilgrims, Simon remembered, if only for a few short days. Could the man have intended to kill one or both of them, and that was why he attacked them outside Compostela? It was possible – but again, why? What motive was there for the attack?

'I don't know enough yet,' he repeated to himself. 'I need more information.'

That wasn't all. He also needed his sleep. He cleaned himself as best he could and slowly made his way, yawning widely, to his bed. Once there, with his blanket spread over him, he closed his eyes, and imagined in front of him the face of Don Ruy, gazing at him sternly, one hand on his sword. Then Ruy moved aside, and he found himself facing Ramón, who stood sadly shaking his head. Behind him appeared first Matthew, then a woman whom he assumed was Joana.

But finally, as he began to drift into sleep, he grew aware of another figure behind them all – the squat figure of a man dressed in leather and cheap cloth, an ugly man with a head set to one side, a man whose hands were covered in blood.

Chapter Sixteen

Matthew's corpse had been lodged in a room off at the northern side of the Cathedral. It was a mere rude shelter, and the next morning, when Simon and Baldwin arrived there with Munio, it was cool in the lee of the massive stone walls.

'I keep bodies here until they can be buried,' Munio explained as he fumbled with the lock. 'You will understand that in the hot weather, we have to bury them quickly . . . and Matthew will need to be placed in his grave today.'

The room was bare. There was a set of shelves over on the left wall, all musty and cobwebbed, while the only light came from a small, high window. The right wall was composed of massive stone slabs, the unrendered wall of the Cathedral itself, and boxes were stacked along it, all with open lids. Some had shovels protruding, some axes, while in a far one stood some long polearms, an incongruous sight here in a church's grounds.

Munio saw the direction of his gaze. 'Where would *you* put them?' he asked simply.

Simon grinned, but he saw that Baldwin didn't hear their talk. The knight stood just inside the doorway, staring at the wreckage of his companion.

To Simon, the body was like a shrivelled husk of a man just as a raisin was a shrivelled husk of a grape. Other corpses struck him with real sadness, like that of the woman Joana, because in their death they had shown the ending of lives which were not yet fully ripened. There was so much that youngsters might have achieved. That was what had hurt him more than anything about the loss of his own first son. Peterkin had developed a fever, and that with the diarrhoea had made his end messily brutal. Worst of all, as he faded, his screams and whimpering had stabbed

Simon like daggers of guilt, because he could do nothing to ease the lad's suffering, and that had caused a terrible desire to have him silenced. It was almost a relief when at last his crying had faded to nothing and Simon realised that he would never again make a noise.

This death was different. Matthew was an old man. He had seen and done much in his sixty-odd years, and a life which had been fully enjoyed – or endured – had not been totally wasted.

Matthew lay untidily. No one had bothered to put his hands together or close his eyes. They probably thought there was no point, not with a beggar who wouldn't be able to afford the simplest funeral. Simon could empathise with that view. There was no point in making too much effort for a man who, when all was said and done, wouldn't be missed by many. Matthew had no wife, no daughter, no son, no mother; there was nobody to mourn him.

But when he glanced at Baldwin, Simon realised he was wrong: Baldwin mourned him. The knight was overcome with sadness. He had slept badly. Simon had heard him tossing and turning during the night, and more than once had thought that he should interrupt Baldwin's thoughts and try to talk, but each time he had slipped away into slumber again. It was hard, but he was so tired with the heat during the day and wine at night, and he simply couldn't keep his eyes open. He vaguely recalled waking and seeing Baldwin sitting at an open, unshuttered window staring out at the stars, but now he wasn't certain that it wasn't a dream. It had all the power of reality, certainly, but his dreams were often vivid.

The knight appeared reluctant to approach closer. For once, Simon felt that *he* was the calmer of the pair of them in the face of death. Rather than waiting, Simon stepped forward and stood over the corpse, staring down at the body. 'Is the girl out here as well?'

'She is buried. There was nothing to keep her from her grave.'

'This man was wounded where?'

As he spoke, Simon was aware of Baldwin walking forward and standing at his side. The knight's eyes looked moist, as though there were unshed tears held at bay, but then Simon saw him blink a few times, and when he glanced at his friend's face again, he saw a kind of resolution there. Baldwin reached down to pull the clothing from Matthew's body, and as he did so, he grew once again into the magnificent logician whom Simon so admired.

'Only the one wound,' Baldwin noted.

'A stab in the breast,' Munio agreed. With his expressive features cast in such a mournful mould, Simon thought he looked as miserable as a hound which has just seen its supper stolen by a cat.

Baldwin waved away a small collection of flies. In hours, he knew, that tiny wound would be heaving with maggots. The wound itself was only a mere half-inch long. It was a narrow blade which had done this. There was no tearing apparent, which tended to mean that the blade had been sharp all along its length, right to the hilt, or that it had not been thrust in with full force, but there were no hard and fast rules with wounds, as he knew. It was largely a case of supposition.

He pushed his little finger into it, and found resistance as his second joint slipped beneath the skin. Thus the wound was only some two inches deep. Either the murderer had used a very short blade, or he had failed to stab with any great effort. This was the sort of wound which could have been inflicted by accident – not that that was likely. There were simply no reasons for someone to want to rob a mere beggar, so this was a deliberate act: perhaps Matthew had insulted a man or his wife, or this was the execution of a renegade Templar. And Baldwin knew which of the two he believed.

There were so many people who might have wanted to kill a Templar, had they learned of Matthew's past. A beggar who insulted a woman in the road might earn himself a knock or worse from her husband, but that would be an instantaneous reward for a real or imagined slight. This, if the witness was

right, was a sudden attack without any hint of conversation or
words beforehand.

'No sign of robbery or theft from the body?' he asked.

Munio looked at him. 'If a man was desperate enough to
steal, would he seek out such a victim?'

'The witness, this other beggar who saw it all happen – have
you tracked her down?' Simon asked.

'No. I am afraid she has disappeared too. I wonder . . .'

'You think she too has been killed?' Baldwin shot out.

'No, but perhaps she was so fearful of the killer, she ran from
the city. She was not well known here. I have seen her a little
recently, but she wasn't a local woman. Perhaps she saw a murder
and feared he might track her down as a witness and kill her
too?'

'It is possible,' Baldwin mused, staring down at the terrible
figure of his dead friend.

It was Simon who asked, 'What was her name?'

'María from Venialbo.'

Simon and Baldwin exchanged a glance. Simon commented,
'It's odd that she was able to help us with first Joana's death and
now Matthew's death too.'

Baldwin said, 'Have you asked the gatekeepers whether they
have seen her leave the city?'

'Yes, but none of them say they have.'

'So we have lost the only witness?'

'She may return, but yes, I think we have lost her.'

Simon touched Baldwin's arm. 'Come. We ought to leave
Munio to his work.'

'Yes, of course. We are grateful for your time and your help,
señor.'

'It is fine. Of course, you would tell me if you learned anything
that could be useful?'

'Yes. As soon as I can, I will tell you what I may,' Baldwin
said, but he knew that he couldn't tell Munio anything. It would
be too dangerous. Especially if there was a man in the city who
was prepared to kill any Templars he met.

* * *

Gregory was disgruntled. That stupid cow of an ex-wife of his had the brain of an ox. Dull-witted and only ever thinking of herself. She had ruined his day. Just his luck that he should meet her here when he was feeling so good. Well – she'd wrecked all his sense of well-being.

He was back in the nave of the Cathedral, praying as well as he could over the din of the newest batch of pilgrims, who were gawping up at the ceiling and telling each other just how magnificent it all was at the top of their voices. They had to talk loudly, because with everyone speaking at the same time, it was impossible to hear anything. Thus it was that Gregory's concentration on the service being conducted forty feet away was regularly being shattered. The priest kept an expression of unconcern fitted to his face, as though this was perfectly normal and that speaking in the sure and certain knowledge that nobody more than two rows away from you could hear was natural, but Gregory was convinced that every so often there was a faint crack in his benign facade whenever a particularly pushy pilgrim braying about the decoration broke into his prayers. Curious, wasn't it, Gregory thought, that so many people who could have declared their religious convictions with absolute sincerity, could behave with such brash insensitivity towards so many others who were trying to participate in the devotions.

To Gregory it seemed sacrilegious, but he knew that it was normal human behaviour. Even in his own home town, people shouted at each other as the service went on. In the Cathedral at Canterbury, the public conducted their business in the nave because it was a warmer, drier place than the market square outside, but here it was infinitely worse. Some of the folks here had travelled hundreds of miles in order to come and have their prayers heard. To have the words of the priest drowned out was a great annoyance, especially to Gregory, when he desperately needed to hear something soothing today.

He was feeling very raw after meeting his wife again. Stefanía would keep popping up. What she wanted with a pilgrimage, he didn't know. Since she had legally divorced him, there was little he could do about it, of course. He couldn't even demand to know what she was here for; as she had haughtily pointed out to him, that was none of his business now. When she set her head back like that, peering at him like some slug she had found munching at her vegetables, he wanted to clout her, the disrespectful baggage. Her tone, when she coldly informed him that, as they weren't married any more, she need not show him respect, merely added oil to the flames of his anger. It didn't help – as she knew too well! It was typical of his luck that he should have chosen *her* for his wife.

At the end of the service, he stood and bowed his head. So far as he was concerned, his task here was over and done with; all he need do was return home now. Somehow he had to try to recover from this journey.

If he had not joined the Templars, his life would have been better, surely. He had gone there less from a feeling of conviction or devotion, much more because he wanted to get back at her for what she'd done. The cow! She'd even ended their marriage in a way that did most harm to him. It was – what? – a month after he joined them that the Order was swept away. One month, one miserable month, sleeping in clothing already foul, the new beard itching at his jaw, the sleepless nights as he was woken at some unearthly hour to go and pray. Good God! It was awful.

Not as bad as the arrests, though. When he had been taken, during his time in the preceptory at Montesa, it was typical of his bad fortune. His wife had left and divorced him, he was a laughing stock at home in England, and he had only joined the Templars to escape, thinking that by joining the richest Order, he could have an enjoyable life of moderate luxury. He had not realised that by joining the Order and being sent to Montesa, he would be going to the only blasted place in the Christian world where there were more Moors than anywhere else in Castile or Aragon. It was a sick joke. Still worse, that he should have been arrested and threatened with torture. How could they have threatened a man like him? He'd done nothing except try to join the most religious of all the Orders, and for *that* he was to be arrested and persecuted, if the Pope had his way.

At least Gregory was saved from that, because he was taken in by the Kingdom of Aragon and, as such, was safe from the depredations of the Pope's torturers. At the earliest opportunity, he left the place where he had been held, and travelled back to his home country, England. But although he certainly didn't feel like a Castilian or an Aragonese, nor did he feel truly English any more. He had lived away for too long. Gregory had been tempted to join another Order, perhaps one of the friars, for he wasn't sure he wanted to stay in a big religious house again. A large monastery or preceptory would feel too much like a prison, after his past experiences of living in what seemed to be a condemned cell.

He bowed and genuflected, then turned to make his way outside, but the press was too great coming in and he was forced like a small eddy when the tide comes in, to retreat to the safety of a pillar, and while he stood there, he saw her again.

The bitch. God, how he loved her! That was why he had helped lay out Joana's body. It almost felt as though it brought him nearer to his ex-wife. Yes, he adored and detested her simultaneously. His ambivalence was fired by her affairs, rather than diminished. He knew what she was like. She had loathed him while they were married, saying that he was too cold, too distant, too religious – yet then, when he finally cracked and said that he hated her, wanting in that moment of drunken fury to tear her apart – when at that precise instant he swore before them all that he would take up the cloth, he saw that terrible delight in her face. The triumph of a woman who has seen her horse win in a race, knowing that her bets will make her rich. She knew that she had won, that she had conquered and eradicated her opposition.

He was the enemy to her. Always had been, ever since the day of their marriage, as though she had decided from the start that she wouldn't make him a good wife and would win her freedom and independence as soon as possible. The marriage arranged by her father had been merely a thorn in her flesh.

Therefore, when he declared his desire to join a convent, she had immediately agreed and stated that it was her aim too. All this before witnesses. Christ Jesus! He must have been bloody mad!

Being English, he couldn't comprehend at first that his rash drunken statement could be in any way binding. As soon as he awoke the following morning, his head pounding like a drum, his belly sick and roiling until he vomited noisily outside the door of their manor, he sought out his wife. His surprise when she visibly recoiled from him was overwhelming. Her maid quickly explained that on the previous night, after hearing him say that he would join the Order of Santiago rather than bed a frigid bitch, on his honour and on his belief in the Gospels, Doña Stefanía had duly stated that she would join the Order herself. Since she apparently couldn't serve her husband to his satisfaction, she hoped that she would be able to serve God better.

'Ah, my dear wife, that is all forgotten,' he said with as much affection as he could muster. 'We had a row. Even the King and Queen of Castile argue on occasion, I am sure. Let us forget our dispute. Come, won't you give me a kiss?'

'Sir, you may forget your oath before God, but before God, I do not,' she said haughtily, drawing herself up to her full height. 'I have chosen my course. I will not kiss you! What, do you think He would forgive us?'

He was enraged – that was his excuse. Perhaps he should have attempted mastery of her before, because it was always said that a woman needed whipping to keep her controlled, but he hadn't . . . he had not *wanted* to. It seemed a harsh way to treat a wife. Today, though, he was furious. She had not wished to sleep with him for the last year, submitting only when he demanded his rights, and then lying like a piece of marble without moving. He had his headache and his belly was rumbling like distant thunder, and he was a little light-headed from the wine of the night before.

Stepping forward he grabbed her, then threw her upon her bed. 'I won't have you deny me again!'

She lay absolutely still. 'If you rape me,' she said, speaking up at the ceiling and pointedly not looking at him, 'I shall declare your rape to the priest. You are raping a Bride of Christ, and you shall be excommunicated!'

'Damn you!' he roared, and he leaped upon her.

That was his sin. He had raped her. Yes, she had been his wife, but the woman he raped had formally declared her intention of withdrawing from the world the night before, just as he had declared that to be his own intention.

Earlier he had forgotten it, but seeing her again had brought it all back. He cast a look once more at the cross on the altar, and for some reason felt a curious elation, as though he had confessed; as though he *was* in fact forgiven. It was a sensation which started in his head, but then moved down to his spine, and he felt it enwrap itself around his lower chest, like a warmth that was spreading itself about his ribs and engulfing him with . . . well, it felt like it was engulfing him with love.

He gasped. The feeling was like an embrace from God, a cradling as though God was putting His arms about Gregory, and then, as he closed his eyes in gratitude and turned his face upwards, Gregory felt the hair on his scalp move as though God's breath had stirred it. He was so stunned, he couldn't move, but merely stood there, basking in the knowledge of God's love.

It was an age before he could collect himself enough to go out, and when he did the sun was unbearable. He stood for a moment at the top of the steps, dizzy and drunk with love. Drunk with delight, too, for he knew that he *was* renewed, that God *had* forgiven him, against every expectation.

The heat was like a hammer beating at his senses, and he knew that he must find a shaded place to sit and collect himself. He wanted to dance and sing and praise God, but his legs couldn't possibly support him. They were too shaky still. There was a place selling cider a little way off, and he made for it, hoping to grab a chair and collapse in the shade for a while.

Arriving at the tavern, he drew up a stool and sat back in the shade. Soon there was a young serving girl, who smiled at his accent but fetched him some good cider in a jug, which she set at his side. Light, cool and tasty, it was perfect for this kind of weather. He leaned back, crossed his arms, and closed his eyes, a beatific smile fixed to his face. This was not contentment, this was ecstasy.

It was some while later that he could open his eyes again and survey the world. He yawned, then glanced about him as he picked up his cup again, and that was when he saw *him*: the felon who had led the attack on the pilgrims. Aghast, he nearly fell from his stool, but his shock hadn't been noticed. Domingo had no time to watch others; the hulking fellow was too busy sitting and frowning at the little box in his hands. The surviving members of his robber band sat around him, obviously the worse for wear.

Gregory's first inclination was to bolt, but instead of making himself conspicuous by running, he pulled his hat over his eyes and got slowly to his feet, preparing to wander off.

Even as he took up his staff again and felt the sun's radiance through his cloak, he heard a man saying, 'What now then, Dom? Will she call the city against us?'

'If you want to talk to me, fool, you call me Domingo! Right?'

Gregory heard the slap of a fist, the sound of a body falling, but dared not glance round. As he made his way out, he couldn't help but hear the next words.

'I told you: she ordered us to attack those pilgrims on the way here. She can't report me for taking her precious box because she knows I'll tell everyone what *she* did. That stuck-up bitch of a Prioress wanted all those poor bastards dead.'

As he walked out into the road, those words still rang in Gregory's ears. That his ex-wife could have done such a wicked thing sickened him – and then he began to wonder *why* . . .

Baldwin and Simon waited while Munio stopped and locked the door again.

'It hardly seems worth the effort,' he commented. 'No one is going to go in there to disturb him.'

'There is surely no need,' Simon agreed. 'He had few enough possessions and no money.'

'That is why it is so odd that he should have been killed,' Munio said mournfully. 'I have never heard that he was abusive to people, and why else should someone decide to attack a poor man like him? It couldn't be for his money.'

'Perhaps he died because of something he had done in his past,' Baldwin murmured. Enough people had believed the Pope's propaganda about the Templars after all.

'What sort of thing could he have done to make a man wish to murder him?'

Baldwin did not answer, and Munio stood observing him for a moment or two in silence. 'I think you know more than you say.'

'I have no idea why any man should want to harm the old beggar,' Baldwin stated, 'and I do not know who did it. But I have to speculate about his death. I should like to meet the other beggar again, the woman who witnessed the attack.'

'So would I,' Munio agreed glumly. 'It is not a pleasing matter for me, having two murders one after the other.' He looked up at the sky. 'And I have other work to see to,' he said with resignation. 'I should return to my hall. Guillem will be expecting me.'

'You can leave us here,' Baldwin said smoothly.

'Yes, I thought you would say that,' Munio said with a faint grin. 'So that you can be left alone to get on with your own investigations.'

Baldwin smiled but said nothing.

'So long as you tell me what you learn, Sir Baldwin,' Munio said with a certain firmness. 'You are not in your own land now. This is my city, and I need to learn all I can about the young woman's death. You understand me?'

Chapter Seventeen

Baldwin led the way straight to the tavern near which Matthew's body had been found. 'The thing is, you'll sometimes find the odd innkeeper who is kindly disposed towards a beggar. Perhaps Matthew came here occasionally and we can learn something useful from the serving staff.'

'Yes,' Simon said, but his mind was elsewhere. 'Why do you think Munio was so insistent that he wanted to know about the girl's death?'

'I cannot imagine.'

Simon looked at him. 'Was it because he thought that you'd run off and find out all you could about Matthew's death and not bother with Joana's?'

'Perhaps. What of it? I am not responsible for what the good *Pesquisidor* thinks.'

'Aren't you? And what if we could find out something about the girl's death?'

'Then we should of course tell Munio. But right now, I want to see what I can learn about Matthew.'

'Very well, Baldwin,' Simon said, sure now that Munio was right, and that Baldwin was more interested in nailing his old friend's killer than tracking down Joana's murderer. From Simon's perspective, this was all wrong, and he would continue to bend all his efforts to solving that crime.

The inn was a pleasant enough place, but the man at the bar could not help them. Yes, he had recognised the beggar, it was María. He knew her well – a sad girl, widowed when she was young. Where was she now? Couldn't say. Hadn't been up for food since Matt's death, poor old devil.

Baldwin and Simon stood out in the shade of a chestnut tree

and chatted for a few moments, Baldwin scowling up at the building, while Simon gazed back along the alleyway towards the Cathedral.

He had a vague feeling of inadequacy. If he was back at home, at his own home in Dartmoor, he would know lots of people who could help with his enquiries. It was curious that Munio himself couldn't tell them where to look for the beggar-woman, he thought. The other man had allowed them to come up here, almost as though he expected them to find out something.

'Seems a bit odd that this man has no idea where she might be,' Simon mused.

'Why should you say that? I wouldn't expect a tavern-keeper in Crediton to know where all the beggars are,' Baldwin said curtly.

'Even the tavern-keepers who feed and look after them?' Simon asked.

Baldwin eyed his friend with a renewed respect. 'What are you suggesting?'

'I think we should go back inside and point out to mine host there that we are acting on behalf of Munio – and that the beggarwoman must be found before her life is endangered. If he still refuses to help, I think that we should sit down inside and make a nuisance of ourselves.'

Baldwin gave a humourless grin, and strolled back inside.

The man to whom they had spoken originally, a runty type with a skimpy moustache and a cast in one eye, looked up unwelcomingly as they re-entered, leaning on a large cask and reaching under his apron to scratch at his groin. It was a big, cool room, with a packed earthen floor wearing a thin scattering of hay. There were some unglazed windows with their shutters wide open down the right side of the place, while at the back, behind the serving man, stood a doorway covered with a large motheaten blanket. There were only two tables in there, for most visitors made use of the floor to rest their drinks on.

Simon crossed his arms and leaned against a large, rough pillar that propped up the roof while Baldwin walked forward and sat on a table, eyeing the man with ill-concealed distaste. 'I want to speak with you again.'

The man looked from him to Simon. Then he shrugged and turned his back.

'If I have to,' Baldwin went on, 'I shall have you arrested by Munio and we'll question you in his hall.'

'I've got nothing to say. I told you all I know.'

All of a sudden, some words he had heard came back to Simon. Someone had said that the innkeeper here was a woman, not a man. It was a *woman* whom Munio had said was kindly disposed towards the beggars of the city. A woman who protected them.

Pushing himself away from the post, he crossed the floor and, as he was about to pass through to the back, the man suddenly flicked aside his apron to pull at a knife in a scabbard underneath. The first Simon knew of it was when there was a harsh rasp of steel; he whipped round to see Baldwin's bright blue sword blade resting on the man's throat. While the latter swallowed nervously, Baldwin reached over with his left hand and took the dagger from him; Simon stared a moment at the man before turning and pushing his way out to the back.

He found himself in a small room, filled with the stench of sour wine and rotten meat. On the floor near a water jug lay the rank carcass of a cat. An open doorway revealed a small garden beyond, filled with vegetables. Two women were inside the room – one short and truculent with a narrow, rat-like face; the other a black-clad beggar who sat at a bucket, sleeves rolled up while she beat clothes clean.

There was a clumping clattering noise, and Baldwin burst in with the servant. 'Aha! Hello, María,' he said. 'We should like to speak with you for a while.'

'Yes, I was there,' she said.

They were sitting out in the yard area, the early sun gradually warming them. Baldwin had demanded some wine, but when it arrived, he found it impossible to drink and asked the man to fetch a skin of good quality wine from another tavern not far away. The woman who owned the place grudgingly agreed, and Baldwin was now sipping a strong red wine which he found more palatable.

For once, Simon had little taste for wine. His head was aching, making him feel a bit woolly, and he demanded a pot of fresh, cold water from the well, watching the innkeeper as she went to draw a jug for him.

He was somewhat surprised by his second meeting with María. With her veil removed, she was a striking-looking woman, with an oval face that, if it had been cleaner, would have been attractive. Her face was lined with grief, and he remembered with a pang of guilt that she had mentioned losing her family. She looked as though she had suffered greatly.

For Baldwin, though, there was no time for kindness. 'Why did you choose to hide?'

'What would you have done? Waited out in the open for someone to kill you?'

'Why should anyone kill you?'

'I saw him. I was there. No murderer wants to leave a witness behind.'

'You honestly believe your life is in danger?' Baldwin said.

She looked at him, and let him see the full extent of her fear. Lifting her hands, she took up her hood and let it fall on her shoulders.

Without the protection of veil or hood, the two men could see her for what she really was. Dressed in her beggar's clothing, she appeared a large, middle-aged woman who could have been any age. Without the camouflage of clothes, she was revealed as a slim, haunted-looking woman in her mid-twenties. Her great doe-shaped eyes were luminous with sadness, and there were bruises beneath them from tears. She had a delicate face, but where her complexion should have been a dark olive colour, she was wan, almost yellow. On her left brow there was an ugly brown and mauve bruise. 'Look at me and tell me I don't fear,' she said hollowly. 'I have suffered everything. I have lost my husband and my children, and now a man seeks my death in order to hide his guilt. I fear every footstep!'

'The man who killed Matthew – have you seen him since?' Baldwin asked.

'If I had, I should have run away!'

'Do you know who he was?'

She stared out over the garden. There was a curse, and the servant dropped a pot, the thing exploding on the hard floor. The sound made María duck with utter terror, a look so petrified on her face that Baldwin half-rose and put his hand on hers. 'Don't fear – it was a clumsy potman, nothing more. You are safe with us here.'

She gazed into his eyes to try to gain confidence from him, but then she shook her head and looked away. 'All you want is to hear me accuse another man,' she said sadly. 'You don't care about me any more than you care about a rat.'

That was the truth. These men wanted a trophy that they could hang on a wall. They weren't interested really, not in a beggarwoman. Why should they be? She was just a victim of her circumstances. It was not her fault that she had been widowed, it was just something that had happened. Because of it, she was without a protector, and had become a beggar, regarded by some as a whore. She had so much to give, but now she must spend her time hidden in case she was hunted down.

With shaking hands, she pulled her cowl up and over her head again. From beneath its protection her voice appeared to gain a little strength. 'His name is Afonso. He's a young man in his mid-twenties, perhaps younger. A handsome fellow, so long as you don't look in his eyes. He's a mercenary – no loyalty to any lord. He was a Portuguese in the company of an Englishman and his squire. I saw Afonso run at Matthew with the knife in his hand. Matthew died; Afonso fled. I saw him run.'

'Do you know why he did it?'

'You think I should have asked him?' she asked with slow, cold sarcasm. 'While his hands were yet bloodied?'

* * *

'The girl, Joana,' Simon said hesitantly, glancing at Baldwin. He could sense that the knight's mind was focused on Matthew's death, but Simon was more interested in Joana's. 'She was killed in such a ferocious manner. I wonder . . .'

'What?'

Simon saw Baldwin throw a look over his shoulder towards the inn, as if he could stare through the walls and see the beggar sitting, still weeping, where they had left her.

'I just wondered . . .'

'It makes no sense,' Baldwin interrupted. 'Why should a young man want to kill him? How on earth could someone like Matthew have offended a fellow of twenty-five or so?'

Simon sighed to himself. 'It could have been anything. You know as well as I do that some men will take umbrage at the way another man looks at them. Remember that Knight of Santiago whom we saw on the day we got here? He was the sort of fellow who was prepared to take offence for no reason.'

'The knight? Oh, yes – the man with the woman.'

Simon gave a low whistle. 'I hadn't thought: it was Ramón, wasn't it? And the woman must have been Joana. Poor girl. She had no idea she was going to die that day.'

Baldwin shrugged. 'Most victims have no idea of their impending end. I wonder if Matthew did?'

The two old friends made their way down to the Cathedral. There they joined a queue to pray at a chapel, and when they were done, they wandered about the square until they saw Munio, who gave them a welcoming smile and waited for them to catch him up.

'So, have you enjoyed any success?' he enquired.

'We have been considering some ideas,' Baldwin said.

'At least you have had some ideas, then,' Munio said drily. 'Which is more than I have done. I have arranged for Matthew to be buried, but that is all.'

'There is one thing that occurred to me,' Simon said hesitantly. He wasn't sure how rational his thoughts were, in the cold light of day. 'The attack was so extreme, I wondered whether it was deliberately brutal, just to conceal the identity of the girl.'

'You think that is possible?' Munio asked. 'You think we were lucky to recognise her so swiftly?'

'*If* we did,' Simon said. 'I was saying to Baldwin last night that the identification was too swift. Perhaps the lady was wrong to think it was her servant. Could someone else have been killed, and this servant girl used her body to effect her own escape from a miserable existence with her mistress? Or did someone abduct her, leaving this other woman in her place so that he wouldn't be followed?'

Munio's face had grown longer as he spoke. 'The lady did say it was her maid. The clothes . . .'

'You say that the body is already buried?' Baldwin asked.

'Yes. We couldn't leave it above ground for any longer. In this temperature . . .'

Baldwin had turned to Simon with an expression of resignation, as though that settled the matter. It spurred Simon to say, 'Of course. But we could ask the Doña whether there were any distinguishing marks on her maid's body. Perhaps those who laid her out would have noticed something. If not, we could always have the corpse exhumed so that we can check.'

'It was Ramón who laid her out,' Baldwin reminded him.

'Yes, with that man Gregory, he said,' Simon recalled. 'So often, matters seem to point to this Ramón.'

'There is one other thing,' Baldwin said, and told Munio what María had said.

'Afonso?' Munio considered. 'I do not know the man, but I shall ask the gatemen whether they have seen him.'

'Good!' Simon said. 'So now let's go and see the Doña Stefanía and ask her whether there's a reason to dig up her maid.'

'A good suggestion, but where is she likely to be?' Baldwin wondered.

'The woman is supposed to be a Prioress, isn't she?' Simon grunted. 'She'll be in a church, obviously – or a tavern!'

The three men visited the nearby churches, and were

disappointed, but when they began to check the drinking-houses nearer the main square, Munio suddenly pointed, and following his finger, Simon saw Doña Stefanía sitting at a bench with a rough-looking man clad in dark clothing of a particularly shabby material.

Baldwin and Simon trailed a few steps after Munio and stood in the background as he went up to her, smiling. 'Doña Stefanía. Do you mind if I ask you a few more questions? There are some things we should like to clear up.'

'But of course,' she said graciously, waving her hand to indicate that he might stand beside her. Her companion looked Munio up and down in a thoroughly insolent way, but the *Pesquisidor* didn't appear to notice. Simon himself felt his ire rise at the sight of his attitude, though, and he walked to join Munio even though he felt the sweat breaking out all over his body. It was unpleasant, because he actually felt rather chilly in his sweat, even though he knew the heat was terrible.

Other than the man at her side, there were a pair of pilgrims who, from their voices, came from the lands about Bavaria; they sat fanning their faces with their great broad-brimmed hats while they spoke in a desultory manner. On the opposite side of the table were two stoic-looking men who appeared to be local traders up to sell their goods at the market. Both seemed unaware of the heat, so far as Simon could see. They slurped their wine and muttered incomprehensibly to each other, to all appearances quite comfortable. It made Simon feel irritable to see them so relaxed when he felt so crotchety and sticky.

Perhaps it was their clothing; their shirts and hose might be made of something that made them feel cooler, Simon thought. As for him, he could better appreciate the Bavarians, with their red faces beaded with sweat, puffing and blowing. Simon reckoned he could leap into a well and drain it, it was so hot. He had never known a place to be so burned by the sun. It was as though the air itself was being exhausted from an oven's vent, and each breath seemed liable to scorch his throat.

Munio stared at the two locals, who were of a mind to ignore him and remain, but then Munio jerked his chin at the landlord, and suddenly the table was entirely empty but for the Prioress and her friend; the traders were whisked away like dirty platters, and the two Bavarians took one look at the way they had been ejected, and decided not to argue. It was always the way for a sensible traveller: while in a foreign land, it was better to avoid disputes.

'So, lady,' Munio said, when they were sitting, 'we wanted to talk with you a little about the murder of your maid. Our apologies for this. It must be hard for you, having lost your sole companion.'

Simon was sitting next to Munio, and he saw the woman shoot the *Pesquisidor* a sharp look, then glance somewhat shamefacedly at the man beside her. For his part, he sat as if unconcerned. Simon waved at the innkeeper for some watered wine, listening to what Munio was saying. After her first startled reaction, Doña Stefanía appeared simply disinterested, as though she had better things to occupy her mind.

'It is hard. I have lost much since I arrived here,' she said in a broken voice. 'At least some have made me welcome and have been keen to comfort me in my sadness.'

Looking at him, she thought Munio appeared less than sympathetic to her. He was a typical, hard-faced man like so many of these tough Galicians. No sense and less feeling. He had no idea how much it meant to her, losing her maid. Of course he couldn't understand how much she had then lost last night. No one could. That relic was all that kept the convent going.

My God! she prayed. Saint Peter, please don't let us lose it for ever! Make that devil Domingo bring it back to me. How can we survive without that relic? Without it, our whole priory must fail!

He had spoken again, but as her gaze moved to him and she tried to concentrate, she saw that Simon had caught the innkeeper's attention and was demanding drink. He seemed a little slow already, she thought, and shifted in her seat, squirming away from him.

'What?' she asked.

'Are you aware of any distinguishing marks upon your maid's body?' Munio repeated steadily in English.

'I don't know . . . What an extraordinary question!'

'Not so strange as that,' Simon said, a little thickly. There was no air in the square, no breeze to cool the forehead, and he really did feel quite odd, as though the room would start spinning any moment. Except he wasn't in a room.

To ease his strangely whirling mind, he concentrated hard on the conversation. Munio was taking too long. Why didn't the man get to the point? 'Look, your maid, she was so badly beaten . . . why would someone do that to her? There must have been a reason! Did she have any enemies?'

'No, but I told you that she was delivering money for me. Surely she was found on the way with my purse, and that was why she was taken. Perhaps someone saw her and took an interest in a pretty young woman like her. Oh, how should I know? And what does it matter? The fact is, she's dead, and that's all there is to it.'

Baldwin glanced at Simon. He had seen the look on his old friend's face, and he wondered: was Simon quite well?

Doña Stefanía could see that her answer had nonplussed them. At her side, she could sense that Parceval was impressed too.

It was Simon, though, who blurted out, 'Go on, ask her about Ramón!'

'What did he say?' She understood English perfectly well, but Doña Stefanía cast Simon a look that would have suited a small toad, convinced that he was drunk. Just like her husband. She could never have respect for a man who was inebriated. He might rape her, just as her husband had that time.

'Doña Stefanía,' Baldwin said, 'I am sorry that we must ask these questions, but we have to try to learn what happened to Joana – and ensure that the dead woman was indeed Joana. Ramón has apparently left the city, so we wanted to ask: could you have been mistaken about her identity?'

'I don't know what you could mean,' she began, and then she saw his expression. 'You mean Frey Ramón . . .? So at last you understand my fears?'

'What fears?' Baldwin asked.

'As I said before, he could have persuaded poor Joana to pretend that Don Ruy had spoken to her and demanded money. When Ramón got the money, he killed her and fled.'

'That is one possibility. Another is that both fled together, with your money,' Baldwin said.

'You really think she *lied* to me?' Doña Stefanía repeated dumbly, and the memory of the shattered face above the tunic sprang into her mind at the same time. 'She lied . . .?'

'The poor girl was so viciously beaten; no woman deserved such a fate,' Parceval said, resting a hand on hers. 'I think I can throw some light on the matter.'

'Please speak,' Munio said.

'I saw the Knight of Santiago riding away yesterday morning. At the time I thought it was odd because he has only recently returned with us, and I thought that a knight in an Order would be told to rest and remain here for some time. It isn't right that a monkish knight should wander about so much, surely! Yet there he was, saddling his mount and riding off.'

Baldwin shot out, 'Was he alone?'

'Yes, so far as I could see.'

'Then surely that dead maid was my Joana,' the Prioress said brokenly. 'You let him escape!'

'In which direction did he go?' Munio asked.

'I saw him heading for the southern gate. Perhaps he turned in a different direction afterwards, I don't know, but he didn't look like a man who was trying to conceal his route. I think he was going to carry on that way. Surely his departure proves his guilt!'

'I shall have men follow after him,' Munio said.

'There may be no need,' Baldwin said. 'We spoke to a groom who mentioned that Frey Ramón had gone, and from what the groom said, he was determined to seek out the Knights of Christ at Tomar.'

'Why would he want to do that?' Munio frowned. 'He was already a member of an honourable Order here.'

Parceval took a gulp of wine. 'My God! Because he was appalled by what he'd done, of course! He killed Joana and then bolted. If he'd stayed here, the *freiles* of the Order would have condemned him and wanted to punish him, so he chose to ride away and seek fulfilment of his penance in battle. The Knights of Christ are the successors of the Templars and the *Reconquista*, aren't they? Ramón must have decided to ride there and seek for war against the Moors. How else would a warrior find peace, but in fighting?'

'It is as I said! Ramón saw my money and took it! He is not going to Tomar; he is fleeing justice!' Doña Stefanía cried. 'Oh my God – all that money!'

Joana had lied to her: she was sure of it now. Joana had intended stealing from her, then she herself was murdered and robbed. While she, Doña Stefanía, sat alone, waiting. Until Parceval finally arrived, anyway.

Suddenly, the Doña felt a lurch in her breast, and her heart began pounding just as it had the night before in the alleyway. She shot a look at Parceval, her attention dropping from his features to his lap. There, she saw, was his heavy wallet. He had said that he was poor when he had journeyed here with her. She wondered about that again, then shot a look at his face. Could *he* have been Joana's killer, the robber of the money?

Baldwin saw the direction of her gaze and thought that she was eyeing her lover salaciously. It was a shock to him to see a Prioress acting so lewdly, and he felt physically repulsed. He was close to passing a sarcastic comment, when he saw that her face was stilled, as though there was a terrible doubt in her mind, and that was when he took in the sight of the well-filled purse.

'You appear to have enjoyed some success with investments,' he said to Parceval.

'Hmm? Oh well, I have been fortunate, but this isn't from investments.'

'Then how did you come to find such wealth?' Baldwin asked, allowing an edge of suspicion in his voice.

'When I left on pilgrimage, I wanted to make sure that I could travel without being recognised,' Parceval explained. 'So I deliberately wore these miserable clothes. I carried no money, for a pilgrim should need none, and instead had a receipt for a sum I had deposited with a Florentine banker. Now I'm here, I have cashed it with his house – that of Musciatto.'

'Most convenient,' Baldwin said. 'But please – tell us where you were when Joana was being killed.'

'She died during the afternoon, you say? I was in church at first, and then went to meet Musciatto. After that, I went to a tavern where I met this good lady.'

Simon, meanwhile, was beginning to feel quite sick. His breathing was abnormal: he was having to take shallower breaths, but more of them. It felt as though he was growing hotter, then a little cooler, and his throat was parched. He had ordered drinks, but the damned innkeeper was so slow, it would be next week before he bloody arrived. Simon tried deeper breaths, and simply doing that seemed to help. Noticing Baldwin's anxious expression, he said with scarcely a moment to think, 'If he was so fond of her, why didn't Ramón stay here for her funeral? He left yesterday morning, didn't he, and that was before the poor girl was put in the ground.'

'True, I did not see him there at the funeral, and I should have expected to,' Munio said thoughtfully. 'Yet if he was filled with gloom at losing her . . . why wait to view the funeral?'

'I think *he* killed the woman, took the money, and bolted,' Simon gasped, but he was scarcely aware of his words, he was so overcome with sickness. He had to concentrate merely on sitting upright. Otherwise he must fall.

'Most men would draw the line at murdering the woman they intended to marry, but I suppose such a thing is possible when a lot of money is involved. One thing that my time as a Keeper of the King's Peace has taught me is that nothing is impossible.'

'Surely it is unlikely, though,' Munio said, shrugging. 'This man was her lover, poor young lady. Even if he did not stay for her funeral, that may have been the impact of his broken heart. Losing her, he lost all. He decided to travel and, who knows, to throw away his life in a gesture of faith to God, joining the Knights of Christ. No, I believe someone else had a part in this, some other man. There are so many strangers in a city like this,' Munio said dejectedly. 'Foreigners from all parts.'

'Even my husband,' the Prioress said. 'I had not thought to meet *him* here!'

Parceval was frowning. 'It must have been him. Who else?'

Munio sat back and gazed at Doña Stefanía suspiciously. 'Your husband?'

'My ex-husband, perhaps I should say. I was married to Gregory of Coventry. We were wedded in 1301, when I was fourteen, and I was lucky enough to divorce him six years later.'

'How did you get dispensation for that?' Baldwin asked, intrigued.

'It was easy. He had an argument with me, declared he would be better living as a monk, and swore before witnesses that he would renounce the secular world and enter a fighting Order instead. In return I swore that I would myself enter the convent, and thus we parted for the night.' Her voice was calm and level, but there was a certain fire in her eyes as she spoke, like a woman recalling scenes that were better forgotten.

'The next morning he didn't remember what he had said, and tried to force himself upon me, but I reminded him of his oath. He was rather shocked at first, but then tried to say that it wasn't a real oath. I had to demonstrate that it *was* genuine, and if he was determined to renege on his word to God, I was not. Then he . . . he took me against my will. I spoke to the priest that morning and managed to install myself in the Priory that very same day. I believe that *he* joined that disreputable and dishonourable band of warrior knights, the Templars. It is terrible to think that I was once married to a man who would be capable of joining such a group. Terrible!'

Baldwin's sympathy for her eroded as he noticed that as she spoke, she put her hand out to Parceval. That man patted it and met Baldwin's gaze with a calm smile. Baldwin's feelings rose in favour of her husband. As she spoke, Parceval met Baldwin's look again; there was a smug expression on his face.

Biting back his contempt for the man, whoring about with this Prioress, Baldwin was about to make a sharp comment when he caught sight of Simon's face. 'My friend, are you quite well?' he asked, concerned.

'Yes,' Simon lied. He felt as though he had a fever and was drunk at the same time. It was difficult to keep his vision in focus, and he must squint even to see Baldwin clearly. 'I am just thirsty. Where's that blasted innkeeper?'

Baldwin stared at him, then bellowed to the serving staff to bring a large jug of water.

Chapter Eighteen

Gregory shot from the tavern as soon as he thought it was safe, and bolted around the corner to stand with his back to a wall, panting slightly after the unwarranted exercise, ears straining for a sound of pursuit. If he could, he'd have laid an ambush for the devil, caught him, then showed his wife that she couldn't catch *him* out so easily. He wasn't just any green squire, he was a knight by birth and training, damn her soul! This fellow was plainly in her employ, a hireling who had been told to hurt him. Why, Gregory had no idea. All he did know, was that he was unwilling to sit about and wait to be killed.

The alley into which he had darted was a quiet little thoroughfare, and as he waited, listening, almost no one passed by. It was good, because it meant he could hear any steps approaching. There was the occasional heavy tread of boots and slapping of sandals, but nothing that sounded like a pursuit, and after a few moments his heart slowed to its normal rate, as his body realised that there was no need to panic any longer. He could have wept. Why on earth had he married that vindictive woman? Obviously she was after him. God in heaven – were those men told to kill all the pilgrims, just to make sure they killed *him*? How could she be so wicked?

He had been standing with his palms against a rough wall, and now he forced himself to pull them away. The left one was scratched. On the wall, he saw that there was a small projecting nail. At the time he had felt nothing, but now he was aware of a throbbing. It must be a sign of his mental distress.

Why should his wife have wanted to kill him? Surely she couldn't still bear him a grudge? She had punished him anyway, ruining his reputation and forcing him to go, like her, into a convent. Rape, she called it. Rape! When it was a wife's duty to her husband. Not that she would ever admit to that. As far as Stefanía was concerned, it was a sign of his brutality, nothing more.

What had he ever done, other than love her? It was just his luck that he should have married a woman who was incapable of returning affection. She had no idea of love. Couldn't understand when he gave her his own unconditionally. It simply wasn't part of her make-up.

Damn it! Gregory knew that God Himself had forgiven him. Why couldn't *she*? Was she so blind? And now she wanted him dead, she wanted revenge. She was prepared to see the felon and his band kill all the pilgrims, just so they could strike him down.

Gregory felt a most peculiar courage take him over. He suddenly wanted to confront her. He had endured enough guilt over the years for his one mistake and saw no reason to continue to suffer. What, after all, had he done that was so wrong? Nothing! It was *her*, with her warped sense of morality. Her, and her airs and graces. Well, damn her. It was nothing to do with Gregory, and he refused to hide in the shadows. He had as much right to be here in Compostela as anyone else. He refused to run scared. Why should he?

Looking at his scratched palm again, he felt a rising annoyance. He wasn't evil. If the silly mare wanted an apology, he could give her one, but he would no longer keep avoiding her and hiding all the time.

With a sniff, Gregory put his nose in the air and set off towards the little room where he had a lodging. Less than halfway there, he was suddenly struck from behind by a massive buffet that made him fall to his knees, dazed. Looking up, he was about to open his mouth and cry for help, when the next blow caught him over his ear, and he collapsed on his elbows. There was a rushing in his ears, and the ground opened up in front of him. With the inevitability of disaster, Gregory felt himself toppling forwards, and he began the fearful journey into the deep darkness.

Just as the roaring noise overwhelmed him, he heard a strange guttural voice rasping in his ear. 'Leave the Prioress alone, you bloody bastard.'

'Stop your damned bellyaching!' Simon said, averting his head from the bowl of watered cider. 'God's Ballocks! If I wanted to fill myself with water, I'd jump in the river.'

'You are lucky to have been with us when you collapsed,' Baldwin said.

They were still in the tavern. Once he was sure that Simon was going to recover, Munio had left them to go and speak to the house of Musciatto to confirm that Parceval had told the truth about the money. The Prioress had hurried away with Parceval while the two lifted Simon and set him down on the table top. Baldwin now stood above him, cooling a cloth in a bowl of chilly vinegar and dabbing it on his head. He had felt a terrible fear when Simon toppled over, thinking that the Bailiff might die. Others he had known *had* died from heat exhaustion – and the idea that his best friend should succumb was appalling.

'Are you sure you are . . .' he choked out.

'I am fine, Baldwin! God in heaven! I was just a bit thirsty, that's all.'

Baldwin could not prevent him from sitting upright. He stood back, wiping his hands on the cloth, then thought better of it, dipped it in the vinegar, and passed it to Simon again.

'Are you sure this is supposed to help?' Simon growled. 'It makes me feel like puking.'

'Better that than dying,' Baldwin said shortly. 'Are you sure you haven't shown any sign of illness until today?'

'Well, only a little,' Simon admitted reluctantly.

'What?'

'I just felt a bit . . . I had a touch of gut rot during the night.'

'Last night? What of before?' Simon's shiftiness made Baldwin exclaim in exasperation. 'Good God, man! You should have told me.'

'I will in future, Baldwin. All right? Now give me more cider, and then we can decide what we need to do next.'

Baldwin sat on a bench and watched as Simon drained his cup. 'I don't know that cider is the best drink for a man in your condition,' he said miserably.

Simon lowered his cup. 'Baldwin, I am not dead, and I won't die either, provided I am just a little more careful. That's all I need, a bit more care.'

'Very well,' Baldwin said. He looked in towards the tavern-keeper. 'He does not seem to like having you lying on his table.'

'Tough!' Simon said unsympathetically. 'If he wants, he can come here and tell me I'm not allowed. I'll settle his mind on the matter.'

Baldwin smiled. He was about to speak when he heard an odd noise outside in the crowds. 'What's that?'

Simon turned his head, wincing a little as he did so. 'Sounds like some sort of upset.'

'My heavens, I hope it's not another dead man,' Baldwin murmured. He sat up and stared out into the roadway, craning his neck to see what was happening.

Simon hopped down from the table and tensed his legs slightly. He still felt rather wobbly, but a great deal better than he had before. 'Any sign?'

'There's a man hurrying here.'

Simon saw him, a large ox-like man with a square head and thick neck. He was running straight towards them. 'I don't recognise him.'

Nor did Baldwin, but soon the man was talking to the tavern-keeper, and the two men came to Simon and Baldwin and indicated that they were wanted.

'By whom?' Baldwin demanded.

'Munio.'

Gregory came to gradually, like an old dog stirring from a deep sleep.

The first thing he became aware of was that his cheek was sore. There was a solid lump under it, and he tried to move his head to a more comfortable position. That was when he realised that not only was the lump hard, his head was very painful too.

'Christ alive!' he muttered.

'You should be careful of your language in a god fearing town like this one.'

Gregory opened one eye and stared at Munio. 'Ah, señor, I . . .' he began, but Munio waved a hand.

'I can speak English as well as Castilian or Basque. Perhaps it would be safer to stick to that.'

'Safer?' Gregory became aware that a small crowd was milling about them, and from the muttering, people were not happy to have found him there. 'What happened?' he asked thickly.

'I was hoping you could tell me that,' Munio said.

'But I was . . . walking. Oh yes, I was on my way to—' He suddenly lifted his head. The pain was like a swift thrust from a dagger, straight in at the back of his skull. 'Christ Jesus!' he moaned, and began retching.

Baldwin and Simon arrived as he ejected a stream of yellowish bile onto the slabs, and Baldwin muttered to Munio, who sent their messenger to a nearby wine-seller. He was soon back with a skin of wine, and Munio passed it to Gregory without comment.

The injured man's mouth tasted foul, as though he had woken from a night's carousing, and the strong wine was a relief. He swilled some and spat it out, then drank a goodly mouthful and swallowed with gratitude. 'That's better.'

'What happened?' Munio asked.

Simon stared at the cleric without comprehending why they had been called here. 'Is this someone else who's been attacked?'

'Yes,' Munio answered. 'Fortunately this one wasn't killed, although he could have been, had he been hit a little harder.'

'Is there anything to connect this attack with either of the others?' Baldwin asked.

Munio nodded to Gregory.

'I was going to see my lady,' the man explained, wiping his lips with the back of his hand. 'I was married to her once, but she left me and took the vows.'

Baldwin said, 'You are Gregory?'

'How did you know my name?'

'Because we were looking for you,' Baldwin said, smiling at Munio. 'You must have heard that there have been some murders here. A man was killed yesterday, only an old beggar, but—'

'And a woman the day before,' Munio interrupted. 'Now we find you here, beaten over the head, just like the first corpse – the woman. Yet you are alive.' The *Pesquisidor* was clearly angry that Baldwin appeared to have forgotten all about poor Joana, and was concentrating all his efforts on the murder of Matthew.

To his credit, Baldwin heard the rough note of anger in Munio's voice and looked abashed. He nodded hurriedly. 'Yes. The woman was beaten to death, and although you have not suffered so much damage as she did, perhaps there is some connection between the attacks.'

'Connection?' Gregory echoed dully, but then his head jerked up. 'Yes! I was going to talk to my wife. She tried to hurt me before, I think – and this must have been her again! Christ, but my head hurts! I saw her man, you see, and I thought that she was trying to punish me for . . . well, for a past misdemeanour.' His voice trailed away.

'What misdemeanour was this?' Baldwin demanded curtly. He had other things to check up on.

'Sir, you are English. I can speak freely in front of you. My wife and I had not enjoyed a happy marriage. She decided to join a convent, and when I was in my cups, she had me agree to dissolve our marriage so that she could take up the vows. In jest I said that I would do so too, and thought little more of it. Next morning, she refused to see me, saying that our union was no more, that she was a Bride of Christ, and I a Brother. I found this infuriating, and sought to make up with her as a husband and wife should, with the result that she accused me of rape and locked her door to me. That day she left my house.'

'What of it?' Baldwin asked.

'She has not forgiven me. On the day I arrived here, she learned somehow which party I was with, and set her men to attack it with the aim of killing me. I just heard them discussing their attack! By a miracle there was a second party, this of honourable knights . . .' A vision of Sir Charles's face came to his mind, but he pushed the memory away. 'Well, they rescued us. Drove off the others and saved us from death.'

'You were with Don Ruy?' Simon asked.

'How did you know that?' Gregory asked. His head was hurting abominably, and he wanted to thrust it into some cold water to try to cool it. When he felt the back of his skull, he found a lump the size of a cobblestone. Merely touching it made his breath hiss with pain. 'He almost killed me! It's just my luck she should get a servant with a strong arm!'

'Who is the man whom you accuse of doing this?' Munio demanded.

'My wife's servant. He's called Domingo – he's a hunchback and he hangs his head like this . . .'

Simon and Baldwin exchanged a look, then stared at Munio.

The *Pesquisidor* nodded. 'Yes, it sounds like the fellow whom Don Ruy said went out through the gate after he saw Ramón and Joana: the felon who led the *malfechores*. Do you know where we can find this man?'

Domingo watched over his men in a surly mood. There were two fewer men now, he saw. Two had left during the day, leaving his group to find better work or pay.

He stood and walked out to the wall behind the tavern, pulled open his cods and pissed. There was a small pebble on the ground, and he turned, aiming and rolling it end over end a few times, chuckling without amusement. A moment later he was smothered beneath the torment of grief.

Sancho was dead, and there was nothing he could do to bring his boy back. It was wrong that people should be happy, when this tragedy had happened. The whole world should have grieved with him.

He reset his clothing and started back to the tavern, a hand touching his purse. There were no coins left to buy drinks. All he had was the little box with its valuable contents, but he daren't try to sell it in Compostela. He needed money, and that meant the Prioress. No one else he knew could help him. Perhaps if he went to see her and suggested an exchange – money for the Saint's relic? The bitch couldn't refuse that, could she? She'd hurry to the nearest moneylender to get her precious box back. Perhaps she could pawn her rosary or something. Domingo wasn't very strong on the sort of belongings a Prioress would have; all he knew was that she was wealthier than his own wildest dreams. He should know that – he who had grown up in the shadow of the Priory at Vigo.

This journey had begun with such optimism, he and his men setting off with the Prioress and his cousin Joana, travelling all the way east to the Basque regions, visiting the church, Domingo and his men trying not to appear too overwhelmed by the people, the money, the buildings, the rich clothes, the shops selling everything . . . everything imaginable! Domingo and his men had gazed in utter awe at the stalls in the town. Only later, when they had gone to the church to give thanks for their safe arrival, had Domingo seen the little casket which Doña Stefanía handed to the Bishop with a grimace.

It had obviously cost her, that grimace. She looked like a woman who had eaten the biggest egg only to learn that it was bad. But what Domingo didn't understand was why the Prioress burst out laughing the moment they were all out of the church. And kept laughing for the next few miles, as did Joana.

Not that Joana would tell him anything. Bitch! His cousin had always had a fond belief in her own importance. Never treated Domingo as anything better than a dog, and not a favoured one, either. As far as she was concerned, he was a necessary evil. He protected her and her mistress, but that was all.

Then, one day when the Prioress and Joana were talking quietly together before the campfire, Domingo heard them mention a relic. They had their heads together over a small box, and he saw them both cross themselves as the Prioress closed it and dropped it into her purse. Joana looked up and saw him staring. It was a short while after that, that she and the Prioress tried to join Don Ruy's band of pilgrims, as though they feared Domingo might steal their most prized possession.

Once they had settled in with the new group, Domingo and his men had been told to leave the two women, but to keep within earshot. The Prioress was a fast worker, and she had soon picked a pilgrim as her lover. Joana had told him about this the next day, giggling at the way her mistress had knelt and prayed, begging God's forgiveness, once she realised she'd been more than a bit indiscreet!

Next morning, way before dawn, she'd come to Domingo with Joana, and insisted that they leave instantly. Luckily they soon met Frey Ramón again, and stayed with his party until Doña Stefanía told Domingo and his men to attack Don Ruy's band.

Domingo pulled the box from his purse again and stared at it, weighing it in his hand. It felt like nothing, and yet he knew it was worth large sums to any number of churches. The trouble was, he couldn't walk into the Cathedral here and offer it for sale. If they believed for one moment that the box contained a genuine relic, they would arrest him and torture him to learn when and how he had acquired it. He could make sure that the Prioress was punished for taking it, he supposed, and that would bring her down off her high horse, but he didn't care about that so much as having a pocketful of money to purchase wine to deaden the hurt of Sancho's death.

Perhaps she would see reason, he considered. She might agree to find money in exchange for the thing. Simply to be rid of it would be a relief. He felt as though it was watching him all the time. There was a strong superstitious streak in him, and he felt that it was bad luck to have a part of a saint on your person when engaged upon less than honourable exploits.

Yes, he would go and see her – right now, before their lack of funds was noticed by the tavern-keeper.

Domingo walked out into the street, and made his way by the larger thoroughfares to the main square. There he saw a large body of men gathering, but thought little of it. Instead, he turned down the road towards the small chapel where he had last seen Doña Stefanía. He entered, looking for the Prioress, but saw no sign of her. Undaunted, he left and turned towards the next. She was bound to be in one of the chapels.

As he reached the door, he heard a sudden roar in the distance, and stood for a moment, his head cocked, listening. It sounded like a fight. He hesitated, but his instincts took over, and he started trotting back the way he had come, towards the battle.

Baldwin was not willing to allow Simon to take part in the actual fight. While Gregory tottered unsteadily towards the tavern, Munio and another man helping him, Baldwin told Simon about all the tortures he would have to endure, should Simon's wife Meg ever get to hear that Baldwin had allowed her husband to go and fight when he was recovering from heat exhaustion.

'And then, I think she'd have me skinned. The death would be entirely unpleasant,' Baldwin finished cheerily.

'Come on! I have to help catch this bastard,' Simon said urgently. The big man wasn't used to being mollycoddled.

'No. Not a chance. I'd prefer to die myself than have to explain to Meg how I let you in there,' Baldwin said lightly, but then he shot Simon a look. 'I mean it. I won't allow you in there.'

'There are several men there.'

'And I won't have you killed by a single one of them,' Baldwin said patiently. 'You can stay out here in the roadway and stop anyone from escaping, if you like.'

'This is bloody ridiculous!'

'Ridiculous or not, it is what will be,' Baldwin said, and gabbled to Munio. The *Pesquisidor* nodded, glanced at Simon, and then muttered something to one of the men from his posse. This man, a short but powerful-looking fellow with a grim expression and wary watchfulness in his brown eyes, had the appearance of one who was capable of stopping even a determined Bailiff. The staff that he gripped in his large hands underlined the message.

Simon sulkily subsided as Baldwin and Munio moved forward with Gregory until they were nearer the tavern. There they paused; Baldwin moved stealthily around a wall and stood in the shadow of a large tree from where he could see the tavern's open yard. A short while later, Gregory came back again as Munio hissed an instruction, and more men moved up to join him.

'What's happening?' Simon demanded.

'The leader isn't there. They're just waiting a while in case he's gone out for a leak,' Gregory said. His eyes were gleaming in the twilight, a flaming torch lending his face an unwholesome yellow and orange colour. 'No! They're going to attack now!'

Simon turned back to see that the mass of men were streaming ahead. Just to the left, he saw movement – then there was a flash, like a burst of lightning, and he knew it was Baldwin's peacock-blue blade. He saw it whirl in the air, over the heads of the men running into the tavern's yard, and then there was a great roar, and the men burst like a torrent into the tavern itself.

The noise now was a mixture of screams, growls, and an occasional short shriek, accompanied by the ringing, clattering and crashing of swords, axes and knives.

'I have to see what's happening,' Gregory said with a most unclerical enthusiasm. He was very pale, but his hopping from one leg to another showed his eagerness.

'If I can't, I don't see why you should.' Simon grumbled, but he was talking to the empty evening air, for Gregory had already darted up and into the tavern. Simon started to move after him, but as soon as he took the first pace forward, the staff swung down in front of him. Resting his hand on it, Simon said bad-temperedly, 'I could shove this up your arse if I wanted.'

The man set to guard him merely shrugged uncomprehend-ingly as Simon turned and glanced up at him.

'In my country, I could have you arrested for holding me here like this, you great hulking cretin.'

This time there was a short grin, as though the man understood Simon's frustration, but had his orders.

The battle was soon all but over. There were only two men still resisting, and Simon could see a point of blue gleaming in a candle's light, moving in an arc to rest gently on a man's throat. The fellow suddenly stopped dead, and stood immobile while Baldwin's hand reached around and plucked the long knife from his hand. It was so smooth and effortless, Simon had to smile. He turned again and grinned at his guard, and then his smile became fixed.

Over the man's shoulder, Simon had seen a face which he recognised from the descriptions. The man's head hung slightly oddly, as though it was a little too heavy on one side. His expression was one of shock and anger, as he stared past Simon towards the tavern, and then at the grim figure of Munio who stood questioning one of the prisoners. Baldwin was walking about the place, his sword still in his hand, while Gregory had returned to join him, and now strolled a little to Baldwin's side, eyeing the sword with satisfaction.

Simon pushed the staff away and began to stalk his prey.

Chapter Nineteen

Domingo stared with amazement. How could any piddling official dare to attack his band? He had never heard of such a thing in his life before. These fools had no right to start hacking away at him and his men!

But if they dared to attack, maybe that was because his men had been betrayed. And that could only mean one thing: the Prioress had informed on Domingo and his men. No one else could have had them all ambushed like this. It had to be her!

Almost before he knew what he would do, he felt his legs turning him as though of their own volition. She had caused the death of his son with her stupid demand that Domingo should attack the pilgrims, and now she'd betrayed them when their only crime was having obeyed her commands. They'd done what she'd wanted, and now she'd made up her mind to throw them to the law.

But Domingo wasn't going to surrender without a fight, and if he could, he would kill her too. She deserved that much.

He shot a look over his shoulder, and took in the scene at a glance. There were the officers, there were his men, one being clubbed and kicked on the ground, and another guard holding a man slightly nearer. Domingo's eye was drawn back to that last man, a tall, strong-looking fellow with a sword on his hip and a serious expression, grim with concentration, fixed upon Domingo.

The robbers' leader turned and pelted away back towards the Cathedral. He would find Doña Stefanía, and by Christ, this time, he would make her pay.

* * *

Simon's legs exploded into action; he raced off after Domingo as soon as he saw the man start running. Simon easily side-stepped the staff and then he moved as fast as he could, left hand gripping his sword's hilt, right one pistoning back and forth as if it could make him catch up with the wiry Galician a little faster.

A dull ache started pounding in the back of his head, but he ignored it. It was just a hangover from his earlier illness, nothing more. He was fine, and he had a focus for all his energies now: the felon ahead of him. This was the man who had led the attack on the pilgrims. He was also implicated in the murder of Joana, and was probably involved in the attempted murder of Gregory as well.

There was something wrong about that last thought, but Simon didn't have time to analyse it now. His mind and body and soul were all focused on catching Domingo. Nothing else mattered.

He saw the robber slam into a woman, who gave a short scream as she was hurled backwards into a wall, her head bouncing against it before she slumped to the ground. Domingo rebounded from her into a small cart, back to a wall, and then he was balanced and running again, leaping over a tray of foods, pounding onwards. Simon hurdled the woman's body, bellowing hoarsely at the top of his voice to clear the path before him, then roaring again to persuade someone to catch Domingo, but he only knew the English words, and no one appeared to understand him.

'Stop that man! Stop him! 'Ware that man! Stop that murderer!'

His breath was a harsh pain now. It felt like pins and needles as he swallowed it, as though the air was filled with steel that scraped and scrubbed his throat with every breath. With the row of his feet slapping on the slabs, there was the thundering of the blood in his veins, all but deafening him, and when he reached a corner, he had to hold out his arms to stop himself from crashing bodily into the wall, shoving away as he carried on running, pushing himself in the new direction. Ahead of him, he could still see Domingo, and the robber was gaining speed now. Simon was slowing, but the Galician, raised in the hills south of

Compostela where he had run throughout his youth, showed no
signs of flagging. Simon felt his breath sob in his breast at the
thought that he was going to lose his man, and then he was on
again, teeth gritted in grim determination, fists clenched, while
he concentrated on Domingo's back, ignoring the pain in his
own legs.

There was a bellow and he snapped a look over his shoulder,
only to see, loping easily just behind him, his guard, the staff
still gripped in his hand. He saw Simon's look, gave a short nod,
then overtook him.

Simon was dumbfounded. He had always been considered
relatively swift over a longer distance, that he had stamina rather
than the ability to sprint, but now he felt as though he might as
well stop and stand still as try to compete. The Compostelan
merely set his head down like a bull, and stampeded onwards.
Simon hadn't heard of the festivals in which the youths of the
towns ran with the bulls, but if he had, he would have been hard
pushed to say whether this man was more human than bull.

A pause for a heart's beat, and then Simon's second wind
came; he chased off after the two men once more. He heard
another shout, a scream, and then a third call, and this time it
was taken up by other voices. Suddenly Simon was in the square
again, and he stopped, leaning against a doorframe while his
face suddenly flamed with heat, his legs wobbled beneath him,
and he felt as though his mouth was too small to swallow as
much breath as he needed. He had to grip the wall to support
himself as he peered into the square.

Domingo was all but incoherent with rage. One fool he could
have coped with, but this second man had prevented his escape,
and now he was held at bay. There was a circle of stallholders
and hawkers about him, all watching him with that measuring
assessment that a man had in his eye when he gauged one dog's
strength against another's in the ring. Three brandished good-
sized sticks, while another had a blade out and ready. Then there
was the thickset man who had pursued him. He stood gripping

his staff as though wondering where to poke it to make Domingo collapse most speedily.

This was the man who was the most dangerous, Domingo knew. While Domingo's legs were recovering speedily, the other's legs were already relaxed, as though he had not just chased Domingo for over a half mile.

Domingo must crush this opponent or be vanquished himself, he knew. He retreated slightly. The man smiled grimly, tapped the staff against the palm of his hand, and then started to advance.

Instantly Domingo moved. He ran full tilt into the officer, head down.

Astonished, the man hesitated, and then it was too late. He tried to bring his staff down to block Domingo's rush, but the weapon bounced off the robber chief's broad back; Domingo's head then thumped into his belly, and all the air whooshed from his lungs before the first of his assailant's punches landed on his body. Bringing the staff down again, he tried to inflict some pain on Domingo, but the latter had the leverage to push him around, and then managed to pound his fist into his kidney. Overcome with agony, the man fell.

Domingo felt him collapse, and kicked once as the man curled into a ball at his feet. He glanced down with surprise at the bloody knife in his fist. He couldn't remember grabbing it. It must have been the officer's own weapon, for it wasn't Domingo's. Furious, frustrated, he kicked again, seeing the thick mist of blood that erupted from the dying man's kidney.

He could see Simon still leaning on the wall. To his surprise, Simon pushed himself upright and began to walk towards him. 'Who are you?' Domingo shouted. 'What do you want with me? I've done nothing to you!'

Simon understood none of his words. He approached steadily, drawing his sword as he came, watching Domingo's hands, his feet, his eyes – the way that his body moved – for those were the indicators that showed a martial artist's skill.

Oh God, there was that dizziness again, but he wasn't going to surrender to it. He would arrest this felon if it killed him.

Domingo saw the steely determination in Simon's eyes, cast a look about him, saw the reluctance of the others to come to his aid, lifted his blade and gave a shriek of defiance, and then ran at the youngest man there. The fellow gave a squeak, tripped and fell, and Domingo was already over him, and running on.

But this time he'd been forced away from the Cathedral. He wouldn't be able to catch the damned Prioress, the woman responsible for all his woes; he wouldn't be able to kill the vixen! There was a hill ahead, and he hurried up it. Behind him he could hear footsteps pounding after him; and every now and again a missile would hurtle past his head.

He came to a small open space with a couple of donkeys tearing at a patch of scrubby grass. He hurtled down an alley to the right, hoping to deflect some of the hunt. Forty yards or so into it lay another alley, and he ran up it. This ended in a wider space. An old barn stood in the middle; he slipped through the part-open door, hoping no one was close enough to see him, praying that they wouldn't be able to hear the painful thudding of his heart in the still air.

Simon was convinced at first that the man must have darted down another alley. He wasn't the first of the pursuers to reach what he thought of as a cross between a yard and a green, and there were already three or four men milling in confusion when he reached it. He had to stop, leaning against a low tree, desperately trying to catch his breath. 'Where is he?' he gasped. 'Did anyone see him?'

It was clear that no one understood a word he said, and beyond a couple of quizzical looks, he was ignored.

He couldn't blame them. This area was roughly triangular, with their entrance in the middle of the longest side. From here, three main lanes ran away, and two smaller alleys as well. Domingo could have taken any of these and would be well out of sight by now. There was no means of telling where he could have gone.

Simon permitted himself to sink to his knees, the breath
sobbing in his throat as he realised that they had lost the man
responsible for so much pain and suffering, Simon had been
determined to catch him and bring him to justice, but he had
failed. Worse, he had led one of Munio's men to his own death.
In his mind's eye, Simon saw that man's body twisted with agony
after Domingo had stabbed him, writhing as Domingo kicked
him. Another death. Another victim.

Then, through a veil of tears, Simon saw it: the faintest
smudge of ochre. Hastily wiping his eyes, he stared. A half-
moon of blood lay on the ground. Looking back the way he had
come, he could see no sign of footprints of blood, but then he
realised that here, emerging from the alleyway, Domingo would
have had to alter his pattern of footsteps, slowing, then hurrying
again. Perhaps as he came out into this yard, a different part of
his shoe hit the ground, and that was why he had deposited
blood here.

The mark pointed towards a narrow alley which headed up
away from the Cathedral. Simon was about to take the men up
that way, when he saw what looked like another print – except
this one pointed to a barn door. The door looked slightly ajar,
and Simon, looking up, thought he saw a flash, as though there
was an eye in the gap, watching to see what the posse would do.

Simon looked along the alley again and nodded to himself.
He stood, whistled, and, when he had the attention of all the
men, he ran straight at the barn's door, kicking at it with a foot.

Domingo saw Simon slump to the ground in defeat, and smiled
to himself, but he wanted these men to leave. He didn't want
them idling away their time here, he wanted them to run off in a
different direction. There was a group of three who were pointing
away from the Cathedral, and he willed the others to take their
advice. 'Go on, go on!'

The whistle cut through his thoughts. It was as loud as a pig's
squeal and Domingo's attention shot back to Simon. He saw the
Bailiff look about him with satisfaction at all the other men,

then he saw Simon's gaze turn back towards him and the door, and realised. 'No!'

He retreated as Simon began to run. In moments the door shivered to pieces and the whole barn filled with particles of rotten wood and dust. By then he was already partway to a screen at the back of the barn. He hoped that there was a room beyond, maybe with an exit to another building, thence to an alley where he could escape, but as he ran in, he realised that this was only a garderobe. His feet took him almost into the small chamber, and then he had to stop, before he got trapped.

Turning at bay, he felt his lips draw back from his teeth in a snarl of animal rage. He shouldn't be in this position! *He shouldn't!* Grabbing at his purse, he pulled out the relic, and muttered a prayer for protection to Saint Peter, but there was nothing; no reply. He grasped the box in his fist, shaking it furiously. The Saint could save him if he wanted, but he had no regard for Domingo, and the outlaw knew that even that last hope was gone. He uttered a curse against the Saint, his parents, and all his descendants just as the door cracked and fell, and Simon hurtled in.

It was all the Bailiff could do to duck under the swinging knife; he felt no more than a slight grabbing at his shoulder as the knife caught at his jack. Luckily the quilting saved him from being scratched. Domingo couldn't escape, for the door was blocked with the other men from the pursuit, so he turned again to face Simon. If he couldn't get out, he could sure as hell take the foreigner hostage, keep him at knife-point until they paid him and released him.

Simon was feeling quite faint now – and that was his excuse later. He should have been able to disarm the Galician without killing him, but at the moment, all he could think of was that knife and stopping it from hurting him. His reactions were too slow; he still felt queasy after all the running, on top of his earlier fainting fit. As Domingo charged towards him again, he lifted his sword.

Domingo felt the steel slip into his breast with a sense of disbelief. There was no pain, just a curious slithering sensation, but when he looked down, he saw that the sword was buried in his chest. He opened his mouth, tottered, and then lifted his knife to dash Simon to the floor, pushing himself onwards, using the full force of his weight and malice to try to crush Simon.

All Simon could see was the insanely grinning features of Domingo advancing. It was a scene from hell, with the mad face approaching and the wet red knife held wickedly high overhead. Simon felt himself being pushed back, until there was nothing but the timbers of the garderobe behind him and beneath him; and then he heard a great cracking and wrenching, and felt himself freefall, that smiling face above him like a devil's, pulling him down to hell.

'How is he?' Baldwin demanded as soon as Munio returned.

'Not good. I think it is the heat. It can sometimes affect a man who is not used to our weather, yes? He was very exhausted.'

'Exhausted!' Baldwin repeated. All he could remember was that foul stench.

They were in Munio's house, a long, low building with a garden that was planted with more plants than Baldwin could possibly name. The whole place seemed verdant, and filled with vibrant colours – rich purples, reds, yellows and everywhere green.

The house itself was white-painted with simple shutters on each window and a small stable for Munio's two horses, to whom Baldwin had already introduced himself. The knight always liked to investigate the horseflesh wherever he went, but it was scarcely worth the bother in Munio's household, he saw. One plain and rather old rounsey and a skittish young mare made up the total complement. Munio was not poor, but neither was he wealthy.

When Simon had set off after the felon, Baldwin had been helping to disarm one of Domingo's men, and had not noticed his friend's sudden disappearance. Later, when he and Munio wondered why Simon had not come to help interrogate the members of the band, Baldwin was only just in time to hear of the accident, and then he had bolted after the messenger to go and supervise Simon's rescue.

It had been one of the most repulsive tasks Baldwin had ever witnessed. The two men had fallen through the floor of the garderobe, toppling together some fifteen feet into the relative softness of the heaped sewage underneath. It was fortunate that the toilet did not fall straight into a stream, as so many did, for then Simon must surely have drowned. As it was, he fell backwards into the muck, Domingo on top of him, embedding Simon's sword deep within his torso. The robber was already dead when Baldwin arrived; the knight had thought Simon was as well.

It was a terrible shock. Baldwin had known many comrades die, and he would have said, had he been asked, that he was all but inured to loss. True, he would not have felt that way about his wife, nor his daughter, but he would have thought that losing the companionship of a man was something he had been long seasoned against fearing. The idea that a man's death could bring him up so sharply had not occurred to him. Yet here it was. His hand grasped his sword hilt as though to keep his grip on reality, but all he could see was the terrible future, of returning to England without his best friend, of telling Simon's wife and family that he was dead. He could imagine all too easily the appalled horror in Meg's eyes.

He wanted to fall to his knees and beg for his life, to demand that God return him, to say that God had made an error, and that Simon should recover; he wanted to deny what he knew had happened. His best friend was dead.

Yes, he felt the odd emptiness in his throat, the heat at his eyeballs, the utter despair that hammered over his soul. Simon had been his first acquaintance on returning to Devon, his closest confidant. It was Simon who had recommended him for the new post of Keeper of the King's Peace, who had involved him in his most interesting cases. And now all that was over.

Baldwin could not help it. He covered his face in a hand and wept silently, while men hauled the revolting mess of Domingo's corpse from Simon's body. He wept while the men curled their lips, averting their heads; he wept while one fetched a bucket and threw it over Simon's face; he wept while men reluctantly grabbed Simon's clothing and dragged him from the wrecked box. He wept while Simon choked and spluttered as a second bucket of water was emptied over him. He was still weeping when his eyes opened, and he saw Simon weakly trying to flick away the ordure that had so besmottered his face and hands. Sir Baldwin was still weeping as he jumped forward, his joy leavened with a natural unwillingness to touch Simon in his present state.

If, for Baldwin, Simon's recovery was a delight that was all but unhoped for, to Simon it was nothing more than a hideous nightmare, worse than his drifting off into insensibility beforehand. That had been terrifying, feeling the world, as it seemed, cracking about him as he was forced down, down, down by the demonically grinning Domingo. He had genuinely thought that the devil had captured his soul. That was one thing, but coming to, lying in a box filled to overflowing with sewage, was enough to make him freeze in a blind panic, his fingers clenching rigidly, all his muscles tensing as his mind refused to accept what his nostrils were telling him. He closed his eyes just before the second bucket hit him.

That was when he found his voice again, although he had no wish to open his mouth. He started mumbling and swearing, but revulsion soon made him shout to be pulled free. Baldwin berated the men standing around, kicking two to make them pull Simon out, but even then refused to hear of Simon standing. Simon was desperate to get up, as though movement itself could clean him of the filth in which he was smothered, but he was forced to lie back on the broken remains of an old door rescued from a building nearby. Once there, Simon passed out again, thankfully just before more men arrived and carried him to Munio's house.

'He will be well,' Munio said.

Baldwin nodded, but he felt empty. Simon was his closest friend, probably the only man living who knew quite so much about Baldwin and his past, other than Edgar, Baldwin's steward. Seeing him so weakened made Baldwin realise how vulnerable a man could be. Loneliness was a terrible thing, he realised. To live alone, with all one's friends dead or gone, that must be the worst possible penalty God could impose.

It was the punishment which had been meted out to Matthew. The poor man was without any companions. Even the beggars in the streets were apart from him – although whether that was because they disdained *him*, or because he ignored *them* was a moot point. His pride would make it difficult for him to accept that he was a part of their fraternity.

A man like him, a noble knight, brought so low. And then to be murdered by some inconsequential peasant in an alleyway. Why should a common churl attack a beggar? It was inexplicable, or it was simple. Either a man had taken a sudden dislike to Matthew's face – Baldwin had seen that before – or it was a long-held grudge.

'I forgot to tell you before,' Munio said. 'I had Guillem ask at the house of the money men. Musciatto confirmed that they had given Parceval money. He is wealthy in his own right.'

'So as one door opens, it is slammed in our face,' Baldwin muttered.

'So it would seem. So there is nothing to suggest that Parceval had anything to do with the murder. He didn't get that money from Joana's purse. Now I have heard from the gatemen. The southern gatekeeper remembered this man Dom Afonso. He left the city yesterday, with an English knight and his squire.'

Baldwin nodded, but the news gave him no comfort. If anything, being reminded of Afonso simply added to his mental confusion. There was no motive for this strange man, this mercenary, to attack Matthew, as María had said. An older man, perhaps, who had a grudge against the Templars – that could have been comprehensible, but María had said that he was a younger man – quite a lot younger. So what could have been his motive? It made no sense. A richer man trying to rob someone with nothing; a man with position killing a man with none; a young man killing an old one at the end of his life. There was no logic to it. Baldwin had mused over it all through the night while sitting at Simon's bedside, and all day today it had never been far from his mind.

He needed more information. There was not enough to allow him to speculate. All he was convinced of was that Matthew had not died because he was a beggar. Beggars were sometimes killed, usually by drunks or arrogant fools who thought they were better than them, when the only difference between a knight and a man like Matthew was good or bad fortune.

There were men who believed that Templars were evil, but men who thought that way would not kill like an assassin in the street and run, they would usually confess and throw themselves on the mercy of the local court, expecting all other rational men to thank them for ridding the world of a foul parasite. Any man might execute a heretic, after all, and the Pope's entourage had succeeded admirably in persuading the population of Europe that all Templars were little better than lackeys of the devil.

Munio was still toying with the little casket. When the men pulled Domingo away from Simon, this little box had been gripped tightly in his hand. Munio had cleaned it and opened it to reveal the bone; both he and Sir Baldwin were convinced that it must be something with religious significance, but there had been no reports of any missing relics. Maybe Domingo and his men had stolen it in France or further away.

'I wish I could make sense of Matthew's death. Why should this Afonso kill him?' Baldwin fretted.

'You are greatly exercised by the death of a single beggar.'

'Even a beggar deserves justice,' Baldwin said sanctimoniously.

'Perhaps,' Munio said, but without humour. 'But so does a young woman, whose life has been cut short.'

'I know. Both are equal in importance.'

'Are they?' Munio asked. 'Forgive me, but you appear to have discounted the girl's life already.'

'Not at all,' Baldwin assured him. 'I am as keen as ever to catch her murderer – but with Ramón gone, I do not see how to proceed, whereas a witness gave us the name of Matthew's killer.'

'I keep thinking: but where is the money?' Munio said.

'Well, we now know that Domingo and his men were penniless. So that makes it less likely that they killed Joana,' Baldwin acknowledged. 'And this box and its contents is hardly the sort of thing that could be easily sold. Unless they intended selling it here to the Cathedral?'

'If they had, it would have involved lengthy negotiations. The Church does not approve of buying back things which are Her own.'

'The lack of money does not justify assuming that Ramón was the murderer,' said Baldwin.

'I do not like to accuse a Knight of Santiago. But he left the city, and no one here appears to have suddenly grown wealthy,' Munio pointed out. 'Surely the money could have been removed from the city. Where better, than to be taken out of Galicia itself, carried by a man who has declared himself to be so overwhelmed with grief that he must leave the country? Ramón was there, he saw Joana, he lied to you and he fled. Who else can I suspect?'

'We know Ramón was there,' Munio continued sombrely. 'Domingo went up there later, but if Domingo took the cash, he'd have spent it or run. Yet he did neither.'

He stood, the casket still in his hand. 'This man Ramón has many questions to answer.'

Chapter Twenty

Simon came to feeling groggy and lethargic, and stared at an unfamiliar ceiling. For some reason it was very dark, and he thought at first that he must have woken during the night, but then he saw the light in thin streams that reached across the floor. There were shutters here which were covering the window.

For a moment, he wondered where he was. He had woken expecting to see the rough thatch of his own home at Lydford, and he reached out an arm for his wife, but his hand encountered emptiness at the same time as he realised that the ceiling was not his own. The beams weren't pale logs split into planks, but appeared to be blackened poles, all unsplit. That was odd, but when he turned his head to stare at where Meg should have lain, he saw that he was not lying on his own bed. This bed was too small for sharing, and that was no doubt why the woman was sitting on a chair. But this was terrible. As he lay and mused over this mystery, his overriding concern was that Meg might learn he had been here, sleeping in this woman's bed. Who was she? She certainly looked very attractive, with her dark skin and black hair, but he could remember nothing about arriving here. It was very peculiar.

He moved to sit up, and as soon as he lifted his head from the mattress, he felt the nausea and weakness washing over him. With a groan he sank back and, hearing him, the woman awoke and walked to him, putting a cool hand upon his forehead.

'Am I in heaven, or are the angels visiting the earth?' he asked hoarsely.

'You look much better,' she said. He could see marks of exhaustion under her eyes. 'Your high temperature is gone.'

'I have been in a fever?'

'For two days. I think it was the sun. It has been very hot here for a little while, and your friend told me that you were not used to it. You need to drink more.'

Simon was sure that he remembered her, but his mind seemed unable to focus. Then: 'You're Munio's wife!' he blurted out at last.

'Of course,' she said mildly, taking a cool cloth to his brow and wiping it. 'I am Margarita.'

She brought over a pot of wine that had been diluted by water and held his head up to it. He drank greedily, and could feel the chill drink washing down his throat and into his belly. It felt wonderful, but it served to remind him just how weakened he was. 'Where is Baldwin?'

'He is out, but he will be back before long,' she said, and her smile was gentle, but exhausted.

'You have been looking after me for long?' She was very beautiful, he thought. In the absence of his wife, Meg, he was fortunate to be nursed by such a kindly woman.

'All the time that your friend was not here, I was,' she nodded. 'You were very unwell.'

'I was fortunate to have so capable a nurse,' he said with an attempt at gallantry, but in reality he was thinking of his own wife, struck by a pang of homesickness. He missed her and he wanted to return to her, away from this strange country with the people who spoke their odd language.

She laughed. 'I think you are well enough now,' she said, and left him with an order to call if he wanted more to drink.

As she was leaving, she heard him murmur, 'God bless her, and keep my lovely Meg safe for me. I love her.'

Inside, as Simon relaxed, the investigation came back to him slowly, and he recalled the conversation at the tavern. They had captured Domingo, he recalled. The man had run at him, and it was all Simon could do to defend himself, he was so weak. That much came back to him – but if he had been lying here in a fever for two days, surely Baldwin must have discovered the meaning behind the girl's murder. Perhaps he had also learned why the old beggar had died.

Baldwin arrived back much later in the afternoon. Simon heard his voice calling loudly, and then there were running steps and the door was thrown open as he strode inside. 'It is true, then? You are all right again?'

'I'm fine,' Simon grunted peevishly. Not only had Baldwin left the door wide open, with windows in the passage behind him, but although Simon wouldn't admit it, he had been dozing, and Baldwin's sudden eruption into his room had made him leap from sleep to wakefulness in a moment. It was not good for his humour.

'Good. Then you will be all right for the journey.'

Simon felt his belly lurch. 'Journey? What journey?'

'We sail for Portugal in the morning,' Baldwin said with a flash of white teeth. Then he gave a bellow of laughter that made Simon wince. 'Christ's Blood, but it'll be good to see the place again!'

In the large bed at the inn there was little privacy. The owner of the establishment was enormously proud of his massive mattress and the great wooden structure that supported it, and usually Parceval would not have been fussy about sharing, but when what he wanted was to cradle and cuddle Doña Stefanía, he needed a bed with rather fewer witnesses than the six pilgrims who shared it with him.

The room that he had rented in preference was ruinously expensive, but as Parceval reflected, he could afford it now. He had won by his speculations and now he was floating on a tide of success. As he knew, death could meet a man at any time, and it was sensible to enjoy the good things while you could, before a knife or runaway horse put an end to your earthly worries.

In here, the warmth from their two bodies was all but unbearable, the general temperature was already so high. They had the shutters drawn, and reflected light was thrown up on the ceiling from the pool of water that stood outside, dancing and swirling in yellow-gold ripples. It was soporific to watch as he lay back, Doña Stefanía beside him.

She wasn't asleep. Her gentle breathing was not as shallow as when she dozed – he had seen her when she was exhausted, truly exhausted. Yet the memory of sex with her was not enough to make him grin. There was nothing really for either of them to smile about, he knew. His own story was miserable enough, a story of horror and shame, one which only a saint could forgive, and yet he had been granted no relief. There was nothing for him but death.

The Prioress was little better. There was something that was holding her here, although she wouldn't talk about it. He couldn't make it out. If she'd wanted to, she could have thrown herself on the mercy of the Bishop. That must surely be better than sleeping with Parceval and the damage this could do to her immortal soul – not to mention the ruination of her career here on earth. Yet instead of asking for help, or even leaving town and heading back to her convent, which wasn't that far away – only a few leagues – she stayed here, gazing at the beggars and thieves about the place, making it her business to talk to the whores and sluts as though she was thinking of taking up their cause before God. As though a stale who plied her trade in the Cathedral yard could hope to receive God's sympathy!

Not many men could make it to Compostela when the whole of the van Coye family was determined to skin them alive. He had been lucky at times, certainly, but generally he'd been clever and one step ahead. That was why he was here, and not lying dismembered in a ditch somewhere on the way.

Doña Stefanía was suspicious, he could tell. She looked at him just a little bit warily, as though wondering whether he had in fact killed her maid and gone off with the money. Well, why shouldn't she wonder? He would too in her position. She already knew he was a dangerous man, that he had killed before and was here because of that fact. There was no secret about it.

He felt rather than heard her movement as she stretched out a hand, and he sniffed and cleared his throat. Instantly the hand withdrew. They deserved each other, he thought bleakly; she was only there because she wanted his money, and he was there because he wanted her body and the fleeting forgetfulness it provided. She detested him, in all probability, and he didn't trust her an inch.

'Are you asleep?' he asked gently.

'Mmm.'

'Odd, that man putting up such a fight – the one who attacked our band of pilgrims.'

She grunted, but he was sure that she was listening carefully.

'He was the leader – I told you that, didn't I? And yet he was no coward, apparently. He tried to take the Englishman with him. Failed, though. He got killed but the Englishman lives.'

Yes, he was lucky to have reached Compostela. Van Coye's family had tried to have him murdered, no doubt about that. Bloody bastards! Van Coye had deserved his end. He was ever an argumentative arse, was Hellin van Coye. From the first day he arrived at Ypres to the day he died at Parceval's hand, he had been a bastard. Big, strong, and proud of his power, Hellin used to bully all about him into submission. He'd push anyone, just to see them retreat. Mastery over others, that was the thing.

Well, one day he picked on a man who wouldn't back down. Hellin saw him in a tavern, and when he saw the girl with him, he was smitten, by all accounts. The youth was not half Hellin's age, but that didn't worry van Coye. If a man was smaller, younger, weaker and less experienced, so much the better.

Parceval was very drunk when Hellin began his assault. Well, they all were. There must have been seven or so customers left in the inn by the time Hellin noticed the boy arrive. The lad walked with his girl to a dark corner in the tavern – a stupid error. He was away from the door, and must pass by Hellin again to escape the place. Not that Parceval knew this at the time. He was outside, spewing again. He'd already been forced to go out and puke once to make space for more ale, and now he was feeling the onset of the next bout. His skin felt too tight, his face was hot,

his body clammy, but he felt marginally better and was rising to
return when he heard the noise inside.

It was strange how some men lost all control when they were
drunk. Hellin was one such. Whenever he had too much to drink,
he wanted to fight, and tonight was no exception. Apparently he
made a great game of laughing at the couple, jeering and making
stupid comments about the man. He'd a fair group of his friends
about him, and they kept on and on until the couple rose to
leave, the maid hiding her face beneath a veil. Then Hellin stood
and blocked their path. The tavern was only a small place, and
there was nowhere else for escape. The youth pushed the girl
behind him, and Hellin held out his hands innocently, the brutish
features – Christ *Jesus*, how Parceval hated that face! – express-
ing apology, as though he suddenly realised that he had gone too
far and wished to apologise, but when the boy trusted him,
Hellin van Coye drew him to his breast, snatched the boy's own
knife and plunged it into the side of his neck, thrusting down
with all the force at his command. The lad fell without a murmur,
probably dead before he reached the ground, and then it was that
Hellin took the girl.

He was nothing if not democratic though, Hellin van Coye.
When he had enjoyed his game with her, he held her thrashing
form for his friends. He wouldn't have wanted them to miss out
on the fun.

Many wouldn't believe the story afterwards. Ypres had been
such a lovely little town, but things had changed, perhaps forever,
when the famine struck and swathes of the population were
struck down. In one month in 1316, a tenth part of the city's
people had died from hunger. After those days, the murder of
one young man and the rape and subsequent suicide of his woman
was of little note. There were many more things for the folk to
concern themselves over, such as would there be any food on the
table that night?

Parceval had coped very well with things. Until that hideous
night, he had been a cheerful fellow, always the first with the
offer of an ale or wine when the taverns were open, always the

first to open his wallet, the first to see the humour in a youngster's shame or embarrassment. It all changed that night, though,
because of Hellin.

For Parceval, that scene haunted his dreams. Drunk, confused,
he returned to see the boy dead on the floor. The girl was
discarded at his side, eyes screwed shut, her wimple and veil
gone, her dress torn apart, her skirts clutched to her in the hope
that she might cover herself.

He could do nothing. His horror rose, choking him, searing
his soul, and as he reached towards her, Hellin and another
grabbed him and pulled him from that hellish room.

The lot of them callously left her shrieking to herself in the
middle of the floor, covered with vomit and her lover's blood.
The men walked down an alley, two trying to support Parceval,
but they had only gone a short distance when Hellin bethought
himself that it would be amusing to pick on someone else. He
did that sometimes; he was as unpredictable as the thunder. This
time it was Parceval's turn.

Hellin turned on Parceval and accused him of not taking his
chance with the girl. That, he said, was disloyal. Or was it because
Parceval had no ballocks? Here was Hellin, providing them with
a pleasant chicken to stuff, and the least Parceval could do was
show willing and pile in. All this was said with that customary
glowering mien with the twisted lip, that meant it was either a
joke, or that Hellin was working himself up to a killing frenzy.

Parceval had said nothing at the time. He was recalling that
face – that pure, white, terrified face. It was appalling. He felt
his stomach react, and he emptied his ale over the roadside to
the hilarity of the companions, but then he lurched away, and
while his 'friends' spoke and laughed, he sought a trough and
washed his face and hands.

That poor girl had screamed as though her soul was being
torn from her with pincers of steel. She had screamed as though
the entire legions of heaven were powerless to help her, as though
there was nothing, nothing in this world that could ever rebuild
the life that was shattered that night. When the men had all left

her, she had taken up the knife that had ended her man's life, and
slit her own throat, rather than suffer any more. What could life
have been to her after that night?

Parceval had washed himself and felt the drunkenness fall
away as he thought of her. Then, while his companions sat or
sprawled in the roadway, he walked up to Hellin and stabbed
him in the back of the neck, shoving the knife in and up with all
his might, clinging on to his blade as the great meaty hands
reached up and over to haul him away, ignoring the punches and
slaps from his 'friends'.

'Friends'! These were the men who had raped his daughter.
He had no friends.

'Why do you want to go there?'

'It is only right that a man should seek a murderer, surely?'

Simon eyed him doubtfully. Baldwin was suspiciously
enthusiastic for someone who was talking about scouring a
country for a fugitive. 'Come on. This is not only about some
dead servant girl, is it? I can understand your wanting to speak
to Ramón, but you were all afire to seek out Matthew's
murderer. Why are you now so keen to leave here and go to
Portugal?'

Baldwin's smile dropped a little. 'Is it that obvious?'

'It is,' Simon yawned.

'In the first place, as you say, I want to question Ramón; in
the second, it seems that the man who killed Matthew was with
a small band, and he's in Portugal too. We have heard that he was
seeking a path to Tomar when he left here.'

'That makes more sense,' Simon said. There was a terrible
lethargy stealing over him again. 'So you want to catch him too.'

'It is not only that,' Baldwin said and stared out through the
open window. 'It is hard to explain, Simon. When I was in the
Order, I was a young man. For the first time in my life, I had a
purpose. Before that, I was idling my way through life, enjoying
it as I could, but always knowing that my older brother would
inherit the manor. At last, when I went to Acre and witnessed a

magnificent city brought down and destroyed by the Moors, I realised that I had a purpose. At that time, I thought there was no more honourable thing that a man could do, other than join an Order and defend pilgrims by fighting as many Moors as he could. And then the city fell and I was injured and saved by the Templars.

'I suppose if I had been saved on a Hospitaller ship, I might have joined the Knights Hospitaller instead, in which case you and I would never have met, because I would still be in my Order. But I wasn't. I was saved by the Templars, and because I owed them my life, I gave my life to the Order. My happiest memories of all are of the Order, of warm sea breezes, of the scent of orange blossom, of fresh lemons, of . . .'

Baldwin fell silent. In his memory there were so many different scenes. Rocky coasts, sun-baked hills, lush olive groves, vineyards, slim, dark-skinned women with black hair that gleamed in the bright light. It was more than a series of unrelated memories; it was his life.

'You want to go and see it again?'

'I was in Portugal for a while. It has happy memories for me, but it also has the great fort of Tomar.'

'So what?' Simon yawned. It felt as though his entire body had been pummelled by a gang of miners with their hammers, and he winced.

'If this Ramón was heading for the Order of Christ, Tomar would be the first place he would go to. It is where I shall find him.'

'And the killer of Matthew.'

Baldwin's smile hardened. 'His killer also seems to have headed in that direction. I think I shall find him there as well.'

'How long would it take to get there?'

'I am told that on horseback, a man travelling at his ease could do the journey in fifteen days without any strain, or perhaps as few as eleven if he was prepared to make his mount suffer.'

'I've been here for two days. You'd have to travel swiftly to catch them.'

'I have an easier method. We shall take a ship and sail there.' Simon caught a yawn. 'If you think so,' he said unenthusiastically.

'You'll be fine, Simon. It's only a short ride to the port, and then we take a ship down the coast. Travelling night and day, not worrying about a horse's stamina, we can get there speedily.'

'I'm sure,' Simon said, but now the exhaustion was overtaking him again.

'When we are there . . .' Baldwin began, but before he could complete his sentence, Margarita appeared in the doorway behind him. Baldwin turned and gave her a shamefaced smile. 'I see I am not allowed to overtire you. Rest, Simon, and I shall speak to you again later.'

Simon nodded, and although he tried to give the woman a cross look, because he would have liked to know what Baldwin had been about to say, he failed. His eyelids were too heavy, and he needed to close them, just for a few moments.

Before Margarita could silently close the door, he was already snoring.

Chapter Twenty-One

Baldwin found it hard to contain his enthusiasm. He left the house and went out to the small garden that Munio was so proud of, and when Munio's steward appeared, Baldwin asked for a cup of wine.

It arrived, carried not by the steward, but by Munio himself. 'So you have had some good fortune?' he enquired.

'It seems so,' Baldwin said lightly. 'With luck we can soon take our leave of you and board a ship to Portugal. I will be reluctant, but it will be good to try to find this Ramón.'

'And the other,' Munio said. His usually doleful expression looked today still more mournful than usual.

'It would be good to catch him as well,' Baldwin agreed.

'It would have been more satisfying if Joana's murderer had been that felon Domingo.'

'Yes. But his men deny anything to do with her murder and there is no money. If a common felon found himself in possession of such wealth, he would be incapable of saving it or concealing it. He would surely spend it at once,' Baldwin said. He had seen it many times before.

'Yet he did go out there that day. Of course, one of Domingo's men once said that he and Joana were cousins.'

'Which makes murder neither more nor less likely,' Baldwin observed.

'As you say,' Munio said. 'And have you given any thought to what you would do if you caught one or other of the two?'

'Oh, Ramón I should like to question, if the *Mestre* allows me. As you said, he could have had something to do with the death of the girl. We think he saw her up there but lied and left the place. If he is guilty of her murder, I should wish to bring him back here.'

'And the other?'

'Matthew's killer is clearly evil,' Baldwin said shortly. 'He was witnessed murdering a harmless old man. He deserves his fate.'

Munio turned upon him a look of such piercing intelligence that Baldwin blinked. 'I fear you think me a fool, just because I do not speak your tongue so well as you.'

'Not at all, you speak my language better than I speak yours, and for that I honour you,' Baldwin protested.

'But still you treat me as an idiot. You think me a country bumpkin, not an astute fellow like yourself. Oh, do not try to argue otherwise. It is clear enough. Now, Don Baldwin, let me tell you some things. I know you have a burning desire to go to Portugal. Why not? I hear it is a lovely country. But you want to punish the murderer of a beggar. That death offends you more than the ending of the life of a beautiful, defenceless child, when the motive for her death was either her rape or the simple theft of the money that was on her. That means to me that her murderer was either exceedingly fortunate, because he found a suitable woman to rape just at the time that she was carrying a fortune in money, or that he already knew she would be there with the cash. Which means he knew her, knew of the blackmail, and knew she had the money. That man could so easily have been Ramón. He picked up a stone and smashed that poor face into nothing, then stole all the money. If that is the case, he is a cold-blooded murderer and should be punished.'

'I agree, of course I do. But where is the proof? Why should he run if he had killed her?'

Munio was scathing. 'If he didn't, why did he run away before seeking out and killing the real murderer? Can you imagine a chivalrous man leaving his fiancée's corpse like that? Any knight would try to seek the murderer.'

'I have no power to arrest him in Portugal or anywhere.'

'So you will question him,' Munio said. 'And he will go unpunished.'

Baldwin nodded slowly. The thought in Munio's mind was easy to read. The *Pesquisidor* wanted the man killed. 'If he is a Brother in the Order of Christ by the time I get there, there is nothing I can do to have him punished. The Brothers will protect him.'

'And meanwhile you will go about and in his place, seek the killer of an old beggar.'

'If I can bring the man to —'

'Yes. You want him more than Ramón. You think he deserves his punishment and you will visit it upon him. Why is that?'

Baldwin couldn't meet his gaze. There was a deeper understanding in Munio's eyes than he had expected, and he felt ashamed. Yes, he had been determined to go to Tomar, both because he wanted to find the murderer of Matthew, but also because he wanted to see a Templar site once more. He had heard that Tomar was unchanged, that the Portuguese King Dinis had no wish to lose the powerful army that had helped to protect his Kingdom, and had therefore allowed the Order to continue in all but name. Striking the words 'and the Temple of Solomon' from their name satisfied the Pope, as did the statement that the new Brothers were all recruited from untainted men who had nothing to do with their forbears, although Baldwin suspected that many among them must have had some links to his old Order.

It was not only that, though. Munio had hit the nail on the head with that astute comment: Baldwin wanted to serve justice on the murderer of a man who had once been his companion-at-arms. This confession made Baldwin feel ashamed. He had truly sought to treat one murder as somehow more worthy of justice than the other. When all his life since the destruction of the Templars had been focused on seeking an equality of justice for all, he now saw that in this strange city he had forgotten the basic principle of his own creed: that any murder victim deserved the same benefits from the law as any other.

Munio had not ceased to gaze at him, but now his expression was less bitter, and he poured some wine into a cup for Baldwin, lifting it to him. 'Have a little of this.'

'Señor, my shame knows no bounds.'

'A little humility is good,' Munio said while he poured himself a large cup. He took a gulp and swallowed with satisfaction. 'Ah! A good wine, that. Yes, but too much humility is self-indulgent, I always think. I knew a man a little like Matthew once, and he burned at the sight of any injustice, just as you do. He was formed from much the same mould. Once he had been a *clavero* in the Order of Santiago, a very important man, as you can imagine: the man who held all the keys for a great fort. One day that good man learned that some of the Order's expensive goods had disappeared, and he sought to find the thief, but the Order's *Maestre* accused *him* of taking it – saying that he was bound to be the one responsible since he had all the keys in his possession.'

'And was he the guilty man?'

Munio gave him a steady stare. 'Who can say? Only God knows a man's heart. For me, it was enough that from that day onwards he became an indefatigable seeker of the truth. The fact that someone had dared to accuse *him* made him realise how thin is the covering of honour that envelopes even the highest in the land. No family is free of crimes. The French King himself has shown that. Consider his daughters.'

Baldwin knew what he meant. Some ten years before, the French Crown had been rocked by the wives of King Philip the Fair's two sons; both young women had been found guilty of adultery. Their lovers had been castrated and burned alive, of course, and the two guilty women were incarcerated at the castle of Château-Gaillard. One died of cold in the first winter, but the other was still living, so Baldwin had heard, in a monastery.

'Certainly no family is free of the stain,' he agreed quietly.

'Yes. So it matters not what a man *was*, but how he behaves now,' Munio said with satisfaction.

Baldwin let out a breath slowly. He was sure that Munio had divined his past life in the Templars somehow – although now he thought about it, his behaviour regarding Matthew had been less than discreet. If he had shouted his interest in the old Templar from the *Pesquisidor*'s roof, it would scarcely have been less plain.

If Munio was to ask Baldwin about his past, the knight was not sure what his position would be.

'There were always many Templars here,' Munio continued thoughtfully. 'I met them and grew to respect them in Oxford. When I returned here, I met even more of them. They came here on pilgrimage, for they were constant travellers and keen to ensure that their souls were as pure as they could make them. That was my impression of Templars: that they were honourable and devout. I could not censure such men. Even Matthew, who had suffered so much, he deserved better than to be left desolate as he was.'

'But as you say, a religious man who has been killed at the end of a long life is less cause for vengeance than a woman whose life was ended so early,' Baldwin ventured.

'No, not less cause, but no more cause. I believe that justice must reflect equally on all. It is not a view which meets with universal approval,' Munio said, and shrugged, 'but it serves for my personal creed. Thus, if you go to Tomar, I would like you to spend the same amount of time seeking the killer of Joana as the killer of Matthew. Would you swear to do that?'

'Yes. But I may learn that they are innocent, too. What then?'

'The innocent go free.'

'Yes, but if they are guilty . . .' Baldwin spread his hands helplessly. 'What would you have me do? I cannot murder them myself. That would make me no better than them.'

'True, and if they have joined a religious Order they are safe from our justice,' Munio agreed. Then he leaned on his elbows.

'But tell me, how would the *Mestre* of a religious convent respond if it was shown to him that his latest recruit was a murderer and violator of innocent Catholic women? Or that he was the executioner of a Templar knight who was already so reduced in his position as to be forced to beg in the streets of Compostela?'

Baldwin drew in a breath sharply. 'Any Master would surely feel that the culprit should lose his habit. He might insist on the vow of obedience, and demand that the man should leave and join a religious Order with a vastly more onerous round of duties.'

'Yes,' Munio said with satisfaction. 'And then, if the man was innocent of the crime, God will ease his toil, because if the man was so devout as to want to join an Order to serve God, he would be comfortable no matter to which Order he was sent. But if he was guilty and had expected to escape, how much more painful would be his punishment. I have always thought that, contrary to belief, the Church is not so generous to failed priests as our secular society is. We only hang a man. The Church keeps him imprisoned for ever.'

'You will allow me to go with your blessing?'

'Yes. But not Simon, friend.'

Baldwin felt as though he had been slammed in the belly. 'You mean to hold him hostage?' he asked, choked.

Munio looked up, hurt. 'I called you "friend" because that is how I consider you, Don Baldwin. No, my reservation about Simon is caused by his illness. My wife says that he should not travel, and I am inclined to agree with her. Look at how he was today when you saw him.'

Baldwin was unconvinced, but when Munio gave a whistle, his wife came to join them both, and she argued forcefully and vociferously that Simon should remain.

'He is not well enough to travel, Sir Baldwin. Look at him! You may return and see him at any time you wish, for I doubt you will wake him. He was close to death, and to take him on a voyage now would be fatal. Think of the perils which afflict the healthy at sea, from fevers to sicknesses. If he were merely to become seasick, his body could not cope. Please consider him.'

Baldwin was aware of a horrible feeling of separation. In the past he had always had an able man-at-arms beside him, his Sergeant from the Templars, Edgar, but Edgar was back at the manor near Cadbury with Jeanne, Baldwin's wife. He had preferred to know that she and Richalda, their daughter, were safe in case of an armed gang, or even the risk of war. Edgar was competent and entirely capable. He would see to it that Jeanne and Richalda were safe.

At all those times when Edgar had not been with him, Baldwin had been pleased to have the sturdy, stolid Bailiff at his side. Simon was resourceful, bright, and a doughty fighter when one was needed.

'I do not know if I can do this without him,' he said slowly.

'Of course you can,' Munio said briskly. 'You'll find these men. If you don't, persuade the *Mestre* at Tomar to help you find them. These men all appear to be heading in the direction of the town. If they have already arrived, good, and the *Mestre* can see to it that they pay for their crimes; if they have not arrived, so much the better, because you can save the Order from recruiting dishonourable souls who should never have been considered for a holy fort.'

Baldwin shook his head doubtfully. To travel so far, without friend, without companion, without even the power of the law to support him, felt foolish in the extreme. Better, perhaps, to wait until Simon was quite recovered, in which case he could have a friend to count on.

How long would that take, though? Days? Weeks? The men already had a good head-start on him. Ramón had left on the morning of Matthew's death. That was four days ago, now. Even sailing instead of riding on horseback took some time, and these men were some hundred miles away by now. A longer delay might mean their escaping.

'How long will it take to get to Tomar?' he asked.

'The sooner you start, the sooner you'll get there,' Munio said unsympathetically, then chuckled. 'I think three to four days to sail down the coast, then another two or three to travel inland, if you can make good time. I can't help much, but I can at least give you some currency. I have some *libras* and *soldos* which you can use.'

Baldwin stood. 'I should pack and make my way to the coast if I am to catch my ship in the morning.'

The next three days were, for Simon, unremittingly tedious. Always an energetic man, he loathed lying about. His indolence was a strain on himself and, he admitted, on all about him, but he couldn't help it. When things grew too much for him, he couldn't curb his tongue.

If he had been in England, in some part of Dartmoor with a pair of miners, he would at least have felt more or less at home, or if he had been in a city like Exeter, where he knew many people and could count on their dropping in to chat, it would have been different, but here, with all the language difficulties, he felt awful, as if he was being imprisoned by people who could not understand him. Even if he had a simple request, the servants would tend to seek Doña Margarita, or Munio himself, rather than take it upon themselves to try to understand his words. He could ask for water or wine, and one grizzled old devil appeared to comprehend fully when he demanded bread, but that was about it.

If only, he kept telling himself, he had gone with Baldwin. At least he would have been moving, doing something. Not only would he and Baldwin have been able to keep each other's spirits up, Simon would surely have felt better if he had been occupied. All he could do here was keep on wondering where his old friend was, and how he fared. There was no point telling himself the truth – that he might have suffered a dangerous relapse, nor that he would have slowed Baldwin down; all he knew was the boredom of loneliness and uncertainty.

For there was uncertainty in any journey. The grimmest and

most fearful outcome of Baldwin's trip to that place . . . what was it called? Oh, Tomar! Yes, the worst possible outcome was that Simon would never hear from Baldwin again. There were so many dangers – rivers in spate, bandits, mountains, rockfalls – even if Baldwin survived the terrible risks of a sea crossing. Having once sailed over the seas to Galicia, Simon had thought that the perils of seafaring would diminish, but he was perturbed to learn that his own travel had merely given him a livelier appreciation of the dangers, and now his every thought was bent towards Baldwin and his safety.

He was standing by the window in the late morning on the fourth day after the knight's departure, feeling glum and lonely, when Margarita stole in quietly and studied him.

'So, you are ready to ignore my words and climb from your bed?' she asked with mock seriousness.

Simon smiled. 'My lady, how could I remain in that bed knowing that you were about to arrive? Besides, my very bones ache from inaction. I'm not used to this!'

He would have said more, but he had a natural inclination to avoid rudeness before any woman, especially one who had nursed him through an illness.

'It is like being caged, I suppose,' she said, studying his body. He had lost much weight, and his face was quite haggard, with deep lines at his brow. What made him look worse was the constrained expression on his face, like a prisoner who can see and hear real life continuing outside his cell, but may not go out and experience it himself. She thought it made him look a little like a vulnerable boy-child, petulant at the unfair rules that held him here, but accepting their authority nonetheless. 'Would you like to join me on a visit to the market?'

'Madam, I should kill for the chance!'

In the bright sunshine, he put on the hat again. The long peak that felt so stupid did at least reduce the overpowering glare of the full sunlight. He wore a thin shirt and one jacket only, on Margarita's advice, and although he could feel the enormous power of the sun's heat, it did not make him feel queasy or weak as it had the day he collapsed.

'You should drink more,' she said. 'That is probably what affected you.'

'I had drunk plenty,' he retorted, but without rancour. 'I had gone that morning with Baldwin to one of the troughs near the stables, I think.'

'Sometimes the air in certain areas can be bad,' she said. 'If you can smell rotten eggs, the air can affect you, I have often observed.'

'Malaria, yes,' he said. 'I have heard of it. But I thought that it caused yellowness of the flesh and similar ailments?'

'In some people, yes, it can,' she agreed. 'Others are affected like you, and find that their bowels are loosened and they have a violent fever. I do not think you were so badly stricken, but it must have been a cruel fever.'

Simon nodded, but his mind was already on other things. A hawker was selling cockleshells, and when he looked past her, he saw a man with intricate little necklaces of shells. It was exactly the sort of trinket that his daughter would adore, especially since it came from a place so far from her own home and experience. He indicated the seller, and nothing loath, Margarita took him to the man and haggled on his behalf.

Afterwards, she was keen to acquire meat for the evening meal, and she walked enthusiastically along the benches on which were set out all the bleeding cuts from the animals which had been slaughtered that morning in the shambles, the blood still staining the cobbles where the apprentices hadn't yet washed it away. While she was studying the slabs of meat and consulting with the butcher as to how she wanted it prepared, Simon went for a stroll. He saw a table set out with wines and made his way over to it, ordering a pot of red in a loud voice and draining it in two gulps. It was strongly flavoured and had a metallic taste, but Simon had been told to drink more after his illness, so he gulped down a second dose as soon as the man had refilled the cup, and found that his attitude to the city was marginally improved.

Although he was used to working for long periods alone on the moors, this place was too alien for him to feel entirely at home. The heat, the crowds, the odd tones of the voices, all assailed his senses and made him feel more than ever like a stranger, or an outcast.

It was while he stood at the wine counter that he saw Gregory again. The cleric was standing pensively at a stall which sold many pewter badges for pilgrims to display on their clothes, and as Simon watched, Gregory picked up a large cockleshell and purchased it.

'That should suit your hat!' Simon said.

Gregory jumped and turned with a face bright red. 'Ah! I had thought you were gone with your friend.'

'You heard that Baldwin had left?' Simon said, rather surprised.

'I . . . I asked,' Gregory said hesitantly. 'You see . . .' He was suddenly shy, glancing away from Simon and looking about them in the square. Taking the plunge, he spoke so low that it was all Simon could do to hear him over the noise of hawkers. 'When we attacked the tavern that day – the day you were knocked down?'

A polite way to put it, Simon reflected. Aloud he merely prompted, 'Yes?'

'That day . . . I saw his sword when he drew it.'

'So?'

Gregory looked at him quickly. 'It's nothing to do with me,' he said, and would have turned away, but Simon realised what he had seen: Baldwin's sword, the special little riding sword of which he was so proud. The sword into whose blade was etched a Templar cross in memory of his service and his friends.

Simon caught his shoulder. 'I know what you mean,' he said, speaking quietly, 'but why should you ask about him because of that?'

'He was . . . Well, so was I. For a time. A short time,' Gregory said miserably. He looked up at Simon. 'I was not faithless.

When my wife divorced me, I chose to take my own vows. It was just my luck to have married such a vicious shrew, and as soon as I could, I joined the Order. Best thing I ever did.'

Simon was aware of Margarita. 'Shall we share some wine, Gregory? Let us take a seat for a while.'

Margarita wanted to return home, but she was prevailed upon by Simon to remain with him. To his shame, he insisted that he felt weak, and must have a few moments sitting. The call on her generosity of spirit was effective, although Simon saw that she did not believe him entirely, and he wasn't certain whether the expression in her eyes was hurt and offence at being lied to, or simple amusement.

'Now Domingo is dead, what will your wife do?'

'Ex-wife,' Gregory said dismally, his hand holding a cup. 'I wouldn't mind, but I still love her. It makes me feel a fool, but I can't help it. Even after she had her servant attack me, and had him kill all those people, and clobber me again the other day,' he said, his hand rising gingerly to touch the egg-shaped lump on his tonsure, 'I still can't bring myself to hate her.'

'What will she do? She will need some form of guard to return to her Priory, won't she?'

'I suppose so. From what I have heard, she will have the services of another bully boy. Some damned Fleming she's taken up with.'

'I seem to recall . . .' Simon murmured, and was then quiet. The man with whom she had enjoyed an affair: Don Ruy had said that he was a Fleming. 'Wasn't there a Fleming as well as Don Ruy in your band of pilgrims?'

'Yes. That was the same man. I had heard that he had a fling, but I had no idea then that the woman he had had a fling with was my own wife!'

'So Domingo actually attacked the very same band in which you travelled, along with her own lover?' Simon mused. Two things had occurred to him. First, Domingo was evil and dangerous, but he clearly wasn't mad. Second, Domingo was a very competent killer. He didn't draw back at the last moment. If

he had struck down Gregory, the latter would have remained
down. He might have killed Joana, but there was no possibility
that he had knocked Gregory down as well.

So the man who had attacked Gregory must have been
someone else altogether.

Chapter Twenty-Two

The ship rocked gently as it passed down the Portuguese coast, and Baldwin was content. In the glorious sunlight of a summer's day, his wide-brimmed travelling hat pulled down tightly against the breeze, his head rammed deep into the bowl-shaped crown, he felt as though he was achieving something – and he was filled with excitement at the idea of seeing a Templar church.

In the distance off the port side of the ship lay another small town. Fishing boats painted in bright colours with large sails, moved slowly over the clear, blue water, the crews throwing their great nets into the water or hauling on the ropes that would pull up the pots for catching lobsters. These were the things that Baldwin remembered from his last visits to Portugal – the prevalence of fresh fish throughout the country, and the broad, azure sky.

When he boarded, he had asked the master of the ship where they would dock, and he had told Baldwin that their course would take four days to reach the estuary that led up to the great city of Óbidos, which the Portuguese still called the 'Wedding City', since King Dinis had given it to his wife as a present when they married some forty years before.

'Not long now, Dom Baldwin,' the master called.

To port Baldwin saw a series of white beaches, and then there was a gap, a narrow space, filled with water, at which the master was pointing. Baldwin felt a slight anxiety to think that this was the place where he would leave the ship, which must continue on its way to Lisbon, where the master had material and leathers to sell. Baldwin himself would be set on land so that he could either sail to Óbidos, or perhaps hire a horse. That, he considered, glancing about him, looked unlikely. There might be a sturdy mule or two here, but he reckoned that a boat would best suit his purposes.

He climbed from the ship into a small fishing vessel, and that set him down safely on shore. Knowing little Portuguese, he felt daunted by the thought of explaining himself to the fishermen who stood idly watching him while their hands automatically moved wooden lumps through old nets as they threaded new string through holes. So this, he thought, is what Simon felt like in Galicia. It made Baldwin realise how disorientating a total inability to communicate could be.

By signs and regular repetition of the name 'Óbidos!' he managed, he thought, to make his wishes plain, and many of the men about the nets smiled contentedly, their sun-browned faces wrinkling, eyes all but hidden in the tanned flesh from long years of staring at the sun glinting off the sea. It was only when a black-robed priest appeared that he realised that they had understood not a word.

'I wanted to sail to Óbidos,' he explained in Latin.

The priest looked a little bemused and when he spoke, his accent was so strong, Baldwin found it very hard to understand. 'Aha. The city is easy to reach.'

He had a fawning manner, which put Baldwin's back up at first, but then he reflected that this man was probably unused to meeting strangers from over the seas, and knowing that Baldwin was heading for the great city, he might feel that respect was a suitable response.

There were no boats sailing that afternoon. Baldwin had to content himself with sitting outside a small, cheap inn on a sun-whitened bench and sipping at a rough local wine. Tomorrow he would be moving on. With luck, once at the city he would be able to buy or hire a horse. Tomar was some way beyond Óbidos, maybe another fifty miles, which meant at least two days of travelling in this heat. Perhaps he could make up time by riding at night, he thought, but that was dangerous without a guide. Munio had given him some gold to help him, arguing that Baldwin would need more than hope to carry him onwards, and as the murders were committed on Munio's land, he had an interest in seeing to it that his colleague was successful. That was his argument, and Baldwin had little enough money with him, so he was in no position to refuse.

It would be a hard journey from Óbidos, he knew, and he must make it as quickly as he could. Perhaps he should hire a guide. It would make the expense much greater, but it would probably shorten the journey time.

Yes, when he reached the city, he would try to get a guide, he decided. But for now, all he was aware of was his sudden hunger as he caught a whiff of fresh sardines roasting on a charcoal brazier nearby. They smelled and, so he soon learned, tasted delicious.

The next morning, Baldwin was woken by an insistent pulling at his shoulder. A weather-beaten face peered down at him, dark eyes shielded by heavy lids, and he was glad at first that a man had come for him. Then the old woman cackled to see his dull, unaware expression, and he jerked upright, pulling the sheet back over his nakedness.

Last night the weather had been delicious, with balmy breezes wafting over his body out here on the bench by the door. The warmth and the gentle sound of waves slapping at the sand had made his sleep all the better, and he had not been disturbed by dreams but had merely sunk down into the deep slumber of the exhausted.

He dressed quickly, feeling more comfort, for once, in donning his hose and tunic than in slipping his sword belt on and tying it about his waist. The comforting mass of metal was one thing, but as he heard that loud crowing laughter and glanced about to see a group of women all pointing at him, the one who had woken him standing in their midst, he felt the blood rush to his face.

The boat was waiting for him when he arrived in the estuary, a small, single-sailed craft with a crew of three. They appeared to be fishermen who had bought a cargo of fish from a sea-fisherman, and were transporting it up the estuary to Óbidos.

Baldwin was now feeling the itchiness of the traveller who wished to be on his way, and he climbed aboard the small vessel with a sense of relief. The master of the ship, a grizzled old man with a thick beard and skin the colour of a walnut, dressed in a long tunic like a dress, with the skirts tied up to a waist belt to leave his legs free to climb the ropes, appeared to be in less of a hurry, though, and the sun had climbed steadily before the craft finally slipped its moorings and set off at a leisurely pace up the great estuary.

The nearer he came to Tomar, the more convinced Baldwin became that he was on a fool's errand. If Ramón had truly murdered Joana and taken the money, this was the last place he would come. He would want to enjoy his money.

That was the thought that gradually eroded his motivation. Afonso, yes – he could be sure of that man's guilt on María's testimony, but Ramón? All Baldwin knew was, he had seen his fiancée's body and appeared genuinely distraught. Yet he had lied. Why was that? Simply to win himself a little peace?

Joana herself was probably deceitful. Baldwin had come to the conclusion that she had invented the blackmail to enrich herself, and then an accomplice had taken the money. Could it have been Don Ruy who stole the money and then killed the maid so brutally? Maybe Baldwin should have remained in Compostela and sought *him* out again . . .

The boat moved along at little more than a slow horse's walk, the wind gentle, and Baldwin began to wonder if he would arrive faster if he were to walk, but although they did not appear to race, he was surprised, when he peered back over his shoulder, to see that they had already covered some miles. It was only two hours or so later that the master touched Baldwin's shoulder and pointed ahead. They were rounding a broad hill, the river a calm, smooth blue that reflected all the clouds. Closer, it was a pellucid expanse, through which Baldwin could see weeds waving gently and fishes darting to and fro. Following the master's finger, Baldwin found himself studying a hill that rose before them from the water like an island.

'Óbidos.'

Simon woke to find that he was feeling much stronger. After breaking his fast, he walked out into the garden, sitting in the shade near the gate, where he could watch the people walking past.

'So I find you well?'

'I am very well, Munio, I thank you.'

Munio cast an eye over him, and nodded, pleased with what he saw. 'You have recovered greatly.'

'It is all because of your wife's kindness. Without her nursing, I am sure that I would have been much slower to recover,' Simon said.

'I am sorry that I have left you to your own devices so much,' Munio said, 'but sadly there are many matters for a *pesquisidor* to look into.'

'At least there have been no more murders,' Simon said.

'True enough,' Munio said, and sighed. 'But whatever happens with Baldwin when he questions Ramón, I should still like to know where on earth the relic came from.'

Simon nodded. He had seen the casket a few times when Munio had turned it over in his hands. 'You still do not wish to give it to the Bishop?'

Munio smiled. He had already told Simon of his feelings for the Bishop and his men. 'What would you do? If the Bishop had lost something like this, he would have told me immediately and demanded that I take the city apart stone by stone until I found it. Yet if I go to him with it, he will be bound to state that it is his and demand that I give it to him.'

'In truth, it is the Church's,' Simon said. 'I can't think of a better place to install it than in the Cathedral. It should be safe there.'

'Yes. Except what if it was stolen from another church which needs the intervention of a saint more? No man can say that our

Cathedral is deprived of the good offices of saints of all ages and crafts. This could be the sole relic owned by a small provincial church,' Munio said with slow uncertainty. 'I do not know what to do for the best.'

Simon was still musing over his words long after Munio had left to go and see Guillem. It was noon when Simon stirred himself and, bored, decided to find some food. He could have remained in Munio's house, for Margarita had made it clear that he was very welcome, but even with her happy and cheerful presence, it was growing a little claustrophobic and he felt the need to leave the place and find some peace in the city itself, in among the throngs of pilgrims and traders. Just being out and with other people would be soothing to his soul.

He was walking towards the small tavern where he had met Gregory, when he saw the fellow again. Gregory was sitting at a bench, chatting amicably with Don Ruy.

They made an odd-looking couple, the knight with his aquiline features and faintly supercilious manner, as though he was convinced that he was better than anybody else and had been punished only because the judge had been bribed or misled; and the priest with his hard done by appearance, but they appeared happy enough chatting together.

Simon was about to walk past them, seeking a quiet niche, when Gregory saw him and pointed him out.

Don Ruy eyed him unenthusiastically, but stood with a polite bow and invited Simon to join them. They were not eating, but if the Bailiff wished, they could ask for bread.

'I was relieved to hear that you were unharmed after your fight with the felons,' Don Ruy said, Gregory translating for him. 'I heard that you had fought with the leader.'

'Yes – the man you saw leaving the city as you returned,' Simon said.

'So at least that child Joana's death is avenged,' Don Ruy said.

Gregory stared as he explained to Simon, and then added, 'Why does he say that?'

'Her killer is dead,' Don Ruy said, as though explaining to a fool.

'Why should Domingo kill her?'

'We are not sure that he did,' Simon explained. 'We know that Doña Stefanía slept with the Fleming, and we have heard that others got to know. Don Ruy here heard of it from Joana herself, which is why *he* believes Domingo killed her.' He hesitated, then said, '*I* don't.'

'But why not?' Gregory exclaimed.

'Because someone arranged for Joana to go to that ford. He or she concealed your ex-wife's horse so *she* couldn't go, knowing that there was a blackmail attempt. Domingo did not get the money, though. The real killer must have done so.'

'Unless the money was hidden by her.'

'Or someone else,' Simon agreed, his mind elsewhere.

Don Ruy's voice rumbled again.

'He says that he did not hear anything about any blackmail until later, when you spoke to him about the dead girl. Until then he had no idea,' Gregory translated.

'Yet someone must have known,' Simon said. He was suddenly quiet as a fresh thought occurred to him. There were two others who definitely knew of the affair: Doña Stefanía and the Fleming.

'The blackmail stood to damage the Doña's reputation,' he mused. 'And she lost all her money.'

'I understand that she has nothing left,' Gregory said. 'She is living on the alms of the Cathedral – and the Fleming,' he added with a hint of vitriol.

The Fleming, Parceval, Simon thought. He had Munio's confirmation that he had collected money, and afterwards he was with Doña Stefanía: she had confirmed that herself. Yet Simon felt there was something not right about the man – and the Prioress herself. She had arranged to have a band of pilgrims killed, if Gregory was right, just to avenge herself on her husband, but now she was living with Parceval more or less openly.

Gregory looked distressed. 'I still don't understand why my wife should have told her man to kill me. Twice she did so. Once when she set the whole gang on our band of pilgrims, and then secondly when she had him strike me down in the city. Why should she want to do that to me?'

'A good question,' Simon responded noncommittally.

'Just goes to show my luck,' Gregory said dismally. 'Who else would be so unlucky as to marry a woman who could seek her own man's murder?'

'Strange that Domingo didn't actually manage to kill you,' Simon observed. 'He was very practised at murder.'

'It *was* odd,' Gregory agreed. 'It is hard for me to remember much about the attack, as my head was exploding. But I remember him warning me off my wife. Ha! He called me a "bloody bastard"! Can you believe that?'

'In Galician?' Simon asked.

'No. Now you mention it, I think it was in English. I didn't think a peasant like Domingo would speak English.'

'No. I wouldn't have thought he could,' Simon agreed pensively.

That night, Simon felt the shaking and nervousness in his body again, as though his bones had developed a cold. He felt oddly sick, his appetite completely gone, and the rumbling in his belly boded ill. As soon as he could, he took to his bedchamber and closed his eyes, wishing away this malady before it could take hold.

As though denial might prevent anything worse than a temporary affliction, he had not mentioned his concerns to Margarita or to Munio, but they had noticed his lack of appetite. When he was woken in the middle of the night with terrible cramping pains in his belly, and vomited over the floor while sitting on his bedpot, he scarcely noticed his hostess and servants cleaning him and gently helping him back on to the clean sheets, but when he later fell asleep, he was enormously relieved to feel a woman's cool hands calming him.

'I love you, Meg,' was all he said, and Margarita blinked in surprise, but said nothing when she saw he was already asleep.

Chapter Twenty-Three

It was two days after leaving Óbidos that Baldwin at last rode up into the town of Tomar, feeling bone-weary and filthy after riding or walking throughout the hours of daylight.

Óbidos had been useful. It took him little time to find a horse, although he regretted buying this one in particular, and while it was being saddled, he had bought two loaves and a little dried meat, which had tided him over the journey. A friendly priest had given him a blessing for his journey and rough directions, and Baldwin had covered several miles before nightfall.

His horse was, however, a skittish, evil-minded nag, a pony which had been broken-winded, and whose nostrils had been slit with a knife for several inches to improve its breathing, an operation which had not improved its temper in the least.

So far as Baldwin was concerned, the thing deserved to be killed for dogmeat. Especially when they arrived. Out of kindness, before going to the fortress, Baldwin rode to the river, the Rio Nabão, to let the beast drink. There was a ford here, and he rode halfway over to let the animal cool down, but once there the froward beast began dancing, and he was forced to cling on for dear life.

In some ways he couldn't blame it. Sitting in the saddle in the middle of the river, Baldwin looked up at the great square lines of the walls and the central block tower, wondering whether he would be recognised, whether he could be arrested. Perhaps the horse had merely picked up a little of his own nervousness. There was something particularly unsettling about this place, a great fortress in which once he would have been welcomed with open arms by all the warriors living within, but where now, with the destruction of his own Order and its replacement by the

Order of Christ, he was unsure how he might be greeted. All he *could* be sure of was that if there were a priest in the place, the man would want Baldwin arrested.

There was a tavern at the riverside, and he bound his horse to a post, then sat outside with a jug of wine and some bread, dipping the bread in olive oil, and eating shavings of strong-flavoured, dried ham. The wine was delicious, just as he remembered it – pale, cool and thirst-quenching. When he had finished his meal, he felt invigorated and ready for the horse again.

Baldwin could see its eyes rolling wildly as he approached. He had to spend time calming the thing before he could release it, and even then he had to mount it in one smooth movement before it could make its protests felt.

Soon he was walking it up the roadway towards the fortress. The town's streets were all narrow, but bright under the high sun. There were few clouds, and the breeze, although welcome, was still hot. Baldwin knew full well that his friend Simon would have found this atmosphere all but unbearable, judging by the way he had responded to the warmth of Compostela, but for Baldwin this was marvellous. He could feel the heat seeping into his body, and he felt as though, having absorbed this warmth for the last few days, he had stored up a resource of heat that could keep him through any number of cold, snowy, wind-swept Devonshire winters.

He looked up at the hill. From here, the castle was only visible as a massy square tower up on the right, with a wall that reached around the top of the hill, following a concave sweep. Baldwin's mood darkened. It felt almost as though he was slowly approaching his own doom, and that on top of this hill, he would find himself accused and held as a renegade Templar, a man to be treated as a heretic, to be arrested, tortured, and burned to death. And all, perhaps, for a pointless mission.

With that thought, he stopped and dismounted, wondering why he had thought that coming here might solve anything. This castle was no longer a Templar site, it was a fortress for a new Order, and nothing to do with him. If there were people here who felt pious, it would be their duty to arrest Baldwin and hold him until the authorities could deal with him. He had travelled here remembering his old Order as though he could return to his youth, or recover some of the happiness he had known as a young man – as though mere proximity to a Templar site could ease his soul and undo some of the foul injustices of the last decade. Yet how could it? This place was nothing more than a series of blocks of stone. It had no soul, no life. All it was was a place in which men lived and worked. It was no better nor worse than the men who lived in it.

And looking up at it from the bottom of the hill, Baldwin suddenly wondered how pious and good the men of the new Order were. This castle was intimidating, a place built to protect those who lived inside, and to threaten those who lived without. Yet Baldwin had sworn to question the Portuguese. He had given his word to Munio when Munio gave him money to come here; he would not return without attempting to honour that vow. With a sigh, he led the horse up the pathway.

It was only a dirt track, and Baldwin could see through the trees as they thinned, taking in the view of the lush green lands on all sides. The ground was hilly, but not in the same way as Devon, where it was impossible to see much more than the next two hills from another. Here, it was possible to see for many miles, to far-off hills coloured blue with the distance, each plainly visible in the rolling countryside because none was of any great height. It also made the sky seem much broader, like the skies Baldwin had known as a youngster, when he had spent time in the islands of the Mediterranean. There too the sky had appeared larger, bluer, and more wonderful. In England, it was ever grey, he considered.

He could feel his heart begin to beat faster as he wound upwards, and suddenly found that on his right was a great mound of rock, on top of which was a wall, the first part of the castle's outer defences. Each block was massive; daunting in its size. It made Baldwin wonder how men could have moved, shaped and installed such huge lumps of stone.

But pondering on such things was merely a ploy to delay his arrival. He turned his horse resolutely to the front. To reach the entrance, he must walk about the base of this wall of rock to a final flat wall, in which was a large arched gateway. With hesitant feet, he undertook this journey, and then stopped.

It was rather anticlimactic to see that the gate was wide open and that men stood laughing and lounging in the sun.

Afonso clattered along the roadway. There, downriver, was the great castle, and he burned with excitement at the thought of actually arriving there at last.

'It is a good location for a fort,' Sir Charles said. 'Astonishing place. Good height. Difficult for anyone to scale that hillside. Plentiful water at the foot, which should mean that there is enough to fill a well, and the countryside here looks marvellously fertile. The peasants must be well-ruled. They don't seem so lazy as English ones.'

There was a sniff from Paul. 'Perhaps they are happier with their lot,' he commented.

'Paul is sometimes prone to such cheerful comments,' Sir Charles said to Afonso. 'He agrees with me, by and large.'

Afonso nodded, but he was only half-listening. For the most part, his mind was focused on the castle and his reception there. He had longed for the day when he would reach this place, having achieved his goal, and yet now there was that strange feeling of relief. Both relief and joy at success; balanced with the recognition that he had not in truth achieved all he could.

That old man, Matthew. His face kept returning to Afonso, that last expression of happiness – at his death. That curious acceptance.

No matter. Afonso had done his duty, and now that he was done, he had one last act to perform – and that must be done here at the Castle of Tomar. He wondered how Charles would react when he heard what Afonso intended.

As Afonso knew, this was the place where the Templars had managed their affairs in Portugal. It was the centre and hub of their Portuguese operations. The place where a man who had sought to harm them would go.

Baldwin waited at the gate while a cheerful-looking lay Brother was sent to ask what they should do with the stranger at the door. Before many minutes had passed, a tall man strode around the side of the gate, and stood eyeing Baldwin closely, but without rudeness. He had the manner of one who was delighted to see that he must welcome an equal, but he was also convinced and confident in his power.

It was not only the set of his shoulders and the way that his hand rested on the hilt of the large sword that hung at his hip; Baldwin thought that the power resided in the slightly hawkish set of his face and the dark and intelligent eyes, perhaps also in his white tunic with the red cross, so reminiscent of the Templars' own uniform. It made Baldwin's heart feel as though it had missed a beat for a moment.

When he started to speak, welcoming Baldwin, the man's voice was deep and sonorous, and although his Latin was slightly archaic, it was nonetheless easily comprehensible, and that was a relief after the last days of trying to make himself understood to a succession of ill-educated, or not educated at all, priests between Óbidos and Tomar.

'You look like a man who has travelled far, my friend.'

'I have travelled from Santiago de Compostela in the last week and a day,' Baldwin agreed. 'I am called Sir Baldwin de Furnshill, from England.'

'You have come a long way to see us here. But I should be reluctant to interrogate you without offering you a little wine. I am called Frey João, the *claveiro*. Please come with me.'

He walked at a swift pace, taking Baldwin around the mass of the huge tower on the right, a continuation of the mound of rock which Baldwin had followed to the gate. They were in a cleared area between two gates, a perfect defensive killing ground, Baldwin noted. Then, suddenly, they were in the open. Stables, kitchens and stores were set out, leaning against the castle's walls, while men hurried about their duties. Wagons and carts rumbled and squeaked, and smoke rose from braziers, some heating bolts of metal for smiths, while others were more prosaically being used to cook fish.

'Welcome, Sir Baldwin, to Tomar. The castle-convent of the new Order of the Knights of Christ.'

Simon was drenched in sweat. His face was suffused and his nose bled profusely, and although Margarita washed him carefully, when her husband entered the room quietly and stood at the foot of Simon's bed, he could smell that odd odour. 'How is he?'

'No better,' she sighed, standing and stretching. She had been at Simon's side for much of the night. 'It is no surprise. After falling into that sewer, I can only wonder that it has taken so many days for him to succumb.'

'He seemed so hale and fit yesterday,' Munio observed.

She nodded, but there was no need to say anything. Simon's eyes were open, and bloodshot, and he had a rash over his belly, chest and back, but he was not awake. Instead he appeared to have a form of muttering delirium.

'I hate to have him here like this without even a friend to sit with him,' Margarita added.

'With you by his side, he is fortunate enough, Wife,' Munio said gruffly.

'It is not the same as having his own wife here,' she said tiredly, pushing the hair away from her face. 'And he is so weak already after that first attack. He is not ready for this.'

'All we can do is try to build him up,' Munio said comfortingly. 'There is nowhere better for him than here. Do you want more wine for him?'

'Yes. I think he will need more. And I should get some sleep, too.'

'Do, and I shall arrange for someone to take over here,' Munio said.

His wife nodded and took his proffered hand, but as she rose to her feet, Simon gave a low moan, and his head began to move from side to side, his hands clutching at the bedclothes. With a patient look at her husband, she sighed and sat down at Simon's side once more. She had nursed enough people, including two sons who had not survived to five years old, to know that the next few days would be the most crucial for Simon. If he was to live, he must get through the next week.

Baldwin followed João through a small doorway near the vast cylinder of the church. It gave out onto a cloister, in which white-clothed monks and novices were working at their desks. Walking silently around them, the *claveiro* turned left through a doorway, and into a small office, in which a pair of clerks sat bickering over their work.

'If you cannot be silent, leave us,' João said calmly, and the two men bent their heads to their work again. He gave a thin smile, clearly unamused by the clerks' behaviour, and then waved Baldwin through to a larger room which was empty but for a table and some chairs.

'Please, come and be seated,' the *claveiro* said, motioning towards a chair, and sat himself nearby. He made no effort to go to the other side of the table, but then Baldwin could feel the strength of his character. This was not a man who needed little props to enhance his authority. He sat easily, his hands upon his thighs, the picture of comfort and relaxation. 'Now! My gate-keeper told me that you were asking for me. You had an especial request?'

Baldwin, now he had arrived here at this place, was in two minds as to how to broach the subject. João was obviously a man with immense power and influence, and Baldwin felt like a mere rural peasant in his presence. He had not wielded the same power when he was a Templar, for then he was a mere knight whose most important commandment was that of 'obedience'. Although today he was a Keeper of the King's Peace, he still felt the almost superstitious awe which he had felt before for men of such importance, men who were senior in a great religious Order.

'My lord, I am here on a difficult mission,' he said at last when the silence was growing too oppressive. 'I have come, as I said, straight from Compostela. While I was there, a young woman was murdered. I helped the *Pesquisidor* to investigate the case.'

Gradually, taking care to tell João only the relevant facts, Baldwin recounted all that had happened – the killing of Domingo, the suspicions, the reason why people wondered whether Ramón could have appropriated the money.

João nodded, but his face grew grim. 'And you ask whether this man might have murdered his own fiancée, then stolen the money and fled? It is a great deal to absorb. It would also be ridiculous for him to do so, surely? If he was to run all the way here, what would be the point? He could not possibly keep all the money while he was here, in my castle. No, a man coming here to join the Order must first take the vows. Chastity, obedience *and poverty*! Why should a man come here, knowing that?'

'That is a part of the proof,' Baldwin said. 'If he did come here, without money, then that perhaps is the best proof of his innocence. Unless his guilt took him over, and because of that he decided to live the rest of his life in penance. But when I set off from Compostela, I did not know if he would come here and take the vows.'

'Is there more I should know about this man?'

'I do not think so. Not this particular man,' Baldwin said.

'Then there is another?'

Baldwin could not meet his astute eyes. 'Yes. There was another man – a fellow who killed a beggar, a mere feeble, washed-out beggar. Yet this man stabbed him to death. I do not know of any reason why he should have done so, other than a simple desire to kill. Others have told me that this man is a mercenary, with no allegiance to a lord.'

'And you want his head?' João asked, his eyes narrowing.

'If it is possible I should like to ask him why he killed this man,' Baldwin said.

'Why? Was this man a companion or friend?'

'He had been a companion once,' Baldwin said a little stiffly. He was unused to responding to such personal questions. 'But my interest is in what caused the killer to strike. The man he killed was of no earthly danger to him, and a man who can do that is a danger to all, like a rabid dog.'

João moved. A hand rose from his lap and went to his chin. It rested there a moment, his forefinger tapping thoughtfully against his lips. 'So you say you are here to question a man who may be one of my *freiles*, that you wish to ask him about a woman's death, but you are more emotional about another man who is nothing to do with him or me. You seem driven by powerful emotions, my friend.'

'I . . . I seek justice, that is all.'

'All? I thought that justice was in the hands of the Lord,' João mocked gently.

'Justice is also my work,' Baldwin said simply.

'Then you are a unique man. This fellow you seek – what makes you think he might have come this way?'

'A chance comment overheard by another.'

'And on that mere chance you came all the way here? Perhaps he died on the way. It is many hundreds of miles from Compostela.'

'He was not alone. He had an English knight as companion, and a squire.'

'So he may arrive here safely.' João gazed out of the window pensively. 'A Portuguese man with an English knight. It should not be too difficult to find such a pair.'

'Your country is a large enough land,' Baldwin said drily.

'True,' João said, and stood, all evidence of dreaminess gone. 'Return here at noon tomorrow, Dom Baldwin. I shall consider your request and give you an answer then.'

'I thank you,' Baldwin said.

João clapped his hands, and one of the two clerics poked his head around the doorway. 'Sir?'

'Take Dom Baldwin to the gate.'

There was nothing more. Baldwin bowed to the still faintly

smiling João, and trailed back out into the sunshine. He walked over the courtyard and through the double gates. Only when he was outside the castle did he feel he could take a breath of fresh air. Until then, tension had gripped his chest like a band of iron.

'Tomorrow,' he murmured as he mounted his horse. 'And if I learn nothing then, why, I shall return to Compostela.'

He had spent the last days willing the time to pass until he could get here, and now he had arrived, he found that all he wanted was to be away again.

That night, Munio put his head around the chamber door to ask his wife if she needed anything. By now, Simon's illness had changed in character. Munio could almost hear the sick man's muscles grating and working against each other. It seemed as though the fever had turned the sick man's body to stone, with every bone, every tendon and ligament made as stiff and brittle as flint. His jaws grated tooth against tooth, his fists were clenched, and over all, there was the springing of sweat at his brow and beneath his armpits. Munio had only rarely seen a man who looked so unwell and who yet survived without harm.

'Margarita?' he whispered again.

'Leave us,' she whispered back, reaching forward with a cloth to cleanse and còol Simon's brow. 'I shall let you know when he recovers.'

If, Munio thought as he softly shut the door and returned to his chamber. He lay back on his bed, put his arms behind his head, and prayed that Simon would get well. It would be terrible to think that their guest could die without the comfort even of an old friend.

Chapter Twenty-Four

Baldwin had slept in a comfortable inn near the river. When the sun was up, he woke early, and walked out to the water. Where the ford lay, he trod into the waters and knelt, splashing it over his face and beard, scrubbing with his fingers at the coarse hair.

Looking at his reflection in the water, he studied himself for a moment dispassionately. There were more grey hairs in his beard now, and the wings of silver at his temples were rapidly expanding.

Suddenly he had what he thought was an insight, a view of what he must look like. He had the feeling of being a teenager still. That was how he saw himself – a fellow barely old enough to wear a sword in anger – and it was how he felt, still young. His views hadn't changed, his opinions and beliefs were the same as they ever had been, and that was why he was here now.

Yes. It was why he was here. A knight errant trying to avenge a comrade who had been murdered. The death of Matthew was unnecessary, and worse, it was pointless. There was no sense in striking down an old man like him. But if his death was pointless, then how much worse was Baldwin's own journey here?

He had come here, as he told himself, as he told Simon, and as he told Munio, because he wanted to find the killer of the girl, when in reality he was growing persuaded that her murderer might be dead: Domingo. He found it hard to believe that Ramón was responsible. The man had obviously been in love with Joana, and if he craved money, he would not have come here to forswear all wealth.

No. He was here for Afonso. This Portuguese was guilty of Matthew's murder. María had witnessed it. Perhaps Afonso was annoyed by Matthew's demanding whine, or perhaps he simply disliked his face. There was no sense in it, no sense in wiping out a life for so little reason, but so often death was like that. Meaningless. It happened because God decided that a man had enjoyed or endured enough.

But here was Baldwin, prepared to fight this Afonso, and for as little reason. Matthew was dead, but he had lived a full, worthwhile life. He had not expired young like so many. Not for him the death of a martyr in Acre when the walls collapsed, nor the tortures or flames in the French King's dungeons. No, Matthew had lived to a fair age. Did Baldwin have the right to kill another man simply to avenge a long life? No! It was ridiculous! As ridiculous as a middle-aged man coming all this way because his interest was piqued at the thought of seeing a Templar castle like the ones he had lived in. Simon must be wondering whether he had lost his mind completely. Staring down at his face in the water, Baldwin wondered whether there was a touch of insanity in his dark, intense eyes.

He would go to see João, and as soon as that meeting was finished, come what may, he would return to Compostela, he decided. And then, when there was a fair wind and a ship heading in the right direction, he would set off for home, and go back to real life, to his wife and daughter and the serious business of his manor and his court.

Voices gradually intruded upon his consciousness, and he realised he was hungry. He finished his ablutions, and walked to the shore, rubbing his scalp vigorously. As he made his way to the inn, he did not know that he was being watched.

Sir Charles eyed him from beneath his broad-brimmed hat. He was sitting on a bench at a tavern on the opposite bank, waiting for his companions to wake, but as a man who was perfectly aware that he had many enemies, he was always on the lookout for anyone who could be a threat, and seeing this middle-aged stranger with the build of a warrior, Sir Charles was sure that here was someone who could be a threat to him. Sir Charles kept studying him with care as Baldwin shook the water from his hands and set off up the lane to his inn.

'Olá! Bom dia,' Afonso said as he came out of their room, stretching and casting an eye about the place.

'So far, perhaps,' Sir Charles muttered.

João was sitting in his room when a novice tapped nervously at his door to tell him that the Englishman was back. The *claveiro* told him to fetch the man, and sat staring at the empty desk before him.

It was not an easy job, managing a castle the size of Tomar, and for João, it was doubly onerous. In the past he had been with the Order of São Thiago, and moving to a new Order was not what he had wished for, not at that time of his life. If he could, he would have taken a post with a peaceful Order, perhaps the Cistercians, and spent the rest of his life in quiet contemplation. But the man who wishes to serve God must follow where He commands, and in any case, like so many pious men who had positions of importance in other convents, there were good reasons for coming to the Templar sites and restoring them in the public eye. João had felt the keen urge to come here and do all he could for Tomar.

The Englishman was a driven soul, he thought again. He had seen that in the fellow's eyes the day before. Now, if anything, he looked more torn than before. He had the appearance of a man who had come to a decision, but who disliked the result. He was not going to like the responses he would get today either, João thought to himself.

'Sir Baldwin. I am pleased to see you again.'

'I thank you,' Baldwin said as João motioned to the novice who had led Baldwin inside. The boy brought in a tray of wine, which he set between the two men. He poured a little into two goblets, then quietly withdrew.

Baldwin sipped at the wine. 'I am here, as you asked, to hear your answer.'

'My answer – yes. I did not feel it was an answer I should give,' João said, toying with the stem of his goblet. 'If the man whom you sought was guilty, that guilt was for him and for God.

If he wished, he could speak to you, but I saw no justification in forcing him to do so.'

'So I have wasted my journey,' Baldwin said.

'You are a hasty man,' João said, and there was a flash of steel in his voice. 'Please hear me out. As I said, it was not a decision I could take. However, I do not wish to have even the most pious woman-murderer here in my castle. Piety is important in a knight, but a knight who can rape and kill a Christian woman is not worthy of his robes. So I went to speak to him last night.'

'He is here, then?'

'Yes, he is here. And he will speak with you. He has agreed.'

'I am most grateful.'

'I shall be with you while you talk,' João said as he clapped his hands. In a moment or two, a novice had entered, listened quietly to João's instruction, and scurried off to fetch Ramón. While they waited, the two men sat without talking.

Baldwin was hard put to control his impatience. No matter what he had decided that morning, he knew that he must still try to find Afonso and learn what had made him stab Matthew. Although if Afonso admitted to the crime, what then could Baldwin do? Kill Afonso in his turn? That was ridiculous. It would be perpetuating the endless round of revenge.

Over the table, João studied him with interest. He knew that Baldwin was struggling with a bitter internal argument, for he had seen the signs before. A man who is in charge of a convent soon begins to spot those who have need of most support. Every man, João thought, would come to God in his own time. He thought Baldwin was probably coming to find God in his own way. For his part, João was content to remain silently watching Baldwin. There was nothing he could do to help. Baldwin was no doubt being spoken to by God.

There came the sound of boots tramping steadily along the corridor, then coming to a halt outside João's door. A knuckle rapped on the door, and João called out permission to enter.

Ramón walked inside with the truculent demeanour of a man

expecting to be accused. He glared at Baldwin as soon as he entered the room. '*Claveiro*, you wanted me?'

'You know why, Frey Ramón,' João said mildly. 'This is not a court, and you are not accused. This good knight would like to speak to you, though.'

Baldwin had stood when Ramón walked in, and he remained on his feet. 'To see you is to be more certain that you are innocent,' he began placatingly.

'After my woman was murdered, I chose to leave Compostela,' Ramón stated harshly. 'Why should you seek to follow me?'

Baldwin was unsure how to conduct this inquest. Eyeing Ramón, he tended to think that a direct approach would be most effective. 'There are some who say you yourself killed her.'

'Me? I loved her!'

'Yet she was carrying a large amount of money when she went to the meeting at the ford. We know that you were there with her, for you were seen by Don Ruy.'

'Yes, of course I saw her there. She had asked me to go and meet her.'

'What, in order to guard her? While she negotiated with the blackmailer?'

'No. She made no mention of any such thing,' Ramón said with apparent surprise. 'All she wanted was to ask me if I would protect her if she left her mistress. Obviously, I said I would. We were betrothed, and I hoped to marry her this year.'

Baldwin felt sure that the man was concealing something. Before Ramón could move on to a fresh topic, Baldwin said, 'What then?'

'That was all. I returned to the town, and shortly afterwards her body was brought back.'

'That is *not* all, is it? You were walking with her for some while. What else did you talk about?'

'Nothing. We spoke a little, and separated. That was all.'

'What did you speak about?'

'That is none of your business!'

'I am trying to convince myself that you are an innocent man, Brother! Can you not tell me what passed between you?'

'What does it matter?' he spat.

'It matters because another could be arrested and hanged for the murder if you don't help us to resolve things,' Baldwin snapped. 'Do you want an innocent man to be blamed, just because of your high-minded desire to protect someone?' This last was a guess, but Baldwin was sure that Ramón must have a good reason for keeping silent on the matter.

Ramón shot a look at João, then looked down at the floor. He hated the idea of telling the truth, but he hated still more the idea of lying, especially if that might lead to an innocent man being accused. He had no idea that Baldwin's 'innocent' was already dead. 'I don't know that I should tell you . . . it reflects upon my lady's virtue.'

'Tell me, please,' Baldwin urged.

Ramón glanced once more at João, who remained impassive, but then lifted an eyebrow. Ramón knew what that meant. A Knight of Christ was supposed to tell the truth to the glory of God. That reflection stabbed at him coldly like a shard of ice, and he shivered, but at last told his story.

'I was surprised when she asked me to see her there at the ford, because she and her mistress had already told me that Doña Stefanía must go out to a meeting and that was why I couldn't see Joana until later. Then she whispered to me to find a means of getting to this place. When I arrived, she was there. She had a bag with her, and she told me that she had taken it from her lady. Doña Stefanía was a dragon and a thief, she said. She had served her loyally, she said, but enough was enough.

'During the journey to Compostela, the Doña had slept with men, she said. A woman with loose morals was no mistress for her. So Joana had invented a blackmailer, a man who knew of the Doña's affairs, and who demanded money. Joana asked me, would I run away with her? We could keep the money, she said, and she showed me her bag.

'There was more gold in there than I had seen before in my life. Thirty to thirty-five *libras*. She had taken it from her lady.'

Baldwin interjected, 'How so, when the lady herself was going to bring this money to the blackmailer?'

'She hid her lady's horse. There was a cousin of Joana's travelling with her and her lady, a man called Domingo. He was there to protect them. Joana told him to take her lady's horse and move it so that the Doña wouldn't be able to leave immediately, and then Joana played on her lady's fears, pointing out that it would be easy for a man who was so dishonourable to capture her and take her hostage. Doña Stefanía,' he added drily, 'was easy to convince that she would be safer left in the town.'

Domingo was Joana's cousin! Baldwin felt a tingling of excitement in his belly. 'I see. So she showed you all this money?'

'And I told her to take it straight back to her lady. I'd have nothing to do with stolen money,' Ramón said, but to Baldwin's consternation, a tear began to run down his cheek. 'And that, Sir Baldwin, is the cause of my guilt. For I killed her, as surely as though I beat her about the head.'

'What do you mean?' Baldwin demanded.

'I left her there. I shouted that I wanted nothing to do with a common draw-latch, and that if she wished to marry me, it had to be as an honest woman. I told her to take the money back to her lady and quit her post. Then, I said, I would marry her. But on her way back, someone who must have heard us shouting, captured her, killed her, and stole all the money. If I had been kinder, if I had ridden back with her, instead of angrily riding off and leaving her alone, she might still be alive today.'

'That was Domingo, perhaps? He could have killed her for the money?'

'Perhaps. From his reputation, he would not have thought anything of murder for thirty *libras*. But I did not see him there.'

'Did you see anyone?'

'Don Ruy was there. I saw him after I had spoken to Joana and refused to accept her money. I was not in a good temper. I was thinking that I should leave her alone. If she could be so faithless to her own mistress, was she really the sort of woman who would make a good wife to a Knight of Santiago?'

'Don Ruy, you say? Where was he?'

'At the ford where the women wash their clothes. I saw him there. I remember it, because he was exchanging foul comments with a whoring beggar, and both were laughing at their lewdness. I thought it was disgraceful that a knight should be so crude. Don Ruy thought nothing of it. I dare say he took her for a tumble afterwards.'

Later, when Ramón had left them, Baldwin and João sat for some time in silence.

To João, it seemed as though Baldwin was at a loss for words, and he thought it better to leave him to mull over all he had heard without interruption. It was necessary sometimes, he knew, to have time to order one's thoughts.

Baldwin at last broke the silence. 'I think your Frey Ramón will make a good Brother.'

'We have need of faithful brethren,' João said. 'You were persuaded by his evidence?'

'I was,' Baldwin said heavily. 'Which carries the double pain for me of a wasted journey and the knowledge that I could have remained in Compostela seeking the real murderer there. I have no idea who was responsible. There is still this rape, murder and theft.'

'Perhaps a means of finding the murderer will come to you when you return to the town.'

'I can pray.'

'I shall pray for you.'

'I wonder . . . It would mean much to me to be able to pray in your oratory to ask for guidance. Would it be possible . . .?'

'No, not with the Brothers, of course. But you could join in a service in the chapel with the lay Brothers.'

'I should be very grateful. It would ease my mind.'

'Yes,' João said, and then, although he was not sure why, he said, 'Would you prefer to pray with me here, alone?'

Baldwin looked at him, and nodded. 'I would be very glad.'

It was afternoon when he and the *claveiro* left the chapel and wandered down from the little cloister around the church.

'My heart is full,' Baldwin said simply. 'I feel renewed.'

'I am pleased for you,' João said. He looked at Baldwin. 'You speak Latin very well, my friend.'

'I was fortunate to be educated.'

'And you say the *paternoster* fluently.'

'My brain has always been retentive,' Baldwin said defensively.

'Many men are fortunate to have good minds,' João said comfortably. 'Especially those who have lived in places like this for a while.'

Baldwin could not meet his gaze. There was a terrible silence between them. It was a gulf into which all noise was swallowed, as though if either were to speak, it could only result in death and disaster. Baldwin waited. He was convinced that João would call for men to capture him, that he was going to be thrown into a gaol and held. His worst fears were about to come true.

Then João idly kicked a stone from the path. 'I think,' he said quietly, 'that those who served here were not evil: they were heroes and martyrs. If they had been evil, do you not think that the demons they had summoned would have frequented these places? No, if the Templars were guilty of anything, it was of arrogance. And who, living in a place like this, wouldn't be prone to that sin?'

Baldwin was unable to speak. They had reached the level area before the circular church. A young child was running past, and Baldwin watched him speed over the ground, laughing as another boy chased him. 'I am sure you are right, *claveiro*,' he said huskily.

'I believe so. I find it painful to think of all the violence inflicted on men whose only crime was trying to obey God.'

They had reached a small gate in a wall, and João motioned to it. 'I wondered . . . it is a pleasing little area. I must leave you, but if you wish, you may enter and rest for a while.'

'What is it?' Baldwin asked.

'A graveyard.' João looked about him sadly. 'It is where the monks who used to live here were buried. Wait here, and meditate quietly. Leave your sword sheathed, and you might learn something useful.'

Afonso climbed up the roadway with Sir Charles. The English knight stood at the gateway peering out over the view, while Afonso entered the castle's gates and walked into the courtyard.

The place was enormously loud, with men shouting at each other, the beating of hammers and chisels, bellows making the flames roar, and over all the sonorous tolling of the massive bell in the church. Afonso gazed at it with wonder. It was nothing like a church as he knew it. Instead, it looked like a citadel, a castle's keep. It was a tower that dwarfed every other tower in Tomar.

The place he wanted to go was near the church, and he entered it quietly by the small gate. Immediately, the noise died to a background hubbub, and he found himself in a small cloister with a pleasing area of lawn. There were no seats apart from some stone-carved benches, and he walked to one and sat, staring at the grass.

There was another man in there with him, he saw, a man in a white tunic, and at first he wondered if it might be a Knight of Christ, but then he thought that they must all be in the church for a service, for the bell had ceased its clanging invitation.

Afonso was not worried. He bent his head and clasped his hands and began to pray as he had been shown by his father all those years ago. At once he felt the calmness return and envelop him. All the frustrations and worries of the last ten years began to disappear. It was as though he was able to tell his father what had happened, as if he could talk to his father properly again. Not that it was possible, of course. He had died many years ago. But simply confiding in him would, he hoped, make his father's soul happy.

When he was done, he sat back. After a few minutes, he heard footsteps approaching. A man sat on a bench nearby.

Baldwin cleared his throat. 'I came here to try to find you.'

'You have succeeded.'

'May I speak to you?'

'Not here.'

Afonso stood, and without a backward glance, walked from the cloister out to the courtyard, Baldwin following. As soon as Afonso opened the gate and stepped out, there was a shrill cry, and the little boy whom Baldwin had seen before, ran past, clipped Afonso's leg, and fell headlong. For a moment, there was no noise from him, but then he began to shriek with pain and surprise.

Baldwin saw the lad sit up, his mouth a blood-filled hole where he had fallen and dragged the inner surface of his bottom lip along the gravel-strewn ground. Baldwin felt his courage quail within him, but Afonso had no hesitation. He picked up the boy, and with a piece of his tunic, began to hook out the stones and grit which had been caught in the little fellow's mouth, not stopping until he had most of them out. Then he walked to a hut and demanded some watered wine for the boy. Only when he had seen the boy drink a little, still crying pitifully, and had found another to look after him, did he turn back to Baldwin.

'Why did you want to talk to me?' he demanded.

'Because I wanted to kill you,' Baldwin said seriously. 'And now I am not sure.'

Chapter Twenty-Five

'Yes, I wanted to kill him. I hated him – I still do,' Afonso said passionately.

Baldwin felt his hackles rise. 'An old man like that? What had he ever done to you?'

Afonso gave him a ferocious stare and his mouth opened, but then he shook his head and stared out over the town below them.

They had walked out from the castle and were sitting on a low wall a short distance away. Afonso had been quiet all the way, as though helping the boy had exhausted all his energies, but Baldwin was seething with a curious emotion. He wanted to strike the man, but something restrained him . . . probably João's words. '*Leave your sword sheathed.*' Why had he said that? João must have known that Afonso was going to be here. How had he guessed?

'Were you told to go there to the graveyard?' he asked.

'No. I went there to find some peace and to pray. The *claveiro* said I might meet someone there and he suggested it could be good for me to tell my story,' Afonso said. 'If you wish to hear it, I can tell you now.'

There was a strange listlessness to him still as he began his story, as though he had been on a long journey, but had at last finished it. He was home.

'I am called Afonso de Gradil. I was the second son of Dom Álvaro, but my older brother died when I was young. My grandfather helped fight the Moors and won back our lands, and my father felt the debt to God deeply. When I was young, he renounced the world and took on the white robes. He became a Knight Templar, living here in Tomar.

'Like my mother, I was proud of him. I honoured him for taking up the sword in God's name. When she died, I thought that I might wish to come and join him here in the castle, but before I could do so, the Templars were arrested.'

He looked at Baldwin. 'The accusations against those men were false. I know this. And then they began the foul process of destroying the Order – all on the words of a few lying men.'

'I know,' Baldwin said impatiently. 'So why did you choose to punish another innocent Templar?'

'Innocent? Brother Matthew was an agent of the French King sent to destroy the Templars!' Afonso spat. 'He was here for a while, but he invented stories about worshipping a devil's head, about urinating on the cross . . . all kinds of nonsense! Then he took those stories back with him to France and gave evidence against the Templars, helping to have them destroyed. And one of the men who died was my father.'

Baldwin fell back in his seat, and he felt a hideous crawling sensation over his flesh, as though tiny demons were enjoying his discomfiture. Suddenly the remoteness of Matthew, the 'otherness' of his behaviour, made sense. It was why he had never been tortured; he had no need of torture. He had willingly given evidence against his own brethren. 'No!'

'My father heard of the courts being held in France and travelled with others to give evidence in support of the Templars. Many were listened to, but because of Matthew, my father was captured. In 1310, he was burned to death with fifty others outside Paris, in a meadow near the Convent of Saint Antoine.'

Baldwin knew that place. Saint Antoine des Champs, on the road to Meaux, was a huge fortified precinct, entirely walled and moated. The Templars had been taken there to break the spirits of those who still denied guilt, and had been led there on wagons, shouting their innocence still. Chained and manacled, they could not escape when the King's men slipped the horses from their harnesses and set fire to the wagons, not even giving the men the dignity of a stake.

'I knew Matthew . . . are you sure he was guilty?'

'My uncle saw the records.'

'Your uncle?'

'The *claveiro* here. He came here willingly to restore the castle and convent to its previous glory,' Afonso said. 'After the shame brought upon the convent and my father by Matthew, he felt the need to do all he could to put matters right again. As did I in my own way.'

'So you killed Matthew.'

Afonso looked at him again, and there was a sadness in his eyes. It was enough to stay Baldwin's hand. He remembered this fellow picking up the child in the courtyard and helping him so carefully and kindly. Then he remembered Matthew. Conflicting emotions rose in his breast, but if Afonso was right, and Matthew had indeed survived the ordeals of the Templars by confessing to crimes and accusing his own brethren, then Afonso was justified in his revenge. And Baldwin would be merely perpetuating an injustice by killing him.

'I think you know I am speaking the truth,' Afonso said.

'I believe so.'

'Aha, that is good news!' a strange voice broke in. 'I would hate to have to harm an Englishman so far from home.'

Baldwin felt the muscles at the back of his neck tense. Slowly he turned and faced Sir Charles, who stood there smiling happily. 'So you aren't going to kill my friend, then, Sir Baldwin? That, I think, is an astonishingly good idea. Why don't we have a chat over some wine instead?'

'I should be glad of it at some point,' Baldwin said. 'But first I should like to finish this conversation.'

'Please do so. My friend here is leaving my companionship now, which I feel is very sad, but no matter. I shall be in our tavern, Afonso, if you change your mind.'

He turned and walked away, whistling, down the lane towards the town, and Baldwin raised a questioning eyebrow at Afonso.

'My task is done. I have decided to come here and join the Order. Many men from the Templars are still here. King Dinis did not believe the allegations, and he has merely changed the name, but the Order remains. My uncle will see that it remains pious and Christian. I shall join the Order, and then go to Castro-Marim. There I shall be able to kill Moors, and fulfil my father's aim.'

'If you thought Matthew was responsible for your father's death, then your killing him was understandable.'

'It would have been.'

Baldwin felt his breath catch in his throat. 'What do you mean: *would have been*?'

'I didn't kill him.' Afonso shrugged. 'Someone else got to him first. I merely reached him as he fell to the ground. And the thing that surprised me was that he looked glad. He was grateful for his life to be ended. I found that hard to imagine.'

Baldwin stared at him for a short while, then turned away and gazed out over the low lands beyond the river again. It was speculation, but Baldwin knew enough about how the Inquisition had gathered their evidence against Templars to be able to piece together the story.

'He had lived with his shame for such a long time,' he said slowly. 'All his life had been spent as a Templar, and he was as committed and honourable a Templar knight as any – until the arrests. I expect he was captured with others in France. He lost his courage while in the gaol. The Grand Master, Jacques de Molay, and the leading members of the Order were held *murus strictus*, with small walls, which meant that they were held alone and manacled for years, but the others were held *murus largus*, in large cells with many men together. That is where Matthew would have been held. And when the torturers did their work, they did it in the same large cells, so that all the other Templars could see what would soon be done to them. One at a time, they were taken and scorched, whipped, broken . . . Is it any surprise that a man like Matthew, proud, haughty and handsome, should find his will breaking as he saw all his comrades being tortured? He agreed to give evidence against them, and he was released. Except now he had no one to call friend. All his friends were dead, or they despised him. He had no profession, no livelihood.

His past career was closed to him for he had betrayed his companions. Ah! Poor Matthew! So he sank and became the lowest creature whom he himself would have disdained. A beggar'.

Baldwin sighed deeply and turned to the younger man. 'Yes, Afonso, I think he would have been very glad to have been killed. Whoever was responsible saved him from ever having to look himself in the face again.'

Munio's head was uncommonly heavy. He had sat through three days of court deliberations in the city and after all that, he was more than a little exhausted, although not so tired as poor Margarita. That was why he was sitting beside the sick man tonight, leaving his wife to go to bed early. After sitting up for the past three nights, Margarita was close to collapse, and Munio was worried about her. At last she had submitted to his insistence, and went to her bed a short time after eating a light supper, but it meant that in her place Munio must watch over their guest.

Simon's breathing was a little improved, Munio noted with a feeling of hope. It was not much, but Simon had been so close to death, from what he had seen, that any faint sign of improvement was a source of joy. Munio dreaded the thought of telling Sir Baldwin that his friend was dead.

Munio was not scared of Baldwin, even though most men would have known fear of a greater or lesser extent when harbouring the best friend of a knight. Knights were so dangerous, generally. They were prone, so Munio thought, to acquiring the same attributes as their favourite clothing: steel. In place of flexible thinking, such as a man like Munio himself might develop after wearing soft clothing all his life, the average knight was incapable of the limited pliancy even of a shirt of mail. Most knights understood only one response to any stimulus: drawing a sword. There were many indeed, Munio knew, who would, on hearing that a companion had died of a disease in another's house, immediately rush at the poor man who had only done his best to protect a guest. True, there were some who would happily speed a man's death just for the coins in his purse, but that was rare enough. Most Christians were kindly behaved towards their own.

In any case, Baldwin was not one of that type. Munio was sure that the knight would be more likely to berate himself, were Simon to die, rather than blame others. For Baldwin, Simon's death would be a cause of shame, because as Munio knew, there had been no real need for him to leave Compostela at this time. He could easily have demanded that Munio send another man to question Ramón and the other fellow, the one whom Baldwin thought might have killed the beggar.

'Come on, Simon!' he muttered. 'You have to get better. How else am I going to find out who killed poor Joana? I need your help.'

Simon made a slightly choking noise in his throat, and Munio shot him a nervous look, wondering whether he would need to wake his wife to look after Simon again, but the Bailiff gave a short cough, smacked his lips, and turned his face to the wall. Munio wiped his brow gently, but Simon's forehead wrinkled, as though annoyed by the service. He twitched his face in rejection, and Munio drew the cloth away, a feeling of relief thrilling him. Putting a hand on Simon's brow, his lips relaxed into a smile as he felt the relative coolness of the flesh.

'Ah, my friend, you will never know what glad news this is,' he whispered.

It was hellishly bright in the room when he slowly swam up through the warm seas of sleep to the cooler shallows of wakefulness, and Simon winced as he opened one eye a crack.

'I am as thirsty as a blacksmith who has drunk nothing but water for a week,' he said hoarsely.

Opening his eye a little wider, he glanced down at his body. He felt as though he'd been thrown in the path of an entire host of chivalry riding at full gallop. Terrible. And his voice was as rough as a sawn oak log. 'What's happened?'

'You have been very ill,' Margarita said gently.

'How long for?' Simon asked in a croak.

'Five days. I think it was the foul air from when you fell into that pit with Domingo,' she said. 'But you are over the worst of it.'

'I owe my life to you again, my lady,' he said with a smile. 'I should like to thank you.'

Her face was not glad, but rather remained anxious. 'Your health is all the thanks I need, Bailiff. Now, drink this cider and try to rest.'

'Rest? I've done nothing but rest for five days, if you are right.' Simon grimaced, but he took the drink and sipped it slowly.

His recovery was slower than before. He had suffered a serious fever, and he felt as weak as a newborn puppy. Daylight itself was painful, and he found himself squinting even early in the morning, and to it was impossible for him to do more than rest in his bed when the sun was at its height.

The languor to which he had succumbed was not merely physical. His mind was scarcely able to concentrate for more than a minute at a time. He was too tired to worry himself about Joana's murder, or any other matter, come to that, apart from the fact that he missed his wife, his own little family. The fact that Baldwin was not with him was an extra blow. Simon was not a man prone to feelings of self-pity, but on that first day after he woke from his fever, his soul was weighed down under a leaden gloom that prevented his taking pleasure in anything. The mere thought of food was enough to make his belly clench like a fist; he could drink little other than cider and a tiny quantity of white wine, and all he felt able to do was sit and doze. It was a relief to be nudged awake when the night approached, to be carried indoors to his room and sleep.

On the second day of his recovery, he felt that life was improving enough to justify taking a little meat, and although the stuff took an age to chew and try to swallow, it did eventually go down. At first he felt as though it was going to come straight back up, and ten minutes later he had the conviction, judging by the noises emanating from beneath his belt, that he might soon need to hasten to a chamber pot; however, his worst fears came to nought, and he did find later that afternoon that he was feeling much better.

When he went to bed, he did not sleep so well as he had. The bed felt too warm, the blankets too itchy, the air too muggy and uncomfortable. He rolled over, trying to settle, and eventually slept, but even as he did, he was aware of that same parade of people passing by which he had seen so many days before. There was Doña Stefanía, Ramón, Don Ruy, Domingo, María, and then Gregory and Parceval – both together, and smiling at him as though they knew something he didn't. Even as Simon tried to draw his attention away, he saw that Parceval was holding up a hand, and in it was clasped a large stone.

Chapter Twenty-Six

The next morning, Simon woke feeling tired still, but at least fully refreshed. He was able to roll out of bed, grunting at the pain in his aching muscles, and lumber to his feet. Drawing on his hose, then a thin shirt and jack, he forced himself to tie his belt about his middle. The weight of his sword was comforting. Heavy, he told himself with a curl of his lip at his weakness, but comforting.

Munio was already gone, running to view a body in a tavern. Some men had been drinking all night, and although they had started as the best of friends, they had ended the night as mortal enemies. Now one was dead, and the other unconscious after being hit hard by the cudgel in the hands of the innkeeper, the bloody knife still gripped in his hand.

Margarita looked glad that he was well, although she insisted that he should rest about the house all day and rejected absolutely his suggestion that he might go into the city and sit at a tavern for a while.

'If you want to make sure I am all right, you could join me, lady. We could send for your husband.'

'It would not be right for us to walk about the city,' she said quickly. 'No, you must remain here. I shall make sure that you are comfortable and one of my men will remain with you.'

'Perhaps I could merely walk along a road, or—'

'Master Bailiff, you will stay here,' she said firmly, and so, he found, he did.

The pain in his joints was already going by lunchtime, when he ate a bowl of pale, watery soup with light ham-filled dumplings, followed by a mixture of fruits – not usually a meal he would care for, but today he was enormously grateful for it, and ate an orange and some grapes with enjoyment. Afterwards he lay back on his bed and dozed for an hour, before waking feeling much more hearty.

Pushing open the shutters, he saw that there were clouds over the sky and the afternoon had cooled a little. 'Perfect,' he said as he walked from his room. Outside there was an old man nodding on a stool. Simon passed by him quietly, but some alarm stirred him, and he woke startled, gabbling quickly in his incomprehensible tongue.

Simon smiled broadly, then nodded, ducking his head, widening his eyes and nodding again, before walking away, ignoring the man's entreaties. 'As if I can't look after myself,' he said.

The weather was delightfully cool compared with the previous days, and he walked easily down to the square.

It was quieter now, perhaps because there was a service going on in the Cathedral, and Simon found himself walking along almost empty streets. The market had finished and the stalls were deserted. It gave the place a curious feeling of death, a feeling which Simon did not enjoy after the grim misery of the last few days. He needed life and happiness, things to remind him that he was alive, that he had not expired. This deathly hush was alarming.

There was a bell from somewhere in the Cathedral, and suddenly people appeared in the doors, hurrying about again. It was just like Exeter Cathedral when the priests finished their ceremonies and the choir trooped out, and all the congregation of merchants, prostitutes, hawkers and haggling townspeople who had gone in out of the wind and rain sloped off back into the open.

Simon sat down on a bench and ordered a small cup of wine. It tasted rough, but as he sipped, the flavour improved and he wondered whether his reaction to it could have been caused by his fever. Nothing tasted quite right since he had recovered.

The air was warming, and when he glanced up, he saw that the clouds were clearing. He moved along the bench until he was shaded by a building at his side, and when he was there, he saw Doña Stefanía leave.

She was swept along by the mass of people. Simon saw her glance in his direction, but he was fairly sure that she averted her head, as though he was a reminder of a sad experience. He wasn't sure why she should blame him for the death of her maid or the loss of her money, nor was he interested enough to want to find out. It seemed unimportant, compared with the illness he had suffered, or compared with the pleasure of sitting in the warmth and feeling the sun heat his bones.

As she carried on around the corner of the Cathedral, Simon saw another familiar figure – Parceval. Simon wondered about him. Parceval was a curious fellow. His clothing was shabby, yet he had somehow managed to seduce the Prioress, so either she was a shameless wench, or Parceval had the gift of persuasion. Simon had not spoken to the man, thus had little idea whether he could have been involved in the murder of Joana. The only time Simon had seen him was when he himself had collapsed, and he had not been on his best interrogative form that day.

There was one way which always, in Simon's experience, persuaded a merchant to come and chat. He gave a wolfish grin to Parceval and held up his cup. The Fleming smiled with a gesture of acceptance, and walked over to Simon.

'Take some wine with me,' Simon said, gesturing politely at the waitress.

'I thank you.' The Fleming sat down gratefully. When the wine arrived, Simon poured from the earthenware jug, topping up his own cup as well as filling one for Parceval.

'You speak good English,' Simon observed.

'I am a merchant. I deal more with the English than any others, because your wool is such good quality.'

'We are proud of it.'

Parceval nodded. There was a coldness about him, Simon thought, but that could well have been the reserve of a man who was conversing in a foreign language.

'You are here for your benefit?' Simon asked.

'Ah yes. I always thought it a strange thing, to go on pilgrimage for another man,' Parceval said.

'I agree. Although it is easy to see how a great lord, who swore that he would go on pilgrimage but then died, might leave in his will an instruction that one of his staff, or perhaps his child, should undertake the journey in his place.'

'For the good of his soul, he should ensure that he can make the journey himself,' Parceval said. There was a hardness to his voice. 'No man should force his child to do something against her will.'

'I have a daughter,' Simon said. 'She wishes to marry a boy I think a fool. He is one of these youths to whom costly parti-coloured hose are more important than a warm home, a good flock of sheep or a herd of cattle.'

'And you are sad at this thought?'

'Very.'

Parceval leaned forward, his face animated. 'If you take the advice of a man who lost his daughter, you will indulge her.'

'You have lost yours?'

'She was a beautiful girl – my pride and delight. But I told her not to see a boy because I did not approve of his father. She went to see him without my knowledge, and that night, she died with him. He was murdered; she was raped, and she took her own life in despair.'

Simon gave a groan of sympathy. 'My friend, that is terrible. My own worst fear is that I could lose my daughter. Did you find the man who had done this?'

Parceval's face hardened. 'Oh yes, I found him, and I killed him that same night. And I think I too died that night'.

Dead, he thought. Yes, I am dead. I have been dead since that night. There has been nothing since then. Only transient pleasures. Perhaps she wouldn't have committed suicide if I'd stayed with her – or did she recognise Hellin as my companion? My *friend* even!

He had hoped that the journey here to Compostela would have given him some ease of mind, but it had achieved nothing.

The only result had been his affair with the Prioress, a matter of convenience to him, but one of necessity for her. She had no money. Of course she could have gone to the Cathedral and demanded alms, but she appeared chary of that. Instead she preferred to wander the grounds watching all the visitors. Parceval had wondered why, because she should surely have been more worried about being seen consorting with him than about any shame at being poverty-stricken. Still, the ways of women, as he had so often thought, were usually incomprehensible.

Simon left Parceval to his own thoughts for a moment. Then, 'She seems a good woman, the Prioress.'

'You think so? I suppose so. She is lonely since the death of her maid.'

'It was a peculiar thing, that,' Simon said.

'A man saw her, a man raped her, robbed her, and killed her,' Parceval said harshly. 'There is nothing strange in that. Just one more bloody bastard who feels nothing for the death of another person. Life can be cheap.'

'Do you think so?'

'Me? I value life. I know the value of things: it is my job to make an estimate so that I can buy in and sell at a profit. Lives are the same as any other thing a man may buy or sell. Some are expensive: they are bought dearly, whether with money or lives. Look at the three men who rescued me and the other pilgrims on the day we arrived here: they were expensive. They cost the felons several men, without harm to themselves. The felons were cheap. They died quickly and easily.'

'Like that maid.'

'Who, Joana? Oh, yes. She died cheaply.'

'Did you know her?'

'Only vaguely. I saw her on the journey here.'

'I heard you met the Prioress on the way, too.'

Parceval smiled. 'Yes. I am afraid so. I was the cause of some embarrassment.'

'Because of . . . ?'

'Because we were seen together by that man Ruy.'

'She spends much of her time with you still. Does she not fear exposure?'

'Doesn't seem to. She lost all her money, so maybe the advantage of a few luxuries outweighs the risk of discovery.'

'Perhaps,' Simon agreed.

'That Ruy, though – he didn't *have* to tell anyone. That was shameful. I think he was just jealous.'

'Really? Why?'

'I caught him sniffing around a few times. He was like a desperate hound after a bitch. All over eager. On the journey down here, he was after the maid, you know, the bloody bastard.'

'Joana?' Simon asked. He was trying to recall where he had heard that phrase before.

'Yes. He was attracted to her, so I heard. That was what she thought, anyway. She told her mistress that too.'

Simon nodded and poured the remainder of their wine. Then he smiled as he remembered where he had heard those words. 'Why did you beat up Gregory? Were you worried that he might take your woman away from you?'

'Good God, no,' Parceval sighed. 'No, I only wanted him to stop upsetting the Doña. It was silly, but the little shitbag seemed to pop up wherever she went. So I tapped him and told him to leave her alone. And he did.'

'Probably because of the pain in his head,' Simon said grimly.

Parceval laughed unsympathetically. 'It was a light tap, nothing more. He should count himself lucky.'

'One thing more than anything else worries me about the girl's death,' Simon said. 'It's the money. The Doña didn't keep it – she is plainly desperate for cash. Then there is Ruy. He appears to have little, as did Domingo. I wonder who else might have taken it?'

'There was her betrothed, Ramón.'

'It is possible – but not likely. He was a Knight of Santiago, after all.'

'So? You think knights are any better than ordinary
folk? Look at the French royal family! Three daughters, and
two of them adulterers! Then there were the Templars, the
most evil men ever born, and *they* were supposed to be
religious. No, friend, you can't trust to a man's birth. The man
I killed . . .' He stopped momentarily, feeling his anger reaching up to strangle him as he allowed a vision of Hellin's face
to appear in his mind's eye again, but then he rushed on again.
'Yes. I killed him. You know why? He got me and some
others drunk one night, and for sheer malice, he killed a boy
and then had us gang-rape the girl. He thought it was great
sport, very funny. I knew something was wrong – I was so
drunk at the time, I didn't join in. I don't know. I was busy
vomiting everywhere, and we left her there afterwards, but it
was later, when I grew a little more sober, that I realised. Oh,
God!'

Simon waved to the waitress and poured more wine as
Parceval's eyes streamed with tears.

'God in heaven! How could he do that, eh?'

'It was your daughter?' Simon asked in a hushed voice.

Parceval nodded, sniffing. 'And I killed him. What would you
have done? I struck him down like a rabid dog. Like a demon.
He was evil, though. He had already given me a mortal blow.
And that, my friend,' he choked, trying to recover himself, 'was
the most powerful man in Ypres at the time, a knight and son of
a knight. So don't tell me that a knight is incapable of rape and
murder.'

Munio returned late in the afternoon, and when he saw Simon
sitting out in the front of the house, he gave one of his slow
smiles.

'When my wife told me that you were much better, I hardly
dared to hope that you would be so greatly recovered,' he said.
'Are you sure that you are quite well enough to be up and in the
open? Perhaps you should stay indoors, away from dangerous
airs?'

'No, I think that the open air is better for me, thank you,' Simon said, but his mind was elsewhere, and Munio could see his distraction.

'My friend, are you still in pain?' he asked solicitously.

Simon's brows rose in surprise. 'Me? No, I've a few aches, but nothing more than that. Why do you ask?'

'You seemed to be thinking of other things, and I wondered . . .'

'Ah, no. It was just a conversation I held this afternoon with that strange fellow Parceval the Fleming.'

'I have heard that he is keeping the Prioress,' Munio said with a stiff air. 'She appears to have forgotten her vows. It is strange, is it not? She spent so much time after arriving here trying to conceal her affair, and yet now she is living with that man so openly that even I, the *Pesquisidor*, have come to hear about it.'

Simon had given the matter of Doña Stefanía and Parceval a great deal of thought. Alone in this city, lonely and adrift, he felt he understood the Doña's feelings perfectly.

'She arrived here with men, a maid, and money. All is gone. She must feel that her life has been turned upside-down. For a woman like her, what could be more natural than that she should turn to the only friend she has? She probably doesn't fully realise how obvious her sins have become. Do you think the Bishop has heard of it?'

'Not necessarily. He doesn't trouble himself much about the town.'

'Yet there must be a risk. It seems odd that she should have exposed herself to it. Why not merely go home: her Priory is not far, is it?'

'No,' Munio said. 'But if all her money was stolen when her maid was killed . . .'

'That is the other problem I keep returning to,' Simon said. 'Where is the money? What has happened to it? If a thief had stolen so much, I should expect to hear about it. Is there no man in the town who has been said to have spread *libras* around?'

'There is nobody who has apparently received a marvellous gift, no,' Munio said.

'I do not understand it,' Simon said, his face reverting to his scowl again. 'Why should someone steal the money only to hide it away? Merely to keep it secret until it can be used and flaunted safely? That time may never come!'

For a moment he felt as though someone with greater intelligence and less confusion was hammering at the back of his mind, but the sensation faded, and he resorted to glaring at the view as though daring it to continue to hide the truth from him.

Baldwin jumped from the boat into the shallow sea with a grunt of relief. He turned to wave his gratitude, picked up his meagre pack, and started off up the loose sandy incline towards the houses.

'I am beginning to feel that all I have done this year is travel,' he muttered.

'This year? Extraordinary. Myself, I feel as though travel is all I have been doing since my lord died.'

'Aye, and before that,' Paul added.

Baldwin grinned at Sir Charles. The knight and his man still had their horses. A knight would not allow his horseflesh to be taken until he had lost absolutely everything else bar his sword. The mounts shivered and tossed their heads, glad to be free of the ship and the stinking reek from the hold. Patting Sir Charles's horse on its neck, Baldwin said, 'And yet you decided to come back here with me?'

'It is difficult to deny that your companionship, as an Englishman, would be more attractive to me than . . .'

'A stranger from Portugal?'

'Afonso was no stranger,' Sir Charles corrected him. 'In fact, he saved my life once, and I had grown quite fond of him in the last few months. But when all is said and done, he is determined to be a monk and take the three vows. Now, forgive me for being a rather conventional knight, but I never saw the harm in wine, women and song; the three, sadly, are not to my friend Afonso's taste.'

'What will you do now?'

Sir Charles's expression did not seem to change, but a certain grimness came into his eyes. 'I am an Englishman. I am unhappy away from my own lands. I think it is time that I rediscovered my own country. Perhaps I should return home.'

Paul shot him a look. 'Are you sure?'

'Paul, where else can we go? We speak no other language apart from a smattering of French, and wherever we stop we appear to have enemies. At least in England we can comprehend the insults being thrown at us.'

Baldwin had not asked them in whose service they had lived. During the four-day voyage up the coast, he had not felt the need. Their dialect and accents spoke of the North Country, and from the amount of time that they had been travelling, it was clear to him which magnate they must have served.

'There are some in the West who would be glad of two strong men-at-arms, if you can find no other service to your taste,' he said.

'You interest me strangely,' Sir Charles said, glancing down at his stained and worn tunic ruefully. 'Any man who can introduce me to a lord who possesses a good tailor would earn my undying friendship. You could name your own price.'

'I only have one question remaining now,' Baldwin said. They had reached the grass, and now they climbed the steep pathway up the cliffs, leading their horses. The wind whipped about them and they must grip their hats to stop them from being snatched away in a gust. 'Who killed that woman, and why?'

'The maid?' Sir Charles looked blank.

'Herself.'

'An odd death, that. I saw her body in the square when she was brought in and thought to myself, Where is the man who could do that!'

'What on earth do you mean?' Baldwin asked, stopping on the path.

'Just this. If a man had raped her, he'd stab her or throttle her to silence her, but I've never seen anyone smash a woman's face about like that before. If he found her attractive, he'd never wreck her like that, would he? No. I thought at the time – still do – that it was more likely that another woman killed her. Through jealousy, perhaps.'

'She was raped,' Baldwin pointed out somewhat caustically.

'So? Some women have friends and companions who may be tempted,' Sir Charles said lightly.

Baldwin was about to comment when he stopped. Was it possible that there had been *two* people involved in Joana's murder?

Chapter Twenty-Seven

Simon had no idea that Baldwin was almost home when he took to his bed that night. He lay back on the mattress, feeling the finer points of straw scratching at his back like tiny needles, and sighed contentedly. There was a pleasing odour of herbs, and the bed was a good quality one, with a rope-slung mattress; he felt enormously comfortable, and his body was soon overtaken by a delicious lassitude. Closing his eyes, he was aware of a wonderful sensation of slipping away, as though he was falling through the bed and down, to be swallowed up by the earth.

No. There was something alarming about that. He opened his eyes again and stared up at the ceiling. It was made of bare poles of saplings, with the thatching looking as though it was haphazardly thrown on top and bound in place. Now, in the darkness, he reckoned it looked like a strange forest, in the same way that the idle mind can see faces in clouds on a summer's day. Especially after a pint or two of strong cider.

In a way, this ceiling reminded Simon of a wood, and then, when he viewed it slightly askance, he thought it was much like the trees leading up to the ford where he and Baldwin had found Joana's body. There was the same large gap through which the ford itself could be seen, the same close-set meeting of branches where the girls hung up their drying. Beyond, he thought that the contours of the grasses in the roof were much like the rocks on which the washing was beaten and scrubbed. He could even imagine that the little hillock on the left side there, was the lumpy form of the dead body. On this side of the river.

So the horses had been tied up there, and the two had crossed over the water and walked together, perhaps made love in the sunshine: Ramón and Joana. Later he had gone back to town, but she had remained there.

Domingo had turned up after Ramón had left, had killed his cousin, beating her in a frenzy, and then taken her money. And raped her at some point, of course. He must have taken the money back with him to the town – except there was no sign of it amongst his possessions. Unless he had used it to buy the relic. Relics could be expensive, after all. But no! Domingo was not that sort of man. So maybe he had stolen the relic too.

Simon swore softly to himself, rose and padded out to the hall, grabbing a long shirt to cover himself with as he went. Munio and his wife had retired to their own quiet solar, leaving all the servants snoring or grunting here in the main hall. Simon donned his shirt and went out to the buttery, drawing off a pint or so of wine. He took it with him out to the cool garden and sat listening to the night's creatures.

Domingo had *not* taken the money. He couldn't have. All Simon's experience rejected the notion. Domingo was not the sort of thief to hide his good fortune under a bushel. If he had won a small fortune from the Doña, he would have spent it, especially on his men. But the men whom Baldwin and Munio had captured proclaimed their poverty, and there was nothing on Domingo or in his pockets. Ramón might have it, but Simon doubted it. If the man was honourable and intended joining another religious Order, he could hardly do so with money acquired by stealing from a Prioress and murdering a maid. No, that made no sense. It was possible that Baldwin's other target, the Portuguese, could have taken it. In fact, that made more sense than any other possibility.

Then his mind began to work with a sudden clarity. The assumption so far had been that this was an accidental murder, that the crime intended was blackmail, and that the killing of the maid was merely incidental to that; the maid's attractiveness was simply the spur to the rape and murder, neither of which had been planned. But perhaps the murder of Joana was no accident after all. She was there because Doña Stefanía's horse had been hidden by Domingo, her cousin. What if her death had been planned?

That gave Simon much to consider for the rest of the night, but it was not until the eastern sky was lightening that his face cleared suddenly and his mouth dropped open as the other possibility occurred to him.

She was already dropping with exhaustion. The work was repetitive and dull, but at least washing clothes brought in a few *dinheiros* and still left her time to sit in the square.

Standing again, she closed her eyes as she drew herself upwards. The pile which was the result of her efforts overnight was a pathetic sight, and when she looked at it, she was close to tears. All this misery – all this shame, sadness and poverty – and all caused by the conjunction of some terrible events that were nothing to do with her. And as a result, she must sit here every night while her fingers ached, the skin cracked, and her eyes grew sore.

Now she was done. She would go to buy a little wine, something to put the feeling back into her fingers and toes. It would cost more than half the money she had earned tonight, she knew, and that made her choke back a sob.

The woman at the bar gave her a hard look as María walked from the place, as though she felt that the beggarwoman was enjoying herself too much and the rent should be put up. If she did so, there was nothing María could do about it. For now, the most important thing for her was to gain enough energy to be able to survive the remainder of the night.

She walked out into the roadway, past the small triangular patch of grass, pulling her hood up over her hair. It was while she was decorously trying to hitch the veil up that she saw a dark shadow pissing against a tree.

It was a perfectly normal sight in the evening, but something prompted María to hurry her steps, and as she did so, the man turned and saw her. She recognised him immediately, as he did her. Even with her hood and veil, there was no mistaking the form and size of María the beggar, and he hailed her with a sudden grin.

'Where to, woman? May I buy you a cake and some wine?'

She hurried her steps, saying nothing, but she could hear his chuckle and his footsteps as he set off after her. The way took her down the side of the hill; she turned right along an alley, then left, hoping to lose him in the maze of smaller streets, but it was no good. She was clad in her heavy black skirts, while he wore hosen. While she kept feeling her bare feet getting tangled, he moved without impediment.

The pursuit ended when she tripped and fell headlong.

'Come, María, why the panic? It's not as if I'm a murderer, is it?' he teased from above her. 'And if you sleep with me again, I'll pay you for a whole evening's work as well as paying you.'

It was tempting to believe him. God! She could do with the money, and he was not unappealing like so many of the men she'd been forced to accept. But how could she trust a man like him? He was another so-called honourable knight, just like the ones who had taken her home away from her.

He saw her face hardening. 'Please!' he said, more quietly.

There was a curious expression of hurt in his eyes, as though he wished to have her company for its own sake. Perhaps he did, too. She was brighter, better educated than most wenches in the city. More companionable.

'It will cost you more this time,' she warned him.

'I don't care.'

'The money now, then,' she demanded, holding her hand out.

'Come, you can trust me,' he said.

'You say I can trust you?' she repeated cynically. 'I can trust no men. One only who married me, and one who saved my life – but both are dead now. You, Don Ruy – you must pay. The money first, and then you can have me.'

While Baldwin awoke with a sore neck, glaring up at the grey sky and trying to imagine how long it would take to dry off his sodden clothing after being so effectively soaked by the dew,

Simon was waking to a pot of warmed wine that had been watered and sweetened, with some aromatic herbs and spices added. To set it off, there was the fresh juice of an orange. It was tasty, refreshing and, in short, the ideal drink to wake a man from a deep slumber.

He stretched with only a slight feeling of stiffness in his lower back and one knee. That was an old wound, from a bad fall when he was a lad, and it was growing to be his most efficient means of predicting the weather. Whenever it was about to alter, his left knee twinged. Perhaps the weather would soon change, he thought. It was possible, but then again, it could merely be the last after-effect of his illness. If there was one thing he was certain of, it was that he was not going to tell his wife Meg about any of this.

The door opened just then, but with his eyes closed, he thought nothing of it. He murmured, 'Meg, I adore you and miss you. God keep you for me and for me alone!'

Opening his eyes, he saw Munio's wife, who stood silently with a plate on which was a flat lump of the local bread, some plain cheese and a little ham. She said nothing, but set the plate beside him, and walked from the room with an abstracted air.

Simon did not notice, for he was immersed in the sudden insight which had come to him last night: that the murder had been planned. The money had either been taken away from the town, perhaps by a pilgrim who had stolen it and now was a hundred miles away, or it had been stashed away for a rainy day. If so, Simon thought, it was an astonishingly restrained person who had committed the crimes.

He finished his meal and donned his tunic and hose, still pursuing the new direction of his thoughts. The more he pondered on it, the more sure he was that he was right. There was only one link missing now, and he was sure that he would soon discover that.

Pulling on his jack and binding his sword about his belly, he left his chamber and went to seek Munio.

The *Pesquisidor* was sitting at his table in his hall with a somewhat doleful expression on his face, and Simon could not help but notice it. 'Is all well, Munio?'

'Yes. Why – should it not be?' he demanded.

Simon was surprised by his snappishness. 'My apologies, friend. I did not mean to upset you.'

'That is right. An English freeman would hardly insult his host, would he?' Munio said.

Thinking to distract Munio from his strange mood, Simon said, 'I think I can see what happened out at the ford that day when we found the body. Will you allow me to command some men? Perhaps you too could come with me?'

'You think I have time to drop all of my official matters on some whim of yours?' Munio grated, but then he took a deep breath. 'My apologies, Master Puttock, but I have received some disturbing news today.'

'But of course,' Simon said mildly. 'Shall I ride out alone, then?'

'No, I shall find a man to help you,' Munio said, eyeing the man who, so his wife said, desired her.

He was as good as his word. No sooner had he left the house to find Guillem, than two men arrived at Simon's side. One spoke a form of English, and Simon was convinced that he could explain what he needed. They would walk while Simon rode, as he was still feeling weak. He borrowed Munio's horse for himself, and the three set off as soon as they could.

Simon wore a small goatskin filled with weak cider about his neck, and as they left the city, he unplugged it and took a long gulp. This weather was peculiar. It was so hot, he wondered how people survived it for long. Surely most people must die young, withered away until they were nothing more than the dried-out husks of the folks they had been. Even Munio, he thought, had been affected. It couldn't be healthy to live in so hot and inclement a climate. Not like his Dartmoor. There at least there was always abundant moisture. It kept the flesh full and elastic, healthy; not like these thin-skinned foreigners.

It took the trio less than half an hour to reach the ford. Simon sat on his horse, hands crossed over his mount's cruppers, contemplating the land before him.

The body had been found up there on his left, but Don Ruy had said that Ramón and Joana had been walking over on the other side of the stream. Simon kicked his horse onwards. At the ford the river was only shallow, if broad, and the water came no higher than the men's knees. Not that they cared. They stoically ploughed through it, without glancing at Simon on his horse.

Once on the other side, Simon began his search. The land here was separated into fields, with a footpath of some sort. On the right-hand side was a ditch, which was a little damp in the very bottom. It looked as though it was used for some form of irrigation. Bushes and a few thin, tormented trees tried to grow here, and there was a thick thorny mess beneath them.

It was here, Simon guessed, that Ramón and his woman had walked, and he rode along at a gentle amble, explaining as simply as he could to the men with him what he expected to find.

Once they understood, the two men set to with a will, and began to shove plants and twigs aside in their search for Simon's proof. He had hoped that from his vantage point on the horse, he would be the first to see it, but it was the man who understood a little of Simon's language who suddenly gave a delighted crow-like cry, and pounced. Grinning widely, one hand bleeding with a slash from a vicious thorn, he held up a large leather purse, an expensive, soft, decorated purse filled with gold and silver coins.

'Well, well, well,' Simon said with a grin that threatened to separate his crown from his jaw. 'So I am not so stupid as I feared!'

There was much more to be done, once Simon had proved that part of his theory. Now he was keen to check on other aspects.

Leaving the horse at Munio's stable for the groom to see to, he walked with the purse into town. Once there, he found a tavern, and sat in full view of the Cathedral, the purse safely tucked inside his jack. He still had the skin about his neck, but set it down and bought a jug of wine. Soon, he began to feel comfortably somnolent in the warm sunshine, watching all the people in the square.

They were all hurrying, but slowly, he noticed. In England, everybody tended to look as though they were hastening every-where, when they had little reason to; here everyone seemed to move in leisurely fashion and yet they covered the land faster than their Devonshire counterparts.

Simon soon spotted the person he had come to see. The Prioress walked about the place with an anxious expression on her face, turning this way and that, catching the eyes of many people, and as quickly looking away. Her manner was that of a woman who was looking for someone, although she appeared half-terrified that she might find the target of her searching. She caught sight of Simon and he smiled at her, beckoning, but she gave a graceless shake of her head and turned away, walking towards a small group of beggars.

'You won't find her there,' Simon said, comfortable in the knowledge that his simple test had been proven. Now there was only one more trial that he need make. For that, he must have assistance.

If only, he thought, Baldwin was back. He could do with his friend's help.

Had he but known it, his friend was already back at Munio's house.

Baldwin, Sir Charles and Paul arrived back at the house a little after lunchtime, just as Simon was sitting at the tavern and waiting for any sign that his assumptions were correct. Baldwin went straight in to find his friend or Munio. Instead he found Margarita, in her hall with a steward, but looking very troubled.

'My lady! I am so glad to be back and to be able to thank you for your great kindness to me and to my friend.'

'Sir Baldwin, I am glad to have been a friend to you.'

'Where is Simon?'

'He is gone out. I expect he is in the town.'

Baldwin nodded, but he was aware of a certain frigidity about her. 'Lady, Simon is well?'

'He was very ill with a fever, Sir Baldwin, but now, yes, he is fully recovered.'

'I am glad to hear it,' he said heartily, and again, he thought that her manner was a little off. 'Um. Should I go to find him in the town?'

'Yes. That might be a very good idea,' she said as though considering the matter carefully.

He nodded and gave her the best bow he could manage, but when he left the house, his brow was furrowed. There was something very odd in this, he felt sure. Had Simon offended Margarita in some way? Surely that was impossible. Simon was a polite, reasonable, trouble-free guest generally. Perhaps it was simply because he had been so ill. Some men could become pests when unwell, he knew, and yet he had seen Simon when his friend was close to death, and he had never been difficult. If anything, great illness made him more pliant and amenable. No, it was surely not that.

In the yard, he surrendered himself to the fact that he did not know what was wrong and could not, until he had spoken to Simon himself. Perhaps he could throw some light on the matter?

First, of course, he must find Simon.

'What now, Sir Baldwin?' Sir Charles asked.

'Well, after enjoying your companionship for the last four days on board ship, may I repay the compliment by buying you both a meal? My friend is in the town, I believe. We could do worse than go to see him.'

'We could indeed,' Sir Charles said with a smile. He was starving hungry. Almost the last coin he possessed had gone on the passage from Portugal to here, and now he was famished.

'So long as he has a joint of beef and a slab or two of bread,' Paul muttered, but Baldwin didn't hear him and Sir Charles chose to ignore the comment.

*   *   *

Simon stood and glanced about the square. Doña Stefanía was standing near another group of beggars, casting her eyes over them all, the kneeling man, the stooped and wailing woman, the girl on crutches, but Simon could see that the one she wanted was not there. No, he thought, she's hiding still, isn't she? Can you blame her?

He felt quite relaxed. The whole picture had at last fitted into place, like a mosaic seen from a distance: he could see the individual hints at the overall picture, the tiny chips of stone, but now he could see the totality of the scene as well. Each clue was fitted into its own logical place, each related to the next, each pointed to the overall solution. Nothing was difficult, once you had the basic idea, he knew. No, it was quite simple when the theme was at last divulged. It made the solution laughably obvious, as so many mysteries were, when you had the key that opened them.

It would be good, he thought, to explain to Baldwin how he had come to this conclusion, although he knew that it would upset his friend. Still, it was important to know the truth, and Baldwin would appreciate it. It would set his mind at ease to hear what really happened, even if the facts were painful.

As he was about to leave the tavern, he saw Doña Stefanía again. She was walking about the edge of the group of beggars, and she caught a glimpse of him just as he looked her way. Her face was pale and drawn, a picture of sadness, and he wished he could ease her torment. 'But I can't ruddy help you unless you let me, can I? If you won't let me speak to you, I can't do a thing,' he muttered irritably.

He drained his cup and sat back. Until Baldwin returned, Simon felt unwilling to expose the facts, just in case his assessment was wrong. If he was right, Doña Stefanía was going nowhere until she had found what she sought – and she *couldn't* find that now.

Chapter Twenty-Eight

Doña Stefanía could *feel* his eyes upon her. It was infuriating! The shabby fellow with the bright eyes and unhealthy white skin was staring like a man ogling his first woman. If she could, she would have run to the nearest Cathedral official and demanded that the impudent churl be punished for his lack of respect.

She couldn't, though. There was no official in the Cathedral to whom she could turn. She shouldn't have remained here. Oh, if only she had gone back to the Priory . . .

It was mostly due to Parceval. Doña Stefanía was confused. Without Joana, she felt as lost as an unmasted cog on the open sea. Worse was when the foul monster Domingo had demanded her relic. Losing that was a disaster! But so was the loss of her companions. She was all alone, with only Parceval. He was her sole friend here.

Parceval had money, but she no longer suspected him. No, he couldn't have robbed, raped and murdered Joana *and* returned to meet herself in the tavern. He would have taken longer. Anyway, he had satisfied Munio. No, Parceval was innocent. Someone else had stolen her money and done those terrible things to her poor young maid.

Doña Stefanía felt the beginnings of panic. There was no one to whom she could turn. Of course, when that devil Domingo had robbed her of her only valuable, the Saint's relic, she had submitted to Parceval's generosity. She joined him in his own room, an offer she had felt forced to accept. At the time, she had believed that he had stolen her money. She meant to take it back – except there had never been the opportunity. Every time she had tried to reach out and search his belongings, she became aware that he was awake. It was as though he needed no sleep, damn him!

She wanted her relic back, but Domingo must have sold it or just thrown it away. At that thought, ice entered her bowels. The idea that a saint's holy remains should be cast away, perhaps into the river, or even into a midden near the town – that didn't bear thinking of. Her religious soul quailed at the thought that her innocent theft of the relic could have led to it being discarded by a heathen like him. It would mean that she herself would be considered as guilty as Domingo, should the Bishop ever learn of her trick.

So she had to wait here. And then she had learned that the Fleming was not a liar, and he wasn't a thief. The money wasn't taken by him. She went with him and saw how the house of Musciatto treated him, like a deeply honoured client. This was no common churl, but a wealthy merchant who had chosen to dress like a peasant. That was up to him. It at least made her feel a little better. A man's breeding would out, she considered. She hadn't fallen for a bit of rough serfdom, but a rich man. It was some consolation.

What was not in any way consoling was the fact that although now she thought she had guessed the truth, she *still* couldn't find her relic, her money or her maid.

Because Doña Stefanía was sure that her maid had not died. Joana was still alive, and in possession of her money, and Doña Stefanía wanted it back.

'Wait a moment, Bailiff.'

Simon had stood as the Prioress disappeared around the side of a wall, and yawned. There was no point hanging around here, he thought, and he was about to make his way back to Munio's house, when he heard Gregory's call.

The cleric was approaching with the tall figure of Don Ruy at his side. 'Perhaps we could share a jug of wine? This town, for all its gaudy baubles and trinkets to be sold to pilgrims, is surprisingly short of intelligent conversation.'

'I should be happy to,' Simon lied. He had no desire to speak to the miserable fellow. In his private opinion, Gregory spent too much time whining about his lot and not enough getting on with his life, but Simon *was* interested in speaking to Don Ruy.

'Could you ask the knight,' he said to Gregory when they were all seated on benches and each had a jug of wine before them, 'whether he recalls that day when your ex-wife's maid was murdered?'

Don Ruy looked a little startled on hearing the question and shot a look at Simon, but he nodded, then shook his head with apparent sadness.

'A terrible waste,' Gregory translated.

'Certainly,' Simon agreed. 'Such a young life. And I under-stand you rather liked her?'

Gregory looked from one to the other as he translated. 'He says she was a pleasant enough woman.'

'With the legs and bosom to make her still more appealing,' Simon said. 'After all, Don Ruy was seen watching her closely as he followed her out of the city.'

'He says he's told you this already,' Gregory said as Ruy affected an elaborate yawn.

'Yes,' Simon said, stifling his own yawn. He was feeling more than a little lethargic himself after so much wine so early in the afternoon. 'But he said that he left the city for a ride and came straight back here again afterwards. He said that he *didn't* follow the girl. But he saw her walking over on the other side of the ford with Ramón.'

'Yes. That is right.'

'He told us he saw another person there.'

'There was no one.'

'Come! There was a washerwoman at the ford.'

'That is true.'

'Who was she?'

'He does not know.'

Simon chewed his lip thoughtfully. 'I wonder. The hostler at the stable told us Don Ruy was away most of the afternoon. Don Ruy said he was out for a short time. I had forgotten that until I started thinking about the sequence of events. And thinking about them, I remembered the washerwoman. What happened to her?'

'He does not know.'

'Let me prompt his memory! After all, anyone there could be suspected of Joana's murder.'

'Don Ruy says he has better things to be doing,' Gregory said nervously as the knight stood, tapping at his sword hilt.

'Tell him to wait. I want to ask him about María, the whore . . .'

With an incoherent roar, Don Ruy swept out his sword, and it sparkled in the bright sunshine.

Suddenly he shot forward, and the table went over, the edge striking Simon in the lower belly, its weight trapping his legs. He cried out, more in surprise than pain, and then the table top was thrust at him again, and he felt himself toppling backwards, the full mass of the wood on top of him. With his mouth wide in alarm, he flailed with his arms, but there was nothing he could do, and he thumped backwards, his head taking an unpleasant knock on the stone flags.

Gregory had remained rooted to the spot as he saw Don Ruy explode into action, and he jerked back as the table went over, and Simon flew backwards, but then he saw Don Ruy grab for his sword, and he responded without thinking. He was standing now, and he had no weapon to hand. Simon's own was sheathed and hidden beneath the table, out of reach. But behind him was a pilgrim who, footsore from having just arrived, sat massaging his bare, horny feet, a strong, iron-shod staff at his side. It was the work of a moment to snatch it up and take it in the quarter-staff hold, one quarter of its length held between his hands, three quarters projecting like a polearm.

Don Ruy was about to stab at Simon, but the staff jabbed hard forward, catching him under the breastbone. It was painful, but more than that, it was shocking, like being suddenly molested by a rabbit. Don Ruy fell back, his mouth working as he tried to accommodate the concept of the feeble cleric Gregory suddenly becoming a ferocious avenger, and then he leaped to the attack.

But Gregory had been an experienced fighter before being thrown from the Templars, and most Englishmen were raised with a staff from childhood. Using it as a half- or quarter-staff was second nature. Gregory easily knocked aside the knight's first thrust, parried the second, and then automatically poked hard at Ruy's face, the iron ferrule striking the man's right temple. Withdrawing the point, Gregory realised that the knight was not immediately attacking again, and he struck once more, this time catching the back of Ruy's hand.

The tip had been fixed upon the staff more than five hundred miles earlier, when the pilgrim passed over the mountains near Roncesvalles. It had worn down progressively until now it was a thin sliver of metal that was as fine as a razor on one side.

It was this that had caught Ruy's temple and hand, and as Gregory drew the pole away, he saw that there was a fine mist of blood pumping from Ruy's head. The knight realised at the same time and, reaching to his skull, stared in disbelief at the blood that smeared his fingers. He turned to stare at Gregory, his face now devoid of any emotion but rage. Whirling his sword about his head, he swung it at Gregory, and although Gregory held the stout staff in its path, the blade thunked into the wood and tore out a massive chip. The blade came out, almost tearing the staff from Gregory's grip, and whirled again, this time catching the wood a glancing blow and cracking a great splinter from it; and when it glinted in the sun and appeared to slice straight at Gregory's head, he was sure he was about to die.

There was a ringing crash, an echoing, heroic sound like bells and trumpets and glory all together, and a second blade blocked it. Gregory was thrust aside, and he saw a flashing peacock-blue shimmering in the air before him, and then he was dancing away, the shattered remnants of the staff still gripped firmly in his hands, as Baldwin moved in.

It was as Don Ruy lifted the table that Baldwin had reached the square. All he could see was Don Ruy apparently attacking Gregory and he rushed forward to try to prevent bloodshed, but then he saw that there was another body on the floor, and even as he realised it was Simon, his anger was kindled. His sword flashed into his hand, and he leaped between Ruy and Gregory, his blade sparkling in the sun. His senses quickly became attuned to his opponent. Ruy gave way like a man who was hard-pressed from an unexpected attack, but then Baldwin saw his eyes narrow, and he had just enough time to prepare before Ruy darted to the left, then sprang forward. His sword made a sharp thrust toward Baldwin's throat, but then slipped down and up again, and if Baldwin hadn't been ready, it could have opened him like a chicken from gizzard to groin.

Baldwin slammed the blade away with his own, grasping his sword like a staff, his left hand on the blade, pushing down with both hands. Ruy, for all his strength, couldn't control the full weight of Baldwin's body over his own blade. He was already crouched in a difficult position trying to thrust, and Baldwin's move unbalanced him. Falling, he could do nothing to protect himself, and he landed heavily on his right shoulder, forcing him to grunt, and then he gave a louder cry as Baldwin kicked him hard in the belly. Don Ruy was infuriated by that blow. It made him roll over to stab upwards with his sword, but before he could complete the manoeuvre, he felt the ferocious chill of a bright blue blade tingling at his throat.

'Submit!' Baldwin hissed through clenched teeth.

Don Ruy stared at him, his eyes glittering with resentment, but then the blue blade moved and he could feel the flesh begin to part. He cried, 'I yield!' and his sword clattered on the pavings.

Simon grumpily accepted that he had few grounds to object, but he still did, volubly, as the rather alarmed-looking men gathered together by Munio lifted him gently onto a door and carried him back to the *Pesquisidor*'s house.

'You should not have taunted him,' Munio said, gazing at him mournfully.

'I only tried to get him to talk,' Simon said indignantly. 'How was I to know that the damned fool would jump on me for that?'

'He said you accused him of rape and murder! What else would you expect him to do?'

'I *didn't* accuse him of that. I said he knew where the murderer was, and he does, I'd bet, from the way he went for me.'

'Oh, I see. He attacked you because you *didn't* accuse him?' Munio said. 'Yes, of course. That makes perfect sense!'

'No! I accused him of knowing who the murderer was, and he was protecting her, more than likely. He's a fool, that knight.'

'I can at least agree with that,' Baldwin said. He was walking on the other side of Simon's makeshift bier, and he cast a look at Munio. 'He went quite mad. Good thing he's in gaol for the night.'

'Potty!' was Simon's conclusion. 'He damn nearly broke my head, too.'

They had reached the house now, and the party turned into Munio's entrance, the peasants carrying Simon carefully up the cobbled track. It was quite rank with weeds, and they must mind their step so as not to jolt Simon too badly. None of them wanted to risk Munio's wrath, because he appeared to be in a particularly sour mood today.

Sir Charles and Paul had trailed behind them, hoping that a meal of some kind might be in the offing. Munio glanced at them bleakly, then motioned to them to enter as well.

As they sat about the table with a thick stew ladled into their bowls and plentiful supplies of coarse bread, Baldwin told them all he had learned about Matthew from Afonso. There was a strange feeling that, by telling this story, somehow his own sense of betrayal was diminished. Matthew was a weak man. There was no crime in that. He was as other men were – a human being. Fallible, he could be twisted by those who were more corrupt, ruthless, or simply more brutal than himself. And once he had agreed to lie to protect himself from torture, he was lost. There was no one who would support him. His former companions and friends would not look at him, either because they knew of his perjury and despised him for it, or because they too had committed the same crime, and avoided any man who might remind them of their evil deed, condemning all their friends in exchange for their own freedom from torture. The men with whom he had colluded thought him a coward and ignored him, while those who knew nothing, merely believed the accusations against the Templars and assumed that he was as foul as he had himself confessed. No man would have dealings with him. Thus he was forced to beg.

'It's sad to see people begging,' Simon said meditatively. 'There are many such here. Not because there are more poor folk here than in other towns, but because many people here will give alms. The beggars know that pilgrims are likely to have been sent here, or to have set off to come here, because they have committed some crime and will be willing to give money away to the poor. And beggars are faceless people, who are used to being ignored. It must be rare indeed for a beggar to be heard, watched or threatened.'

Baldwin glanced at him. 'Matthew wasn't threatened by Afonso, Simon. He would have been killed by Afonso – but Afonso found he was already dead.'

'Yes. And we know who did it.'

Baldwin nodded. 'I think so, yes.'

Munio gazed from one to the other. 'Who, then?'

It was Simon who responded. 'Pour me a little more of that marvellous wine, and I think I can put in place a means by which we can show you.'

'When?' Munio demanded.

'In the morning, I think,' Simon said. 'That will give that fool Don Ruy time to clear his head and calm himself. It will also make him appear more vulnerable. And should give us an extra little piece of incentive.'

The next morning was grey and cool, and when Baldwin threw open the shutters, he felt that the weather was suitable for the end of this grim little affair.

He had set off for this pilgrimage with a heart that was keen to purge itself of the hideous murder he had committed, and he had hoped that when he arrived, his soul would be lightened; instead he had found an old comrade, lost him, and finally learned of his perfidious behaviour. It was a sad man who stared out at the roadway before the house.

While the household stirred and readied themselves for food, he went out and walked away through the city until he reached the gates. He left Compostela and walked up along the river again until he came to the ford. There he sat on a rock and studied the ground once more. Simon had been mysterious all last night. He and Baldwin knew the culprit, but Baldwin had only guessed because of Matthew's death. As to why, he thought he knew that as well, but Simon's twinkling smile made Baldwin wonder whether he had got completely the wrong end of the stick.

He would not learn anything here, though. Walking quickly back to the city, he felt himself grow a little out of breath, and told himself sternly that today he must make time to practise with his weapons. It was his normal regime at home to play with them for at least as long as it took for his blood to heat sufficiently to make his muscles ache and burn, and the sweat to run.

At Munio's, he was surprised to see a massive bowl set at the door ready for beggars. The norm was for one tenth of a household's food to be given up to the poor, but this was almost enough for Munio's entire staff and guests. Roasted fowls, pies, even a large cheese, were thrown in higgledy-piggledy, and Baldwin remembered that he had not yet eaten. He hurried into the house to see if there was any food left after the others had broken their fast.

In the hall there was still a little wine, watered and flavoured with spices and oranges, and some bread. He took a large piece and a handful of olives, and stood chewing while servants arrived to clear the room. The tables were emptied, then their cloths removed while the tops were stacked against a wall and their trestles folded and put away. Soon there was only Munio's own table standing on its dais, and before it a wide, clear space.

Sighing, Baldwin took his seat on a bench.

He did not have long to wait. Munio arrived soon after the last of the tables were removed, and shortly after him Guillem hurried in, carrying his pots and parchments. He sat down and began to prepare his tools, glancing about him enquiringly as he did so. Then the other interested parties filtered in.

Simon came in and looked about him, walking to Baldwin's side. Sir Charles and his man arrived and stood at the back of the hall as though interesting themselves in the strange and obscure practices of a foreign court. After these came the spectators – the rowdy, the nosy and the plain silly, who could always be counted upon to witness another's potential execution.

Munio had a small hammer with him, which he used to call order. 'Bring in the man.'

To Simon's delight, Don Ruy was a dishevelled figure after a night in the gaol. His beard blued his jaw, his hair was unkempt, and his clothes were marked with more recent stains. There was a tear in his sleeve which hadn't been there the night before, Simon noticed, and he hoped that the madman was content with the result of his attack. The Bailiff was happy to forgive and forget an insult, but not a sword.

'Don Ruy. You are here because last afternoon you attacked this man, Simon Puttock, and caused a disturbance which could have grown ugly. Do you confess?'

'I don't. He accused me of a crime. I was protecting my honour, as is the right of a knight.'

When Baldwin had translated, he had to put a hand on Simon's wrist to stop him leaping up and accusing Ruy of lying. 'It will not help matters.'

'It'd make me feel a lot better,' Simon said, but he was already cooling. Instead of watching Ruy, his attention was concentrated on the door at the rear of the hall. Occasionally he saw a black-clad figure arrive, but each time he shook his head, and the person was left alone.

'That man accused me of murder,' Ruy said, throwing out a hand towards Simon with justifiable anger. He was humiliated, standing here like a common felon, while the man who had dared to accuse him stood there with his honour intact. It was he, Don Ruy, who had been the injured party, not that smarmy, block-headed English Bailiff! 'What would you expect a man of honour to do? I defended myself, as is my right!'

Simon was pleased to see that at last a proud, slender figure had appeared. He quickly lifted his brows and nodded his face towards her: Doña Stefanía de Villamor, and not a moment too soon, because only seconds later he saw the person entering anxiously behind her. That was when he smiled to himself, glanced at Baldwin and saw his brief nod of approval, not unmixed with confusion, and settled back in his chair with his chin on his chest. There was little more he could do for the moment.

'You launched an unprovoked attack on the good Bailiff, and for that you must suffer the consequences.' Just then, Munio caught sight of Baldwin's glance and followed his look towards the back of the room. At this point he changed his speech.

'But first, before we decide on the punishment, I should like to mention something else.' He reached into his purse and brought out the little casket. 'This was found recently. Does anyone recognise it, or claim it as their own?'

There was a sudden hush at this unexpected interruption to proceedings, and Ruy himself looked as though he might protest, but before he could do so, Doña Stefanía stepped forward eagerly.

'It's mine! It was stolen, but it's mine!'

'It was stolen, lady?' Munio said heavily. 'You realise that there is a law demanding that a theft must be reported? To whom did you report this crime? It was not to me, was it?'

'I did not know that I had to report the theft. I thought that my loss was my own cost and should be put down to my own foolishness as a woman.'

'Your humility does you credit,' Munio said sarcastically. 'Do you know where it was found?'

'No.'

'On the body of a dead man. A man who was in charge of a gang of thieves. Perhaps you have heard of him? His name was Domingo.'

'Domingo?' She brought her brows together. It was hard to feign ignorance, but she was determined to try.

'Yes, Domingo. He led his men against a band of pilgrims on the day that they arrived. Afterwards, he was reported as having stolen your horse, I think?'

'I didn't report him.'

'Another theft that went unreported. Curious, because that theft apparently prevented you from going to meet someone.'

'My maid was able to go instead.'

'And she died in your place,' Munio pointed out.

'Yes,' Doña Stefanía said, her eyes downcast.

'And your money was stolen from your maid.'

'Yes.'

Munio glanced at Baldwin, who nudged Simon. The Bailiff gave a beaming smile and flicked aside his coat. From beneath it he brought out the purse he had found at the ford.

'Is this yours?' Munio asked.

Her face was answer enough. 'I had no idea . . . how did you . . .'

'It was easy,' Munio said, and motioned to Simon.

Simon stood now, and strolled to Munio's table. While he spoke, Munio translated. 'The money was never stolen. The attempt was made, of course. Your maid, Doña Stefanía, as you suspected, wanted to leave you and take a nice little nest egg with her. She had spoken to her lover, Don Ramón, about getting married, and he agreed. He was delighted; he loved her.

'But first she must get her hands on the money. To do that, she told you that someone had heard or seen of your affair with another pilgrim, and that he had approached her, demanding to meet you and be paid off. You were enraged, of course. You thought that you had done nothing wrong . . .'

Munio's tone was ironic, and a chuckle rippled through the hall. Simon smiled winningly and continued as the Doña's head shot around to glare at the audience.

'. . . so you told her you would go and pay the man. But when you went to fetch your horse, you learned that Domingo had taken it already. Perhaps he wanted to sell it for himself. So you had no horse. Instead, you told your maid to go.'

'She wanted to go. She said it was safer than letting me go. If there was a felon there, he might have molested me – ransomed me, perhaps!'

'Perhaps. You should be glad, whatever is true. It was easier for her merely to go in your place. She arrived there, and met her husband-to-be, Don Ramón. He was thrilled to see her. They went for a lovers' walk – but then things went wrong. She produced your money, Doña, and presented it to him.

'But she had not reckoned on Ramón's integrity. No sooner had he heard how she came to have your money, than he threw it from him. He refused to listen to her blandishments, but left her, telling her that if she wanted to marry him, she must take the money back to you and confess. Then he mounted, and rode away.

'He did not know that her plans were already set in train. One part of her plan was to have a woman arrive, someone who was similar in appearance to her, who was of the same build, the same shape. As Ramón rode away, she saw this person who was to take her identity. She was going to kill her and disappear with the money.'

Doña Stefanía nodded. 'You are right in every respect, I believe. I have remained here in the city in order to find where my Joana has gone, but she has been in hiding.'

'A beggar may walk the streets, but she can be found if she is unique. That is why the woman you sought has been hiding.'

Something in Munio's voice made Doña Stefanía frown. Then her mouth fell open and she whipped round. There, near the door, she saw the tall beggar. 'That's Joana! Don't let her get out!'

There was no need for her cry. The figure leaped for the door, but before she could reach it, two sturdy peasants moved before it, arms folded. Seeing their stolid figures, the beggar sagged, as though she realised that there was no escape.

'Joana, you evil child!' the Prioress raged. She forgot all about the other people in the room, and marched up to the beggar, slapping her across the face. 'You would steal everything from me, would you?'

Then, to Baldwin's amazement, she fell back.

The beggar's veil had been knocked from its moorings, and Doña Stefanía could see that this was not Joana. 'Who . . . who are you?'

It was María, but Baldwin now glanced with consternation at Simon. He had thought that María was merely Joana renamed. Apparently not.

Simon took up the story again. 'However Joana was not able to kill her victim immediately, Doña. She was in hiding, about to spring, when a man rode up – a man of strong passions, who when he forms a desire, will have his way. This noble knight,' Simon said drily, eyeing Don Ruy, 'had seen you both on the pilgrimage here, and he had developed a fancy for your maid. When he rode past, seeing another woman of a similar build, walking by the river on her own, he offered her money to lie with him. Nothing loath to make a few *dinheiros*, she agreed, and the two lay together on the roadside. While they were coupling, Joana could not move even to retrieve the money. She was pinned there like a rabbit by an arrow.

'After he was done, the man left the woman. She rose, and found herself being berated by Joana. She was reluctant to stand and listen to this, but Joana set upon her to kill her, and she must defend herself.'

'No. Joana waited until her cousin was there, her Cousin Domingo. He was to have half the money for himself,' María spoke up. 'I knew nothing about this. Domingo did not realise at the time that I was to be her victim. She thought he would think nothing of killing me because I was nothing to her. Although I was her cousin, she saw me only as a useful thing to be destroyed for her profit. But Domingo! She thought he would kill me because I was no longer part of his family.'

'You were related to him, weren't you?' Simon pressed her.

'Yes,' she admitted, her head downcast.

'And you use a different name to save your family from shame, don't you?'

'Yes.'

'Your real name is Caterina. María is solely a trade name for begging and . . . other activities.'

'Yes.'

'What relation was he to you?'

'I was his sister, but our father dispossessed me and refused to acknowledge me when I married,' she said with a firm pride. 'I married a *mudéjar*, you see. None of my family would help me from that day onwards.'

'But Domingo drew the line at killing you?'

'Yes. Joana tried to beat me to death, but her first blow missed its mark and only served to hurt. I saw she had a rock, and she started shouting to Domingo to hold me, to knock me down, so she could kill me, but he reached around me and beat at her with *his* rock, crushing her head, then her face, and beating all to a mess. It was horrible!'

'It must have been,' Simon agreed. 'Especially when Domingo deliberately made the corpse look as though it had been mutilated after a rape.'

'Yes.' Caterina lowered her head with revulsion. 'He said he had to make it look like a rape so that people wouldn't realise anything else had happened. He wanted to hide the truth as far as he could.'

'Why?' Munio asked.

Simon answered, 'I think because he knew that the Prioress would leave no stone unturned to find her money. If Joana's body was found and she appeared to have been murdered during a robbery, Domingo knew he'd be suspected. A rape would make him, as Joana's cousin, less suspicious in the Prioress's eyes. Joana could have had a chance encounter with a rapist before she ever met the blackmailer, or the blackmailer himself could have raped her . . .'

The Prioress spoke. 'He knew that I'd seen Don Ruy staring at Joana while we travelled here. He intended me to think Don Ruy was the guilty man.'

'So, to continue,' Simon said, 'after this, Caterina left. She had no idea about the money. Domingo didn't think that his cousin would have thrown it into the bushes, and didn't know where she and Ramón had lain, even if he had guessed, so he could not find it. He searched about the horses, I expect, but then grew worried that he might be seen, so he rode back to the town, probably thinking Ramón had taken it. The body remained where he'd left it.

'If all this is correct, then of course Caterina is innocent of any crime so far,' Simon went on. 'And so she would have been, but she grew worried. Someone else knew that she was there, I think – another beggar. Someone who happened to hear Joana and her talking about meeting. Perhaps this beggar put two and two together. He heard about the money which Joana had carried, and he demanded some of it for himself. Caterina knew nothing about any money and refused. In which case, he said, he would tell his very good friend, an investigator, and see her arrested . . .'

'No!'

'I saw this person go and talk to Caterina only a few minutes after we told him that a sum of money had been stolen from Joana. We helped to ensure his greed got the better of him. What else would a beggar do?'

He looked over to Baldwin now, and he could see the realisation dawning on his friend's face. Baldwin's eyes were glistening, and he blinked quickly, sniffing. Beyond that there was nothing. He had already come to terms with the sort of man that his comrade Matthew had become.

Simon shrugged. 'Caterina followed after Matthew the beggar, or perhaps she simply waited at a place where she knew she would find him. And when he arrived, she thrust once with a sharp little knife. The death of Joana was undoubtedly self-defence, Munio. But Matthew? That was simple murder, nothing more.'

Chapter Twenty-Nine

The only man who appeared shocked and unhappy was Don Ruy. 'Don't touch her! She is no murderer, but a victim of other men's crimes.'

'Perhaps in your case that could be true,' Munio said. 'For you have defiled her yourself, forcing her to accept you for money.'

'I have done no such thing!' Don Ruy said forcefully. 'I have never taken a woman against her will, and this one has been paid handsomely.'

'What of your wife?' Baldwin asked.

'He's married?' Caterina said, and stared at Don Ruy. 'You said you—'

'Enough!' Munio commanded. 'In the case against you for murder, I doubt that you need fear. We'll keep you in custody until tomorrow when we can hold a court to debate the matter.'

Munio sat in his hall later that day as Guillem finished writing up the notes of the court's events.

Doña Stefanía had left clutching her casket and money like a long-lost child, and the crowd had gone. Now only Guillem remained, and Munio. He wondered idly how a man like the cleric could enjoy life. No woman at his side day and night, no companionship other than that of men. It was a life upon which Guillem appeared to thrive, but Munio could not comprehend it. To live through the rest of his years without his Margarita was a terrible thought. A man needed his woman, and to live without her was a dreadful concept.

He was a fortunate fellow; he knew that. When he had met his wife for the first time, he felt as though he had found more than a companion. She was another part of him; they shared the same soul. Her kindness and generosity of spirit were a delight to him. Unfortunately, it was that which had caused them their troubles now, of course.

Margarita could no more see a man or woman in pain without helping, than she could have murdered a child. That was why she had tended to Simon so carefully through his two illnesses – because she was inherently kind.

He sighed. The trouble was, so often people thought that because a woman cared for them, necessarily she must love them. Oh, Munio had heard of it happening elsewhere, when nuns looked after the ill in their convents, and then the men who recovered found themselves deeply in love with the nuns. It was all too common. And now Simon had apparently fallen in love with Margarita. She had heard him praying that she would love him or something.

Munio stared out through the window, listening as he heard the footsteps approaching. They were the steps of two happy men. Simon's gait was still a little slow, and there was a vague shuffle to his left leg, which had caught the brunt of the table at the tavern, while Baldwin's was faster and lighter after all his travelling.

'Guillem, I should prefer that you were gone,' Munio grunted.

The cleric stopped and stared at his *Pesquisidor*. There was a strange note in Munio's voice, he thought, a sad, lonely tone. 'If you're sure,' he said, and packed his remaining bits and pieces into his scrip before making for the door. He reached it just as it was thrown open by Simon and Baldwin, and the two entered, Baldwin grinning broadly.

The last Guillem saw of them was Simon marching up to Munio's desk, and the *Pesquisidor*'s face assuming a smile of feigned pleasure. It was so close to being a mask of horror that Guillem felt his heart lurch in his breast.

Simon and Baldwin had no idea of Guillem's insight as they crossed the floor to Munio. It was Simon who reached him first, thrusting out his hand. 'I am so very grateful for all you have done for me, Munio. Especially your wife as well. I am sure I would have died if it were not for her careful ministrations.'

'Perhaps so, but all she did was her duty to an unwell person,' Munio said pointedly, but the two were not of a mood to pick up on subtle hints.

'You expect me to believe that?' Simon said with a laugh. 'No woman could have treated a husband with more care and consideration than your wife did me.'

'And it cannot have been easy for any person to look after so repellent a knave as this Bailiff,' Baldwin said lightly. He was perched on the edge of Munio's table now, and Munio looked away. He liked Baldwin. In fact, he liked them both, but his wife thought that she had heard Simon praying for her, asking God to keep her for him. That must mean that Simon wanted Munio dead. It was a terrible thing to do, to ask that a woman be widowed so that she might be taken.

'Anyway, it will soon be time to go,' Simon said. 'I should like to say goodbye to you and your wife, and then we must leave Galicia and return to our own homes and wives.'

What about mine, then? Munio thought. Would you keep her in your house like a Moor with his harem?

Baldwin nodded. 'Simon has a new home to find, down on the coast, and I must go back to my own home in Devonshire. We will both have much to do.'

'Yes,' Simon said with a noticeable lessening of his pleasure. 'My wife doesn't want to come and live with me in Dartmouth. Nor does my daughter. Poor Meg. She wants to remain in Lydford for the rest of her days.'

'Meg?' Munio asked. 'Who is Meg?'

'My wife,' Simon explained. 'Her name is Margaret, but I always call her Meg. She doesn't want me to go so far from Lydford, but it is where my new job lies. The Abbot of Tavistock has asked that I go there, and there's nothing I can do to refuse him. He is my master.'

'What . . . what will you be doing there?' Munio stammered.

'The Abbot has just been made the Keeper of the Port of Dartmouth, and I am to be his representative.'

Munio took a deep breath. 'Then we should celebrate your new position, Bailiff!' He roared for a servant, and demanded that his wife be brought in, and Guillem too, so that all could share in Simon's pleasure.

And his own. 'I have a terrible murder resolved thanks to both of you,' he said, and put his arm about his wife. 'And let us drink to your wife, Meg,' he added. 'I hope she grows to love your new home as much as your old one!'

It was cold in her great church when Doña Stefanía arrived home again, and she closed the door quietly behind her as though to shut out the possibility of any of the other Sisters hearing her. Today she knew that she had to beg forgiveness for all her sins on the way back here, and she must also plead to be able to keep the relic.

'Oh, God,' she sighed as she knelt on the freezing flagstones immediately before the altar. 'What else could I have done? That man could have tempted an angel from heaven with his honeyed tongue. I tried to disregard him, but it was impossible. And when I thought he had my money, it seemed only sensible to stay with him, so that I could try to take it back.'

That was not all, of course.

'No. I didn't have to stay with him when I realised it was in truth his own money. But by then, it would have been difficult to find somewhere else. And I thought that Joana was still alive, and if she was, I could have won back my money still, and perhaps even found my relic . . . *Your* relic, I mean! I thought that after Domingo took the casket from me, he perhaps gave it to Joana for safekeeping, because surely if she hadn't died there at the river, he would know. That devil knew everything. And I thought that if Joana had lived, and that the whole of her death was staged, then Domingo must have been involved with her. They were related, after all. Cousins.'

She tugged the casket from her scrip and held it aloft. 'And see! I did succeed. Not in the way I expected, but I did manage to bring it back to You, and here it is! Please accept it, and let us keep it here, for if you do, it will be greatly to the glory of Your Church!'

There was no answer. No thunder-roll, no fork of lightning, nothing. But if there was no heavenly choir singing her praises, nor, reflected Doña Stefanía, was there a bolt from the heavens to strike her down either.

Lowering her arms at last, which were now growing a little tired, she murmured a reverent *paternoster* before setting the little casket on the altar.

'I shall announce that the relic is here, and people shall come from all over the world to sing Your glory, Lord. I shall have it mounted in a gold box, with rubies and pearls and emeralds and . . . and all manner of gems to show how highly we value Your generosity. Holy, holy, holy, Lord. Lord of all . . .'

On the morning they were due to leave, Munio was pleased to accept the decision of Sir Charles that he and his servant would leave with Baldwin and Simon.

'I am sorry to hear it,' he lied politely. It was best, he thought, always to be polite to men such as Sir Charles. He had the look of one who would be swift to take offence.

Sir Charles smiled as though he doubted the depth of Munio's sorrow. 'It is a shame, but there is nothing here but expense. You have no tournaments in Galicia or even in Portugal. What I need is an opportunity of fighting in the lists and winning wealth and renown, or a new lord whom I might serve, and a lord like that will be in England or France, not here. I shall have to return home and see what is happening in my country.'

'Well, I wish you a happy voyage and Godspeed,' Munio said.

'We are thankful for all your kindness to us,' Baldwin said. 'And I especially thank you, Margarita, for your careful treatment of Simon while I was away. It must have been terrible to have the fear of his decease before my return.'

'Let us not even think of such things,' she said with a shudder.

'No,' Munio agreed. 'Not when you are about to embark on another long journey. Godspeed to you all.'

Simon and Baldwin made their farewells, then Sir Charles; and the four men, Paul bringing up the rear, set off north-wards, aiming for the coast and hoping to find a merchantman which would convey them back to Dartmouth or perhaps Topsham. There were many good, sizeable ports for them to strike for.

'Let's hope that the weather holds,' Baldwin said with a glance up at the gathering clouds.

Simon had not forgotten his prostration on the way to Galicia. 'Aye, let us hope so,' he said with a frown.

'It should be easier than the way here,' Baldwin said lightly. 'The weather looks hardly bad enough to ruffle the sea. I am sure we'll have an easy time of it.'

'Good,' Simon said. He looked up again. There were storms gathering, he thought, but he relied on the knight's greater knowledge of the sea and understanding of the weather in these parts. He had spent more time here than Simon.

Surely he must know better.

It was a few days after Baldwin and Simon had left that Munio stood with Guillem on the walls of the city near the eastern gate and watched the crowds entering the city.

'Don't you think she should have been executed?' Guillem asked quietly.

Munio looked at him. 'What useful purpose would it have served? I think that this way justice is seen to be done.'

'She murdered the beggar Matthew.'

'Only because he threatened her. If he had not demanded money, saying that if she didn't pay him, he'd tell the Prioress who she was, she wouldn't have been panicked into killing him. That is the point, I think. She was forced into killing him by his actions, that evil fool!'

'A Templar,' Guillem said, crossing himself. He shook his head. 'I can understand how the Pope felt that they deserved destruction if they were all formed in the same mould.'

Munio remembered Baldwin and was silent a moment. He

did not know, but he suspected Baldwin's background. 'No group can be entirely evil, Guillem. Even if there was one like Matthew, there were others who joined the Templars because they wanted to do good, protect pilgrims and serve God. Just think: those men, Sir Charles and Dom Afonso, both served no man, but when they saw pilgrims being attacked, they leaped in to defend them. They would be looked down upon by most people because they are lordless and landless, but they still did what they could to protect the pious.'

'And no doubt rob them.'

'That is not kind, Guillem.'

'No. But realistic.'

Parceval sniffed and then tipped the rest of the pot of wine into his mouth and savoured it as he swilled it about. He had to sniff as he finished the drink. The tears were never far from his eyes now.

It was hard to lose a lover. He knew the Doña wasn't really in love with him, but that didn't matter because he could lie to himself. She had shared his bed for a while, she was an enthusi-astic lover, and while she was with him, he could tell himself that she was there because she wanted to be with him, not because she was desperate without any money and wanted only to take his own purse.

He had loved her, he told himself again.

When his daughter died – he couldn't bring himself to recall how – his wife had gone. She heard what had happened, and that same day she left, taking his son with her. There was no love there when the assumed rape of his own daughter became common knowledge. Perhaps that was why he was so desperate for the love of another woman. Maybe it was just that he was mad for someone to comfort him and give him the solace he craved: companionship and sympathy. Not that the Doña had given him much of that. She had been too self-obsessed. And yet even when she was completely focused on herself, there was something there: he had felt it. Perhaps it was simply the fact that both were lonely people. Their mutual despair made them companionable.

She had gone, though. And all there was for Parceval now was the long, blank road of the future.

He had wealth, it was true, but what use was his money, when his wife was gone and his son with her? All the time he lived in his house, he would be forced to confront that terrible picture in his mind. He had tried to forget it by coming here. The court at Ypres had sent him, but he had not demurred. There had been a hope in his mind that perhaps by coming here, he would be able to forget that scene, his daughter's wide, screaming mouth.

'My God!' he muttered, and waved for another jug of wine. It helped him to forget, and that was all he wanted: to forget the loss of his family, and now the loss of his woman.

Perhaps he should think of her as 'his last woman'. She was surely the last. He couldn't possibly find another. He was too old, and even with his money, he obviously wasn't the most attractive of men. No, in future all he could count on were whores.

He poured and drank steadily.

The woman was right; she had gone back to her church. She could do good there, whereas with him, what sort of future would she have? There was the possibility of finding a new life, he supposed, but more likely the Church would send people to recapture her. The Church did not easily give up its nuns and monks. They were sworn to God, and that oath would last for ever.

What sort of life could he offer a woman? He could go home to Ypres, live again in his house, pretend his wife didn't exist, but all the time he'd be looking over his shoulder, expecting to hear the steps that heralded the assassin, the man hired by Hellin van Coye's family to avenge his death. For surely that man would come. Parceval's danger would start from the moment he arrived home again. He would never be able to relax. Even if he had the good fortune to find another woman, he couldn't live normally. It was impossible.

He stared at the cup in his hand. It was empty. So was the jug. The third jug. He felt overwhelmed with the thought that he could never know peace. There was nothing here for him. Nothing. Nothing here, nothing at Ypres. Where could he go? Where could he live?

Standing, he stumbled, and had to lean on the table. What was the point of struggling when all was stacked against him? Better to take away the success from his enemies. He would steal their thunder.

Steal their thunder, he thought, slipping and toppling against a wall. That was it. He would take his own life. Prevent the bloody bastards from killing him. Yes! He'd stop their fun. He'd hang himself. Here. Tonight!

He belched. No one could stop him. It was his life. He was nearly at his chamber. Leaning against the wall, he tried to focus on the door handle, but it was terribly hard. His hand refused to coordinate with his eyes, and it was some time before he could lift the latch. As soon as he did so, the door flew wide open, crashing against the wall. He staggered inside, and his hand went to his belt. Pulling it free, he heard his knife fall and make a cracking noise as the bone handle struck the packed earth of the floor. His purse rattled loudly as the coins struck. For a moment he stared down at them, but his misery made him shrug. There was no point in picking them up. Better that he should . . .

'Señor?'

Blearily, he turned his gaze onto the woman who owned this place. She stood anxiously, a small figure in her fifties, with sagging, greying flesh. He thought she looked little better than a corpse.

But then his interest quickened, for behind her was another woman. She was slim, elegant, fair-haired, and younger. Parceval gaped foolishly, and then ridiculously tried to stand a little more straight, to look a little less inebriated. 'My lady, I am going to kill myself.'

'Oh! Not here, señor!'

The other smiled. She had been looking at the floor, at the heavy purse, but now she turned her eyes upon him. 'Is there really no other way? Perhaps the señor would reconsider. There is always something to make life worthwhile.'

And Parceval, drinking in the sight of her, reflected that perhaps she was right.

The wind blew like a demon, howling in the rigging, whipping into shreds the sail above their heads, and Baldwin stood staring out to sea with the feeling that the whole of his pilgrimage had been a disaster.

He had gone to Compostela in order to pay for his murder, but the journey had been a failure from the first. Surely he could have gone on a simple journey to Our Lady of Norfolk, or Canterbury. It would have been easier, and safer – although he wondered whether he would have felt that same sensation of release and forgiveness. There had been an unmistakable feeling of love and warmth as he stood in that Cathedral. Perhaps the journey was worth that. As was the chance of seeing Tomar.

But the pleasures were offset by the sadness of Matthew's death, and by the grim reality of his descent into poverty and dishonour. It was terrible to hear how a man had sunk so low that he was finally killed for his attempts at blackmail.

As if that were not bad enough, Baldwin had the guilt of what he had put his friend Simon through. The Bailiff had willingly joined him here, but when Baldwin left him, he had almost died of his fever. True, the careful nursing of Munio's wife had protected him from death, but it had been close, and there was always the possibility that the next few days would put an end to all of them.

He glanced up as a wild cry came from the master, and suddenly he heard an awful snapping noise, as the mainsail over his head tore from top to bottom. He was almost shoved from the ship by crew members as they ran up the ratlines and battled with the sails against the wind, desperately trying to rescue what they could.

Baldwin pulled himself hand over hand to the little cabin at the rear of the deck, and hoisted himself into the reeking interior. Vomit puddled all over the floor, and the three men inside were a uniform green colour, Simon lying on the floor near the stern, Sir Charles and Paul looking faintly better because they were at least vertical, both sitting with their backs to the curved wall.

'Has the devil come to claim his own yet?' Sir Charles asked pathetically.

'He would not have to cast his net far, would he?' Baldwin said, and would have essayed a chuckle, but then as the boat lurched, Simon spewed, and Baldwin fled for the open deck again.

And while Baldwin and Simon prayed for salvation amidst the howling horror of an angry sea, while Parceval sat in a tavern with a new lady, and while Doña Stefanía sat at the side of her altar and watched with greedy pleasure as the first of the queue of pilgrims entered her little church and walked to the relic to give thanks and pray to Saint Peter, hundreds of miles away to the north and east, in the great church of Orthez, the priest sighed as he picked up the casket containing the relic.

It was cool here, down in the undercroft, a good place to preserve things. He knew that perfectly well, for after all, it was where the hams and sausages were hung until they were wanted, deep in this cool, dry interior. Perfect.

The box was beautiful. He held it reverently in both hands, then walked with it to a slanting shaft of light. In it, the box gleamed. There was a fingerprint on the cross, and he wiped it with care on his sleeve, and breathed on it to polish it. Then he made his way up the stairs to the main body of the church itself. There, he bowed to the altar, and moved along the choir to where his Bishop stood. The Bishop held out his hand.

'You have it?'

'Yes, my Lord Bishop.'

He passed it over and bowed again while the Bishop tentatively opened it a crack and peered inside. 'Wonderful to think that so little can be so marvellously efficacious.'

'It was a Saint.'

'Yes.'

The Bishop picked up the box which Doña Stefanía had returned to them. 'You can burn this,' he said as he reverently laid down the other casket in its place. 'As if we'd have let that poisonous mare have the real relic! She must have tried to thieve it at the outset.'

'She has told the Bishop of Compostela that she has the relic, and she is already winning many pilgrims.'

'I know,' said the Bishop with a chuckle. 'She says that she swapped over the bones because the Saint wanted to remain at her church.'

'When will you tell her that we only sent her a bit of the tailbone of a hog?'

'Later,' the Bishop said with satisfaction, kneeling before the casket. 'There's no hurry. Later.'